I0819787

FALLING

Novels published by Midnight Fire Media

Your Own Fate
Night on Earth
Dreams Belong to the Night
ShadowWalk
Alarums of Reality
Afterglow Dust
Black Dragon

The Janus Clan series:

The Defenseless
The Slaves
Birds Flying in the Dark
At the End of the Rainbow

Poetry:

Amos Keppler: Complete Poems 1989 – 2003
Secrets - Descriptions of what cannot be described

(A few of the) novels to be published:

Afterglow Rain
Season of the Witch
Thunder Road: Ice and Fire
Red Shadow
Lewis of Modern York
Fangs and Claws of the Earth
Forsaken

For a «complete» list of current and current future Amos Keppler and Midnight Fire Media projects see the Midnight Fire/Midnight Fire Media web pages.

One story of Nine

FALLING

BY

AMOS KEPPLER

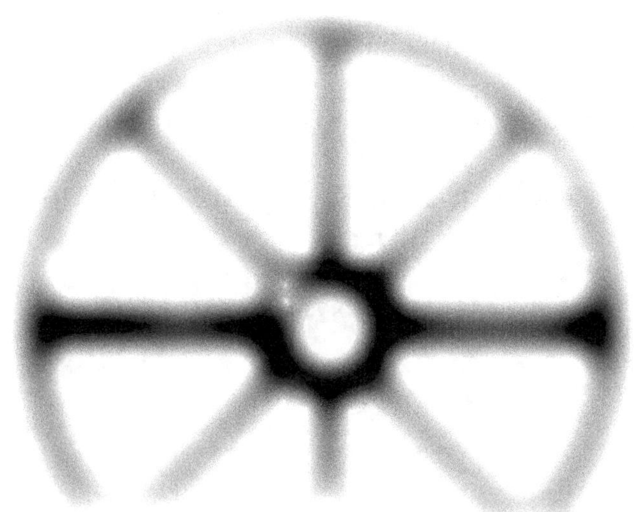

∞

MIDNIGHT FIRE MEDIA
2016

Midnight Fire Media

http://midnight-fire.net/mfm
For more about Janet of the Blue Flame and the Nine:
http://midnight-fire.net/thenine

E-Mail:
Amos13@midnight-fire.net
manofhood@yahoo.com

Cover, text, design, premedia, art and photos Amos Keppler

ISBN 978-82-91693-19-4

Part One: Falling

Chapter 1

The dream from last night, from many nights returned to her. She writhed on a bed and stared at the white ceiling. It turned dark, dark and menacing with clouds and faces. Suddenly she was up there, among them. Dark laughter mocked her and she was falling. She fell down and when she landed and hurt herself, when her body and soul hurt horribly, the laughter grew louder and more powerful.

The city of Auburn, on the Island was filled with hectic activity this day, both stressful and exciting. Various markets set up for the day dominated most of the central parts of town.

The young girl stared at the woman across the table with swollen eyes.

– There is a vast black hole in your path, the fortuneteller hissed at her. – It will suck you in. You will fall into its dark embrace, and it will leave only a shell of a human being in its wake.

Janet backed off, wide-eyed and with cold sweat pouring from all over her body, the horror of the moment burned into her memory. She saw the woman's nice, pleasant face, saw it contort into a twisted version of itself, and the wicked laughter followed her as she ran off.

The erratic sounds, the loud noise of the crowd and the market closed in on her. She pushed her hands at her ears, to no avail.

Toby and the guys caught up with her fast. Rosa, operating a stall displaying her art nearby, also rushed to her the fastest she was able. They saw her distraught face, her watery eyes and the cold drops of sweat forming on her brow. They saw that, even though they saw nothing else.

– That hag! Rosa cried. – And she seemed so nice.

Toby rubbed her back, gently, slowly calming her shaking form.

She nodded, sending him a sweet smile.

– I am okay, she replied. – You guys relax. I just need some ice cream.

– She needs to sate her craving for ice cream. Eleanor looked at the heavens.

– C'mon, guys, Rosa said, – she is okay. Our dear Janet is okay.

They vanished, in a blink of an eye. Janet watched them as they returned to Rosa's stall, as curious people approached Rosa and studied her obscure paintings and designs, in a vain attempt at basic understanding. Janet could not help but smile and good-humored shake her head.

– You have always attempted to scale the wall that can not be scaled, the fortuneteller hissed at her from her recent memory. – You will fail and fall, fall down. Your father's fate will be yours.

Her father had committed suicide as a very young man.

The woman kept talking to her, a prevalent harpy in her troubled thoughts.

Janet sniffed and walked in a daze to the ice cream parlor. She had noticed it on her way in, but deliberately avoided it. As she walked the details of her surroundings emerged extraordinary clear and crisp. A girl crossed her path. Janct saw her face, and it was like the image froze in her mind. There was a pimple on the girl's nose, and a mole on her cheek. There was a whirl, a wave rolling through the air, and it seemed to come from all directions simultaneously.

I see, she thought. I see more.

She bought the ice cream, a big, generous helping unseen in ordinary parlors. Her tongue, long and versatile reached out to touch the sweetness and bring it into the hot embrace of her mouth. She sighed happily as it happened, as the piece melted in the moist cavity behind her teeth.

A shadow fell on her. She trembled.

– They care, he said, – but they do not understand.

She turned, and met the eyes of the stranger. He had long, dark hair, darker than hers, and a glare in his eyes she feared would gut her in half.

– They can not, he nodded. – They do not See.

– I am sorry, are you talking to *me?*

She responded, feigning the arrogance of a Lady, one of gentile birth, and far from boring, mundane Janet.

– Of course I am talking to you, Janet, he grinned viciously. – Do you see anyone else close by?

Taken aback, Janet stood frozen on her spot.

– Your friends, he nodded, confirming something to her, something she did not understand, – even the more interesting and capable among them, can only follow you to a certain point. *I,* however, can take you far beyond that, far beyond your wildest dreams.

Janet blinked. The day had been so normal, so mundane, and suddenly, someone had snapped their fingers, and…

– Yes, he said. – I snapped my fingers.

She blinked.

– You are special, he told her. – Most people today are mediocre fools, and they want to make everyone else like them. I, on the other hand, will want to make you *more* special. I want to cultivate your uniqueness, take that fire within you, and make it grow; grow to a Storm.

And just like that, he was gone.

And thus ended her day, everything happening after that gone from her mind like a candle snuffed out by a breath of wind.

Night came again, and she stared at the white ceiling above her bed, and the dancing clouds and faces there.

2

The classes and the classrooms and Learning the next day did not feel real to her. But then again, it never had. Instead of paying attention to the teacher, she tended to look out of the window with dreaming eyes.

Yesterday was a blur of conflicting images and emotions. The both nice and twisted face of the fortuneteller kept haunting her. The features of the man, *the tall, dark stranger* reappeared in her memory at odd moments.

She heard the bell, heard it from far away. Eleanor grabbed her, and pulled her with her across the yard, and all the way to the classroom.

They sat down as two of the last. The teacher, Mrs. Orniston stared sternly at them. She wore her dull, gray clothes, fitting her personality.

Everything was closed in here. The windows had been closed in an effort to keep the heat from the outside from entering the building. She sat at her desk, writing. All the pupils wrote. Papers rustled. They blew in the wind, even though there was no wind. Toby looked at her. Why did he look at her? She felt everybody's accusing stare, and a rush of heat overwhelmed her, and she stank of sweat from one moment to the next.

And in the moment… in that moment was eternity. She rushed out of the room, pushing a palm at her mouth. Aching feet carried her to the bathroom, to a toilet stinking of bile, a clean, clean toilet smelling fresh and shiny. She fell on her knees and threw up. Time passed slowly. Everything felt frozen, still. She knelt there, leaning over the toilet bowl, hardly moving, hardly more than swaying, her entire body hurting. The sour stench from the bowl hit her in waves, growing worse by the second.

She fell over. Her head hit the floor with a dump sound. She threw up again. The bile flowed across the floor like a tide. Ages passed, without her being able to move. She just crouched there, suffering, the world turning hazy and blurry. Hands grabbed her. She hardly noticed that they did. Faces swam before her eyes. They belonged to her friends. Worry dominated their indistinct features.

The nurse practicing at the Learning House examined her quite thoroughly, taking blood and body fluid samples, the works. Janet sat there, and let herself be examined. It did not feel real to her, not real at all.

The nurse pointed a little flashlight at her left eye, while she moved the eyeball around with her thumb. It did not hurt, but it felt weird.

– Has this ever happened before?

– A few times when I was younger, Janet replied, attempting to nod while the woman held her head. – Not for years, though.

– Is there anything else you can tell me that might help?

– I have occasional vivid dreams, the girl whispered. – In them I am always... *falling*. And it hurts, as if I am really hitting the ground. There is a darkness enveloping me... They feel so real.

The nurse did not seem interested. Janet clammed up.

The examination ended, the puzzled frown never straying far from the nurse's expression.

– You seem healthy enough, she finally said. – It is hard to be sure, of course. We have to wait for the blood tests for that. And you should take a scan as soon as possible. I can give you an appointment at the health center if you wish.

It was more of a command than a request. Janet nodded meekly.

And she was out of there, feeling so much better.

Her friends surrounded her, cuddled her, just being there for her. She returned their smiles, ignoring the worry she spotted in their eyes.

– You are still not sleeping well. Rosa stated firmly. – Do not deny it. Those bags under your eyes are a dead giveaway.

– I am all right, guys, Janet assured them. – Really!

The sounds from the yard attacked her, hurting her ears, the multiple sights smarted her eyes. It was as if her senses had grown to a kind of constant overdrive mode.

She put up a brave front. It convinced them. She saw that easily.

The guys nodded slowly, her words of assurance making them grin in relief. They did not push her further. They immersed her in their circle and she felt better, a little better, a little worse.

Mrs. Orniston watched them, watched her with small, sticky eyes.

– I can not stand her, Fran said. – Is she such a gray mouse or just pretending?

– I bet she is a hungry sex goddess in real life, Toby remarked.

That earned him a good-humored elbow in the ribs from Janet. He yelped in feigned pain.

That small movement alone, every big and small movement made Janet's world turn. She put up a brave front for the guys, for her friends and managed to hide her plight to them, at least to some degree.

She stood alone by the rail later, focusing on managing the sensation overload hitting her. The sounds and impressions created by the crowd, by everything around her, close and far away made her squirm. A woodpecker pecked at a tree several blocks away. She saw its eyes, as if it was right in front of her, felt it as if it pecked her skin, her sore skin. Her hands hurt, as they turned into fists, and her long nails buried themselves in her palms, drawing blood. Shockingly, suddenly startled she smelled the blood. The sensation made her dizzy, and she had trouble standing. She looked for her friends, but they were not there.

– You are a god's daughter, and that makes you potentially very, very powerful.

At first the cold voice seemed to come from the very air in front of her, but slowly he faded into her view, and she saw him clearly for the first time.

– Your transformation has already begun, he said. – Sometimes it does not take more than a small jolt to set it off. Every single powerful adept throughout history has suffered dizzy spells similar to and as bad as yours. I will help you embrace the Change, instead of running from it, like so many have done and do,

Light seemed to bend around him, to hide him, but except for the slightly indistinct frame she saw him clearly, even though nobody else did. If she was not very much mistaken, they did not see him at all.

A thousand thoughts raced through her mind, and none made sense.

– You are confused and conflicted, he said softly. – That is perfectly natural, and expected. There will be a lot for you to handle in your Time of Change to come, but I will help you with all of it, if you let me.

She wanted to say something, something clever, something silly, anything, but was unable to. Janet, the stricken girl stood there and watched as the sorcerer gave her one last, reassuring smile, and faded from her view.

One, undeniable realization struck her, vivid and true.

Magick is real.

– Magick is *real!*

She said it out aloud, the excitement tangible in her voice and her face.

– It is real, she whispered, worry and joy warring within and without the young girl.

The return to the class was kind of anti-climatic, uneventful. The rustling of papers picked up almost immediately. It was like a wave was crossing the classroom in concentric circles. Some of the girls held on to their hair, looking more than a little distressed. Janet sat down, grinning all over her face. The teacher, Mr. Corcoran made a major effort to not meet her eyes.

Are you afraid? She thought. Are you daunted face to face with the unknown?

The other girls left the wardrobe after the gymnastics lesson. She saw them file past her, as the room faded from full to empty. The emptiness surrounded her, and danced on the still waves circling her. She sensed it. It opened up to her like a vast black hole. She stood in the front of the mirror, staring at herself. The tall body, the large breasts, the wide hips, the muscled thighs and upper arms, the strange, violet eyes and ebon hair. For the first time she looked dispassionately at herself. There was a cold hunger behind the smile. She sensed it, and could identify it, could taste it in her mouth, and she savored it.

She joined her friends outside, in the bright and warm sunshine, and she savored it. The five of them walked off, heading home for the day, home to the nice neighborhood and pleasant gardens. She wanted to tell them, sharing herself with them all, the way she and all of them had always done with each other. She did not want to tell them, fearing they would not understand. The fear was a worry in her gut, making her dizzy and weak, and she scolded herself. She could not even tell what was worse: That they would not believe her, and think she had turned insane. Or that they would believe her and back off in horror.

The teen writhed in bed late at night, waiting for sleep to come. The sounds of the night played in her ears. Its shadows danced on the waves. She could see the waves, sense them, and the bells hanging from the lamp would not let up, no matter how hard she focused on it. If anything it made them chime louder.

She finally gave up and grabbed the bells, and put them on the floor, on the soft carpet, where they could chime no more.

Night gave way to day, to a row of smiling faces. Janet blew out the candles on the cake in one blow. Then she stepped back and accepted the enthusiastic accolades from the gathering, blushing slightly.

– Janet is sixteen, sweet sixteen, Eleanor said, – and her time has come.

That sentence, those words, for some unfathomable reason, struck a dark chord and made Janet shiver. She could not tell if it was the words itself or something in Eleanor's voice.

Eleanor had behaved strangely lately.

But so had Janet, and Eleanor might just be responding to that. Janet did not know, and everything was so puzzling, so confusing.

Everything was shards, slivers of reality. That, at least was how she experienced it later, as time raged on. They took the bus to the quay, and the ferry to the twin cities on the mainland. Janet smelled the sea. She recalled the walk to the bus stop, the crowd of girls they had encountered.

– The white brown bitch is at it again, the hen leading the hens had cried out like a curse.

– What do you skinny dolls know? Rosa had responded on Janet's behalf.

Janet had grown her wider hips and larger breasts and forms not that long ago, and since then, for some reason, representatives of the popular girl

groups at Learning had singled her out.
– Nobody but brown bitches has hiiips like thaaat, the cheerleader of a given cluster had declared.
Her snickering court had laughed very, very loud.
– You silly gooses never cease to AMAZE me, Toby had shouted angrily after them.
Janet was hurt by both the support and the attacks, and she wished she had not been.
The travel to the mainland, to the city of Howell with the ferry was uneventful. Janet recalled the wind in her face on the quay and hardly anything more.
They went to «Youth Freeze», a place for underagers, where they did not serve alcohol. It said so on the door, in very specific terms.
– It is a bit insulting. Eleanor nodded to herself.
– It is fucking offensive is what it is, Fran stated empathically.
– I do not mind, Rosa said lightly. – It is a fun place, anyway.
They sort of got that confirmed as they stepped inside. It was still day outside, and the place was already packed with sweaty, dancing teenagers. The hard beating of both modern and older types of drums played by two women and two men shook the room and the people gathered, and the newly arrived felt it immediately, felt it in their bones.
There were no seats left. All had been taken.
– I knew it, Rosa said. – We are hours late, as usual.
– So, we will stand, Janet said. – There will not be much of that, anyway. Let us *celebrate.*
– Yeah, let us. Eleanor smiled. – It is your day, Sweet Sixteen, and I will put a curse on everybody doing anything to ruin it.
Once again, there was that strange quality in her voice and stance.
The dance floor was filled with hard-dancing teenagers. Janet felt the weight of the pulsing drums even before the omniversal sound surrounded her and bathed her in their beat. Ancient rhythms rocked flesh and bone. The sharp drums sounded like shots, shots in the dark hitting and penetrating everybody, and Janet felt herself bleed.
They stood by the wall, resting a bit, all those without a place to sit, sweaty girls and boys, roused by the dance, haunted by unfamiliar feelings and notions.
Janet noticed a boy looking at her. Both quickly looked away. But she looked some more behind the back of her friends. They grinned at her.
– It is not like that, she insisted, – not like that at all. There is just something very familiar about him. That is all.

– That is all, huh? Rosa said mockingly.
– That is all there is, Janet blew her off.
And approached the boy. The others looked astounded at each other.
– Hi, she greeted the boy with a coy smile.
– Hi, he replied.
And then courage failed her, and awkward silence rose between them.
– Want to dance? He wondered.
– Sure, she shrugged.
He took her hand and they walked out on the dance floor. She blushed when he looked at her, when he studied her.
It was a slow dance. Couples danced, while holding on to each other. He stared at her with his strange look, and she surprised herself by calmly (fairly calmly) returning the stare.
– I have not seen you here before…
– That is probably because I have not been here before, she grinned. – Mother finally decided to let go of me a little.
– A little girl away from home for the first time, huh? What is the occasion?
– It is my sixteenth birthday today, a rite of passage kind of thing, I guess.
– I know, Janet.
His voice turned darker, menacing. She froze, as she witnessed how he changed, how his features changed from a boy to an older man.
But it was the same person.
– I need you to make up your mind, Janet, the sorcerer said to her. – You need it. You need to decide if you wish to become a seeker, a traveler of the winding ways, or remain a mundane dabbler in Magick. I will come for you tonight, for your first lesson, and know that if you accept that first, initial step, there is no going back to the dull, uninformed life you have led.
She ran. Even though she walked, she ran. And when she looked back it was only the boy standing there, looking after her with those dark eyes of his.

3

Janet sat in her room. She sat on the floor with her feet pulled up and crossed. There was a piece of chalk in her hand, and she made a clumsy attempt at drawing a pentacle. She had a book in her lap, one worn and with a lot of ears and tears. Its pages were filled with handwriting and drawings. Some words and sentences she understood. Others were totally undecipherable. She sat there with the book in her lap, clutching it in her arms. Memories assaulted her.
– This is yours, a voice told her, her great grandfather's voice.

And it brought tears to her eyes.

– It has been waiting for you, for someone like you for so very long.

And she found herself nodding with burning, clear eyes.

On the cover was written *Book of Fate*, with a strange, transparent ink.

Her hands moved, opening the book on page one. She read the words, tasted them on her lips.

– «Whisper these words of malice and spite, and dream them true».

She shivered in a sudden cold spell, a strike on the senses only increasing in strength when she read, when she did whisper the words below.

– «I spite thee, world, a spite you so well deserve. I crucify people and leave them on the wood to hang, and return at night to admire my great work».

She slammed the book shut, suddenly short of breath, sweat breaking on her forehead. In the corner of the room the shadows turned darker and she heard whispers, flattering, malignant whispers.

Shaking fingers reopened the book. The whispers faded. She read, or tried to, making an attempt to fathom the words and symbols.

– Hello, Janet, it said at the top of page three.

And it was almost a voice, making her look around the room.

She gasped. It was not her great grandfather's writing. She would recognize that anywhere, no matter the setting. But far older, a bit faded, though still easily readable. She breathlessly scanned the page. There were other greetings there, as well, other names.

«Yes, Janet, this book has been waiting for you, perhaps even more than it waited for your ancestors, and will be waiting for your descendants. It is yours, to do with as you please».

Words are like riddles, she read. Or better yet: they *are* riddles. Speech is a barrier, and words are a way for us of interpreting our inner life, our deepest emotions. Magick, and this is important, even crucial, does not come from the words, but from you. The words are merely a way of aiding you towards enlightenment, self-discovery. Through them you share, though imperfectly experiences of witches' past. As your understanding grows, so will your understanding of words. Words are Power.

She closed the book, and put it down, pushing the heavy load under the bed. The girl sat there, on the dusty floor, with her knees pulled up, rocking back and forth. She rose, with some effort, to her full height. Janet, the witch stood before the window, looking at the landscape bathing in moonlight, and more than suspected that she had stood like that, like this a thousand times before, in many a strange land.

That thought brought a stream of hardly comprehensible images and sensations.

The days had passed so quickly lately, in such a rush that she had not been able to think.

But now she did, in her fevered mind. And it was not enough. She wanted… she needed more time. She…

There was a whoosh behind her. She had learned to recognize that sound, learned its significance. The witch wondered, she did, if it in truth was a sound, or something she really could not hear with her ears, but only sense with her increasingly active mind. She turned, somewhat calm, and stood there, face to face with the Sorcerer.

– Peter? She asked him, recalling the boy's name.

He laughed softly.

– I went by that name long ago, he acknowledged. – I chose another name for myself, like all witches do, like you will eventually do as well.

– Do not be so sure! She snorted arrogantly.

He laughed some more. He laughed a lot, did he not?

– Do not play games with me, girl. I can look straight through you, and know, beyond knowing that you have made your decision. What remains is simply for you to acknowledge the obvious truth of it.

She looked at the silver landscape again, at the moonlight, doing so without turning. It looked different for a moment, looked so vast, an entire land of the moon imposing itself on her.

I want to know. She heard a voiceless voice. I want to *be*.

– Yes, she heard herself say. – I want you to teach me. I want to be your… your apprentice. I want to learn all the secrets of the world.

– Excellent! He exclaimed.

She took that one, crucial step forward, into his shadow, his dark embrace.

– I accept your plea, he said. – I take you as mine.

There was a subtle change, a seething within that was not, could not be her imagination. Weak-kneed and smothered by his powerful presence she could not speak and cast her eyes down.

– Bring the book, too, he said.

– The book? She frowned.

– Precisely. It will most certainly be useful, as it contains a lot of arcane, powerful knowledge.

She knelt on the floor and bent down under the bed, and pulled the old book out, fully aware that her hips and butt were exposed to him. The blushing could not be stopped. Its heat almost overwhelmed her completely, until she managed pull herself together and fight herself back on her feet. She stood there, before him, with the family inheritance in her arms. He did not move, but he grabbed her. His embrace sent a thousand cold daggers through her body and mind.

The room faded before her eyes, and what surrounded them in its stead was a place of mist and shadow, and totally unfathomable impressions and sensations. There was nothing there, nothing to focus on, to grab hold of. She shivered visibly. Fear touched her, and bravery and endless curiosity, as she realized what this was.

He brought her far away from everything she had known.

Chapter 2

He brought her to the mountaintop across the sound, above the city. Suddenly they were there, and she gasped, and she continued gasping, her face lit up by a huge smile, as she looked down at the numerous buildings below.

– Impressive, is it not?

She nodded, looking at him with her youthful enthusiasm and admiration.

– It is always special the moment you realize, you know, beyond knowing that Magick is real, the certainty that the world is at your feet.

She kept nodding, stopped a bit and nodded again.

– That was… that was the *Wasteland?*

She gasped, beyond impressed.

– It was.

– You can access it, just like that, move through it, to other places?

– I can, even though it takes a bit of preparation and extreme caution.

There was a whistling of wind from the forest to their left and the sound of flapping wings. The sound the wings made was not anything like she had heard before, and she shivered.

– We are warned not to climb this mountain, and to keep away from the forest. They say Bad Things live here.

– And it is not hearsay or tales to scare little children either, he grinned. – Frightening creatures do live here. But do not worry: we are perfectly safe. I can protect us both.

The Triangle, the Triple Cities councils had, in plenum had plans for a guesthouse up here, and an entire recreational village. The first group they had sent into the wilderness, to survey and plan, had discovered that the centuries old folk tales about the area had been essential correct… and the surviving members had returned to the city, frightened out of their wits.

Janet had known about the stories from an early age. She had always been a *curious* girl.

– My friends and I were on our way once, she said, her lips shivering. – But I froze the moment we sat foot on the trail and refused to go a step further. My fear sort of convinced my friends, too. We turned around and never made another attempt.

– Your instincts are important. He nodded. – You should always heed them.

He grabbed her, and she let herself be grabbed, and in yet another prolonged flash of mist and shadow they were on their way.

They reappeared in a room lit by candles. She took it all in, in a flash, every little detail of the room. She looked at the man by her side in unbridled admiration.

– That was so cool, Peter, she gasped. – So very, very cool.

– That is Malone the Sorcerer to you, apprentice. He corrected her. – I have done quite a bit of growing up since I was that sniveling brat.

– Of course, Master. She bowed her head in inevitable respect. – Forgive this stupid apprentice.

– By all means, Malone the Sorcerer nodded mercifully. – You may now take the tour, familiarize yourself with your new home.

His words… they sounded so final, so ominous, but she quickly quelled the momentarily sting of regret. He left her alone, and she was free to roam, to explore. She walked around and stared breathless at her surroundings.

There were two rooms, really, making out one bigger. The place glowed in the dust of old things, and she looked at each and every one of them: furniture, books, maps and an assortment of stuff she could not even classify. She realized she walked around in a library, a true library of time, unlike the mostly boring, mundane ones she had visited earlier in her life… before she had been born.

You feel it, do you not? He spoke to her, even though he was not physically voicing anything. The glow inside, the awakening fire, the Universe being born?

– Yes, she whispered.

He put her Book of Fate on one of the lower shelves. It was the only book there.

– Feel free to put any book here, he said, – also any from the library. I want you to look at it as your personal space.

She got a warm, fuzzy feeling inside. He was so kind.

Her hand touched the edge of a table, another antique. Restless dust rose into the air. She coughed, and rushed away from there.

– The dust is your first challenge, he commanded. – It will be your job to keep our home nice and clean and tidy.

– Why? She asked, before she managed to catch herself.

– Because your mentor says so, he reprimanded her.

She blushed in anger and embarrassment.

– Yes, Malone, she said in a low voice, casting her eyes to the floor. – Your apprentice is sorry, and will aspire to better herself.

– Your apology is appreciated, but not really necessary, he said. – You are young and bashful, and you will learn eventually. Now, continue your exploration.

He turned, and a door, a door concealed until this moment opened up before him. The tall man waved his cape, and was gone. Fear and admiration continued to rattle her.

Her feet began strolling, seeking to go where her eyes brought her. Or… she wondered if it was the other way around. The place had turned quiet, the presence of the Sorcerer only sensed, not felt. The girl was alone, and she cast apprehensive looks at the dark corners. She walked around the room, around and around, her eyes discovering ever more details for every new pass. Slowly her boundless curiosity and excitement won over the anxiety. A table setting caught her attention. There were nine rather large miniature statues standing in a circle, and one, larger standing in the middle. A male at the center. Four females and five males in the circle. The entire table had been… carved, been made into a representation of a… of something. It reminded her of pictures or drawings she had seen of ancient places of worship… of sacrificial tombs. She touched one of the statues, and it seemed to turn a brighter shade, to come alive at her touch. She pulled the hand back as fast as she was able.

Something resembling a carnival half mask hung on the wall. She was pulled to its vibrant violet shades, its dark raven feathers and light blue jewels.

It was like it gave her a jolt when she touched it. Her hand fell down and she backed off.

She walked out into the hall. There were stairs there, going both up and down. There was bright light upstairs and impenetrable darkness below, so she walked upstairs.

But still the darkness below beckoned her.

It was fairly ordinary upstairs, bright painted walls, naked floor and walls, except for a few carpets, a bit of furniture and paintings. People coming here and visiting only upstairs could easily be fooled into believing this was only an ordinary house.

Walking outside on a balcony she realized she was back on the Island. She recognized the streets below, as one in the town of Auburn on the other side of where she lived… where she had lived. A thrill shot through her when she realized what house this was.

She opened the doors to all the rooms. They were basically the same: One bed, made up, and that was all. She opened all the doors and looked inside methodically. There were nine bedrooms, all quite similar, one bigger with a distinctly bigger bed, and one larger bathroom at the end of the hallway. There were no windows anywhere. She frowned and returned to the first, bigger bedroom by the staircase, opening its door and peaked inside for the second time, and this time she noticed the maid uniform on the bed.

It was clearly meant for her. She knew that and had stepped inside well before she heard Mallory's voice speak to her from the air somewhere to her right.

– *Put it on.*

Fingers touched her clothes, and began removing them. She glanced into the wall mirror before a touch of embarrassment made her look away. Then shrugging, she deliberately returned her own mirror stare. She stood there nude, for one second or ten, before she began putting on the maid uniform.

She did wonder, when she looked at herself afterwards, at the different her, if Malone was into… kinky stuff. But she did not think so. If he wanted something, anything at all from her, it was not that.

The tentative young girl returned downstairs. The light changed from fairly bright to deep orange/red. There were no windows down here either. No door out either. She sought for minutes without finding one. There was the kitchen, with no windows. Another bathroom. Every new room had that deep, dark light.

She stepped through the door Malone had walked through. He sat there, in a deep chair, observing her as she entered the room. It was basically empty, except for him and the chair. He waved his hand, and another deep chair appeared opposite his.

– Sit!

The command rattled her. She quickly obeyed. The chair was comfy, pleasant. She fit it like a glove, as if she snuggled there, like a cat on people's lap.

– This is the house on Altram Hill, she stated. – It has been empty for generations. Several people, entrepreneurs and enterprises have attempted to take possession of it, and even demolish it, in vain.

– It has waited patiently for its next sorcerer, he explained.

She pondered those words, everything she experienced, striving to make sense of it, but it was like a whirl, even a vortex in her mind. Understanding eluded her.

– There is no entrance door here, she blurted out. – Why is there no door out?

– Why, do you need one?

He looked like he was enjoying himself.

– I just wanted there to be one, she whimpered.

– There is no door out, he told her sternly, – no way out of here, or in, for that matter, except through your awakening magick. In the meantime I will be happy to bring you, of course. You would want to see your friends and your mother, I trust, and you will be allowed to, at least up to a certain point, *the* certain point.

She wanted to ask him about that, but she was tongue-tied, and fearful, and so ashamed of herself.

I did not say goodbye, she thought.

– You will now clean the house. You will do nothing but work and feed and sleep. You will be exhausted, but that will only be the beginning. You will work until you drop, and when you wake up again you will keep working, and eventually you will be so tired that everything you used to be just *goes away,* and you will be nothing but that function, a shell, and then, when you are empty, I will fill you, fill you to the brim.

She rose and curtsied quickly, numbly, and left the room. The vacuum cleaner waited for her outside, where there had been no vacuum cleaner before. It was big and heavy, but she was tall and big and strong, and she gritted her teeth and did her best to prepare for what was to come. There were electrical outlets in the house. If there had not been any before there were now. She began with a sigh, sensing the insistent push in her back. The noise from the vacuum cleaner's working sounded strangely mute, as if the house or the air itself absorbed every sound not in immediate proximity to her ears. She dusted the books with a broom, and coughed, coughed hard while doing so. Clenching her teeth she pulled each and every book from the shelf, and dusted them. She sneezed, and she imagined she heard a loud crack rocking the house.

Her eyes flowing with tears she kept cleaning every scrap of surface in the room. The strange carving on the table did not seem to need cleaning, but she cleaned it anyway. The moment she touched it for the second time, it seemed to change, to transform into something strange and unknown. The small statues gained a semblance of… life. The eyes in the mask on the wall glared at her. She hurried on.

It took time and effort, this room alone. She dusted it, vacuum cleaned it and washed it clean, and she was half exhausted before the first hour, and then she moved on to the other rooms. Eventually it all looked and felt the same to her, turning into one, blurry impression.

She stood by the stairs, leading down to the basement, suddenly, once more aware of the passing of time.

It moved and breathed, the darkness below. She sensed light, from the torches on the walls down there, but she did not really see them. Her feet moved. Her soles touched the wood forming the stairs, as the wood turned to stone, and she stood on the ground below, into what resembled more a cave than a cellar.

It revealed and unfolded itself to her, to her known and unknown and unfamiliar senses, as if it… downloaded itself into her.

She saw a large room, one bigger than it was supposed to be, its space larger than the ground the house itself covered. It was a hall more than a room… or a cave. She looked at all the dirt on the floor.

– How can I clean up this? She cried out.

– You rub every spot of rock, and make it shine.

He told her from the air, from the corners and shadows of the room.

She shivered, biting her lip, determination visible in her eyes, as she kept working.

– My back hurts, she sniffed.

There was no reply, not even the hint of one. She poured water on the stone and began polishing it. And repeated the process. And walked back up to fetch more hot water and soap, and clean washing cloths. How many times she repeated the process she did not know, and eventually she did not care.

It was all just a blur of pain and despair and hardship.

– Feed, Malone commanded. – Replenish yourself.

She stood on her knees on the cold floor and fed herself the porridge he had put before her. Hunger assaulted her as something physical, a tangible thing scratching her insides. She ate like a pig and knew it, and she did not care.

Then she was back working, working, working. She took on the upper floor, and the attic, hardly registering anything anymore. Vacuum cleaning the floor, washing it, and polishing it. She did not see anything before her but a fog of indistinct embers. Her entire body hurt. But it did not really matter anymore. It had all become numb. She had become numb all over. There was no pain anymore, no thought, and no mind.

Her hand moved. Her sore skin held on to the swab. She stumbled down the stairs, rubbing the banister on her way. It was queasily clean by the time she was done. She returned to the living room with a sick smile on her face.

Malone was not there, but she still sensed him, sensed his eyes on her, sensed them preying on her. Her limbs hurt. Breathing hurt.

– I am done, she called out. – The work is complete.

There was no response. She did not even sense his presence anywhere, and she usually did. The house seemed quiet and empty.

But it was not, she realized startled. It… spoke to her, breaking through her fatigue, whispering cautious words of warning and danger.

She frowned, as she put her foot down. There was something making her frown, a nagging worry in her gut. She put it down one more time, hard. Dust rose from the floor.

– No! She cried out. – NO!

She rushed to the shelves, to the table, to all over the room. The thick layer of dust had returned everywhere, as if she had never removed it.

Her fervent search for a dustless spot proved fruitless, like she knew it would. She sat down on the floor, burying her face in her hands, shaking in frustration and exhaustion. A timeless time passed there on the floor, while she slowly, painfully pulled herself together, somehow.

She rose, stumbled back into the hall, pulled herself up the stairs. It held no surprise for her that the dust had returned here as well, and in the attic, and she knew beyond knowing that the stone floor in the basement was just as dirty as it had been before she had started on it. The vacuum cleaner waited for her, faithfully at the top of the stairs. She carried it back down, and began repeating her horrendous task.

There was no sleep, no rest. She slept, rested while she worked, while she struggled and suffered. Food arrived in the form of a large bowl on the floor in the kitchen, like to a pet. She went down on all fours and began feeding, licking up the thick, unsavory soup-like fluid like a cat, her hair coming in the way. No matter how many times she brushed it from her face, it returned and got in her mouth with the soup and she feared she would swallow it.

Leaving the empty bowl behind, she returned to work, and work and more work. She cleaned the table with the statues. They glowed even stronger and looked even more human-like now.

I cut you, the Master said. I gut you like I would a fish.

They frightened her. She shook like a leaf when they looked at her with their living eyes. The cloth in her hand dusted them, and it was as if it moved by itself, as if she was merely the tool of its quest to clean everything. The sound of the vacuum cleaner resounded inside her, and as it sucked in the dust, it felt like it sucked her empty as well.

She even looked like dust. The few glimpses she caught of herself in the mirrors did not encourage her to investigate the matter further. It did not do that at all. The darkness of the living room gave way to the brightness of the upper floor and the attic, to the dungeon below. She cleaned and rubbed and dusted, and she could no longer recall how many times she had repeated the performance. It was all a blur, a vast, empty hole inside of her.

Clean yourself, he told her in contempt. You are filthy.

And his contempt made her cringe in shame.

She showered. The deluge fell on her and washed her away. She cried, cried bitterly, but the tears did not show in the deluge falling on her. Drying herself seemed like a soft, dreamlike experience. Clothes, casual clothes, pants and sweater and socks, the works, had been put on the bed this time. She dressed in a slow, pleasant movement. The mirror did not really show much, as if she was hardly there at all. She walked through the house. There was no more dust or shit or anything anywhere, except a few spots she easily identified and took care of. She smiled in elation, and that smile, strange as it was, seemed to light up her entire self. Her very body smiled.

Music flowed from somewhere. She could sense it, sense its flow from the very air, and she followed it to its source, exactly like a moth to a flame. The young girl's face had a trance-like quality. She walked in a daze, not really seeing or registering her surroundings.

He sat in his chair by the fire, listening to the music seemingly flowing from the ether at the other end of the room. She saw a nice room, one with tables and chairs and shelves and carpets.

– It is not empty anymore?

– That is because you see more. He nodded. – I have torn the blindfolds from your eyes.

He stood behind her, suddenly. She jumped out of her skin, or that was how it felt. He turned her around, easily, a puppet in his hands.

– And now… I am going to *open* you, crack you open like I would a nut.

He put his hands on her shoulders. She wanted to pull away, but could not. He tore his claws into her skin, into her very being, his atonal voice filling her mind. An eerie, ghoulish and colorless glow began rising from her chest. She looked at herself through his eyes. He let her. As she watched it was as if her chest split in two. It felt strangely pleasant, almost sensual. She swayed from side to side with closed eyes and that weird, ecstatic smile.

– Feel it, he hissed. – Feel the *Magick!*

Pain shot through her. Her eyes opened wide and saw him stand there with a knife, cutting her open. She screamed, screamed her throat raw.

– You came here to learn, Janet, and learn you will. His mighty shout cracked her skin, all over the body, and she was crumbling, crumbling in his hands. – I open you. I open you wide. I fill you up, fill you to the brim.

She lay on a bed, one of fire and mist, and shadow, and she was burning, and she was screaming, her shrill echoing through an endless void, one she felt and sensed everywhere around her. The bed burned and no matter how much she fought to get up she could not move. Patterns formed in the ceiling, in the air above her, and she could not tell what was what. She glimpsed faces, brutal angry faces snarling at her. On occasion they came close, close enough for her to see their long, sharp fangs, and she screamed, howled in fear.

It was morning. She awoke on the bed in her room. Her eyes had been locked open, locked so hard that she was unable to close them. She pulled herself into a fetal position and lay there shivering for hours, days, years, and during all that time she did not dare close her eyes.

Stand up.

When the voice finally called to her she was relieved beyond words. She had missed it, believed it to be gone forever.

Are you ready?

– Yes, Master, she replied, calling out to the air.

Good. Make yourself presentable and come to me, and we will continue your education.

She showered. Water seemed fluffy, like snowflakes. It melted on her body, instead of hitting it. She rubbed herself slowly with the large towel, enjoying the touch of the fabric on her skin. It felt so very, very good. Her skin had become so sensitive, as if every touch was a million. She turned and saw the lovely dress on the bed, not really surprised. She put it on before the mirror, and then she proceeded at grooming herself, brushing her hair, applying make up, determined to look her best.

The face in the mirror looked like that of a stranger. In one way it looked the same, but in another, inexplicable way completely different compared to only a few days ago.

The eyes remained open, opaque, like glass, staring at the world in an unnerving and deep manner.

She left the room, walking barefoot on the cold floor, the soft carpet down the stairs. The house loomed silent around her, but she could still hear music. A dark organ solo rumbled in her mind. She noticed the long table in the sorcerer's room the moment she walked through the door. The scent of food played in her nostrils as never before.

– Ah, there you are, my dear, Malone greeted her with a bottle of wine in his hands.

He popped the cork without using any kind of aid she could see. The smell of wine reached her, and mixed pleasantly with the scent of the food inside her nostrils. He poured the blood red fluid into the two glasses. She walked to one end of the table. He was there, pulling out the chair for her, like a gentleman. She felt faint. He was everywhere around her, no matter where she turned.

They sat at each other's side of the long table, having a thoroughly civilized meal. The wine burned strongly in her stomach. She hardly noticed the food.

– How is the food? He inquired. – To your satisfaction, I trust?

– Yes, Malone, she replied eagerly.

They sat close, the long table shrinking before her eyes, until she felt she could reach out and touch him. He raised the glass.

– A toast, he said, – to Magick.

– To Magick, she voiced her agreement.

They drank. She felt the fluid pass her tongue and mouth and slip down her throat.

– It is so good, Malone, she said giddily. – I have never had wine before, never wine tasting so good. It is such a great taste, the flavors playing strings inside me I never imagined existed.

– It is not really the wine. He nodded. – It is you.

And the glow reached yet another level of power inside her. Power! She tasted the word, sipped it, and felt it flow down her throat.

She wondered if he was making a pass on her, if he… wanted her, and if she wanted him to. He had made no overt move regarding that, but he was older than her, far more experienced. He had probably learned the value of patience, of… savoring the hunt. She had heard the older boys at school speak thusly.

They sat in each their deep chair before the fire, the dancing fire. He studied her, over his meeting hands, his direct stare making her queasy and uncomfortable and hot and cold.

He reached out a hand, grabbed her jaw, opening her mouth, appraising her teeth as if she was some kind of beast. She choked, helpless in his grip.

– Your fangs are visibly longer than average, he noted.

He let go, of her body and mind, allowing her to respond.

– Yes, Master, it is a well-known, inherent trait on my mother's family tree.

He did not comment on that or visualize any reaction, but kept studying her, the leaf blowing in his wind.

– I wonder… what did you *feel,* the first time you walked down the stairs, to the basement?

She considered it, not certain what to say, not knowing what she would say, before saying it.

– I could hear it calling to me. I still can… I think. It was more than a calling, much more… a *compulsion.*

What am I saying? She thought.

– So, heed it, now.

– Excuse m-me?

– Stop fighting it, he said gently. – Give in, give in… to Power.

She sensed it, felt it inside, something breaking, a flow, a release. The wind began blowing. She rose. He nodded his approval. She walked. He followed her, out of the room, down the stairs. She saw his patronizing smile, even with her back to him, but she could work up no anger. He played her, and she wanted more.

The cave welcomed her. The hall seemed even larger than before. She spotted the altar almost immediately this time, the altar and the sacrificial stone, and her feet, crossing the scrubbed-clean floor were washed in a river of blood.

– This is…

– A Place of Power, she completed his words, her intonation sounding strange in her ears.

– An endless line of sorcerers has come here through the ages, he said, – using it as they saw fit, and now that honor has passed to Malone… and his apprentice.

Pride touched her yet again. Joy touched her. She focused, attempting to empty her mind, to fill it with the calling growing to the irresistible compulsion in her gut.

She heard the sound, a deep, clear tone resonating between the walls, and yet not of these walls at all.

There was something in the air, a shimmer, almost indistinct. But she saw it, even though she doubted many others could.

– Touch it, he hissed. – Touch Power.

She reached out with her left hand, sensing his smile, his triumph as she did so. Her fingers first, and then her hand vanished into the mist-like property.

– This isn't much…

She frowned… and screamed short and sharp.

– Do not, he snapped, – do not pull the hand back!

Pain cut through her. She watched, petrified, as large wounds appeared on her arm, and drops of blood jumped from her skin like rain.

– And now your other hand, he commanded. – You need to toughen up, remove yourself further from the sniveling brat you were.

She looked at him through tears, before resolve hardened her face, and she turned back towards the vortex and buried her second hand in the horror in front of her. Lips shivered, and the beginning of a wail turned to a prolonged scream. A molten wave of destruction heated her bones and blood, filled her being, and she could no longer scream, or even utter a single sound.

Her body stood there, frozen, shaking apart at the seams, in what seemed forever, while her blood boiled, and unimaginable images and impressions filled her, filled her to the brim, until she fell, and he caught her in his strong arms, and he carried her away.

She came to, awoke from her stupor, from the deepest of unconsciousness in the room with the fireplace. She rested on a couch, finding him bandaging her arms.

– It hurts, she said numbly. – My entire body hurts.

– Of course it does, he said unconcerned, indifferent. – You have touched the untouchable and survived.

She discovered that she was naked, that small wounds and bloodstains covered her body. The left arm was clearly the worse off, though. The hand looked like it had been caught in a vice. The wrist and lower arm like a shriveled vine.

– What was that? She whimpered.

Jumbled impressions kept jolting through her mind, making no sense.

– It is the Ascension, he said, eager like a boy, like the boy she had known. – Some of the sorcerers have merely been safeguarding it, guarding it, while others have sought the higher realms through it. I intend to do the latter, leaving you your inheritance. You will aid me in my quest, and will, in turn take my place.

A warm, warm glow filled her. She realized he had grabbed her hands. It hurt momentarily, but then the pain faded to a tiny buzz of the past. She looked astonished at her arm and the rest of herself. Malone had healed it, and healed her, healed all her wounds.

She looked at him with doglike gratitude, soundlessly mumbling his name. He rose and he reached out a hand for her. She gave him her hand, and he took it, and he pulled her up, pulled her hard, and it hurt, and she looked at him with eyes filled with gratitude, and only a little bit of fear.

And he led her away, and the two of them melted into the background, into the shadows.

She had showered again and changed clothes. More practical again, pants and a shirt, and a jacket, another of his visions of how he wanted her to appear and be.

They stood on the balcony turning south. It was a warm, pleasant night, filled with mist and shadows. There were houses, ordinary houses in a long row down the street.

– Can they… see us? She wondered.

– No, he replied with distinct pride and arrogance in his voice, – I am masking us from their view. They may hear us, if they listen hard, but not like anything but distant whispers in the wind.

She looked down. It was not far, not really. She could easily jump down without fear of injury or anything.

He turned towards her.

– You said you wanted to learn all the secrets of the world, he said sternly. – Now, I am asking you: Did you *mean* it?

– Yes, Master, she said instantly, potently. – I did. I *do!*

– There is no room for doubt, he said, the stern edge even sterner. – There was, but not anymore, not where we are heading. There are dangers ahead, places where a single moment of doubt and hesitation can bring disaster. It is very important that you are aware of this. This is the moment of final decision, of no return.

– I understand, Master, she assured him, close to panic, fearing he would reject her. – I will not fail you, I swear!

– I know you will not. You are exactly as eager and able as I envisioned.

The praise made the warm wind of pride rise within her, made her skin glow.

This time he gestured and opened a hole, a portal in the air in front of them. It impressed her so much and made her gasp in awe. He stepped through and vanished into the dancing mist and shadow, and after a brief hesitation, she followed. There was a momentary spell of dizziness, of the mist and shadow surrounding her, before she gasping and blinking stood in a hallway lit by torches. She noticed the walls, the walls and ceiling and floor of stone, and looked astonished at the sorcerer. They were in a cave, and far away from where they had been. She knew this was not the cave beneath the house. It both looked and smelled… and *felt* differently. Her senses, so much keener than they had been told her so.

She heard voices. They were close and far away, in all directions. The whispers close seemed to be whispering in her ears, hissing, flattering and cajoling. But there was no one there, no matter how many times she turned.

– Pay them no heed, Malone coached her unconcerned. – They are only dangerous if you allow it, and less than annoying if you ignore them.

– What *are* they? She cried exasperated, attempting to swat what was not there, like she would flies.

– They are spirits of a sort, he replied, – both of the living and the dead.

The chill crawled down her spine like spiders.

She heard music, but it was not like any music she had ever heard. It did not seem to come from anywhere, except from everywhere around her. It surrounded her, embraced her.

– You can hear it? She heard the distinct sound of excitement in the sorcerer's voice, and that, in turn excited her as well. – Tell me you can hear it?

– I can, Master, she cried. – It is overwhelming.

A gasp escaped between her lips. She felt like doubling over, but stood straight, stood her ground, smiling excitedly when she noticed the Master's nod of approval.

– Do like I told you, he told her, – use your power. Grab the air and move it.

She began moving her hands, hesitatingly at first, but then in something very much resembling confidence. Her hands touched the air, the waves assaulting her, and she bent them, pulling them inside her, pushing them away, at her convenience. She realized that she was actually emitting them and that they were hers to command. A smile broke on her face, and made a strange… twinkle appear in her eyes. She saw that though Malone's eyes. He let her, showed her what she could not see.

– Eventually you will not have to move your hands, he revealed to her.
– That is just the crutches of the novice. You will be able to do it with the power of your will alone.

The reaction to both the praise and contempt he showed her warred within the nebulous sorcerer.

He led her further down the passage. The light, fire red at the beginning shifted slowly. The torches on the walls changed to a bluish flame, turning darker. She realized startled that the light no longer was torches, no longer was stuck on the walls, but levitated in the air on both sides of the sorcerer and his apprentice. Dark blue lights showed the path in a place where there were no longer any walls, but a landscape of mist and hardly anything else.

She heard voices again, different from before, closer the further they walked. The ground below her moved, *swayed.* She realized startled that it was not really ground beneath her feet, but a bridge of sorts, and that only the dark blue lights marked its boundaries.

– Do I hear a river? She wondered.

– A river, yes, he replied, clearly preoccupied.

The curious girl looked down, but there was nothing to see, except the mist, the twilight, swirling mist.

– How long is the bridge? She wondered, speaking in a whisper.

Or so it seemed. All sound faded here, into the mist of the nothingness surrounding them.

– Long, he replied, still preoccupied.

She heard sounds, snarls reaching them from afar, occasionally closer, and realized why he was preoccupied. His entire body was strung like piano wire.

They reached solid ground again eventually, after a walk seemingly lasting for hours. The blue lights faded in the mist, into nothing.

He visibly relaxed. She noticed that without trying. They walked on a road covered by flat stones. She glimpsed them like she did her feet, before the mist slowly dissipated a little, and she noticed buildings ahead of them, realizing startled that they were already inside a small township, something reminding her of descriptions she had heard of a medieval village, even though that was not exactly right.

A man, a bard, a singer, a poet stood on a corner ahead, calling out to people passing by, calling out to her. They passed him. Malone basically ignored him. She did her best to do so, as well. He faded in the mist behind them, like the few others venturing outside this twilight.

She frowned. His voice seemed to grow stronger, not weaker.

And there he was again, on the next corner ahead. She heard his voice, heard it close and she understood the words.

The nine resided in the land of the moon

Stepping out into the courtyard an enchanted night

Finally being born to their destined life

Suns have been born and died

Moons have set and risen a million times

Awaiting their long prophesized birth

He played something resembling a guitar, even though that was not exactly right either. She shivered as the chords and the words and the strings cut into her. He stood there, on every corner they passed, and when she looked at him, there was nothing there, no features in what went for the face he revealed under the hood, except a dark texture of nothingness. His fingers seemed to be more mist than flesh, nothing more than the air and twilight surrounding them.

She looked for him at the next corner, but he was not there, and when she turned her head and looked back, she did not see him there either. He was nowhere to be seen, and she realized that she could not hear the music anymore, and she felt herself in the grip of panic.

Malone touched her shoulder in a comforting grip.

– It is okay, he said. – We are outside again.

And when she glanced around her, at their more mundane surroundings she believed she understood what he meant.

– I miss it already, Master, she said eagerly, with a touch of sorrow in her voice.

– I know you do, he nodded.

They arrived at a clearing, an open space among the houses. She sensed it, a resistance in the air, something guarding this place, whatever it was, keeping out the unworthy. Only the powerful could find and visit this place. She pushed forward, through the protecting membrane, and joy and triumph shot through her, as she appeared on the other side.

People appeared to her, fading in from many gates, entry points. The open space had transformed into a house, a tavern. Youthful exuberance lit her face, before she glanced at the Master and caught herself.

But the glow in her eyes persisted.

They were here, wherever here was, and her heart swelled big and beat hard. She recognized the significance of the moment, and looked at her mentor with infinite gratitude in her eyes.

Chapter 3

The place looked old, old fashioned and recent both. Janet took it all in in a flash, or a series of flashes. One moment there had been nothing there, and then everything. She shook her head in an effort to rid herself of the sudden dizziness, but it persisted.

– Am I looking at the world upside down? She asked Malone.

– Nothing so mundane, he replied.

Other people, both those sitting and new arrivals, like themselves gazed at them, like everybody did at everybody, studying them with hungry, penetrating eyes.

– Does the attention bother you? He asked sternly.

– No, Master, she replied instantly. – It probably would have before you took me away, before you revealed the much bigger world to me, but now it seems merely a trifle, one to be rejected with a shrug.

He did not say anything, but she knew he was pleased with her, pleased with his apprentice, and joy spread within her like lava would flow down a mountainside.

Everything was red and orange here, though not in any obvious way. The very air, people's flesh and tables and desks and chairs and ale consisted of fire, of dark and dancing flames. The thought, the realization came to her easily, even as it startled her.

A dark red light was hanging, hovering above the bar, and could sort of create the impression dominating her perception, but everything seemed so different that she could not be certain.

This place had been created by mist and shadow, and in-between was the invisible fire. She saw it. It impressed itself upon her, no matter where she looked.

– Do not study the Masters, Malone commanded her. – Study their apprentices.

Her attention had been drawn to the masters. It had been easy to pick them. They were mostly older, and wore, like Malone an aura of confidence around them like a glow, their authority like a dusted coat. Their shadows were just that, a pale, unremarkable reflection of the sun they made pitiful attempts at emulating.

She obeyed her Master instantly, without consideration and thought, and then, remarkably the thoughts entered her empty mind, as she began measuring her equals.

They were her age, practically all of them, with flickering eyes and with tongues sticking out and constantly wetting dry lips. She recognized herself in every face she closed in on.

Malone walked to a table, one in the corner, and she followed right behind. He sat down. She was about to sit down in the other chair when he stopped her. He produced a coin, the strangest coin she had ever seen, and threw it to her. She snapped it in the air, overjoyed because she did it so easily, so effortlessly.

– Fetch ale, Malone commanded her.

She looked towards the bar, at the queue forming, instantly disheartened.

– Right away, Master, she acknowledged.

The girl rushed forward and began pushing herself forward in the queue, slipping past those she did not push aside, and amazingly she was one of the first getting served. Many an evil eye followed her when she returned to the table with two huge glasses of ale in her hands. She put one glass down before Malone, excitement making her blush hard.

– Now, that was not so hard, was it?

– No. She shook her head excitedly. – Not hard at all.

– You should prepare yourself for more true hardship, though. That is always wise.

– Yes, Master. She bowed her head, taking a sip of the cold ale, looking at him from beneath lowered eyelashes.

He was clearly pleased. She sensed his anticipation, or rather perhaps impatience and also something beneath that she did not quite understand, but something that reminded her very much of apprehension, and she wondered what could make a man like Malone the Sorcerer feel such a thing.

She took a large sip, using it to camouflage her observation of the other apprentices, as they returned flustered to the masters with ale, and she realized startled that, aside from the female bartender there were only masters and apprentices here. Some of the other youngsters looked at her with scorn and worse in burning eyes. She returned the scorn and added spite, instantly sensing Malone's approval and the glow rising inside.

The bartender had served the first round to everybody and had started polishing glasses. Janet's eyes delved briefly by her, an act the girl instantly regretted when the big woman caught her with her piercing eyes. The girl looked away, the hand holding the glass visibly shaking.

Malone looked at her. She felt it, actually felt it and looked at him.

– You are wise to show respect for Florence, he grinned. – She has young sorcerers for breakfast.

Something else dawned on her. She studied him carefully, pulling herself together, looking up from beneath her lowered eyelashes.

– Why have we come here, Master?
– You are such a bright girl, he chuckled, clearly condescending.
Shame and need burned within her. She did not lower her eyes again.
– It is your Path, he told her sternly, – a rather important part of your education. During the next days and nights and weeks and perhaps even months you better be at your best, or I would not want to be in your shoes.
– I will be, she said numbly and animated both. – I will not fail you, Master. I will not!
– I know you will not, he shrugged. – I would not have chosen you otherwise.
And once again she sensed that strange ambivalence in him, of excitement and trepidation, or rather unease, and she wondered what he feared.
She frowned, her mind going further down strange and rarely tread paths.
– I hear many different languages, she mused, her ever-growing curiosity piqued, – but mostly English, even though people are clearly from many different realms. How can that be?
– The explanation, he replied dryly, – even though it instantly raises far more questions than it answers, is fairly simple. What is now called English, amazingly enough without that much change in its original form, has been the preferred language of a considerable majority of sorcerers for hundreds of generations. Thus, since sorcerers tend to dominate their societies it has also spread to the general population. On one hand, English developed in the distant land of England just a few centuries ago. On the other it has been in use for a very long time. It is another Great Mystery.
Thirsty, she was so thirsty. One more greedy and huge sip of the ale merely whetted her… her hunger.
She heard a sound, and looking at the others, she realized that they all heard it, the masters with satisfaction and expectation, and the apprentices with wonder and curiosity.
One of the walls faded away, like the gossamer and mist it was, and revealed a much bigger room, an entire hall beyond. The bar became a part of the hall, and suddenly they were in the hall, still sitting by their tables, their tables bigger, and their chairs turning into benches, the wood literally stretching and changing beneath the guests until the process was complete.
Janet looked stunned at Malone.
– What *is* this place?
– It is a Learning House, he shrugged, – a place of Magick and discovery unique in creation, or at least on this plane of existence. You will not be done learning when you leave this class, but you will be pushed many times beyond your current level of proficiency. Florence will beat it into you and

fill you until you are ripe.

Ripe for what? The girl wondered, but she did not voice her concern.

They were served at the table here, by insanely tall and big wraiths, vaguely resembling males and females, human youths in hoods and robes, their faces hidden in shadow. All of them looked transparent, somehow, but they held on to the tray and the glasses, so they could not be… intangible.

Janet figured.

Fear touched her again, though she could not say why.

– They are out of phase with this reality, Malone told her frankly, sending elephant shivers down her spine. – You will be like them in a few hours, when the doorway opens, and you will not return until you are a full-fledged sorcerer's apprentice, and *then* the teaching can begin in earnest.

Something dawned on her, with the chill and the fear.

– You are sending me to… boot camp? She cried. – To a training ground?

He laughed out aloud.

– You never cease to amaze me, he said, very pleased. – I commend you, my apprentice. You use wording and phrases that have not been in much use in your society for generations, even centuries, and you can even use them correctly.

– My goddess, she said, shaking her head, giggling anxiously.

– Florence can teach you things I can not, he said curtly, darkly. – She is a cruel, very cruel bitch and will prepare you for what lies ahead.

– What lies ahead? She whispered.

– Everything, he shrugged.

He leaned forward, and in his eagerness she saw glimpses of the boy she had briefly known. In his cruel eyes she saw the man he had become.

– You do not know, but I do. I know everything that is going to happen to you. I see your entire, glorious path as an afterglow of what will be.

– How? She pushed herself into saying it, even though she did not want to. – You are not psychic, not… a Seer, are you?

– No, not psychic. He shook his head, grinning his cruel smile. – Not a Seer.

– So, what is going to happen? Please, please tell me.

There was no reply, except his cruel and excited smile.

She awoke from what resembled a deep sleep, or trance.

People had approached them, and she had not seen them coming, and that scared her, scared her badly.

It was a Master and his apprentice, a young, sullen boy.

– Well met, Malone, the scowling man in the funny hat said.

– Well met, Grayson, Malone replied fairly relaxed.

The old man looked at her as if she was a heap of garbage, stinking like years' old rot.

– So, who is this child? I do not think we have had the pleasure of gazing at her beauty before.

He visibly took notice of an apprentice, and even inquired about her. That, in itself was so unusual, even «scandalous» that it made Janet hold her breath.

– This is Janet, Malone introduced her. – She will take me to the Heights.

Surprise, puzzlement and more revealed itself in Grayson's face, as he stared hard and incredulous at Malone, and something passed between the two men. Janet rose and curtseyed quickly, casting her eyes to the ground.

– Well, at least she is well trained, Grayson snorted patronizingly.

– She has learned the value of being polite towards her betters, Malone replied evenly. – But do not be deceived. She is a firecracker, with all the qualities necessary for the ceremony.

Janet blushed, Malone's praise mending the anger over Grayson's words.

– I may try for the Heights myself, Grayson pondered.

– YOU? Malone laughed out aloud and very, very sarcastic. – How many times exactly have you tried and failed by now? You hold a kind of record, in that regard… do you not?

There was laughter coming from all over the place. None of the apprentices was laughing, but quite a few of the masters were. Grayson turned red as a tomato, rushing off in a rage, hissing something to Malone that Janet did not catch.

His apprentice trailed him like a worm in mud.

She did not get the words, but their meaning was loud and clear, and she shivered.

– It was not a curse, was it, Master?

– Do not be afraid. He chuckled some more. – I and Grayson are too evenly matched to throw curses at each other. His words literally translate into «the ashes of the Master», «the remains of his fire». It is an insult, meant for both of us.

And Janet felt a little better, a little worse.

She felt, literally felt everyone's eyes on her, very aware of the cruel fact that she had just been elevated from obscurity to the talk of the evening.

Florence's sticky eyes burned her neck and she shuddered.

A bell sounded, seemingly from the very ground beneath their feet, one, two, three times, repeated in sequence.

– It is the portal, an apprentice cried excitedly, – it is opening.

– It is not an ordinary portal either, another, equally excited corrected him,

– but one accessing the *Crossroads*.

Malone emptied his glass and so did Janet, and so did every other person in the room that had become a hall. Some of the youths had already gathered at a central point, and the others were already hurrying towards it. She looked at Malone. He sat there, gazing relaxed at her, shrugging.

– Some paths must be walked or traveled without cutting corners. That is just the way it is. Go, now, fledgling and return to me like the hawk you are.

She swallowed hard, glancing around her, a stubborn look slowly manifesting in her young, incomplete face.

– Nothing, she nodded. – We all leave with nothing, except what we carry inside. So be it!

She walked towards the center, holding her head high, not looking back, melting into the mist and mass before her. Other bundles of nerves surrounded her and she felt comforted in a way, but did not really allow herself to entertain such thoughts, and in the mirrors she glanced at she saw the same stubborn reluctance reflected back at her.

The woman Malone had called Florence joined them in the gathering of mist and shadows. The moment she crossed that invisible circle, reality itself began shifting around them. The world turned ice-cold in an instant, turning Janet and the others outside in. The surroundings changed completely around them. They stood there gasping, in a realm of harsh winds and foul air, weak as kittens.

– Walk! Florence commanded, her voice at least as cold as the world between worlds they had passed through.

She walked ahead, and they followed her, stumbled in her trail. There had been no need for her to say anything. Janet realized that in a flash. They would have followed her anyway. But she had wanted to make a point.

Janet spotted a structure somewhere ahead. It looked fairly close, beyond two or three minor small ups and downs in the terrain. All the apprentices started walking with a fairly optimistic outlook present in their features.

The frown appeared on those faces fairly soon. They had walked a long while after that and the frown had deepened into a furrow so deep that it threatened to become permanent. Janet, like all of them realized that their objective was far away. After walking until twilight she realized it was very far away. They had moved straight forward for what had to be close to a day, and the structure seemed no closer.

One of the boys fell. Florence was over him instantly. A stick appeared in her hand, from nowhere, and she began striking him, striking him hard. He screamed short and sharp and jumped back on his feet.

They kept walking.

It turned dark, but never completely dark. They were able to see the ground and the far away structure easily enough. Florence drove them further on, on the invisible trail, never saying a word, striking them every time they even showed sign of slowing down. She seemed completely unfazed, walking with a steady, murderous speed, while most of them stumbled forward and had to practically run most of the time, with acid, blinding sweat in their eyes.

– Stop! She said, at what had to be close to dawn.

They stopped, looking very attentive at her.

– Sit!

They sat down in the dirt without thinking twice about it. Janet glimpsed the others through a haze of exhaustion, sick and nauseous. They all looked as bad as she felt. Florence walked to them with a tray of baby bottles in her hands.

– You are newborns, she told them, – helpless and frail. I am your mother. I will nourish you and teach you about life.

They opened their mouth. She pushed the teat between their lips. They closed their mouth and began sucking, sucking greedily.

It tasted awful, and it was so damn humiliating, but they drank, sucked the hardest they were able. Janet felt it, as it spread throughout her body, as it hurt her and changed her. She wanted to protest, to voice her displeasure, but it was as if there was a blanket covering their mind, keeping them from speaking up or even think.

They walked on. It was the next day and the hot sun boiled them in cruel and merciless ways. They rested. There was no shade. They whimpered and opened their mouth, and Mother gave them to drink. Feet moved, and moved endlessly. Janet could not tell if this was the next day or if an endless number of days had passed. She feared there had been another brief night or ten, but she could not quite wrap her mind around it. On occasion she cast her swollen eyes, like they all did at the Structure.

It was no closer.

She came to look at it as elusive as a dream, a mirage fading away as they drew close. They crouched on the ground and threw up, puking their guts out. It truly felt that way. She hurt so much, believing she would be unable to take any more, but she did.

– Focus on the pain, the mirage walking among them commanded. – Let it take you over and be transformed, be forever changed.

It was not difficult. The pain became Janet's friend, her only companion, as the wraiths walking with her turned ever more ethereal and unreal and even invisible at times.

And there was Florence, kind, strict, brutal and kind Florence. Janet looked at her with love in her eyes when she was given to drink, mirroring all the other wraiths around her. She loved the drink so sweet, the taste of the teat in her mouth.

Life before this quickly turned distant. They had been born from the cold womb, out here on the ragged, hostile hills, and that was all there was.

They crouched on the ground, screaming, as their bones broke and reset themselves, as they changed, and grew taller and stronger, like Janet dimly remembered the wraiths in the beer hall.

– I want to go HOME, the boy from earlier whined.

Florence beat him until he fell silent.

They ran, ran towards the distant Structure, and in doing so lost even more of themselves to the run and to the battering winds, and to the Change.

– Humans can not survive here, Florence told them, – not without the elixir. It makes you sturdier, stronger and changes you inside out, making you more than human.

The ten felt an enormous gratitude towards her, as they rested there in their stupor, on the hard ground, exhausted beyond exhaustion.

Ten pair of weary eyes looked up, after the tenth or the hundredth day. The Structure loomed over them, blocking half the sky, and they realized, beyond certainty that they had finally reached their destination.

– You have made it, Mother told them. – Congratulations. Welcome Home!

It was something in the subtext of her words making Janet frown. She frowned and forgot all about it the next second.

They crossed a long bridge, one not bridging a river but another swirling dark and impossible to penetrate mist. Janet shook when she looked down at it and so did the other nine. The Structure was made of rock, but seamless, without any visible cracks at all, as if having been grown, not built. The gate began rising behind them the moment they stepped inside. It slammed close with a loud crack.

The Structure, with stone walls, floor and ceiling resembled a medieval castle, at least their impression of such, at least on the inside. It looked pleasant enough, even through their weary eyes.

They blinked, and suddenly they saw more. Every time they blinked they saw…

More.

Chairs, tables and paintings on the wall faded into their line of vision, shimmering a bit, before solidifying, turning tangible and real.

Shadowy figures, creatures appeared before their eyes, hooded males and females taking their measure, making them shake in their bones.

Large, claw-like hands appeared from the cloak. Janet spotted the ropes and froze to ice, like all of her traveling companions.

– To the Dungeon with them, Florence barked her orders. – Take them and leave them in pieces. If they resist even the slightest you will punish them severely.

Janet wanted to move, to run, to flee, but she could not move, and she, like the rest offered no resistance when the giant, human-like wraiths approached them. The girls and boys' hands and arms were grabbed, grabbed and squeezed, squeezed hard, making them yelp in pain, and their wrists were tied together and they were pulled away by their terrifying keepers. They looked at Florence for mercy, but there was none in her hard, hard eyes.

They were pulled down a wide staircase, stumbling more than walking, and every time they attempted to slow down they were beaten. A large fist hit Janet in the ribs. She almost fell and only the numbing fear kept her on her feet.

The staircase seemed to go on forever, down, down, down. They imagined they glimpsed the end of it far, far down, but it seemed more and more like a mirage for every new step. When they eons later realized they were indeed walking on a flat floor they could not tell how much time had passed since they had reached the end of the stairs. When they glanced behind them the stairs were no longer there.

The Dungeon was exactly that, a wet, cold cellar, going on forever through dark and dank hallways. Janet felt both warm and cold and could not decide which was which. The rope was tight around her wrists and her hands turned even number than the rest of her aching body.

They turned a corner. When they spotted the open cell doors they hardly reacted at all, and that, in itself made it all worse. The first prisoner was dragged into a cell. The wraith put a collar fastened to the wall with a chain around the boy's neck. She grabbed his jaw and squeezed his mouth open and put the bottle, without the teat, now, to his lips and emptied its content into his mouth. He drank, swallowed in a distant, mechanical manner giving Janet more of those dull shivers she recalled so well and had been living with for so long. They were pulled in one by one. No one offered any resistance. Janet was pulled in. Her keeper was a giant hulk of a male. She strived to see his face in the shadows of the hood, in vain. He put the collar around her neck. The metal felt so cold, so very cold on her skin. She wanted to ask him to untie the ropes tying her wrists together, but she could not even work up courage enough to try, to speak or even raise her arms. He gave her to drink and she drank, drank every little drop entering her mouth. She wanted it, the foul drink, wanted to grow strong and powerful and terrifying like him.

He walked back out and closed the heavy door, and left the young girl alone in the darkness. She sat down on the floor, unmoving, unthinking. Other doors closed. She did not move, but sat there, blind and mute, while more and more doors closed, and the same, sickening sound of grinding stone echoed in her numb mind.

– I thought this was supposed to be a LEARNING HOUSE, a muffled cry from a girl reached Janet from somewhere to the left.

Janet feared that it was, feared that it was not.

– No, the girl whined. – I did not mean it, did not mean to speak. PLEASE!

Janet sat there, shaking her head, and shook, shook hard when the screams began, when the girl was *punished* for her indiscretion, for the simple act of opening her mouth. Everybody heard the sound of a whip hitting a shaking body. They could not help but see it through their closed tight eyes.

The Dungeon fell silent. They imagined they heard muffled sobs from somewhere, but they could not be certain. It seemed to invade them, to come from the inside, not through the ears at all. Janet attempted to listen, to study her surroundings, but everything turned muddled, turned gray and indistinct. She noticed that her clothes had become tight, that they were tightening around her limbs to the point of becoming unpleasant to wear. The pain in her hands grew worse, a dull, distant pain slowly increasing. She imagined that she had trouble breathing, to the point of every new breath becoming yet another desperate gasp for air.

And it felt distant, as if it happened to someone else.

She sat there on her ass, unable to move, floating away, becoming one with the floor and the wall and the ceiling and the very air she breathed, and it was not good. It felt horrible. She feared she was disintegrating, that she ceased to exist. Memory failed her. She was unable to recall even the simplest of events from her distant, former life. Agitation ruled her, occasionally, for a moment or two, as she sat there, panting in panic, before slipping back into oblivion and nothing mattered anymore.

Her keeper returned now and then. She did not know his name. He never spoke, but fed her the elixir and left. His brief visits did not feel more real than the walls and the cell itself. He was merely one more specter in what had become her fleeting reality.

They were brought out occasionally, taken for a walk, like dogs, brought to an arena of sorts. It existed within the castle, but there was no ceiling above their head. It reminded Janet of an arena in Old Rome, even though there was no audience, none they could see, anyway. The thought came to her in a glimmer of realization, and the next moment it was gone, like smoke. They were thrown two and two into the pits dug all over the sandy ground. Janet and the other looked confused around them. She spotted a wand right in front of her, a mirror image of the one in front of the boy facing her.

– FIGHT, YOU DUMB BEASTS. Florence's voice sounded from above them, hurting in their ears. – FIGHT UNTIL YOU DROP!

Janet picked up the wand, the fighting wand, bending numb fingers around the wood. The boy did, too. It was surprisingly light, even taking into account their newly acquired strength. She tested it, swung it around in her hands, easily swinging it in the air. They both did, in spite of their tight bound wrists. Images appeared in her mind's eye, illustrating its use, teaching her, forcing it on her, becoming her entire consciousness. The girl, the illustration in her mind struck at her opponent, and Janet did it just a tiny moment later. The point of the wand hit the boy on the head. He yelped in pain and shook his head, but he did not fall. He struck out with a wild swing, hitting Janet in the shoulder, making her cry out in shock and pain and incredulity and fury.

They went clumsily at each other with swinging wands. The sound of wood hitting wood, and flesh and the grunts of those going at each other filled the arena, filled the head of those fighting, those struggling to move to the different beat their lives had become.

She hammered him. He hammered her. It did not seem to affect any of them considerably, except adding to the dull pain filling their very existence.

The ropes seemed to… dissolve. She frowned, as she felt it, noticed it, as the ropes gave way and broke under the onslaught of their enhanced strength. It should make them feel good. She knew that somewhere, inside, but it was merely one more detail in the monochrome scheme they stumbled through.

It went on and on through the day. Every time they faltered and thought they could not go on anymore the silent presence in their mind spurred them on.

The strange, pale sun moved on the sky, somewhat, as the shadows on the ground changed form, but time did not really seem to pass much. They kept striking each other, until the sense of wood against skin and skull was the only thing they could feel.

Days and nights passed there, in the pit.

Stop! The voice inside hardly sounded like a voice at all, but like an incomprehensible collection of syllables. Obedience still struck them instantly.

That is good boys and girls. Now, *sit!*

They did and suddenly they found themselves together again, with everybody else that had come through the gate with them, and they could not tell whether or not they had moved at all. Florence walked among them, a glowing mirage among the pale wraiths.

– Look at you, she spat in contempt. – Someone has just filed you away, left you here to rot.

Janet's head hurt. It hurt all the time. Something told her it was all the hits she had taken, but that same, distant voice also told her that those selfsame hits should have injured her to the point of death.

So, she did not listen to it.

– You will never leave this place, Florence told them. – No one will come and «rescue» you, take you away from here. Accept it and embrace your new reality.

It sounded true, so very convincing and true, and their heart faded further in their chest and soul. The girl understood in her dim mind the double incredulity in Grayson's stare, now. Dull understanding brought an even higher number of dry, bitter tears.

Janet was back in her cell, with the collar around her neck, but without the ropes around her wrists. She could not tell how she had returned, only that she had. Only glimpses, fragments of her new existence were available to her. Every time she attempted to focus on a specific moment it just slipped away.

She remembered the fury. It felt so good, so pleasant in her dead self.

Her keeper returned now and then, to feed her. He groped her, touched her all over her body with his large and strong hands and brutal strength, and she half expected him to fuck her, but he never did, and somehow that made everything worse.

They were let out to fight, and they did so, relentlessly, and they enjoyed it. It no longer felt strange or awkward to them. She looked at her hands afterwards, her bloody and mauled hands. They no longer looked like a girl's hands at all, but, even though still small compared to that of the hands feeding her, large, fleshy hands.

Her keeper returned, and he began groping her, and she, desperate for some contact other than the hard wood leaned on him, pushed herself at him, and his body seemed hard as wood. Her hand reached out, tracing the lines of his hip. He did not seem to notice. She reached the spot between his legs, and stopped for a moment, but she was beyond embarrassment, beyond caring, and grabbed hold of the swinging thing there, began playing with, teasing it.

But nothing happened. She stopped, breathing hard, looking startled at him, finally able to grab hold of something other than a stray thought. He slapped her, and his slap, with his strength was more like a brutal strike. She fell on the floor, actually feeling for the first time she could remember the sweet taste of blood in her mouth.

– What has she *done* to you? She cried. – What is she doing to us all?
Talking hurt, as if her throat had turned to sand.

He pulled back, staring at the floor, shame and indignity written all over the powerful frame. She went to him, caressing the face under the hood.

– You poor thing, she whispered, she cooed.

He pulled further back, and the chain kept her from following.

– No! She whined. – Please do not leave me, leave me here.

The door slammed shut and she fell on the floor, imagining she felt tears flow down her cheeks.

And everything turned dark and non-existing again, as if she just melted and flowed through the cracks in the floor. Flashes returned to her, occasionally of her distant previous life, but they were incomprehensible and granted her only confusion and disarray, and nothing more, not even the dull pain she had grown so accustomed to. Everything faded into the emptiness surrounding her.

Two of them came for her, one male and one female the next time the door opened, and time once again marked its passing to her. They brought her outside, to once again join the line of her sister and brother wraiths. The line was driven along a different route this time. She could tell. The palace was known to her. She remembered all its corners, hooks and crannies. It was more than a map in her brain. It was like she had become the palace, all its bricks and grains of dust.

When they entered the room with the steaming pool she knew they would, before she actually saw it with her eyes.

Their keepers grabbed them and tore the remaining rags off their bodies. Nude males and females, suddenly aware of themselves again and their bodies reeking of stench felt shame. They hurried into the practically boiling water and began rubbing and washing themselves, washing each other. The heat did not hurt them. It felt pleasant in a way. The presence in their mind approved, and that was all that mattered.

They frothed each other afterwards, standing close, like dogs licking each other clean. The next moment they were moving again. Everything happened between moments. Janet choked. They stood in the next room, or the next after that, stood there dressing, in coarse, unassuming fabric.

– Look at yourselves. Florence bid them. – What do you see?

There was a mirror there, right in front of her, Janet imagined there was, but she could not really see herself. There was nothing there but an indistinct, transparent figure. The same dull panic filled her, quickly fading.

They were given the hood and the robe and the cloak, and the image was complete. There was no discernible difference, except for the obvious difference in size between the new and old wraiths.

– Your ranks will swell further today, Florence spoke to them. – You will serve your new brethren, and then they will serve you forever.

Janet did not understand, and she did not try to do so.

She followed the regal woman and so did the other nine. The bigger, older wraiths did not. Janet did not question this, but took it on faith, as did the other nine. They followed Florence like panting dogs into another room, a reception area of sorts. It brought a faint recollection to Janet's dull mind, even though she was unable to identify it.

They saw benches and tables, and seemingly fading in from nowhere people sitting down, ten pairs of people, one young and one clearly older, sorcerers and their apprentices. Janet felt a faint chill, but nothing more. She and the others picked up the trays with the beer, and it felt like they had done it a thousand times.

She served the nearest table. The tray was solid and so were the glasses, but when her hand «touched» the table it went straight through. The young man looked at her. She felt his curious, young eyes on her, as he attempted to gauge her features, but they were concealed in mist and shadow.

Nobody could see her, see anything but the hood, the robe and the cloak, and the indistinct image of the hand on the tray and the glass.

She wanted to warn him, all of them, but she feared her voice would fail her, that no one would hear her, because she was not really here.

Another spilled some beer. It went right through his hand and hit the floor with a splash. She wanted some beer, desperately wanted to taste something other than the elixir in her mouth, but knew it was hopeless.

There was socializing, like before, masters renewing their acquaintance, and measuring each other, and apprentices throwing shy glances at the other youngsters. They felt very brave and cocky these girls and boys, having no idea what awaited them.

Janet and the others walked among them, not there, not present or any factor at all in what was happening. They were merely window-dressing, a way of making the deceit even more effective. She imagined her hand was shaking, but there was no visible sign of that. They were perfect servants.

The bell rang. Janet heard it, even though it sounded muted in her ears. She felt the shaking in the floor and the shift when the portal opened. The young girls and boys bid farewell to their professed masters, having no idea what a betrayal it was.

Janet wanted to know why. She wanted it badly.

But no explanation was forthcoming, or even in the cards.

They were just treated like dirt under Florence's feet, and that was what they were quickly becoming. She used them for her own ends, and did not care about them, did not care about them at all.

The youths walked into the ring. Florence joined them there. Janet blinked, suddenly seeing two Florences. The one in the castle was still here, with them, with Janet and the rest, standing outside the floor, invisible to those in the tavern.

The excited girls and boys vanished, but Florence, the other Florence did not vanish with them, but remained inside the circle on the floor, stepping out of it, joining her fellow sorcerers. They all looked smugly at each other. There was no doubt anymore. The sorcerers were not ignorant, but were, on the contrary in on it.

One nod from Florence, from the mistress of the castle and Janet and the rest turned attentive towards her.

– I am a Goddess, she told them briskly. – I can exist in many realms, both here and there simultaneously.

Her voice turned cruel, menacing, triumphant.

– As I trust you are aware of by now: you are mere wraiths anywhere else. This is the only place you are real. That is your one and only fate.

Janet heard whimpers, perhaps from her own dry mouth, perhaps from others, and she choked in silent despair.

– I will now go and meet your new brethren. You will go on a mission, to prove your eagerness, your dedication to me. It will be days before the new meat arrives, and by then you will be here to greet them, to give them your affectionate kisses, so much stronger and crueler and better suited for your future tasks.

She faded away, and Janet imagined she saw her appear by the portal just as the poor fools arrived.

They were taken the long pathway through the castle. Janet attempted to focus, to get her bearings, to observe her surroundings and imprint them in her mind. It was large, the castle, practically gigantic, almost like a small city, and it seemed to expand occasionally, to… grow, and sometimes even to contract, to shift and change, to a point where one path was never the same. But the wraiths pushing them forward, hounding them knew their way, and did not seem to have any trouble navigating.

Janet studied them, and did her best to emulate them, learn from them, becoming more like them with every new step.

They arrived at something similar to a dressing room. It wasn't exactly that, though. There were pairs of boots and gloves, and nothing else. They put them on, did not need anything but light prodding from the hulks around them. Janet wanted to appeal to them, to beg them to be merciful, but there was nothing there to appeal to, and she wondered, in her sick fear how long they had been in the castle to become what they had become.

The next room was the entrance hall, so familiar, so unknown compared to how Janet remembered it. Florence appeared and pulled a lever on the wall, and the gate was lowered, becoming a bridge again. The hulking wraiths left the castle first and the others followed them. They entered a vastly different world from the barren land earlier, a forest with fresh smelling trees and green, green bushes.

They ran through the twilight land. Running felt easy, now, and they did not really exert themselves at all. Their feet thundered on the ground like horses, and Janet imagined the shaking could be felt for miles. She knew it was. They reached something that strongly resembled a medieval village. She had sensed it from far away, seen and felt its people long before she actually saw them with her eyes. The villagers scurried around, scared and confused. Some attempted to run, to flee. Others just stood there, paralyzed, unmoving like stone. Those running were quickly rounded up. The sheep was gathered by the shepherds, and returned to the rest of the herd. One single wraith caught up with a group, and the entire group just stopped, shivered, bowed their heads in submission, and returned to the village, driven and encouraged by brutal lashes on their backs.

The villagers stood there, at the open space at the center between the huts, shaking hard, terrorized, broken, cut open and attentive, exactly as Florence desired.

She appeared in a blinding flash of light. Everybody cringed and marveled at her presence.

– You have displeased your Goddess, Florence spat, and the villagers trembled. – Now, you will pay a heavy price!

She walked among them and picked children, girls and boys, nearly half of the small children present, and the wraiths grabbed them and pulled them away from stricken parents, to screams and wails quickly stifled with harsh beatings. Any adult, making any sort of protest was beaten severely, but not killed.

– From now on, the goddess told her subjects, – you will raise one male and one female to be the goddess' servants. Ten years from now, when I return they will be ready.

– Yes, my Goddess, a man stepped forward, and choked humbly, with tears in his eyes. – The Goddess' decree will be done.

Florence faded, and the wraiths left, returned to the castle with the children. Janet wanted to feel something, grief, rage, horror, anything, but she did not. The captives were left in the care of the castle's adult servants, those not Wraith, to be taught the ways of the Goddess.

There were other villages, other excursions into the many lands beyond the castle, but it all blurred in her mind, becoming one and the same. Existence was a constant haze, and she was rarely able to grab hold of any given event, and say with confidence that it really happened.

Another batch of ten, of downtrodden dogs arrived at the castle. Janet was there, along with her fellow wraiths. She grabbed a boy, tied his wrists, and brought him with her into the far below Dungeon. He whimpered in her grip, and she snarled and brutally whipped his sore ass. She heard him scream, and it did not faze her, except by the constant contempt coursing through her hazy mind.

The distance seemed so much shorter, now, when she had walked it so many times. The castle was so big, so disorientating that one could become lost, if one did not know the place, was not attuned to its workings, its countless pathways, and she was, increasingly so, as the days passed by.

This is your doll, your toy, her Goddess whispered to her without words, to do with as you please. Do not kill him, or injure him beyond repair. Beyond that do with him whatever you wish.

She groped him, and studied him, filled with curiosity, with desire to understand this strange, unfamiliar creature. He whimpered in pain. She expected him to cry out, to beg for mercy, but he did not.

They reached the cells. The newcomers were dragged into them and collared. She gave her toy to drink. He drank greedily, drank the bottle empty. She knew he was studying her, desperately attempting to find compassion or humanity or anything there. He choked when she ignored him, when she left him, when she closed the door behind her, and left him there to rot.

She joined her fellow wraiths in the line outside, returning upstairs. Upstairs, downstairs, it did not matter. Everything blurred into one, endless haze of nothing. Days passed. Nights passed. There was no sleep, and hardly any rest. Wraiths did not need it. They were constantly on the move, doing their Goddess' bidding. Everything felt like a dream, a waken dream, where everything was light, and emotion was granted by the goddess like a perk, a reward for services well rendered.

Janet passed by a window someday and stopped, suddenly recalling her own name. She looked through the window, at the remote, desolate landscape outside. The glow of the portal, so close compared to how she remembered it, burned in her mind.

The wraiths thundered through the halls, entering the kitchen. She sensed them, and was there with them, facing the major domo of the Goddess'

House.

– There you are, the regal, older servant sniffed. – About time. Well, take this to the Great Hall immediately, or we will all face just punishment.

The woman had spent her entire life in Florence's court, and she was merely a function, no individuality, no desire except the Goddess' mighty will.

Ten wraiths brought the trays to Florence's dinner party. She had guests, nine other sorcerers the girl in the hood and robe and cloak did not know or recognize. But she had no trouble sensing and acknowledging their powers, burning both skin and mind.

They served tea, one brand for Florence and one for the others. Janet recalled now that the Goddess had tea every day, whether she entertained guests or not.

Janet felt nauseas and sick, but did not show it, did not show anything behind the mask.

They served the people around the table, and the people around the table treated them like they were not there at all. Florence glowed in triumph, showing off her power, her wraiths to her fellow sorcerers.

Janet stopped by the window, vomit drying around her mouth, and it felt so good, so good to be sick. She remembered running, running towards this place, this single place where she could see the outside.

– She will never let us go, you know.

The female voice startled Janet. She turned and she saw another formless form stare through the window, stare at her.

– She said as much. We are just mules to her, to all of them. They t-tricked us, and have certainly not *our* best interest at heart.

Janet nodded slowly.

– We have to get away, she heard herself whisper, as she looked fearfully around her. – But *how?*

– This is the place, the other nearly broken, desperate girl whispered as well. – You were drawn to it, like I was.

Janet nodded eagerly.

– You can… glide, can you not, glide through the air? The other girl kept talking, fast and furious. – I have been watching you. My power is levitation, telekinesis. Together we may succeed where both would have failed on our own. We need to get out of here. Let us go, *now!*

They both rushed at the window. Janet could not tell who were through it first. It was high above the ground. There was a tiny part of the roof, a ledge out there keeping them from falling, that was all. Janet tried, tried hard to focus, to remember how it felt like to feel the wind under her feet, to glide on the airwaves.

We must make haste, they told each other with frantic glances, grabbing each other's hands…

And they jumped.

Janet felt it, the powerful jolt of energy coursing through her. It was still there, and she wanted to cry out in joy, but cautiously kept her mouth shut. The shadow of the Goddess was there, with them, and wild panic threatened to paralyze them, but it was what drove them forward, made their power rise, within and without. The land that had taken them days to cross turned indistinct below, and she knew they would not hit it, knew that their bodies would not break like china, as they made contact with the ground. They landed, not far from the portal, the glowing dark hole in the ground, unable to stay afloat any longer.

The portal was wide open, at least on this side. They sensed that. It practically pulled at them, screaming at their senses.

Florence appeared, with a hard scowl on her face. They froze, in fear and indecision.

– You ungrateful wretches, she scowled. – Even if you managed to reach the gate, you would not end up at the place you left. In fact there is no telling where you may end up, in the wasteland that is the Crossroads, and I guarantee you that you will be lost out there. You will return with me, of course, and you will not be punished… too much.

They joined hands, and screamed, shouted at the spiteful creature blocking their way, hitting it with all their mighty and enhanced power… and practically disintegrated her.

There was blood, and skin and bone, pieces of it scattered on the ground, and that was all.

– Was that… her? One girl whimpered. – Or only one of her?

– I do not know, do not care, other girl snarled.

They both snarled, as they charged forward, as they deliberately purged themselves of unpleasant thoughts, and threw themselves into the vortex, into the vast unknown, further than ever from what they had known.

Chapter 4

They held on to each other, for their lives, battered endlessly and brutally by the storm inside the vortex. It pulled at them, weakened them and drained them. Janet felt it, as the desire to puke hit her, as she seemed to be dissolving under the ruthless onslaught.

The other girl began shouting, began *chanting,* reaching out a hand, grabbing Janet's chest. Janet understood the words, and began chanting, began cursing herself.

– «You are my vessel», she chanted, repeating it a million times, as the two of them waged war, – «my vessel, my ride through the storm».

The other screamed, as Janet's hand began glowing, began burning, and Janet began feeling incredibly great and powerful.

A gust of powerful winds and they separated, were cast in different directions at a crossroad, at a glimpse where a thousand different realities and contradictory truths briefly filled her mind.

She stood on her knees somewhere, breathless and totally drained, fearing she was back at the Goddess' realm, but it only looked similar at first glance. This was clearly a different place.

Malone towered above her. She looked incredulous at him through tears and despair and wild, wild hope and distrust, and spiteful hatred.

– I suspected you would come here, he said casually.

She fought to rise, to muster her power, but nothing happened.

– You were lied to, he told her. – You all were. I lied to you, deceived you. Florence was not supposed to teach you anything, except servitude. It was only a ruse to bury you all for good, to make sure you never returned to bother the sorcerers again.

He bowed down, grabbing her hair gently, putting a bottle to her lips.

– Drink this. Quickly!

– Why? She asked him, a soundless word, a mere hiss, more than a word, the rage briefly overcoming her total exhaustion and vulnerability.

– It protects you, from the Goddess' possible vengeance, and also in other ways, contradicting much of the treatment of the so called elixir you have been given. Without it you will burst into flames the very moment she localizes you. Yes, she is alive, and very pissed. You were never meant to escape, never meant to leave that place at all. It is as much a prison as it is her place of power, her kingdom, where she rules supreme.

She drank, too exhausted, too drained to care.

It… helped. At least it served to clear her thoughts, to return her to some semblance of rational thought and will. Slowly, painfully she regained some sense of Self, of individuality, and it felt so good, so very good. He looked at her. She returned his scrutinizing stare, filled with fear, with desperate hope and gratitude, and everything in-between.

– Much of the apprentice-bullshit is just that, Malone confirmed. – An excellent age-old way of getting rid of potential competition. Youths with… prospects are found, gathered and shipped off to nowhere land, and they are never heard from again.

She could not speak, could not voice her thoughts.

– I, myself, however, have loftier goals.

He reached out a hand, and she took it, and he pulled her on her feet. She threw herself into his arms, shaking uncontrollably, her eyes filled with grateful tears.

She caught herself, her eyes abruptly being filled with suspicion and distrust.

– W-what if I had not escaped on my own?

– I was quite confident that you would. As stated I see a bright future for you. But if you had not I would not have shed a tear. You would not be worthy of my efforts, and I would have wasted a lot of valuable time, and you would have deserved your fate.

She held his eyes, and if looks could have killed he would have dropped dead that very instant.

– That is the look of the Janet I love, he chuckled.

She sagged in his arms, bigger than he was now, surrendering to his tender mercies. He turned and she turned with him. The gate glowed before them.

– Do not worry, he soothed her. – It will be all right. I will protect us both, keep us from being torn apart by the tide.

She believed him. He was so protective, so strong. They stepped forward, and crossed the horizon of the gate, and once again she was torn apart by a thousand contradictory thoughts and truths. But when they emerged on the other side this time she was not any worse for wear, was not exhausted or drained, but actually felt a little, just a little better.

– The other I escaped with… she attempted to drain me, to use my power for herself during the traveling, but I turned the table on her.

She dried spittle from her jaw, grinning a little, still shaking, and glaring at him with feverish eyes.

– It is good then, that you were paying attention during the lessons…

She looked around her, at a completely different landscape, one with fields and roads. There was even a bench not far away. This was not home. The skies were clearly different, with several moons and planets prominent in the sky, but it seemed to be a somewhat pleasant, peaceful spot, at least right here. She practically collapsed in his arms, breaking into more tears and far worse shakes.

– I was so *afraid,* she sobbed, – so alone, and I thought I would never see you again.

– You will be alone nevermore, he comforted her, – and you will not be afraid, ever again.

He led her to the bench, and they sat down on it, sitting there for what seemed like hours, and it was so peaceful, so comforting.

She sat there, looking at her hands. They were still large and strong, but she could sense them, see them, feel them, tracing their lines with her fingertips. Slow, painfully slow a sense of life returned to her, and it felt good, felt bad all over. She smelled the stench of days' old sweat, and eons' long shame.

– Come, Malone the Sorcerer bade her.

Janet, the lone and lonely wraith followed him down the trail.

Birdsong filled her ears, and the powerful scent of flowers graced her nostrils, and heat returned to her cold bones.

There was a village over the rise. She heard its sounds, sensed it, as if she was there.

– It is… painful, is it not, to have everything rushing back?

– Yes, Master, she conceded.

Flashes came to her, and she crouched in pain. The wraith she was beat a villager to death, raised the stick time and time again, until there was nothing but a pulp left of the poor man. The memory made her gasp and heave, and there was *pain.*

She curled her left hand into a fist and kept walking.

After a while she glanced at Malone to see if he was studying her, but he was not, at least not in any overt way she could discern.

They joined a market in the village. She did not understand the villagers' tongue. There was nothing familiar about it to her, no words or phrases she could comprehend, but Malone had no trouble communicating with these people, and seemed to speak the language fluently. He bought various kinds of fruit, some strange, some familiar. He handed her an orange. She accepted it, but hesitated.

– I can hardly remember the last time I had something to eat.

– Are you not hungry? He asked her.

She was. Ravenous. She practically consumed the orange without bothering to peel it much.

It strengthened her. She noticed it almost immediately, and a warm glow seemed to spread through her body, warming further the cold, cold bones.

– It feels weird, she noted afterwards, as they left the village, when she was full and content.
– Your body has to, to a certain degree relearn how to work again, he nodded.
– So, I am okay, then? I will be… all right?
The thin, girlish voice bothered her, but she was not able to speak up, to portray the deceit of calm and confidence, and the fact that she knew he could see straight through her did not help either.
– You are most certainly «all right», he snorted. – You are far stronger, sturdier and more powerful than you used to be, exactly the way I want you.
His voice and stance more than suggested that he did not care to discuss the subject further. She shrunk under his pointed stare.
– Yes, Master, she whispered.
They reached a house, at the rise at the edge of the forest. It was a strangely big house, with a strangely big door. They stopped outside. He did not knock on the door.
– You performed to my expectations, he praised her. – You escaped the clutches of that bitch Florence with your faculties pretty much intact, and you gained power in the bargain. Now, your teaching continues. Farrell, the occupant of this humble abode has taught many of your kind.
He knocked on the door. The claws of fear grabbed her. She sought closer to Malone, even as she wanted to flee, flee the fastest her strong feet could carry her.
It took time, before she heard movement from the inside, heard steps and rumblings, and the door opened, and she startled realized the reason why the door was so big.
The man appearing in the doorway was a head taller than them both. She realized, at least to a point why Malone had brought her here.
– Greetings, Farrell, Malone greeted the man in a fairly courteous way, though not without a certain dry irony in his voice.
The giant mumbled or rather growled something. But Janet understood them both. The language they spoke was very similar to her own.
– Allow me to present Janet, another of the few refugees from the Castle Florence.
Janet felt inevitable pride, but also apprehension. She straightened, and for the first time in days without number she removed her hood.
She made an effort at smiling to him, but failed miserably.
Large pools of eyes stared at her, cut through her like knives. She could drown in those eyes, in the pulsing gleam.
– She does not look like much, he grunted, very patronizing.

Janet wanted to say something, anything important, but cat got her tongue, and she remained silent.

– Tomorrow at dusk, he grunted. – And not a minute earlier.

He slammed the door in their faces.

Janet glanced timidly at Malone. The sorcerer smiled.

– Farrell is a mean son of a bitch, but he will not try to turn you into a zombie. He will not even make you paint fences, but teach you exactly what I want you to learn.

– Yes, Master, she replied, suddenly very eager and excited.

– And do not worry. I will remain here, during these trials, never straying from your side.

That comforted her and pleased her. She wanted, needed to prove herself to him, show him that she was not a frail flower, bending at the first sign of trouble. Spikes of rage, hatred, confusion, shame and terror all touched her in that moment.

They returned to the village. He rented a room at a tavern.

– I will have a new set of clothes sent up to you, he said. – Loose the rags and take a bath.

A large, steaming bathtub awaited her when she locked herself into the room. She knew Malone was right down the stairs, but she still felt very alone and lonely.

This was a fairly primitive society, she ventured, medieval by the looks of it, without running water and other amenities the old Janet had grown up with. But that felt so long ago, in another lifetime. She liked it this way. It was quiet here, a peaceful spot in the vortex of reality.

She stood before the mirror, removing what was left of her wraith uniform, fearing she would only see the horrible, indistinct shape she had grown so used to, but she saw a girl, both familiar and different. Everything here, in this room was made for big people. It was easy to understand, now, why she had not drawn that many stares below. They knew or knew of her kind here.

Her kind… She could study her entire body in the mirror. It was battered and bruised, but not that much so. It was a powerful, but yet feminine body, muscled and curvy. The sight… pleased her. An enormous relief flooded the powerful frame, and she fell to her knees, not moving for what felt like hours.

«You are my vessel», she repeated in her mind, reliving the violent, brutal struggle in the Crossroads, where she had prevailed, and the other girl, her opponent, had not. They had fled together, but during that horrible moment she had known the truth: only one of them could survive the brutal battering of the vortex.

Hands curled into fists again. She lowered herself into the steaming bath, and sat there washing and cleaning herself. It felt so good. She smiled.

The skin hurt while she cleaned it. The sharp pain made her smile grow even wider.

She dried herself with the large towel, a thorough but enjoyable task. On the bed was left simple, but nice garments, a tunic with a short skirt, and on the floor light and practical boots. She began dressing. Everything fit perfectly. When next she looked into the mirror she had been transformed into a simple and sturdy farm girl. Her hands touched her hair, so much longer than she could remember. There was a kind of comb, made of bone on the drawer, and she combed herself, combed her sturdy locks in slow, dreamlike movements. She made two braids of her long, long hair and the transformation was complete.

When she returned to the ground floor Malone had ordered dinner. The maid brought it to the corner table by the window the very moment Janet sat down.

– I am so hungry, she cried. – So very, very hungry.

– Feed then, he told her. – Replenish yourself.

The smell, the taste overwhelmed her as she fed. She ate with her hands, like everybody here, including Malone. But to her it was an even more savage feeding, as she stilled a Hunger bigger than she had ever felt. The potatoes, the meat, the vegetables and everything was consumed in a feeding frenzy, and before long she looked astounded at the bare bones on the practically empty plate.

– Would you like some more? Malone inquired lightly.

– Yes, please! She wheedled.

And before long, more steaming food arrived. She ate slower this time, enjoying it more, savoring it, like a flame would a candle.

The window was clean, transparent to such a degree that it did not seem to be there at all. She looked through it and there was no distortion to speak of. Perhaps it was her. She imagined they were sitting outside and breathing the pure and invigorating air uninhibited.

– How many realms are there out there, Master? She wondered.

– I have no idea. He shook his head in amusement. – I do not think anyone does.

– And there are humans in all of them?

– All I have ever heard of and know of.

– Any *aliens?*

– Not in the sense you mean, no, he replied. – Most creatures looking inhuman have been human once, and have, in various ways been transformed or are of human origins in other ways, *or* are of the realms.

She froze in her chair, drilling holes in him with her violet eyes.

– And… Florence?

– Florence will *look* for you, he shrugged. – You have made an enemy for eternity there, my sweet girl. She does not take kindly to those getting away.

– Will she come here, with her… army?

She was relieved to see that he was amused, not angry with her line of questioning.

– No, she will not! One reason is that she hardly spared you, any of you a second glance. You are all like nothing in her eyes. Only by destroying one of her bodies and escaping her clutches you became something more. The other reason is that this is far away from her territory, her *domain*. There is no direct vortex path between the castle realm and here. And your journey through the vortex had a very random quality to it. There is no way to predict where you ended up. She would have to search *thousands* of possibilities, and that is just the first distance. With a second journey any attempt at prediction becomes totally ridiculous.

– But you found me… Master? You knew *exactly* where I would appear.

He rewarded her with a merciful smile, acknowledging her sharp intellect.

– I had the advantage of foresight, he replied unconcerned and very, very lightly. – I knew your destiny, as well as my own from I was very young.

He scared her and excited her even more when he was like that… so confident and arrogant and powerful. She shivered in the afternoon heat.

But she pushed on, like he knew she would.

– Why did Farrell insist on us not coming for the lesson until dusk?

– Because he sleeps during the day. Sometimes answers to a person's questions are wondrously simple and straightforward, you know.

– But you went ahead and woke him up today, anyway.

– I did indeed…

He grinned and leaned back, relaxed in his chair, signaling in small but unmistakable ways that the Q and A was done.

She leaned back, too, sniffing a little, meditating, calming herself, and looking at her mentor in awe and apprehension and impatience.

Day turned to dusk and dusk to night. A fire was lit at the open space by the market. It was tall and stretched far into the darkness. Jugglers, fire-breathers and other performers used a low stage by the forest glen to show off their skills. Malone and his apprentice enjoyed the entertainment.

– Existence is vast. The young apprentice, still a wide-eyed girl shook her head. – And most people are totally clueless about it, about what is out there.

– They do not even see their own realm, Malone said. – Far less the multitude. They see only their pond, and believe that is all there is.

One large and full moon rose on the sky. Janet danced with the other youths of the village. She drank something that was neither beer nor wine or any other drink she had ever had. It had a nice, round flavor, and she drank a lot of it. The others got drunk, and had trouble standing, but she could not quite let go. She kept looking at Malone and kept casting long, worried glances into the deep darkness surrounding the village.

She sat down on the chair opposite Malone, rocking on it, finding herself posing for him, blushing deeply, glancing at him from beneath lowered eyelashes. He ignored her, and disheartened she sagged in her seat. She wanted to sit in his lap, to put her arms around his neck, embrace him and trade passionate kisses with him, but she did not dare, and the low burning, uncomfortable flame in her loins did not spread, did not grow from its initial ember.

The young boys, and even some of the men, looked at her. She both saw and sensed their interest, but did not find any of them even remotely interesting or desirable. Even though she did not show her disdain openly, she made it fairly clear that she was not interested, was not available, and they left her alone. Perhaps they would not have if they did not in part fear her. The fact that she was a former wraith had little or no bearing here, but her being a sorcerer's apprentice made them *respect* her.

Other girls might be seen as young and vulnerable, but she would not.

Magick was evidently, even obviously a way of life here, an integrated part of people's existence. People wore pentacles and various charms, both known and unknown to her openly. A group discussed the man on the hill. They cast long glances up there, their eyes filled with curiosity and fear. Fear was present, even here.

The evening ended slowly. People began leaving one by one or in smaller groups. Janet and Malone remained. They sat there, the two of them, in the silence of the dark surroundings. Janet heard the sounds of the night, gnawing sounds of what she imagined was teeth, as if someone or something was feeding out there, ripping its prey to pieces, and she sought closer to Malone, the closer comfort of his presence.

They retreated to the tavern, and to their room. She was drunk and tired and yawned happily. They both undressed, until they both were stark naked. She did not dare look at him, but stood there, waiting. He walked to the bed and crawled under the blanket. She waited breathlessly. He did not invite her in. She sniffed, and blew out the lamp. It turned dark, and she hurried across the room, and crawled under the blanket on the floor.

He fell asleep almost instantly. She heard him. Long minutes passed, while she listened to his breath. It was completely dark. This was not anything like the surroundings she had grown up in. There were no lights anywhere, no close or distant road lights brightening pitch black bedrooms.

It was quite okay, there on the floor. She hardly remembered how it had been, sleeping in a bed. Her eyes just stayed open that was all. Even when they were closed they seemed to be open. She saw the room and everything in it. Hours passed by, and she writhed and moaned silently there on the soft, soft floor.

She rose, somewhere during the night, with cold sweat pouring from her wet skin. A mirror appeared before her, and she did not see herself, but Florence, Florence holding a chain and a collar.

– I opened you up, the figure snarled, giving the girl her cruel, sadistic smile. – I gave you the world. You are mine. Be a good doggie, now, and submit to your Goddess.

Janet backed off, or tried to. It seemed, for every step she backed off she actually walked closer to the snarling, regal figure. Florence grabbed her, and suddenly she once more wore her wraith uniform.

– That is better. That is so much better, but not completely satisfactory. It needs a final touch…

And the big girl felt herself contract and change. Florence changed her, with her mighty touch, until a four-legged wolf-like creature crouched at her feet.

– Yes, that is it. This is you, and such you will serve me for the rest of eternity.

She slipped the collar around the bitch's hairy neck. Janet felt the metal, heard the sound of the chains making up the leash. Panic grabbed her, total and utter desperation. She sat up on the floor, in the pitch black room, covered in sweat, sick and nauseous. The scream did not stop before Malone shook her, shook her hard and slapped her face sore.

The girl sat there, shaking for long minutes before she managed to speak.

– It was a dream? She whispered. – Just a dream?

– No more tangible or true than a mirage, he confirmed, rubbing her shaking form. – You have undergone a trial, an ordeal worse than any initiation. It is not strange you are plagued by night terrors. I am afraid they will not fade for a long time.

She pushed herself at him, pushing her lips at his, wanting him, wanting him to want her, to have her and ravish her.

– Please, she whispered. – Please, Master.

He held her, shook her, until she focused on him, until she was attentive once more.

There was no light, but she still saw him clearly, and she wondered how that could be.

– You need to be untouched, he said sternly.

She looked at him, with at least one part comprehension slowly dawning in her cloudy eyes.

– It is a requisite for your participation in the Ascension ritual, he told her.

He smiled to her, radiant and full, and she smiled, too, feeling wanted and desired, and content, and a slow, slow gathering calm.

She nodded, nodded again, eagerly this time, conveying her approval, telling him with eyes and a thousand tiny gestures how much she looked forward to, longed for that distant moment in time when they would be together.

He let go of her and returned to bed, and not before long he was asleep again. She could not believe it, as she slowly fell back and crawled back under the blanket. It felt so different. She fell asleep and it did not even take many minutes.

She slept, a restless, troubled slumber, until late at day, when she found herself at Malone's side, walking up the hill to her first lesson in her new class of one.

– I slept so long, she said wearily.

– You had a lot of catching up to do, Malone calmed her, – a lot of necessary rest and recharge.

They walked in silence for a while.

– Dreams are doorways, he taught her, – necessary to live and thrive, but also as lessons to better break through, to the other, hidden realm… or *realms.*

The giant waited for her at the front of his house. He held a fighting staff, a wand in his hand. She felt fear, excitement and expectation, as rubbery legs brought her the rest of the way up. Malone - that shithead sat down on the porch in quite a relaxed pose. She walked to Farrell with a sinking feeling in her gut.

There was another wand on the ground before him. She hesitated.

– Go on, he growled, – pick it up.

He looked like her nightmare of herself in the mirror. He did not. There was no wraith towering above her, but a human being of flesh and blood. She was visibly relaxing. Her hand still shook when she picked up the staff.

– Yes, he nodded. – I am no longer that mindless brute. Neither are you. You have left that behind. Remember forever that feeling of inferiority and helplessness, but never let it rule you, or it will stay with you for the rest of your life.

She shivered, but stubbornly kept her eyes on him, learning anew the shaky skill of balancing the staff in her hands. It was light, as she remembered it. It was the same, exactly alike, a perfect copy of what the enslaved female wraith had used.

– You have a kind of brutish strength, now, he began his lesson, – one quite inadequate without refined skills to use it.

He struck her, struck her hard. One end of the wand hit her arm. It happened so fast. She did not have time to move or even react.

– Come on, you timid bitch, he snarled at her. – attack me, if you dare.

The pain came instantly, reverberating through her already sore body and mind like an ever more powerful, not fading echo. That word, that patronizing word prompted something in her, something dark and horrible. She looked incredulous at him, before her mind was filled with fury.

– You BASTARD, she shouted. – You damn BASTARD!

She went at him with everything she had. Less than a minute later she crouched on the ground, beaten senseless, her mouth drowning in blood, her eyes in tears. She heard his voice as if from far away, so very close to her ear.

– Rage is good. It drives you and fuels your progress and your fighting, but you must learn to focus it, learn to think, to reason, even as your vision turns red with the blood haze, or you will remain a helpless victim.

She fought herself on her feet, drying blood from her lips. He signed for her to attack him, and she did, tried to think, to reason, to feel the staff in her hand, to flow instead of jump when she went at him, the way he taught her, with his words, with a thousand moves and gestures.

But she was still gloriously beaten and struck to the ground.

It went on during the last minutes of twilight and far into the night. She hardly even noticed. The world had turned into one, uninterrupted state of parrying and strikes.

They sat on the ground, surrounded by the silver darkness. She was grateful for the rest, for the fact that he allowed rest, that he acknowledged that it was necessary. He was not patronizing, was not even arrogant, but simply taught her what he taught her with a cold, impassive efficiency.

He grabbed her jaw. She winced in pain.

– It hurts, he said. – You are no longer numb, no longer Hard. Pain, the good teacher has returned to your life and you should welcome it.

She glanced at Malone, knowing he could heal her in a second, knowing he would not do so.

– I was n-numb, she stuttered, having trouble talking because of the swollen jaw. – Now, I am alive.

– Stubborn *and* eloquent, Farrell grinned darkly. – Excellent!

They parried. He let her get away with it for a while, without punishing her, without striking her every time she left herself open.

– Most women lack the strength to even challenge a man if he decides to attack and trash her. You are different, but only to a point, still physically weaker than most proficient males, so you need an advantage, an *edge* to better protect yourself.

He struck her at the hand, almost making her lose the staff.

– And anybody may be a victim, anyway, as you have already discovered. There is no safety anywhere, no safe haven, not in any of the infinite number of realms and planes out there. Even the strongest may fall prey to the dangers and trappings roaming the Universe. The only thing anyone can do is to be prepared the best way possible, to somewhat lessen the chance of being struck down by cruel fate.

She listened to him with a deep furrow on her brow, very attentive and astute, as he hammered his lessons into her being. Violet eyes clouded in curiosity, as she wondered if it was indeed his lessons… or Malone's.

The giant struck at her. She avoided the blow, and was so astonished that she fell easy prey to his next move.

She lay stunned on the ground, during one, two three heartbeats, before fighting herself back up.

– What did you feel just now? He asked her. – Right before I struck you down?

The girl pondered his question, wrecking her brain.

– There *was* something…

– You felt the glow, he stated, – the fire inside. It rose within you like a geyser.

He was intense, behind the stoic mask. It was in his eyes, when she looked into them. She saw a lot there, sadness, faint horror and passion, but no menace.

And she had grown extremely sensitive to emotions lately.

Anger grabbed hold of her yet again, as she clutched the staff, as blood once again flowed faster through her veins, so fast that it hurt. He nodded, as much to himself as to her.

– Feel it, he stressed. – Feel the fire, and next time it rises, let it be the geyser, a volcanic eruption nobody may hold back or put out.

She attacked him. She missed, but it was close. He countered and missed, and she felt the power.

The darkness passed in the light of flashing wands and violet eyes. He was far superior to her, in all things, of course, and showed it to her, showed it down her throat occasionally, when she got too cocky. But…

She… enjoyed this, a fact she realized slowly, with the overpowering taste of blood in her mouth. He kept driving her, kept pushing her, and it was new and great to her, and she would have forgotten all about her horrible time as a wraith, if she had not seen her fresh pain in the eyes mirroring her own.

Memories stirred within her, all those she worked so hard to repress. She crushed a skull, a child's skull in her strong hands, experiencing anew the terror in the parents' faces. He pushed her, until she had trouble seeing anything but nightmare visions.

– Do not repress your memories, he told her curtly. – Embrace them. Use them to grow, to be born.

Her head shook itself, denying his words, his truth.

– Do it, or you will be nothing but a weak and vulnerable girl for the rest of your sorry existence.

Janet bit her lip, bit it hard, nodding determined to herself.

Painful flashes filled her, filled her to the brim. She screamed in anguish and rage.

She slept on the floor at the tavern at the onset of dawn. Malone slept quietly. She could hardly hear his breathing.

They had breakfast the fifth or seventh day. She had trouble knowing what kind and that worried her. It reminded her of the time in the castle, as Florence's plaything and bully.

– I want you to go alone today, he told her.

– No, *please!* She pleaded with him, suddenly totally freaked out with fear.

– It will be good for you, he shrugged, – and I will only be a call away, anyway.

– But he is so strong, she cried. – He can do whatever he wants with me.

Malone was not interested. He studied a flower right outside the window with interest.

She dragged herself up there. Farrell stood there waiting for her, like she knew he would.

He threw one of the wands to her and she grabbed it easily, and felt the pleasure of that simple act, and felt somewhat better.

– You should not wallow in the past, he said, – not once you have accepted it as a noteworthy part of yourself. You should embrace the future. You are your own person, not a product of Florence or Malone or me. And you do not believe that you are either, not really. If you did you would still have groveled at Florence's feet, instead of escaping against all odds. But my words mean nothing, if you can not see this for yourself.

Heat and cold surged through her, and she could not say which was which.

He began swinging his wand, and she did, too, in what had become instinct. She parried his attack and it did not seem hard at all, and she smiled, even as an expression of intense determination changed her face.

Hours days, years later she stood before him with a happy smile on that face. She had a swollen eye and also other spots of bruising elsewhere, but she still felt strangely good and even great.

– Very good, he acknowledged. – Now, I want you to use your power.

– My… She frowned.

– Your power to ride the air, the waves of the ether, he nodded. – In a fight, magickal or otherwise you will need all the advantages, edges you may possess.

He rose in the air.

– Remember, he said. – You have done this. *Remember.*

I do not want to.

She had done so several times, the last time at the top of the castle, reaching deep within herself, flying, escaping bondage and servitude, jumping from the high tower, to certain death, to what would have been certain death for most other people, flying to the Crossroads, to boundless freedom with the other girl, two desperate children holding hands, fleeing to the vortex, to what could never be contained, never be caged.

– We told each other our names, she choked, half crouching there on the ground, – revealed our souls to each other, and then we went for each other's throats, and I killed her, killed her so I might live.

– Only one of you could survive the Vortex, he said. – In your primal state you both knew that. Perhaps if you both had been the cute, defenseless children you once were, you would have attempted to survive together and succumbed together, but you were not, and you never will be again.

She felt it, felt the power, felt her feet dance on its currents, and she rose in the air.

– The air is solid, if you want it to be, he taught her, – as stepping stones for your feet, if you wish it to be, as hard hands or a wall hitting an opponent and there are countless other uses you will discover as you go.

There was the rush of boiling blood and paralyzing fear, as she strived to keep her balance, there, five lengths of her body above the ground. Suddenly she felt rage, because of his smugness, and just like that, control was hers to enjoy.

He began swinging his wand, attacking her, taking it easy on her, and she defended herself clumsily. They parried for a while. He slowly began increasing the speed and intensity, until she felt herself slipping, and she descended slowly, helplessly, until she hit the ground, somewhat dignified and without much pain. Her left ankle hurt slightly, but was basically okay.

– Very good, he praised her, and she felt good, felt joy. – You are a natural at this, and you will be even more so, with the passing of days and weeks and months and years, not just because of your unique or rare power of riding the waves, but because of the fire and determination and the cold, hard place inside that will always be there.

The night passed, as it always did, in sweat and burning eyes, in white knuckles tightening around the wand. Weeks passed, as they always did, without time, without her noticing its passing.

– You will sleep here from now on.

It was more of the same, really. He slept on the bed and she on the floor, on the hard carpet. It did not bother her anymore, but felt right. She slept on hard rock, like a child.

– This week will be different, he said. – This time the physical will take a backseat to the Mysteries, those of the soul and the Magick, which is one of the same.

They sat on opposite sides of a fire. He put his hands into the flames, held them there, calmly.

– Take my hands.

She hesitated, suddenly touched once again by the cold, cold fear.

– Do you trust me?

– No, she mumbled, shaking her head hard.

– Very wise. Now, *take my hands*.

She obeyed, reaching into the dancing flame. Pain shook her, and she screamed in horror, pulling her burned, smoking hands back. She looked at her teacher in terror, moaning in nameless pain, crouching there on the ground.

– It hurts, does it not, far beyond the actual, physical pain?

She nodded, her tears hissing, evaporating, as they hit the scolded skin.

She blinked, and suddenly they sat there yet again, on opposite sides of the campfire. Her hands… she looked incredulous at them… they were healed, as if they had never… never been burned.

– Appearances can be and often is deceiving, he taught her. – I will not hammer this lesson into you, but others will. If there is a reason for us to be here, in life, at all, we are here to learn, and you will learn in spades.

– How do you know? She wondered, suddenly alive with hunger, with curiosity.

– One of my powers is to see destinies. I do not know what will happen to you, but I know that there will be a lot of it and that it will not be pleasant. I know that pain and hunger and rage will make you powerful beyond belief.

She was cold, not only on her back, in the shadow of the fire, but even in her toes, the part of her closest to the flames.

– And… Malone?

– He *knows*. He knew you from he first saw you, and he knew me and many other things, knows what is coming.

Nights passed, weeks passed, she could not tell anymore. It was all just one, continuous state of sleep and awakening and dream and sweat and fire, strands of night and fire dancing before her eyes.

And behind a veil, or a set of veils she glimpsed more, spotted Malone and others, many others, like a string of dark-shining pearls and embers and dancing flames.

Farrell made her read one of his books, yet another of his books, asking her questions, prodding her mind, her depth, beyond skin and bone. She did not know the language, not at first, but it came to her, awoke inside her, slowly, abruptly, like dawn, like the deepest dusk.

– Spells can be useful, he taught her. – Words can be Magick, both in the hands of the uninitiated and initiated, but while the dabbler may wreak havoc easily, the wretched witch can achieve some modicum of «control». «Magick words» make certain things easier, but never forget that the strongest power by far rests *within*.

He gestured, and she knew, instinctively that it was indeed a mere gesture, unnecessary in the bigger scheme of things. She stared in awe, as a hole opened up in the air, in reality itself.

– You have felt it, he said, – felt its exquisite pain.

– The Ascension! She gasped.

– It is called that, and many other things besides. In my realm we call it The Untouchable. It is the place more dangerous than even the Crossroads, the realm where nothing - and therefore everything - exists. All things are possible to those that can travel its freeways and survive.

– And Malone can not, can not travel the Ascension?

– Not without help, no, or he would have done so a long time ago. It is seen as the ultimate prize among sorcerers, among advanced witches.

– And that is why he… needs me? What for? What… ritual are we talking about here?

– I do not know. I do not know anyone that does. I know it is called the Ritual of the Ascension, but since quite a few is called that that information is not very useful. You will find some of them in your books, but it will probably not help you much, not at first, anyway. Many different techniques have been attempted. There are rumors, half-hearted tales of people that have completed the Ascension, but nothing solid, nothing but Mist and Shadow. If anyone has succeeded no one has returned to lay claim to the honor of success, at least not for a very long time.

Silence fell and dreams rose yet again. Dreams fell and silence rose. Words and movement, speech and gestures blended and became the same.

Two people, a sorcerer and his brief apprentice sat opposite a campfire. Farrell put his hands into the flames. The flames danced on his skin, but did not burn it.

– This is true fire, he said. – Put your hands inside it and feel its true power.

She did, and she shook, in pain, but most of all in wonder, in triumph and joy.

– I feel it, she cried incredulous. – I FEEL IT!

It burned her, but it did not hurt. It strengthened her. She felt it and sensed it, beyond sensing. In glimpses she saw the fire turn light blue and violet, saw it shift between those two, and knew beyond knowing that this was her doing.

The fear she spotted in Farrell's eyes confirmed that more than anything, more than the thousand small things bringing her clarity beyond words.

She sat there afterwards, shaking, overwhelmed by the sensory input she had just experienced, what was only slowly fading, what she wanted to both retain and leave behind.

Two fought with wands. They used the air as much as the ground as their arena. Janet felt solid air under her feet. It had become, more than ever a dance.

When she studied him and his moves even more closely she saw without trying that his dance, his ability to walk on air was different from hers, his power different from hers, but in this case the practical application was the same.

He taught her what felt like only a slightly different form of fighting without wands, with only arms and feet, both on and off the ground. That, too, was hard at first, but she already mastered the basics and she quickly mastered that new technique, the shorter reach. Bodies fought in close quarters, flesh to flesh. She felt him, felt herself move and breathe, and marveled even more at her growing agility and skill.

– You can incapacitate, maim and kill just as effective this way, he instructed her. – It is all in the intent, in the mind.

He kept hammering his teaching into her. She took it to heart, with an ever-growing, endless hunger.

She fed, greedily, sensing how every bite supplied mass to her muscles. All kinds of thoughts and emotions raced through her mind as she looked at her teacher.

– What if I do not want the «honor» Destiny has bestowed upon me? She asked enraged and depressed, and the whole range of emotions. – What will happen then?

– I guess you could always go home, to whatever life you lived before Malone fetched you. It may not be too late… but it probably is. And perhaps it is that act that will ensure that your destined path will come to pass? And you are a magick-wielder, soon to be a sorcerer far beyond parlor tricks and appearances. You can never escape that fact. Witches are born, not created, and you chose to embrace your power, your birthright. The Other Realm will always reach out for you, because you are a part of it… forever.

His words returned to her in her sleep, as Magick, as Mist and Shadow, and they burned her with their clarity and pain, etched as they were in her core.

They parried and she grinned, as they exchanged blows. Knuckles no longer whitened around the wand, but handled it easily and lightly. It was as if it came alive in her hands, as if the very air around her was a living, breathing thing, as it entered and left her lungs. Malone was watching. She sensed him, even though she did not see him at first, but even though that distracted her, she was not distracted.

She attacked and Farrell had to back off a bit before compensating and holding his ground. They kept it up a few minutes longer, before nodding to each other, and lowering themselves to the ground. It was a strange feeling to once again feel the ground beneath her feet. She imagined they had spent hours in the air. The young girl was tired, but with an elation far more prevalent dominating her perception.

They faced Malone, as he appeared from behind the bushes.

– She is done, Farrell told him, strangely ambiguous. – I can teach her no more, except what she in time easily will learn on her own.

The girl ran into Malone's arms and kissed him on the lips, free and wild.

– Thank you, Master, he cried. – Thank you!

She turned to Farrell and said:

– Thank you.

They nodded to each other, and Malone brought his apprentice down the hill, through the village and back to the Crossroads. One step forward and they were in its maws, torn apart and reassembled.

She recognized the place they reappeared. It was the village in the mist, where Florence's tavern was or had been. She felt fear, laced with bravery. People approached the gate and appeared from it, behind them. She recognized some of the sorcerers and knew some of them recognized her, and she sent them a challenging stare, but more than anything she basically ignored them.

Malone and some of the others nodded to each other, but she did not.

It seemed so different, so much more than it had been, and she remembered it, remembered every little detail.

The light was bending around every corner, and she saw what was behind each and every one long before she actually walked past it. The houses moved and the mist whirled, and then there was…

She stopped, a brief moment before moving on. The music rose in her ears, in her mind, so much more powerful than she remembered it. It was as if it hit her, like a physical force, but far more potent than any physical force could ever be.

– You have become so much more sensitive, Malone nodded pleased.

The bard stood on the first corner, on the outskirts of the village and his song and music struck her like a hurricane. Malone grabbed her and pulled her with him. The bard stood on every corner, practically paralyzing her with his play. The words… there was no way she could understand the words. It felt like gibberish to her, even though she knew they were not. They spoke secrets to her, drowning her reason in truths. She almost blacked out.

The mist thickened, as the village faded behind them. The music remained, but compared to the edge, the edge of the village muted, manageable, and beautiful beyond description.

– Master, may I ask, she wondered with glowing skin, – what are they, the various portals and pathways? Who made them?

The blue lights appeared before them, leading them where they wanted to go, to the wide, wide Abyss ahead of them.

He pondered her query a bit, before replying willingly.

– The way I heard it, and I believe that to be true is that no one made them. They are natural rifts between realms.

The ground began moving under them. Here, too she sensed more, sensed everything moving in the mist and breathed harder in anxiety, while still listening to her mentor with awe in her eyes.

– Bridges like this one are obviously crafted, though, by various gifted people throughout space and time.

He sniffed.

– The main portals, the main traveling route through the nine realms can be traveled by anyone, most of it fairly safe. All the others are suicide or at least extremely risky without the proper knowledge and talent and constructs such as these.

– You need to be a witch, Janet beamed.

– And a powerful witch to boot, he acknowledged. – A sorcerer without peer.

Behold the witch, the voice in her head said.

She smiled.

And the smile seemed to become the mist, to spread in all direction. The mist returned her grin a thousand-fold and she shook in unease and apprehension, and with her enhanced senses she noticed better his mood and state of being, too, and loud screams and howls shook the bridge.

The river below, dark and troubled roared in the silence. The million voices spoke to her and she could not do anything but reply. The bridge was so long, so very long. She wanted it to end. She never wanted it to end.

The appreciative look Malone sent her made her hot and queasy all over. Excitement rode her like a beam, and the excitement grew when blue lights shifted slowly to red. Dark blue fire turned razing red. Blue, unmoving ice shifted to dancing, glowing red, and they were back in the cave, and would be home soon. They reached the Cave of Spirits, and she felt them. Her sense of them had grown, like all her senses, but they affected her less. They were hardly more than insects now, bugs she easily discarded. She waved her hands and there was no longer any need for him to show her the waves appearing in the air. The torches were just torches again, flames on the walls, He grabbed her, and with a gesture he opened the hole in the air, different from the portals of the Crossroads, or any natural portal between the nine realms. It did not affect her as severely as before. In fact it hardly affected her at all. There was no spell of dizziness when they completed their Journey where it had begun, on the balcony of his house.

Home is where your heart is, she thought.

And she felt his smile, his penetrating eyes on her, and she blushed and she was home, and the glow inside grew to surround her like a warm glove.

Chapter 5

Her bed had definitely, unquestionable become bigger, had practically stretched in all directions. She had grown bigger. When she observed herself stretching on the bed and when she rose and placed herself before the mirror she saw that easily, the muscular arms and thighs, more generous hips and boobs. And it was not only physically, of course.

She had Grown.

Is this whar you desire, Master? She wondered, posing her enticing flesh and smile for whoever was watching.

Or *this?*

A slight concentration, a shifting of focus, and the fire in the violet eyes burned stronger and her frame changed, becoming something far more similar to a wraith than a human being. It did not scare her anymore or made despair rise in her heart, but pleased her, made triumph and expectation rise in her gut, because this was only the beginning, the modest start of her Journey, her Path.

Faint markings, tattoos, more birthmarks than tattoos, part skin and part not revealed themselves on her face when her power soared, invisible to most people when it did not. Distant childhood memories suggested to her that they had always been there. The chill and joy intensified at her core.

After returning from the shower she found her new clothes waiting for her, displayed in such a pleasing manner, floating in the air before her eyes. She marveled at the sight of them. They seemed almost otherworldly, and that very thought pleased her. She dressed, in a soft, velvet robe and hood, both similar and not compared to what she had worn earlier, so much more elegant and beautiful.

The draft in the hall felt warm, cozy. It agreed with her. She descended the stairs, dancing more than she walked. Her body and mind both had become so astute, so sensitive to even the slightest change in temperature and atmosphere.

The house… spoke to her. She used the broom and dusted the living room. There was not much of it and she saw it as a grateful task. And some of the dust was not really that at all, but Dust, a property that would not stand out to the untrained eye, but that to her danced and twinkled in Mist and Shadow. She held out her hands, and started… moving it, making it flow between her palms, and in there somewhere she glimpsed images, impressions of the Other Realm.

– Yes, move the Dust, Malone the Sorcerer nodded pleased. – Glimpse half-truths and the burning of the soul. Open up to Everything.

He startled her, like he always did. She almost lost the focus she needed to uphold the exercise, but held on by a hair.

– Surround yourself with it, he instructed her. – Bath in it. Allow it to embrace you. Feed off it, like you would a scent. Such Dust, like the fire of fire stemming from the heat birth of the Universe is yours to absorb and take advantage of. This entire island is a nexus of realms and this ground, this place, houses even stronger ancient arcane energies adepts may pick up on and use.

It… touched her. She wanted it to. It went right through her skin and flared in her mind. Pain shot through her. She bit her lip, instantly strengthened by the taste of blood. Sweat poured from her brow.

She controlled it. A sense of wonder transformed her concentration-ridded features. She gasped. The house grew in her mind and she with it.

And just as it was about to overwhelm her he spoke:

– Very good, now, let it go.

She did, and stood there gasping for several heartbeats before calming down, before resettling somehow, in her form.

He stepped forward, stopping right in front of her, his presence just as powerful as what she had attempted in vain to contain.

– How was it? He asked her.

– Like being ripped apart by a thousand hooks in my flesh, she whispered with a pained look in her face.

– And still you persevered, he nodded.

She realized he was praising her and she smiled, like a little girl given candy. It melted on her tongue and spread so pleasantly through her body.

– When I power up, when I burn with the blue flame, I look like a wraith, she said subdued.

– No, he corrected her, – you are wraithlike, but not like you looked in Florence's service. Like the tattoos and other visible manifestations, it is a sign of your stature as a sorcerer, not a result of your stay in her care. It will only grow more distinct as you Grow.

His words pleased her, turning her anxiety more towards anticipation.

– Come with me, he told her.

She walked in his shadow, but it was different now. This time expectation rode her like a mare and there was excitement in her gut.

They walked down the stairs to the basement. She sensed it immediately this time, felt the power as a physical force washing over her. There was no need for her to focus or to really heed its call or even consciously giving in to it. It entered her, like a spirit possessing an empty shell.

– Yes, you are *open* now, he stated pleased, – ripe with the forces raging in this world and the next, and all others out there.

The Ascension hovered in the air like a jewel, dark and blood red and like the mists of a thousand seas. She saw no color and all colors.

– It is... beckoning me, she whispered. – I can understand why you want it so much, Peter, why you want to possess it.

– Every single sorcerer or adept that has ever laid their eyes on it has felt the same, he said. – Now, go to it, present yourself anew and reap its favors, its eternal acknowledgement and love.

She hesitated only in marginal ways. Her feet moved of their own volition. Her arms reached out, reached into the seething horror and beauty before her.

The pain was nothing. The scream dying in her throat was a mere trifle, compared to what totally overwhelmed her, the infinity she experienced when she stared into the million surfaces staring back at her. After a million years her feet took that crucial step back. She stared at the open wound her underarm skin had become.

– Very good, now step onto the sacrificial stone.

She almost did not hear him. His voice was faint at first, before once more filling her consciousness with joy. She was not bleeding. There was no skin, but no blood either. She could easily see the veins gutted vertically, from the elbows to the tip of the fingers, but the blood was contained somehow, by the nothing, by the hard air, the stuff she had pulled with her from the Ascension. It surrounded her, waxing and waning, hissing and whispering a million sweet words in her mind.

Her feet stepped onto the circle stone. Then there was pain. It was as if it had been put on hold. Then there was blood, all the blood in her arms. The bloodfall hit the stone and hissed and turned to vapor, and the vapor surrounded her, and she coughed, and she could not move.

– Breathe, the man standing in front of her shouted. – BREATHE!

She crouched, and she heaved, and she felt the change. Every breath hurt, as what the blood had become burned her lungs, as the pain in her arms spread to the rest of the body. A bell, deep and powerful began tolling, its sound washing over her in waves. Impossibly she saw how the altar and the air surrounding it began shimmering, as the jewel changed from blood red to deep blue, and began pulsing in black, in shadow, before stopping, settling there.

The room itself changed, becoming a room, not a cave. She stared at her arms as they healed, as the pain faded, and a heat stronger than any physical furnace shot through her body. The vapor, curiously confined to the circle dispersed. The crouched figure straightened. A pale, pained and sweaty face slowly regained its color. Strength returned. Life returned, stronger than ever, and the ecstatic smile burned the last of the cold from the room, a room coming to life around her.

– Through hardship and determination you have now become the Sorcerer's Apprentice, Malone told her, granted her fondest wish. – Congratulation!

She laughed giddily, still a bit out of it, still riding high from the power boost.

Malone walked to the altar. She joined him there. A pair of eyes burning in violet looked beyond curios at the items lined out before them, lined out like trophies.

– This is the Black Blade of Oradeckt, he said grabbing the knife and holding it up for her to see. – It steals a sorcerer's powers and transfers it to its wielder, at least temporarily and to a point.

He handed her the blade. She took it, cautiously, awe evident in her expression.

– But I thought a witch, a sorcerer is born, not made, and that the power resides in flesh and not in…

– … in inanimate objects. He completed the sentence for her and nodded. – But what you will find in the books and scriptures you read in the coming weeks is that all great objects of power are made of the flesh, the essence of great sorcerers, usually those defeated by those even more powerful, but sorcerers none the less. The blade was made in blood, and tempered by the fire of a woman consuming everything in her path. These and all similar objects, weapons, not trinkets were created, forged during similar circumstances. The stain of spilled blood and broken skin is a part of the metal and carvings Forever.

– Forever… the girl whispered.

He picked up the two shiny bracelets.

– These are the Bands of Kordon. They are similarly charged, though not in the same brutal manner and method. My guess is that the sorcerer forging them did so with a bit more… finesse in mind.

She wanted to put the blade down, but he stopped her, and she looked attentive at him.

– Cut yourself, he told her. – Steal your own power and become even more powerful.

It already… spoke to her, and had done so from the moment she had accepted it from him. There was no need for Malone to show her anything. She cut the meaty part of her palm. First there was only a tiny line in the skin, but then, with each beating of her excited heart the precious red fluid gushed from the wound, as if the heart had suddenly been moved from her chest to her hand. The fluid seemed to spread across the blade, until it practically faded before her eyes. She noticed the energy. It flowed through her like slow, slow lightning, in a closed circuit, increasing with each completed cycle. She savored the sensation. Her awareness grew and kept growing, so amazing, so beyond amazing. She washed her other hand in the stain, and the skin of both turned red. When she closed her eyes briefly, when she blinked all she could see was red.

He grabbed her hands. The blade slipped from her hands and fell on the altar with a sound echoing like the bell had done. In swift, confident moves he put the bracelets around her wrists, and they, too were stained with her life, and another charge passed through her like slow lightning.

– It is done, he declared. – Now, both the Blade of Oradecht and the Bands of Kordon, and all the power resting within them are yours for as long as you shall live.

She felt faint, but not weak, felt charged, felt wanted and empowered and loved, all that and more. When he directed her attention to the remaining tools on the altar she focused on them with all the might she could muster.

– The rest is mere trinkets in comparison, he shrugged, – but may still prove useful on your Path, your Path of Power.

– Power, she breathed, and she knew that the excited smile broke on her face.

The bands felt good around her wrists. Her wrists had naturally felt a little sore at first, but now they no longer did, and when she checked the bloody skin, she found there were no more marks. They had healed. She looked astounded at Malone.

– They have healing properties. She heard his voice from afar. – You will be hard, very hard to kill from now on.

He sounded so proud of her. She felt the swelling inside again.

– Tomorrow we will return to the place where monsters dwell, he cautioned her. – This time I will let you wander by yourself a little, just a little, stretch your legs, flap your wings. You will need to prepare, to be ready.

She knew, knew what he meant, and apprehension took hold of her.

– But you warned me not to go there, she pointed out. – Dangerous creatures live there.

– I did not say exactly that, he corrected her. – I said I could protect us both, and I can. Now, though, I hardly need to any longer.

He caught her eyes, petting her cheek.

– You were not ready, then, to challenge the forces of the mountain and the forest, but soon you will be.

And she knew it to be true. She did not need to take his words for it. Her confidence stemmed from a place deep within.

– You may go to your room, now, he granted her. – I will not need you anymore tonight.

She curtseyed with a smile on her lips, and rushed from the newly made cellar.

Silence ruled her room, as it always did. She stepped in front of the mirror, studying her mirror image, what rested beneath.

Behold the witch, the voice in her head said.

She smiled.

As she began moving before the mirror and before the mirror in her mind, as she pictured every move she made from outside herself. She did not have any wand, but it hardly mattered. The exercise was just as satisfying without it. Her hands and feet and entire body moved with deadly accuracy. Recent memory easily brought forth the moves and the thrusts, brought forth the boiling glow from within. She began sweating fast, and welcomed it, welcomed the exertion and the eventual, inevitable exhaustion.

She sat on the bed, breathing hard, repeating every single movement in her head, gathering power from within, making it rise from her gut, from her center like a burst of fire, a blinding explosion in the night. It rose in her like a living thing. She had sucked it up since entering Malone's service. He had filled her up, maximizing her potential, and she felt ripe enough to burst.

The bands glowed. Her attention seemed to wander. And then her consciousness did. Suddenly she was back at her local Learning House, looking at the boys and girls in the yard doing their thing. They looked older, but basically the same, not having changed at all from the simpletons they were, the limited perspective they lived.

The bands hurt. The pain was so sweet, such an exquisite dish. She moved again, in a blink of an eye, visiting briefly the old house at the end of the road and her mother's sadness, before moving further, exalted and terrified, anxious to see everything ahead of her like a dog on the trail. Disorientation ended again, briefly, when she stopped, surrounded by trees, breathing the fresh mountain air. She realized startled that she was in the forest beneath the mountaintop, where creatures dwelled. A sound reached her from the right, making her turn her head. She saw it. It stared at her. She stared at it, absolutely fascinated. It was not an animal, at least not any she had ever seen, either in pictures or reality. She met its eyes, and it stared at her with its horrible, predatory intelligence. It stood there, naturally on two legs. One moment, two passed… before it charged her. She raised her left arm and a mighty and charged wave blew the creature backwards. It hit a tree hard, while bluish electric flames singed its skin. One moment more passed, before it looked at her with fear in its eyes and set off into the forest.

The witch smiled, a beyond cruel smile, that, she knew frightened the remaining wits out of most and all creatures venturing the forest.

It happened so quickly. She moved again, appearing in the middle of a busy city street, unnoticed by the many pedestrians and drivers. Everything was slow, was fast, as every detail of the slow moving painting burned itself into her cerebral cortex. The girl with the blue eyes had a light brown scarf and red socks. The sweating man with the heavy load lacked one of his canine teeth. The clock on the wall had stopped between five thirty and five thirty-one. Bubbles rose to the top of the beer, as each patron lifted his or her glass to already wet lips.

She crouched nude on the sacrificial stone, gasping and heaving. Her skin was covered in sweat and she noticed, feverishly that she was sticky between her thighs. Malone was there. He touched her. She moaned and writhed on the slab. He pushed a hand between her thighs and touched her in there, rubbed her, raising her heat to a level she could not bear. Release came like a flow, an explosion and she cried out, and then her body sagged and lay still, as she looked up at the male with infinite gratitude in her eyes.

The new day's light flooded the room the next morning. She awoke sweaty and wet and with a happy, dreamy expression locked on her face. Clouds rolled in from the horizon. She sensed the power in the movement, felt the seething energy in the charged air, and stretched merrily on the bed. Nothing covered her and she knew he could see everything, and it pleased her.

She showered, touched herself and cleaned herself. It excited her, excited the water and moisture surrounding her smoldering body.

The maid uniform waited for her on the bed. She put it on. It fit perfectly. She walked down the stairs, and to the kitchen, and made breakfast, made sandwiches. He sat by the fire in the dark room. She blushed deeply the moment he turned his head and looked at her. He beckoned her forward and she put the plates down on the table, and sat down opposite him in the other chair.

They sat there, and had breakfast in silence. She glanced at him occasionally, and kept blushing. Ongoing shivers of joy and anticipation surged through her, as she could not stop thinking about last night, still not certain it had not been a dream.

The plates were empty, and she felt full and content. He looked at her and she straightened in the chair, eager and attentive.

– Listen to the wind on the water, he said.

She closed her eyes briefly, and that was all it took. There was a pond not far from here. She had been there quite a few times with her friends during the summer. It was there, now, right in front of her, a sensation so real that it almost took her breath away.

It was gone. She returned to the living room, and the fire, and Malone.

– I was… there? She said. – All those places?

– To various degrees, he conceded. – Sometimes only in spirit, but sometimes completely, physically and with every aspect of yourself. You were in the forest, treating the beast with the contempt it deserved. The next time you encounter it, it will know you, and it and its fellows will bow to you and treat you with the deference you deserve.

– I was there, she marveled.

– You will learn to control it, control that, too, he told her, – as you grow even more powerful.

– It felt so good, she mumbled, – so incredibly good, almost too good to be true.

– As your confidence grows, along with your Might you will also learn to not think small, he reproached her.

She felt chastised, but it did not seem to matter. Excitement and anticipation ruled her.

– You fear there might be… repercussions, he said gently, passionately, – that you may be struck down by a lightning bolt from the sky for your insolence, because you dare to dream, to reach for the unreachable. But know this: There is no supreme power watching over us, neither good nor bad. We are free to do as we please.

His words turned her warm all over.

– Nothing? She wondered. – No… one?

– There are rumors, he shrugged, – ancient legends you will learn about when studying the books of shadows, about gods wandering the mortal world, but if there is anything to it they certainly do not make their presence known anymore. There are equally insubstantial stories about «Secret Chiefs», Those Sitting in Shadows guiding and judging mankind, sorcerers that have Ascended to a higher plane and observe us from Above. I put no trust in any of it. As far as I am concerned no one has succeeded, and I will be the first.

His words turned her both cold and warm all over.

– But how do you know there is anything there, anything at all?

– I know, he said, with a confidence that stunned her.

There was not a shred of doubt in his voice, in the black eyes piercing her.

She bowed to his words, to his infallible wisdom, sensing beyond sensing his sincerity.

– Undress, he bid her casually.

She blushed, but did not really hesitate. It was not as if he had not seen her nude before, and she wanted to, wanted to expose herself to him, to his deep black piercing eyes. She had already stood up, and opened the first buttons of her uniform, unquestioning and trusting.

The flames from the fireplace reached for her, danced around her, surrounding her. She stood there nude before the sorcerer, her teacher, her master, and she wanted him to come to her and grab her and take her to bed and fuck her, pierce her shield, to stab her with his blade and make her blood flow.

– Dress, he commanded her lightly, with that secret and oh, so attractive smile on his lips.

Her attention was called back to the chair, to the stylish dress, robe and hood, the proof of her stature, which presence she had somehow missed.

She put it on, and was transformed. The figure displayed in the mirror she glimpsed in the darkness was so different and new that she hardly recognized herself. This was different clothing altogether, so soft and luxurious and pleasant.

He rose and reached out a hand. She reached out her hand and eagerly allowed him to take hers. He pulled her into his embrace, and with a lightless flash they were off.

They appeared in a great and dark hall, a place where moonlight flowed through large windows on both sides.

– Everyone else is confined to use the portals, but you are not, she stated, strangely calm. – I guess I knew that, knew it from the first time you did it, but I did not know what it signified.

– To a certain extent, he acknowledged, – in a limited way, within a given Realm similar to the one we are currently residing in. That is my knack, like moving the waves are yours.

She looked around, sensing a build-up. Torches slowly lit themselves, slowly licked higher on the walls. Nothing more happened. She waited, hesitated. Nothing more happened.

– It is empty…

– It is empty, *now,* he cried, and his words, by the power of his voice echoed in the hollow of the hall. – But it will be mine, my castle, my Place of Power when I return from the Beyond, and you… you will be my Queen.

Trickles of heat shot through her like wildfire.

In a whirl of invisible energy, visible to her they were off, going further on their Journey. He returned them to the forest, and this time at its very depths, surrounded by growls and snarls. She froze when she saw the beasts, all the beasts.

She looked astounded at them, as the instinctive forward attack-mode halted and the growls and snarls turned to whining and whimpering. He released his hold on her, and she hesitated only a moment before she stepped away from him, one, two steps, standing on her own in the midst of a horror she had only had nightmares of and hardly been able to imagine beyond those night terrors.

– They cover in fear and respect?

She did not look at him, did not even look at the inhuman humanoid fangs and claws crouching in front of her.

– They recognize us, recognize power and are easily directed and tamed, he shrugged. – They are our servants. You may take one as your pet, if you wish.

– Pet? She brightened.

– Precisely. They can easily be trained to do both menial tasks and as sentries, guarding our castle. They are bright enough to take orders and dumb enough to obey any command, even at the expense of their lives and health. One day we will have an army of these creatures at our disposal, and we will have to begin somewhere.

The girl stared at them, at the empty eyes and docile demeanor.

– Perhaps later, she shuddered.

He did not comment or volunteer any reaction, but allowed her back into his shadow, and they faded away, the world turning inside out once more.

She found herself in the yard of her old Learning House.

– We are invisible to them, Malone confirmed, – to all those that can not see.

The words created more excitement inside her. Everything tingled so pleasant, so irresistible.

– So, do you feel any regret, any sort of ache at all?

She spotted Toby, one of her oldest friends. A bit to the right she saw Eleanor and Rosa in deep conversation with a big and tall new girl. She pondered her emotions and reactions.

– No, Malone, she replied almost instantly, – they are beneath me, now. They always were.

– They always were, he repeated, clearly pleased with her answer.

One more flash and they were in her mother's house.

He did not say anything this time, but let her stand there and study her mother.

– It is so long ago, Janet said unprompted. – It is all behind me.

And she sensed his affection, his warmth.

It invaded her, as they took their leave, and returned to the house in the

quiet street, to the living room, to the library with all the mighty words.
– So what is knowledge? He prompted her.
– Knowledge is power, she heard herself reply.
– So, go ahead and take the Power, he told her. – Take it and fill your empty spaces. Empower yourself!
She walked to the bookshelf, pulling out the Book of Fate, standing there hesitant for a moment, before pulling out several dusty books from the shelves above.
– How do you know which books to pick? He wondered, sounding more than a little amused.
– They… point to themselves, she said, considering her words a bit before nodding. – Yes, they do. They are a glow in my mind, not my eyes.
The young girl heard herself speak, and it felt very strange, as if she did not speak with her mouth, but with her mind. The Master looked smug and clearly high-spirited at her.
– My waves… she said, shaking her head in amazement, – they are part of my… my sensory input, allowing me to see, hear, smell, sense and even taste from afar, from places inaccessible to my… my mundane senses.
Initial doubt became certainly. It suddenly dawned on her, what had not been clear that night in the village in the distant realm.
He looked pleased or smug at her. She was unable to tell the difference.
The dust on the books was real. She tried dusting them, to no avail.
– Do not bother, he shrugged. – They are old and will always be old.
It was yet another curious statement on his part. She wanted to ask him about it, but her shyness, still there got the best of her.
She opened her second book, finally.
«Welcome, daughter», it said. «You read the first few passages in the Book of Fate, and after untold hardship and horrors and the joy of learning you are now ready to move on to better things, to take Power in your hands».
She shivered.
A frown appeared on her brow. She realized that the writing… that the writing was in… red.
«Yes, I write this in blood. Every witch does, write her Book of Shadows, her Grimoire thus. Touch them, touch me, learn from me past and present and future truths, and be forever Changed. You will no longer merely read my words, but experience them, as if you, yourself are writing them».
She slammed the book shut, and sat there, shaking hard, staring at the sorcerer at the other end of the table with wild eyes and with sweat pouring from her frown, her wrinkled brow.
– A wise choice, Malone grinned at her. – What the long dead witch

proposes demands careful preparation. If you had done that unprepared you would have been possessed by her spirit and hardly been more than a passenger in your own body.

He reached out a hand and she did, too and sought his.

– There are pitfalls, he said, once more imposing caution on her. – There always are.

– I know you will lead me through them and lead me to greatness, Master, she said, bowing her head. – Thank you!

– You are welcome, he said, grinning his cruel grin. – And yes, I will!

She shivered in anticipation and anxiety, as the sorcerer's apprentice took her designated place before her Master. He sat in a chair. She sat on the floor, looking up at him with high regard and hunger in her eyes, studying him with blushing cheeks.

– You stem from a family of sorcerers, he began. – It is no wonder you are one. It is in your blood, written in your genetic code. You would have become one without my help, because, as you so rightly pointed out: a witch is born, not made. But you would not have become so powerful. The latest of your line, those before you have basically ignored the calling, and without anyone to learn from you would have had to resort to dabbling, to substandard trying and failing. Now, you are *open,* and as you seek the world, the very existence where we live and breathe destiny seeks you out with its claws and fangs, and as the gods are my witness: you will be ready for it.

As he spoke his words translated in her mind as images, sounds, scents, tastes and touch. She felt touched, felt his hands and eyes on her.

He rose and beckoned her to follow him. She did so, only a few steps, to the center of the floor. He had brought a book. She recognized it easily. It was her family heirloom, the Book of Fate left her by her great grandfather she had read not that long ago. He had split it open somewhat at the middle, and began reciting from it in a strange, arcane language that slowly, chillingly made itself understandable to her.

– Revered ancestors of my apprentice, she who has chosen me as her teacher, grant my wish, open the well of the world to me, to her, so she may drink from it, drink until she is sated. She is ready, ready for her devoirs, to take her destined place at your table.

There was more, but she did not quite get that, the dizziness striking her in waves.

– Are you ready, Janet of the Blue Flame? A voice said, and she glimpsed a dark figure in front of her.

He was not quite her great grandfather, but looked like him, more than enough for her to be drowned in a powerful sense of familiarity.

– Yes! She replied proudly, and hardly recognized her own voice.

– We of our line serving Power recognize you as part of us and acknowledge your right to your birthright and welcome you to our fold.

A large fire rose before her. She took one, two steps back and yelped in surprise and terror.

– Are you afraid, Daughter of the Blue Flame? The voice spat.

– Yes, she whispered.

– Wise, the voice said, a little less unkind, still spitting the words like curses. – But you still want your devoirs, your inheritance?

– Yes, I do! She cried. – I want to inherit the Flame, want to carry it across the troubled rivers.

She sensed the shadow's approval, his dark pleasure and shivered in fear and delight.

– Then drink what is offered you.

The fire, hot on her skin did not burn her. She turned to Malone and he handed her a small bottle filled with a strange twinkling fluid. He had unscrewed it and a kind of smoke rose from its neck. She grabbed it and drank, swallowed everything in one move. It felt right, right as rain.

She had spilled a bit on her hand. It twinkled in blue, in light blue and as she watched the large fire changed to the same color, the same, bluish flame. It whispered to her, beckoned her.

– Step into it, Malone said.

She looked incredulous at him.

– Do it, now, he hissed, – before it is too late. It must be your decision, your will, or it will all be for naught.

One look, one turn of the head was all it took. She looked into the blue flame and was lost. One step forward and the flame began dancing. The whispering and beckoning grew to irresistible proportions. She nodded, and took that final, crucial step forward.

She could see herself in there, as the flame changed, as she seemed to… absorb it, as it shrunk and took the form of her body, embracing her as never before. There was pain, one making her gasp, one making her swallow the flame. She felt it, felt it slide down her throat. The shadow of her ancestor entered her and settled in her and burned within her. She studied her hands, observing in a strangely calm way how the flame slowly faded, and she stood there, without a mark on her, even as her birthmarks showed fully and would to anyone, even the lowest mundane creature. They were visible to her through the Master's burning stare.

– Welcome, Janet of the Blue Flame, Malone greeted her, – to your world.

His words excited her, inevitably. Confusion riddled her for a moment,

before that, too left her.
– It did not burn me? She said.
– Not in a physical sense, no, he said, clearly pleased. – It burned away your past life, everything that is not Magick.
She sensed a pressure building, from within, not without. At her fingertips was not a flame, but a warm, pleasant glow. Her senses reached out by themselves, through the living room, through the house and its cave, and to the world outside. Her bracelets hummed and buzzed so pleasantly.
Malone stood there, inscrutable, studying her with his cold eyes, her enhanced senses not touching him at all, and she shivered in the presence of his Power.
The tattoos had quickly faded again, to reappear each time her power rose high.
She recalled no sleep that night. There was only the teaching and the Power, and the ever powerful presence of her mentor, her Guide on the Winding Ways, the Labyrinth of Life. She sat by her desk, the pupil, and he took her by the hand through the Abyss of existence.
– Spells can be more than useful, he taught her, – as long as you do not allow them to become crutches.
He guided her through the books, every single page and word and letter cast in shadow, moving under her breath, her rapid breath. His finger drew a sign on a paper. He did not use a pen. The paper caught fire and crumbled to Dust at his command. She breathed its dust and potency.
The days seemed endless, and way too short. He drilled her like a sergeant would his troops, but with an intensity that both thrilled and frightened her. Every night she went to bed she had trouble sleeping, no matter how exhausted she turned out to be. She writhed on the bed in her restless sleep, frowning because she felt there was something eluding her, something just out of reach. The days brought more excitement and joy.
It was another day or night of twilight. She could not tell the difference anymore, but she sensed a thousand shades of it. Her eyes and mind seemed ablaze with awareness.
She placed herself before him, standing straight, looking straight ahead.
– Who are you? He asked her curtly.
This was it. This was the time when it all began.
– I am Janet of the Blue Flame. I am born a sorcerer, one with powers of the mind and the body far exceeding those of most others, one in a line reaching far back in antiquity. In this modern age I, like many others was virtually unaware of the potential resting in the murky parts of my being, but *no longer*.

– What is your *name?*

– My name is Janet of the Blue Flame. I proudly embrace my inheritance and disregard my past.

She felt it. Her inheritance filled her. Her past faded like a dull dream.

– So, Janet of the Blue Flame, what was, in your opinion Osiris' secret?

Janet felt pride swell inside before she had started speaking, amazed by how alert and clever she had become, what clarity of vision she enjoyed.

– «He» was secretly Isis, a woman. According to some scholars she lived like that, off and on for centuries, so she became both the god of the sun and the goddess of the moon, both the mother and father of our modern society.

– Excellent, he approved. – You remember more and more about what is in the books, crucial information that is not common knowledge anymore, remember even the innuendo, what is implicit and implied. But you need to do even better: you need to know it by heart, so it will come easy to you, so you will not freeze and fail in a given crisis, when life and death and worse will be at stake.

She knew what he was talking about, knew what kind of horrors and entities that were out there, lurking and preying on the unaware, and she did not even attempt to hide the shivering.

– What do you need to do before using the Black Root?

– Remove its branches, she replied automatically. – They are deadly, not merely poisonous.

He hammered her with his questions and his austerity, making her dizzy. Everything just seemed to be fading around her, until his voice and his face were the only distinct impressions she was able to input.

– *Drink!* He commanded her.

She obeyed the moment he put the smoking brew to her lips. It tasted bitter and stale. She coughed, but not very hard and loud.

The brew started spreading through her body before it had reached her stomach, or so it felt. She began humming, humming the silent music of the spheres only she could hear.

He was pleased with her. She sensed that, and expectation kept rising within.

The questions and hammering continued. She replied eagerly.

– What is the nature of the Green Razor?

She faltered and everything turned to ashes inside.

– It… it…

A sound resembling that of a whip hitting the floor made her jump.

– It heals instead of cuts, he told his apprentice sternly and patronizingly.

– I am sorry, Master, she whimpered. – Your apprentice is sorry.

Her answers were not always correct or sufficient, and each time she made a mistake she fell into a mire of gloom.

– Dance, he snapped. – Dance for me.

She did. Her body whirled and turned on the floor. She had never been very good at dancing, but now she felt like flying, as if she was not even touching the floor, and then she realized she was not. Her body moved on the waves created by her glowing, glowing mind. She performed for him, making herself desirable to him. Time just lost its meaning.

A… stench rose from her lower parts. She realized startled what this was. It was stronger, more potent than she remembered it.

Something hit her, something unbalancing her. She cried out and touched the place of pain on her arm, but managed to stay afloat, to keep dancing.

Time kept losing its meaning. She danced for him, no one but him, and the smile returned slowly to her face.

The snap of his voice and his whip kept hitting her. There was nothing else. She stopped touching the skin and mind touched by his snap and kept dancing.

– What is the nature of the Deep Purple?

– It heightens awareness, Master, she giggled and hummed happily. – It exposes the mind for the user to enjoy.

– What is the nature of the Green Razor?

– It heals instead of cuts, the apprentice replied eagerly.

It was years, eons since he had asked her that question, and she had failed to give the correct answer. It did not matter. She knew, now, and would never forget.

It did not matter that she had to focus on staying afloat. She knew the answers by heart and her response was swift and true.

When he signed to her and she proudly lowered herself to the floor whole seasons could have passed without her being aware of it.

She stood before him, breathless and humble, awaiting his judgment.

– It is time, he declared. – Time to put the last piece of the puzzle in place.

– Of the mystery, she stated proudly, – the trial every adept must face as the final step before the initiation is complete.

A bell started chiming, started chiming again, but she heard it more like drums, like thunder.

– You have entered your fertile period? He asked her.

– Yes, Master, she replied, blushing under his relentless stare and the implications of his question made her warm and hot all over. – It started not long ago, when I was… dancing.

She saw him nodding to himself, her answer to his question confirming what he probably already knew. Excitement rolled through her in waves, her waves spreading inward and outward.

He did not say anything more, but walked out of the room, and she rushed after him, walking in his shadow, down the stairs, to the cellar, the cave. The torches lit themselves, or so it seemed. When she studied Malone she saw no signs, none at all, that he was the one doing it, and he just looked more and more impressive and mighty in her eyes.

The mighty sorcerer stopped between the sacrificial stone and the altar.

– This is it, he declared pompously. – This is the beginning of your final and irreversible initiation into Magick and my Ascension. Are you able and willing to do this, Janet of the Blue Flame?

– Yes, she heard herself say, a whisper, and she hoped: a shout in the night.

– Janet of the Blue Flame, the mighty sorcerer Malone's apprentice once again and one final time places herself willingly and eagerly in his hands.

– Undress, then, and stand naked before your Master.

She slid out of her robe with something resembling practiced ease, and felt pride. Janet of the Blue Flame stood naked before her master.

The chilly draft and the heat from the torches warred on her skin. She was wet below. Everything was throbbing so pleasantly, and she welcomed it. He did not have to order her to lie down on her back on the sacrificial stone, having drilled her extensively in advance. She knew the ritual by heart.

– I accept your offering, he cried. – I take you as my vessel in my Ascension. I hollow you in the name of the older, unmentionable elder gods.

There was a pressure between her eyes, a growing, dulling pain.

– By the Bands of Kordon I bind you.

She sensed a pull in her wrists, and the bands were glued to the stone. The vessel was bound and primed. She wanted him to touch her, to throw himself at her and ravish her.

– What do you need to do before using Black Root? He asked her sharply.

– Remove its branches, she replied promptly, automatically. – They are deadly, not merely poisonous.

– What do you need to do before using Black Root? He asked her lightly.

She frowned, pearls of sweat forming on her brow.

Something cut her. It hurt. She began writhing on the slab.

– I can not remember. Why can I not remember?

He did not reply, except by asking her more questions. He began asking her the questions again. It took a while, but she realized that he did so backwards, compared to earlier.

– So, what was, in your opinion Osiris' secret?

– Did you not just ask me that question?

She looked bewildered at him.

He asked her another question or the same question, she no longer could tell.

– What was the question again?

Fear gripped her, strangely dull. She tried to focus, to master her concentration, in vain. It was so hard to think. She looked terrified at him.

– No, please, she begged him. – *Please!*

Realization struck her, somewhere, but it only hurt more. A whine pushed itself through her teeth and lips. She writhed on the slab, on the sacrificial stone, and pulled her bounds, but she could hardly move.

– Please! She sobbed. – I will be a good girl. I will do anything. I…

– What is your name? He asked her, grinning in wicked triumph.

Horror gripped her, nameless and beyond anything she could have imagined.

Name? She repeated it dully. Or thought she did. His laughter echoed through the cave.

– Who are you?

The sounds he formed with his mouth sounded completely meaningless. There was nothing there she could comprehend.

He made gestures in the air. He spoke, but she heard no words. He spoke the silent language of antiquity. She cringed before the creature growing to a giant in her eyes, submitting to her god with everything she was.

– I change you, he thundered. – I create you in my image, and YOU BECOME MINE IN ALL THINGS.

Something tore into her, a thousand sharp things, but no matter how much she tried, she was unable to recall what they were called.

Pain shot through her, through her body and entire being. Darkness descended on her and she wanted to scream, and she did, she knew she did, but heard no sound.

Everything just… went away, everything Janet faded away to nothing, to a large, empty shell to be filled at will.

Chapter 6

– Without reservation, without reason, he said softly.

The girl lying on her back on the stone looked up at the man towering above her.

– I am your Master, he told her. – I am the star burning you to ashes, leaving nothing but my will and my particular intention.

She listened, listened hard. Listening was hard. A frown deepened briefly on her brow, before fading, until no disturbing thoughts warred for her attention.

The man with the long, dark hair undressed. She felt growing joy the more she looked at him.

– You are my slave, he spat. – You are nothing but a whim of my will.

– Yes, *Master*, she replied.

The sound of bells and the thunder of his laughter rolled through the cave.

She averted her eyes, unable to hold onto the brilliant light he radiated.

– You have no name, he said cruelly, making her cringe even harder in her more or less frozen position. – I feel generous today, though, and feel like giving you one. I think I'll call you… Kitty.

– Kitty, she repeated happily. – Kitty loves her Master.

He crawled on top of her. She was ready for him, wet and yearning mindlessly for his touch, and deep penetration. He pushed and she shouted in joy. His cruel smile filled her, and she sniffed in brief misery, before the rising pleasure took hold over her once again. There was hardly any mind left, and the part of her body not glued to the slab moved to his moves, pushed against him in boundless need and submission.

When he pushed his seed into her she surrendered completely. The bands and spell kept draining her of will and mind. When he emptied himself a second time she forgot the last vestiges of herself, and he dominated her attention completely. She lay there, spent, totally open to his beyond potent will and mind, saliva flowing from her slack mouth.

– You will do simple chores, he told her, – and no more. That is all I require of you.

She shrunk under his stare, so attuned to his emotions and desires, so aware of his thoughts.

He rose and dressed, looking down at her in contempt and scorn. The sacrificial stone let go of the bands and she was able to move. But she did not, not until he nodded curtly. She rose, casting her eyes to the floor. He took her to the kitchen. She made breakfast, and discovered it was not hard, that she came by it without thinking. The chores she came by easy. Everything else was impossible to wrap her feeble thoughts around, no matter how hard she tried. He left her there, confident in his mastery over her and her ability of serving him unconditionally.

She carried the large tray of food from the kitchen to the living room, stopping briefly before the hallway mirror, looking at her darker skin and darker hair, at a female version of the master. He had transformed her and made her his creature. Pride and whatever shame he had allowed to remain surged through her. That brief glance in the mirror was the only memory she retained from her walk. She curtseyed before him and put the tray on the table before him.

He began feeding with a sense of triumph that would not quite fade from his face. He took his good time, before leaving the remains to her. At his command she sat down and began devouring the food.

– You need your proteins, he said generously.

Happiness smoldered her. Kind Master.

Somewhere inside of her, she cried her tears of bitterness and horror, but it never reached the surface, except in glimpses she caught at the edge of her vision in mirrors and smooth surfaces.

She did her chores, morning, day, evening. There were chores and sleep, and nothing else.

People passed by outside. She watched them from the balcony. The sight did not really register anywhere, except as slow flashes of distractions in the glory of service her existence had become.

The morning sickness began one morning. She rushed to the toilet and knelt before it. It took a few heartbeats, a few breaths. She threw up vigorously. Another timeless time later she dried the vomit off her jaw, both while kneeling and standing before the mirror. The face looked totally unfamiliar. She could not grasp its significance. It had nothing to do with her. She rushed back and knelt down before her Master with a frozen, happy grin on her face, sharing the great news.

It grew within her, in the weeks and months to come. She felt it, felt it feed off her, taking her energy and life force. Her belly swelled, from just a tiny bump, to a large ball.

She dusted the house, from top to bottom. It was a pleasant, rewarding chore. She hardly heard the noise of the vacuum cleaner. The brush she used to dust the shelves felt so good in her hand. The mask on the wall stared at her, but she averted her gaze, and proceeded with her chores. It was easy work, practically doing itself, or so it felt.

He made sure she fed properly and she eagerly obeyed his wishes. The ravenous beast she carried in her belly felt like a vast abyss she could never fill. His ongoing control of her took little more than a few added directions now and then. There were no signs of rebellion, no single thought to that effect, nothing even resembling stray notions.

She cooked for her master, slaved for him, the happy smile painted on her swollen face.

Her days and nights filled themselves with chores and service, and she reveled in them all.

Kitty made errands for the master in the neighborhood, dressed in her soft robe and hood. She stepped through the door that was not there, and headed down the street to the nearest grocery store. People stared at her, but she was oblivious to their attention, to their curiosity and gall. She had her chores and that was all that required her attention.

It was early morning, and not many people had found their way to the store. She walked with lowered eyes and avoided contact with them all, just slipped between the human beings like air. They did not matter. She did not matter. Only her chores and the man that was her entire existence did.

She gathered everything in her large basket. It was easy work, and not very trying for her feeble mind. The food pointed to itself for her. The Master had seen to it that she would know her chores and it pleased her to do his will.

Words and commands churned through her mind, repeating themselves, silent but irresistible. She was nothing and wanted for nothing but those things.

The merchant stared at her breasts again, when she stopped before the counter. He always did. She knew he desired her. It was evident in every move he made, in every little glance he sent her. He had trouble breathing sometimes, because of that all-consuming desire.

She began placing her groceries at the counter, and he began registering them on the cashier. When she grabbed the pack of oranges she stumbled and the pack fell from her grip and hit the floor, and the oranges rolled all over the dirty surface.

– Kitty is sorry, she whined. – Kitty is so clumsy. She will fetch. Sorry. *Sorry!*

She crouched and began picking up the wayward oranges, and her swollen breasts fell out of their confines, and the manager began licking his lips.

People stared. She put the oranges at the counter, before finally covering herself, doing so without haste. He completed the registering on the cashier. She paid with a large bill, and he returned coins. His hand lingered on hers. She did not pull away, did not react in any noticeable way. He frowned, pulling his hand away. She grabbed the two full bags, turned around and left the store.

She returned to the house, the whispers and glances and people's condemnation clearly felt. The door, not really there opened up before her, and she stepped through the portal to her little private world. She returned to the kitchen, to its familiar smells and orientation. A sort of calm entered her, settling the unrest plaguing her in the outside world. She prepared the breakfast with fresh vegetables, hams, cheese and bread with practiced ease. It had become a comfortable routine these last months, and she could not recall any other life, and she did not want to.

Any stirring of memory, of her life before this that might be, instantly caused anxiety, even near panic, to rise within her. She was better off without it and did not want it.

She served the Master in his study. He basically ignored her, as he usually did, feeding, hardly taking his eyes off the book in his lap.

Kitty fed, too, wolfing down the food, the energy-rich nourishment, never truly sated, and still feeling hungry when done.

This room always made her feel funny, and that feeling had been increasing lately, with her growing belly. She sensed the little one, even though her sense of him was muted, even though she had expected more. It tried to reach out to her, but was blocked by what she imagined was a thick wall. The Master had decreed it so. The Master was wise.

Nightmarish dreams filled her nights, gone in the bright light of day.

Dry tears fell from her eyes, no matter how hard she dried them. The chores, and nothing more filled her days, gone in the nightmarish dreams of her nights.

Something was… wrong, she knew it was, but every time that fleeting notion touched the tip of her eyebrows, every time she reached for it, it slipped away.

He still made use of her occasionally, but decreasingly so, as her belly grew bigger. He made her suck him, and with experience came greater skill. He made her serve him in any way his fancy struck him, and she became even more his creature. There was nothing for her except that glory.

She frowned, forgetting again the previous thought.

– You will be empty soon, he gloated, – the exact moment you are supposed to be.

He was immensely pleased with himself. She shivered in his shadow. She did not know, and she did not wonder why.

She brushed the small statues in the living room. Her hand moved the brush mechanically without a will of her own. She imagined they were glowing, but she did not see it. Her face did not change expression. A shifting of light did not make her react in any way. Her eyes never wavered from the vacant stare they had become.

The street sounded silent in her ears, the path hardly looked anything more than a narrow trail in front of her, a thread of breadcrumbs she followed vigorously. She followed his vision, and nothing else, and the mere thought set her mind ablaze.

A hand held her arm. It hurt. She released the bags with groceries. The merchant's flustered face appeared in her vision.

– Such a pretty girl, he wheezed. – Prettyyyyyyy

He pulled her close and began kissing her and fondling her breasts. They were sore and it hurt. Her eyes never wavered from the empty stare they had become.

– The Master is hungry, she wailed. – Kitty will cook for him and he will feed, and he will be pleased with her.

– Your «master» can wait, the merchant wheezed, working himself up, – wait just a little.

The words, his and her own did not really make sense to her. They were just empty phrases without content. She did not attempt to free herself, but just stood there, passively, while the fat man proceeded with his task.

He pushed her at the wall in the narrow alley, pushed himself at her, striving with her clothes, so worked up that he could not even do the simple undertaking of lifting her robe.

– Shut up! He gasped. – Shut up, shut up, shut up

She frowned. She was not saying anything… was she?

Then she felt the presence, her master's presence, and it overwhelmed everything else, to the point of her almost not noticing the little fat man staring dumb at the giant towering above him, the dwarf cringing in the corner, whimpering like a child, all reason leaving his sorry ass, until he was nothing but a drooling vegetable.

The master had left again. She felt warm and fuzzy and happy. She gathered the groceries. They were spread across a rather considerable area there in the alley, but she picked up everything with speed and efficiency, humming to herself, oblivious to the world.

She made her way back and immediately began preparing the master's dinner. Everything happened in a happy daze. Whatever she had been before she was Kitty now. Kitty, kitty, kitty

The thought was meaningless, forgotten the moment it strayed.

Kitty changed for dinner. Dressed in a mix between the maid costume and a dress she served the most radiant Lord, Malone the Mighty Sorcerer.

– Are you not a sight for sore eyes, he marveled, and fondled her round belly.

She yelped happily, and redoubled her efforts to please him. A sign, a command from him and she pushed herself at the tall, powerful body, eagerly seeking his approval.

He pushed her forward , over the table, and put it into her, and she sighed in delight. She was ready for him. Her hole was wet and tight. She was always ready for him.

She showered afterwards, at his command, feeling all tingly and wonderful. Each time she touched herself, it was as if it was him touching her, touching her deeply, beyond touch.

Clean yourself, he told her, and wear your best clothes. We are going to a party.

He had showered and changed, too. She joined him on the balcony, blushing and with a bowed head. He grabbed her arm and they were on their way.

They appeared in the middle of a forest, a place filled with life and sound. The stark contrast to the safety and seclusion at home made her instantly apprehensive and she sought closer to the rock by her side. He ignored her, ignored Kitty like he always did, in the terms of acknowledging her presence other than a lowly servant.

A trail lit the way in front of them. Another trail appeared to the left, where others walked, clearly heading in the same general direction.

Another pair, another sorcerer and his apprentice reached the intersection about the same time as they did, and courtesy was called for.

– Well met, Ansgar, Malone nodded.

– Well met, Malone, Ansgar nodded.

That was all. Nothing more was said. Both pairs of sorcerer and apprentice walked close on the trail without further acknowledging each other.

Kitty dared one quick glance at the boy. He did not return her interest. His eyes looked straight ahead, at some unidentified point in the distance. She did, too, unable to hold onto another attention not stimulated, one beside her Master.

It did not rain exactly, but she noticed a drizzle, one covering clothes in moisture. Autumn had recently come to this place. Yellow leaves had just started dropping from the branches. An owl hooted somewhere, even though it was the middle of the day. She recognized the signs of what the inept would call an enchanted forest.

They reached a bridge. It crossed a deep, but not very wide divide. Except for the pleasant fact that she could glimpse the other side this time, it was just like the bridge between worlds she dimly recalled she and the Master had crossed so long ago. When she looked down, there was nothing there but mist, no solid land anywhere in the abyss.

Nothing but the mist and occasionally piercing screams of predatory birds or whatever was down there that made her shiver all over.

She sought closer to the master, like the little child she had become. What she glimpsed down there, in the Abyss she did not dare ponder.

Crossing the bridge was like crossing a tightrope. She was unfocused and unbalanced and would have lost her footing several times if the master had not held on to her. He held her hard and she whimpered in pain. When she reached the firm land on the other side she gasped in sick relief, and looked at the master with boundless gratitude.

The mist cleared slowly and revealed a large, rectangular building placed in a field covered by vapors. It was dusk. Bonfires had been lit to highlight the path to the entrance.

– Remember that this is an important gathering, Malone the Sorcerer impressed upon her. – I want you to be at your very best. Your performance, or lack of it, will ultimately reflect upon me.

– I will be good, Master, she wheedled. – Your fellow sorcerers will look at you with even more envy and boundless respect when we take our leave.

– That is exactly it, he marveled. – You are such a bright and energetic creature, you know.

He patted her cheek and she bristled by the attention he gave her. She choked in her gratitude and tears formed in her eyes.

The frown was present all the time, but it never expressed itself, never was visible to anyone beyond her dim mind.

He walked inside, and she, his tiny shadow followed in his path, into a vast room filled with people dressed in their robe, cloak and hood. This was a gathering of sorts, both planned and not, a place and time where the mighty met. She marveled at everything, everything in her Master's sight.

There was a scream somewhere, but she did not hear it.

– Malone, an older, fat man nodded graciously.

– Tabato, Malone nodded just as graciously.

Tabato's eyes widened slightly. The moment he turned his attention to her she curtseyed deeply, though quite clumsily, of course, because of her condition.

– Is that…

– Your eyes do not deceive you, old friend, Malone confirmed.

Kitty imagined that the bracelets on her wrists grew heavier because of the men's attention. They hurt. They always hurt.

Malone basically ignored Tabato's apprentice. Kitty did, too, even though she noted in passing that he was a nondescript, pale youth. His eyes hardly moved in the immovable face.

Tabato did not care. Apprentices were usually ignored, except when their services were needed or when they incurred the wrath of a sorcerer.

They walked to a table. There were quite a few available tables to go around. The room was not packed. Kitty suspected that it rarely was the case.

She knew she stood out, a sore thumb, a valued possession, even more worthless than most apprentices. Her eyes moved constantly. She could not stop them from wandering, from flickering in curiosity and shame. Smoke and dust danced in the air. She spotted Ansgar, the sorcerer from the forest and his apprentice, and avoided meeting his burning stare by a hair's margin. He showed interest in the Master and his lowly apprentice. She knew that, even though she could not say how and why she knew.

The presence of Magick was palatable in the hall, in the very air she breathed. It tingled from the fingertips to her toes.

– Malone has a *secret,* a female sorcerer insisted to the person she was engaged in a conversation with a few gathering clusters away, – I am certain of it. He is so smug, so damn sure of himself, that prick.

Kitty heard her voice clearly, as if she stood close by her and the winds brought the whisper to her. Cold and warmth warred within Kitty and no winner revealed itself.

– Touch it, Malone told his Kitty.

It came easy to her. She did not have to reach out for it. The tingling changed to stinging.

– Good! Now, suck it up. Pull it inside.

She obeyed, knowing his meaning and desires by heart. The smoke and dust soaked her and its moisture turned her wet and woozy. The bracelets started hurting again, hurting bad. They squeezed her wrists in a vice stronger than thousand others.

Then it happened: she rose into the air. She did not desire for it to happen, but it did anyway. People standing close stepped back, turning pale and anxious. She felt bloated, as if she was about to burst, but still more of the ambient energy filled her, filled the battery she had become.

– Behold, Malone cried triumphantly, – behold the prophecy of the ages upon us.

She saw them, the strands being pulled into her body, into the growing field surrounding her frame. It fizzled and grew there, in potency and power. She did not feel it, had no contact with anything, no control, but it was there.

– Stop! Her Master commanded casually.

He had. He controlled it, controlled her, like the feeble puppet she had become. She choked, wanted to choke in her despair, but could not even do that.

Her body lowered itself, returned to the floor, like a good dog. She looked attentive at Malone the mighty Sorcerer, eagerly awaiting his next command, anxiously longing for the next time he would acknowledge her existence.

He wanted her to stare down the gathering, so she did. They pulled back another step or two. Malone smiled.

– The prophecy of the ages, he repeated, boasted, – and it is mine, mine to control and use as I see fit.

The energy roamed her, changed her, and she was his creature, his to do with as he pleased. The mere thought of it added to the warm, fuzzy feeling within.

Instructions kept repeating themselves in the practically empty space her mind had become.

– You brought this on, someone spat, – brought it on all of us deliberately. Are you *mad?*

– I most certainly did…

Everybody glanced at each other, uneasily, beyond anxious.

– It is like holding on to a beast's tail, the man cried incredulous. – You are also a potential victim.

– I know that, Malone said smugly; – *know* that I will not be; that I will master its challenges.

They stared at him, everybody in the large hall, also those not looking right at him. He had their complete and undivided attention.

– I have seen the future, he told them with a mighty shout. – I sent her to Florence's «training ground», knowing she would return. I know many things.

A stunned silence descended on the hall, on the entire place. Not even a whisper rose beyond the low background noise.

– He is a *Seer,* the woman from before cried. – That is his secret.

There had not been a Seer in the known realms for ages. The prophecies told they would one night return, but it had been so long, and no one believed in prophecies anymore.

He looked at them, stared them down. They believed him. The mere fact that he had the audacity to tell them, expose his secrets like he did revealed to them that they were looking at a man holding all the cards in his hands, his mighty hands.

– Let us take our leave, my apprentice. He deliberately looked at the girl by his side, putting down everyone else present. – There is nothing for us here anymore.

– Certainly, Master, she replied eagerly. – Of course, Master. Your command is my most fervent wish.

The others got the willies looking at her, and hearing her speak. The stink of base fear filled the room long after the sorcerer and his apprentice had left.

Kitty sensed it, sensed them, as they crawled back into their caves and stayed there, shaking in fright before the walking storm that had visited them. She glanced shyly at her Master. Pride filled her.

A carriage, a coach and horses waited for them outside, as it should. A man of her Master's stature *should* be given every possible consideration.

The man dressed in formal dark robe and hood held open the door, and they climbed inside.

– You should enjoy this, the Master told his Kitty. – It is a great ride, with breathtaking sights to more than stun your imagination.

– Kitty will, Honored Master, she wheedled, wheedled, wheedled.

The horses cried out as the man on the coach gave them their whipping. There was a slight pull, and they were on their way. Kitty looked out through the windows with the disposition of an eager child, constantly changing sides in the vain hope of catching every possible detail.

They traveled through darkness, shadow and bright day, everything simultaneously. One moment, when she fixed her attention on a given spot she saw one area bathed in sunlight, while the next brought a completely different landscape clothed in darkness, and only dispersed bonfires illuminated the land.

– The boundaries of reality are highly unstable in this place, on this entire route. Malone lectured her, enjoying the sound of his own voice. – We are not really moving through all the different realms, though, but only catching glimpses of what is far away, of where we may observe but not go, at least not from here.

Lightning, or something resembling it flashed across the various landscapes.

– Crossing a Divide without a carriage is not recommended, he remarked. – Even the most powerful would be lost to its raging mercies if the worst kind of circumstances should arise.

– Even you, Master? The girl said incredulous.

– For now, he nodded, with a smugness and expectation he could not and did not bother to hide.

People began appearing in the flashes, in the tears in reality. They scared Kitty and she pulled back, into the carriage, but she saw them even when she closed her eyes. The images of different lives haunted her, evoking shame and horror and joy, and the one tear falling from her eye.

– We are close, now, Malone hissed in her ear. – So very close.

Kitty frowned, and frowned again, but could not wrap her feeble mind around the hidden meaning contained in Malone's words. One moment she believed she could, but then it slipped away again, like the quicksilver it was, and the murky nothing of her mind returned.

A dark structure appeared ahead. Kitty glimpsed it through the window when the carriage made a turn, and she leaned forward eagerly. It was a building, a castle, one ethereal sight in a jumble of ethereal sights.

– Shall we not stop here, Master? She inquired, with childish longing in her voice.

– We have no need to stop here, he brushed her off. – We have places to go, people to see, and this is a mere distraction, baubles and trinkets compared to what is awaiting us.

The castle faded before Kitty's eyes, before they reached that particular spot on the path. She swallowed hard, the catching in her throat making ghosts of tears form in her eyes.

They passed the spot, the spot on the path and moved on. The carriage rushed forward through the violet mist, between flares of dark lightning and dark rumblings.

This violent pocket of reality seemed to last forever. Kitty suffered through it. She was drawing it inside, unable to help herself, and Master studied her smugly, and with immense satisfaction.

– What do you see? He asked impatiently.

– Kitty sees… Kitty, she frowned. – She does not look like Kitty, but she is.

His expression changed again, his grin filling her entire perception.

– Yes, you will do nicely, he said triumphantly. – You will do nicely indeed. In fact, I actually believe you will exceed my expectations.

They arrived at the fortress at the edge of the plains and a lake at sunset, passing several ruins half buried in sand. Kitty felt sick and resentful, and had no place to direct it. Master rubbed her cheek, petted his pet and she purred in anticipation. She knew what he wanted of her. She always did. It was clear and distinct in her mind.

– This is your final test, Master told her harshly. – If you pass this one you will bring all the joy and satisfaction to your Master that you will ever want.

And that was all she ever desired. She pulled in the restraints he controlled her with like a hunting dog on the leash.

The coach and horses stopped right in front of the closed gate. The fortress had been constructed like a kind of bridge between realms. The gate stood between the way station land and the material realm on the other side.

– Say hello, goodbye to the realm of Avaldami - the forest, Malone said pleased. – We would have needed to walk a practically endless and treacherous distance if that path had been forced on us. Be thankful that your master had other options available.

The Master and his hound stepped outside. Kitty sensed it easily, the barrage, the shield surrounding the structure, the anxious, though fairly confident rabbits inside. The Master had come here before, attempting to gain access, and failed. She felt him loosen her restraints, directing everything inside her into an attack. Her destructive waves flowed from her outstretched hands at the energy shield, and disrupted it instantly. The fortress' physical walls also tumbled down, and the rabbits' screams filled her ears. Pride filled her, as she sensed the Master's approval. He had loaded her, and was now firing her at his stupid enemies.

They walked into the raging inferno the place had become. She looked dispassionately at the scurrying rabbits, as she fired at them, at anybody, men, women and children catching her attention. Flesh and bone itself seemed to disrupt under the onslaught of her enhanced waves. Some attempted to defend themselves, and fire at the two intruders, but the waves protected them as well, forming a bubble around them both, making it virtually impossible to harm them.

She noticed how they all attempted to reach the portal by the nearest wall, but she handled that easily and picked them off one by one. Her control, with his aid was so precise that she was able to kill those he wanted her to kill and leave the rest stunned, but breathing. She had killed children at first, but began differentiating after a while, killing only adults.

– HEED THE MASTER'S COMMAND, she shouted, – SURRENDER OR DIE!

The mighty waves carried her voice. It took a moment or two, a few seconds, while she kept killing, also a few children here and there. People froze. They got the message.

– GATHER BEFORE THE MASTER. KNEEL IN HIS EXALTED PRESENCE.

The rats obeyed, crawling from their various and few hiding places.

They looked shocked and weary and scared at the intruders. They knew or knew of the Master. Kitty saw it in their eyes.

Malone stepped forward.

– Your lives have changed irrevocably, he declared. – From this moment on you are the devoted servants of Malone the Sorcerer. You have no desires or will beyond that. I will give you purpose and laws to live by.

The surviving children stirred and moaned, only slowly regaining their faculties. They tried to move, but was unable to, the proper use of their limbs denied them. Parents glanced at them, but did not move beyond that. A man was dying. He strived to remain on his knees, but failed and fell over, drawing his final breaths.

– Bring me the Orb, The Master commanded.

One man rose with bowed head. No one else moved. He stumbled into a hut. It took only a few seconds before he reappeared with a wooden box in his hands. He knelt before the Master, presenting the box as a gift. Malone accepted it. He opened the box and took one glance at its content, and a wide, bordering on ecstatic smile changed his face.

– Fate has smiled upon you and your children, Malone the Sorcerer declared. – You will raise them to become my servants and sentries. Eventually, one generation from now, you will leave this place and join your King and Queen in their palace. It will take time, but not be that long before my envoy here will come for you and inspect your progress. Your leaders will rule in my place, and rule hard. If anyone among you step out of line, everyone will be punished.

They felt his words beyond the words, in their innermost being. He imposed his will on them in a thousand ways. Kitty looked at them in contempt, at the humbled, sorry excuses for human beings, and she felt pride in her own, elevated position.

The Master had snapped his fingers, utilized his preferred weapon and broken them utterly, made them his creatures. They would never dare oppose him again or even dare entertain the thought.

Malone and his Kitty took their leave. They stepped through the portal and vanished from this realm, leaving behind the ashes of their actions.

It was early morning on the other side. The sun burned in Kitty's face.

They landed on the sidewalk in a street, in a city, one so vast that she could not see its end, even from the elevated position where she found herself. Down the street were the harbor and the ocean. In the bay, shrouded in mist she glimpsed a large red (or orange) bridge. She looked around her, just as wide-eyed as people stared at the two of them.

There was an expression of incredulity and fear in people's eyes puzzling her. People appearing out of thin air was not exactly common, but it was not unheard of, and Malone and his Kitty had not really done anything to cause fear here, had they?

She started coughing. It started as something at the back of her throat she wanted to scratch, and grew in seconds to a compulsion.

– What is that smell, that *stench?* She gasped bewildered, momentarily exerting herself again.

People did not seem to have any trouble with it, at least not in obvious ways.

– It is a poisonous element or two or three or hundred in the air, Malone shrugged. – They have grown up with it and can somewhat handle its foul presence. Do not concern yourself with it. It will not harm us, at least not short term.

She looked incredulous at the cars passing by, and realized that a lot of the stench actually came from them. Her head hurt. Thinking hurt. She shook her head in bewilderment and with a pained, confused look in watery eyes.

Malone stood still a bit, clearly concentrating, reaching out with his power. She realized, attuned to him as she was that he was searching, scanning for something.

A smile broke on his face. He started walking in a fast pace, and she stumbled after him.

He brought them off the main street, where cars breathed poisonous vapors and into the narrow streets and alleys, even higher up in this strange, foreign city. A group of youths followed them. She did not notice at first, but after a while there was a nagging sensation at the back of her neck, and she turned her head, and saw the small tribe with their colors trail the Master and his Kitty.

– Get rid of them, he ordered casually.

She obeyed instantly, sending a focused wave at them. They cried out in horror and pain, and fell, and did not get up.

When she turned her head a while after the next corner there was no one there anymore, no one at all, and she forgot about them, forgot about ever having encountered them. She forgot easily these days, and preferred it that way.

It hurt, hurt to think.

They reached a long, straight and basically empty street. Dry, fallen leaves flickered on gray ground. It was a quiet place, this city, in spite of the constant noise. There was a draft, but no wind.

Malone stopped in front of a derelict house, one with several holes in the walls. A narrow trail between the tall, withered grass led to the broken stairs.

– Kitty gets the funny feeling again, Master, she frowned. – Is that… it looks… reminds her of your house.

– It is and it is not, he replied, very pleased with himself again.

They walked inside, climbing the broken stairs. The door rested, half broken on the floor. The tingling in Kitty's skin intensified.

– This is a nexus of Magick, like your house, Master? She wondered, asked rhetorically, her inquisitive mind working overtime even now, when she was broken and neutered. – Why has not any adept taken possession of it?

– Because Magick is seen as a myth in this realm. He shook his head in contempt. – The ancient beliefs have long since faded from public consciousness, and as a result very few adepts get in touch with their birthright.

– How *awful!* She exclaimed in revulsion.

– The locals probably perceive this as a haunted place, he commented, – and thus stay as far away from it as possible, which explains its rather sorry state, of course.

Yes, haunted, not merely the house, but the extensive yard on all four sides, with tall, withered grass and wild growth.

The shimmering energy hit her the moment they stepped inside the living room. She had sensed it before, and would have been pulled here by her own accord, but now its brilliance made her shield her eyes.

– The Master was looking for the portal, she said amazed. – He has never come this way before.

– That would have been impossible, he sighed. – The tribe guarding the fortress and its portal has been zealously doing so for centuries, making passage dependant upon their good will, which I certainly did not enjoy.

He turned towards her. Did she see affection or possessiveness in his eyes or both?

– You are amazing. He shook his head. – So able and so willing to use your curious mind, even now.

She glowed, bathing in her Master's praise.

But not as much as when they stepped through the portal, and appeared in the living room at the same spot they had left in that other world.

They had come home. The hot blaze within her intensified to an uncanny degree.

– Not much longer to wait, now, he whispered in her ear, as he pulled her close, as he kissed her on her sore lips, as he once more put a hand on her big, big belly.

The next few weeks passed in an even deeper and happier daze, as the last few preparations were completed. She served passionately at her Master's pleasure, and it never occurred to her to do otherwise. The instructions for the ritual were hammered into her, and she knew them by instinct, by her fingers and hair and toes, and she felt blessed.

– He loves me, she hummed, while cleaning the kitchen, – he loves me, loves me, loves me…

She dusted the living room, serving him his favorite meal before the fireplace, while sensing how the fire was growing, growing, growing within her, until she finally was ready to burst.

On the morning, on the day in question she awoke from her troubled sleep, as she always did. She showered, but did not dress, making herself ready with quick, confident moves. When she stepped out in the hallway and walked out on the balcony, it seemed to be a completely ordinary day, but when she turned and glanced inward, at the house and the flesh, it tingled and burned. She returned to her room. Her eyes were drawn towards the flask on the night table. She grabbed it and turned it upside down, and its content flowed pleasantly into her palm. The tingling on her skin grew. She began oiling herself, all over her body, from toe to hair. Oily black, black hair danced on her butt, as she descended the stairs. There was no breakfast today, no food. She felt full and bursting, beyond hungry.

They gathered in the cave, in the cellar. He beckoned her, and she joined him, there, at the altar. She stepped onto the sacrificial stone. The rock began pulsing in dark light beneath her, its beyond powerful energies invading her through her naked soles.

She noticed instantly the change in the Ascension, how its very nature began changing. The building pressure within her seemed to affect it, somehow. Something gave. Excitement drummed in her mind.

Something gave, and her water splashed the stone. The sound of hissing and mist suddenly surrounded her, as if the rock had been red hot. She gasped and her limbs turned weak and wobbly, and she almost fell on her knees.

Malone brought forth the Orb from its casing. He let it go from his hand and it floated into the air, taking its position opposite the Ascension. Kitty's left hand pointed at the Orb, her right at the seething jewel. She knew what to do without thinking about it. The Master was in her mind. She could not read his thoughts, but they still guided her and forced her weak hand. Her limbs and thoughts and everything she was, were his to command.

The contractions began. He stepped forward and began speaking his spells, and it was nothing but meaningless noise to her. She spread her legs. Her arms were pulled above her head, until she hung, partly suspended by the Bands of Kordon around her wrists. They levitated in the air like beacons in the night. She smiled.

– Now, broodmare, he commanded, – do your duty, bring forth the sacrificial lamb.

This she understood, for some reason, and it did not change her emotions one way or another from the overpowering sense of bliss. She moaned, as the pressure began building in earnest below.

The sorcerer's voice rose to a mighty roar, and all the air in the room, in the cellar, in the cave began to shimmer and change. He was sweating, sweating hard. When she screamed in pain he seemed to scream, too. The child, the product of their combined might was coming, was born in pain and power.

It pushed itself out of her, slipped out like a snake, falling, stopping right before it hit the stone. Malone grabbed it, cut the umbilical cord, hitting its back, making it scream, making air flow into its lungs, carrying it away.

She fell and landed on the edge of the stone, and lay still, breathing, breathing, continuously gasping for air.

– You are now a witch, he said, – a sorcerer in your own right. I give you your devoirs, your life, and wish you good luck.

She heard his voice, as if from far away, as she slowly rose from the pit he had placed her, as if his fingers touched her, as his words drew marks on her body and mind and spirit.

He put the small form on the sacrificial altar. She glimpsed, through the red mist of her vision that he pulled the Black Blade of Oradeckt from his robe. It glowed and pulsed, as if in excitement, as if alive. The Orb pulsed. The Ascension pulsed. Malone the Sorcerer raised the blade above his head. He began chanting again, and she realized dully what was happening, what his intention was.

With a strong, unhesitating thrust he brought the blade down and stabbed the tiny body in front of him. Janet felt power then, more than she had ever felt. It washed over her in waves, in waves more powerful than anything she had wielded. Malone's form bulged and throbbed. It leaked energy on every spot. The Ascension changed dramatically. It grew from a tiny jewel to a large circle, a hole in reality itself. Malone placed himself under it. Wind began pulling him, shaking him. His hair rolled back and forth on his head, as if it could not decide which way the wind was blowing.

Then he was pulled into the air.

– IT IS HAPPENING, he shouted. – IT IS REALLY HAPPENING!

The blade slipped from his hand. It hit the floor with a sharp, metal sound.

Janet of the Blue Flame looked up, at an impossible angle into the vastness of the Ascension, at the horrible Nothing there. Peter Malone was sucked into it, growing into a giant in the measureless Void, before shrinking in her view, until there was nothing left but the Void.

The Orb blinked out of existence, once, twice, until it vanished completely. The Ascension shrunk, first back to its original, jewel size, and then fading altogether.

The woman crouched there, on the cold rock. Everything turned quiet around her. Sound faded, light faded, until she was completely alone with the horror of her solitude, and lay dead and still in the dank and shuttered cellar, unable to either hear or see or sense anything beyond the open wound her existence had become.

Chapter 7

She devoured the placenta in an orgy of feasting. There was hardly any thought at first. That came later, unbidden and unwelcome. She could not tell how long time had passed before she began regaining her faculties.

Time did not really exist to her. The pain, the mental agony threatening her sanity was all the measure she needed and wanted.

She rolled her left hand into a fist with a face contorted in rage.

– YOU FEARED FAILURE, YOU BASTARD, she shouted. – YOU FEARED SUCCESS.

The expression of full-blown hatred got no response, except for the dull echo returned from the walls.

She was herself again, whatever that meant, left with all the knowledge and certainty of what had happened.

– YOU PLAYED ME! She howled, writhing on the altar stone like the slab of meat she was. – YOU PLAYED ME LIKE A FIDDLE.

She spent an eternity there, on the cold, hot shame and rage of the sacrificial altar stone, before rage finally proved ascendant, and she fought herself up, standing there on shaking feet.

The house had fallen silent. There was no one here but her. She knew that beyond reason. Her eyes finally sought the tiny, bloody form at her feet. It had stopped bleeding. It was just a piece of flesh. She bent down, and picked it up. The low fall when she stepped down on the floor felt like a mountain. Her foot hurt, and she whimpered. Snarling at herself she stumbled on. She walked up the stairs to the kitchen, and dumped the cold piece of meat in the first bag she could find.

Her eyes sought the bracelets on her wrists. She removed them. They were strangely easy to remove.

She looked at the naked woman in the mirror, at her dark hair and skin, and unfamiliar features.

– You remade me, she said aloud, – *remade* me in your image.

There was blood on her thighs, but not that much, and nothing recent. She was healthy.

The thought made her choke, made it difficult for her to breathe.

She showered, cleaned herself forever. It did not take. When she finally turned off the water she hesitated only for a few seconds, before turning the water back on. She rubbed herself all over her body, rubbed so hard and long that it hurt and the pain felt good.

There was no sleep on the bed later, only a daze of persistent, horrible dreams born of reawakened memory. She wanted to cut off her head to make the nightmarish sensations stop, but did not dare go through with it, fearing it would not work.

Her fists struck her head, and kept striking it, until it started throbbing in welcomed pain.

Her fists struck the wall, not hard, but controlled, and they still did that when she woke up a timeless time later. She fed, gorged on sandwiches and milk, not sure whether or not that happened in the kitchen or somewhere else in the house or elsewhere. Her hands hurt. She looked dully at them. They were swollen, bluish and black. She stepped in front of the mirror again, deliberately staring at the post-pregnant female, with the sagging belly and large breasts practically dripping with milk. Hands rolled into fists. They hurt. She screamed, releasing the dangerous waves through them. She SHOUTED in boundless RAGE. The mirror broke in a thousand pieces before her might.

She rushed to the living room, to the library, and pulled out the Book of Fate, and opened it on the many blood-red pages. A snarl rose from her throat and she touched the pages, the blood-red writing, and it touched her, invaded her, and she let it, and it became a part of her, and that was all. There was no possession, no malignant spirit taking her over, only a better understanding, including the necessary knowledge to see through Malone's machinations, and a bitter choking rose from her throat.

The bracelets called to her from the kitchen. She walked to them, to their glowing, singing metal, and put them back on. It hurt, forcing them across her swollen hands and on her wrists, but it was worth it. They healed her, and not just the hands, but her entire body, bruises and all. It took a few minutes until she noticed, until she was confident it was actually happening, but from then on it took just a few minutes more before she was completely healed.

She knew she could have used herbs, but she instantly snarled at the very thought.

The bracelets hummed and burned so pleasantly, and felt so right against her skin. They belonged on her wrists, belonged *to her*.

Waves flowed through her hands and shattered the chair, and it was easy, not hard at all, and did not hurt, not the slightest.

She walked down the stairs, to the cave, to what had been the resting place of the Ascension.

– Where are you? She cried out with her voice filled with venom, staring at the ceiling. – Are you out there, up there, looking down on me?

She did not sense him, sense his presence, as she had for months.

– Well, come and get me, take me on, she said in a low and dark voice. – Strike me down with a lightning bolt from the sky, «Master». I am ready for you now, and will be even more so as time passes, as the days and weeks and months and years pass.

She walked to her room. It was not her room anymore. She was not that naïve, silly goose of an apprentice anymore. She dressed. The robe and hood fit her better, now, and would fit even better as the days and nights passed. She walked downstairs, to his room, at the end of the hall. It was strangely neutral, only a room, and did not actually raise any particular emotion in her. Malone the Sorcerer had not really made his mark on it at all, not in all the time he had lived here. He had not left a single keepsake or anything that could be deemed personal. The sheets were new and clean. She recalled doing the room on the morning before the ascension. His scent was gone from the room, from the entire place. She could not find it anywhere, no matter how many times she paced back and forth, up and down in the house. When she stopped on the balcony, looking at the neighborhood her doll-like face had gained an almost serene look.

– You have grander plans than this tiny spot, do you not, Peter? She said softly. – Far grander plans?

And this was a nexus…

That thought brought a pleasant trickle down her spine.

This was where he had brought her to the Cave of Spirits, leading to the bridge and The Village. Her senses told her that this was a place, a weak spot in the fabric of reality where he could do that.

But she could not, no matter how hard she tried, she strived. He had let her borrow his power and made sure she soaked up energy from a variety of sources. She still retained some of it, but only a fraction of what she had once possessed. Most of it had vanished with… with the baby.

A boy walking by on the sidewalk glanced up with a look of curiosity in his eyes, and others did, too. They did not stop or pointed or anything, but they *looked*.

She realized that people could see her. It startled her at first, but then she shrugged and accepted it.

They should see her, should notice her, the new Master of the manor.

She walked downstairs, and to the entrance. The door was still there, and it opened when she touched it. There was no handle or anything, but she did not need that. Dark pride coursed through her.

It was early morning. The first light had lit the horizon. The sun had yet to appear. She walked down the street, to the grocery store. People noticed the difference in her. She could tell. When she looked at them with her pointed, unyielding stare they looked away, and she wanted to laugh, to drown them in scorn. She did.

The store had just opened and only a few people had found their way there. The owner shrunk in his tracks the moment he caught sight of her. She smiled to him. The memory of his hands on her made her pull her lips into a thin, thin line. She did like she would normally do, what had been normal for close to a year, now. Malone had had no financial problems, and now she had not either. He had left her well cared for. Her wallet was thick with large bills.

She approached the desk. The fat man would not look at her. He just accepted her money with a silent scowl.

– It is such a nice morning, is it not it? She said sweetly.

He looked up, startled, and froze when the violet eyes twinkled at him.

– I know you were scared to death by my high and mighty protector, she grinned, – but he has left. You do not need to fear him anymore.

She grabbed him by not grabbing him, by not moving, taking him into the lap of her waves, of her buzzing, roaring powerful mind.

– You should fear *me!*

The words, the contempt echoed in his ears.

He gasped and his eyes bulged, and he surely imagined how it would be to meet her alone a dark night. She knew he did.

Janet of the Blue Flame smiled cruelly and left.

She returned home with her groceries, before immediately hitting the streets again, seeking out a suitable tailor. There were quite a few to choose from in the neighborhood, like there were in virtually any neighborhood. Clothing people was a popular and profitable business.

People surrounded her under the arch, swarmed like flies around her, in the streets filled with small shops, little shops of horrors. Janet took her time, savoring the burning sensation of hatred inside.

After a considerable deliberation she chose one store at the edge of the archway, and walked inside. It was quiet there, the place clearly removed from the outside and the other stores. What the difference consisted of was not instantly evident or would not be to most people, but Janet had no trouble sensing it.

A young woman appeared from the deeper parts of the store.

– Good wishes, My Lady, she humbly greeted the dark, imposing potential customer. – My name is Mary, may I be of assistance?

– You might, Janet shrugged. – I assume you employ proficient people here?

She looked very patronizingly, with something bordering on contempt at the other woman.

– This is a family enterprise, My Lady, the woman replied in the same, polite subservient tone. – We pride ourselves of our excellence, personalized service and our satisfied customers.

– I pride myself of giving people one chance and no more, the Lady spat. – Do you understand, worm?

– Yes, My Lady.

This time there was a glimmer of anger in the pretty eyes. Janet grinned cruelly, making the other squirm and shiver in the pleasant temperature of the store.

– By all means, then, lead on. I place myself at your tender mercy.

– Please follow me, My Lady, Mary whispered, or seemingly whispered.

Janet did, followed her to the inner chambers of the building.

They entered a room with a lot of mirrors and two more unpretentious girls.

– These are Menea and Mona, My Lady. They will aid me in the task.

The two girls curtseyed with lowered eyes. Janet began feeling a pleasant hum of triumph and satisfaction.

– We will present fabrics and forms for your approval, and if you find the clothes to your liking, we will sew and adapt them to fit you, and if you find that acceptable you may return to us no less than seven days from now, and they will be ready for your pleasure.

Mary was good at this, so well behaved and polite towards her *betters*.

– Very well, Janet nodded in approval, adding a cruel smile.

It felt so easy, like a second skin.

She let herself be directed and coddled, moving to their directions, very conscious of her power over them, both seen and unseen. They placed her at the center of the floor, between the mirrors, and began working on her.

– You have practically been groomed for this, have you not? She chuckled darkly. – To serve those superior to you.

– Yes, My Lady, Mary replied in her docile manner.

Janet felt how they shuddered in her presence and it excited her. The dark, dark glow inside grew.

But the inaction of the situation got to her, too. A flash of Malone, the enhanced image of himself he had planted in her consciousness danced unbidden before her inner eye.

She focused on the blank wall across the room and he faded away.

The blazing rage remained.

– My Lady has recently given birth? Mary inquired nervously, clearly waiting for the other shoe to drop.

– Yes, recently, Janet replied preoccupied. – Do not worry about it. You are to proceed as if the belly and extra fat is not there. Understand?

– Yes, My Lady.

The bracelets took care of that, too, straightening the skin, returning her body to its predisposed form faster than it would have done on its own.

Mary was clearly afraid. She wore her fear like a blanket, just beneath the surface. No matter the veneer of the proud servant she surrounded herself with. She was afraid of so much, of her costumers, if they would not come, if they would, fearful of losing her reputation. In short she was afraid of everything, of her own shadow. Janet swore that that would never happen to her.

Mary and her girls continued their tedious work. Janet sort of enjoyed it, enjoyed their docile servitude, looking down on them from on high. She only required of them to do a task for her. That was all they were to her and their voices did not really register in her mind beyond the necessity of the moment.

She walked down the road afterwards, aware of the pleased grin on her face and the conscious walk, enjoying basking in the admiration of inferior beings.

They looked so small to her.

She returned to her castle, her fortress of solitude. Living there would require servants at some point, but she was not ready for that yet. She knew she would be.

The door opened to her, opened wide. She did not have to touch it anymore. It reacted to her proximity, like the entire house reacted to her mood. This was not a house, not really, beyond the illusion, but a living, breathing thing, like a heart beating.

It greeted her, made her feel welcome and wanted. She walked straight to the living room, to the library. Like the hall it spoke to her in shadow, in a different dark. The thought pleased her. She slipped her hand along the books, touched them with her fingertips.

– You gave me my devoirs, she said, – taught me about Magick and the world. Thank you!

Slipping her fingers across the back of the books was like playing a keyboard. Faint music reached her ears. It seemed to come from everywhere in the room. She picked one spot, randomly or seemingly random. Her powers had been greater before the Master had left her to her own devices, but she still sensed more now, having changed to a razor's edge.

The sorcerer's face transformed into a silent snarl.

She pulled out a book and opened it on a random page.

Ascension
A place beyond space and time sought by many a sorcerer,
an unbeatable prize, a power beyond peer.
One to rival the gods.
Many have sought its source,
but no one has returned to tell the tale.

It was an index book, giving further directions. She could recall reading about the Ascension in other books, giving more specific, but still totally incomplete instructions.

– Where did you find your information, Peter? She mused. – How did you come by it?

She walked down to the cellar, to the cave. It remained quiet, still. She walked to the altar. Something pulled her there. The knife shimmered in red and fire to her sensitive eyes. She picked it up. It gave her a jolt, not unpleasant, but one charging her. The blade seethed with power, even though only a fraction remained of what had been there the moment it had penetrated the warm, tiny body.

– You are mine, are you not? She said pleased. – I will find many you can drink from. I will fill your cup and drink it empty. I will write names on your ancient tablet, and erase them all from existence.

The blade's surface twinkled. There was a slight pale, bluish shine by the ceiling, an almost invisible reddish glow by the floor, the residue of Malone's Ascension, both present in the black blade.

She watched the walls for a while, studied them, as they shimmered and their surface faded and reappeared. Touching them was not hard. She quite simply reached out with her hand and did it.

– This place is not merely one, she stated, – but several, but many. It is a nexus of realms. You knew that! Are you listening, Peter?

But there was nothing, no one, no sense of being watched or heard. She was alone.

– I guess the Ascension destroyed you, like it has so many others.

The wicked laughter echoed between the shimmering walls.

She returned upstairs. Now, when she had identified it she recognized the same shimmering here, albeit in a weaker form. It strengthened her and her resolve further. She began making dinner, an easy, but somewhat satisfying task. The routine helped her, helped her focus. She brought the piece of meat from the bag, and began chopping it up, sensing its residual power as she did so. The kitchen looked different, like everything did. She selected some pieces for cooking, but most of them she left raw, making one cold and one hot meal. The oven had four plates, allowing her to do everything simultaneously and much faster.

But she took her time, focusing on the pleasure of creating, of making.

The meat boiled in the kettle. Vapors rose from it, and she breathed their sweet scent.

She made vegetables, and she prepared fruit, a variation of a local dish she had seen her mother do many times, but also went far beyond that.

– Any witch can cook, Peter, she said. – It is practically a part of our job description. And with the aid of these ancient cookbooks I can work wonders.

Five books rested open on the desk. She hardly needed to actually look at the words to read them, to know them by heart, by soul, by ear. It turned dark outside. She drank water from the tap while looking beyond the wall with her waves, at the darkening urban landscape.

When she lit the candles the flame pulsed in an eerie light. Her eyes saw so much more, now.

She sat down and began feeding, taking on the warm meal and meat first. Its scent was not mere smell, but sight and sound and more, too, its taste a thousand flavors. She used a fork and a knife, cutting the meat in a relaxed, easy-going way.

The hunger did not decrease with the first few bites, but increased in harsh and dramatic ways. She looked down at the fairly empty plate, at the remains there, the cleaned bones. Then she pulled to her the second plate, with raw meat. She grabbed it with her hands and began chewing, began devouring it. Her teeth, strong and sharp ripped it easily to pieces. This was the first time she had had raw meat, and an expression of savage hunger changed her features. Strength filled her with every new piece.

It burned inside of her, in every cell of her body. She looked at the two set of bones on the plates, and then at the head at the end of the table.

– I know how you taste, now, Peter.

She rose, in one fluid motion. Limbs felt strong and her mind was on fire. She grabbed the two plates with cleaned bones, and carried them into the library. There was room on the lower shelf. She left them there, and returned to the kitchen. The black blade and the severed head were a nice pair, there on the table. She grabbed both and began cleaning the skull carefully. It was soft and would easily crack if too much pressure was applied. She flayed off the skin and removed the soft tissue inside. It did not really require much skill, but she still loved how easily her work flowed. She put the eyeballs and skull on the table and dumped the brain and the skin back into the now almost empty bag.

Her eyes saw even more, now, and all her senses, material and not glowed.

– This house… devours unwanted guests, does it not? No one unworthy can stay here for long without being consumed, without being trapped here forever.

She glimpsed unmoving faces on the walls, caught distant screams with her astute ears, practically smelled and tasted dead and rotted flesh.

The stairwell looked steep, as she returned to the basement, but the sight brought only temporary nausea. The bag remained light in her hand, and walking was easy. She stayed light on her feet.

The basement changed constantly before her eyes, even though it fundamentally remained the same. She felt the meat, the remaining essence of her son being absorbed into her body, granting her increased power. The brain turned slush in the bag still whispered to her, but she resisted its lure. She focused on the blood writing she had absorbed. It spoke to her, even when she was not listening, not making her more powerful on its own, but more knowledgeable and thereby more powerful.

Knowledge was power.

She smiled, knowing her new smile well by now, cruel and cunning.

The remains of the Ascension had changed slightly. Or she had just missed its details in her distress, or it had not merely changed but been metamorphosing, just a faint echo of what it had been and fading, but still present. She bathed in it, using it to further empower herself. It hurt, even in its current, dormant form, but the smile never wavered from her lips.

Something clicked within her, a sign of a reached threshold. She sensed it, felt it like a tangible force. When she returned upstairs, to the balcony the weakness in space revealed itself to her without her having to focus at all. She stepped forward and faded from the house and re-appeared in the Cave of Spirits.

The momentary dizziness faded quickly. The driving glow inside burned that away, like it did everything else. The whisperers pulled back, detracted by her silent snarl of contempt. She heard the music. It held no attraction to her anymore.

She began her descent further into the cave, until it was no longer a cave, and the torches on the wall faded and the blue darkening lights began fading in. Right outside the cave, before the bridge she stopped, smelling the scent in the air, in the quiet draft.

She was far more aware this time around, walking this path. It was amazing how aware she felt.

The sounds turned deeper, menacing. She scowled at them, and once again they pulled back in stunned anxiety.

– Come to me, she cried.

They listened with incredulity, and kept their distance, more cautious than ever. She sensed how they attempted to probe her, without approaching her.

– Come to me. I welcome you. Welcome, children, lumps of clay to an existence in my service.

The hissing sound changed to that of a drill, and she imagined thousands of them drilling into her skin, before she opened the bag.

She turned and turned, as the whispers were sucked into the trap prepared for them. The sudden roar was silenced abruptly and brutally. The sorcerer closed the bag.

– I bind you, she spoke softly her stern command, – I take you as mine to do with as I will, forever and ever, to the only existence you will from now on know. I take your power, your dwelling and thousand thoughts to use and engage. From this moment on you belong to Janet of the Blue Flame and will never hereafter yearn for more.

The form turned into a sphere and swelled to fill the bag, but there was no pressure there, only a state of cowed bliss. She rubbed it like she would a pet.

– Yes, you are happy and eager children in your Master's service, and will remain so for the rest of your time.

She walked onto the bridge. After fifteen, twenty, thirty steps she stopped and crouched slightly, staring down into the whirling layers of mist.

– I see, she hissed. – I see what is hidden behind the veil of time and shadow. Hidden in the boiling river are a million times million raindrops, mirrors of everything that was, is and will be. I know what you are, what you have always been.

The sorcerer held up what had now turned round and shiny, an orb pulsing in eerie light. Her hands and then body began glowing, too.

– As you fall into the Void you will touch all reality and drink of its nectar. I follow you on your Journey. I have your bones and carry your flesh. I will go where you go, and see and sense everything you do. Your experience will become mine, and I will see everything there is to see. As I have cut out your heart and drunk your blood the river will flow all fields, all forests and mountains, and one night you will return to me with the million times million drops for me to drink. The darkest and most potent Magick is mine to possess and wield and all its yields belong to me.

She turned her hands upside down, and the orb dropped from her palms.

– To ME…

The trinket she had dropped fell into the sky below. She needed only to blink to see its path. In such a single moment was the world, and in yet another such single moment was the world, the world, the world.

She could not tell how long she stood there, frozen, in awe and triumph and spite. Her wicked silent laughter was cast between the many walls on its path.

– It *worked*. No corner and shadow are hidden from my vision. Thank you, ancestors, for this precious gift, this unparalleled might. You did not know what to do with yourself, with your potential, but I did. I do! I will put everything to good use, everything I glimpse and will glimpse.

The draft from behind made her turn. It felt good and warm at her back and her front, as she walked, returned to the cave. She did not see the cave's entrance, but had to strive a bit, stray from the path, move outside the shimmering blue lights and red fire in order to reach it, to reach out and touch the wall. It did feel like rock, even though it slithered and burned to her touch, and taught her more new and exciting secrets.

When she turned to return to the path it was not there. There was only the mist, as far as her eyes could see, but she did not really experience any significant anxiety. Her waves, her mind ablaze saw far more. She snorted, a brief, cold laughter.

– I imagine some people will be lost, will they not Peter, after straying from the path, after being distracted beyond words with the lure of tantalizing secrets? But I will not. I am beyond such trifles.

The pathless path split in a thousand directions before her, into a literal crossroads of pathways, but she never took her eyes off the cold blue light hovering in the vast distance, one she crossed in seconds, and then she was back, between the lights, on the Trail of Mist.

She returned to the cave, and heat rose from its base to embrace her and burn her. There was a moment, when she reached the point where she had appeared not that long ago she had no trouble noticing and marking. It lingered as she moved on, as she crossed narrow rock bridges across vast depths and worse. In turn those moments lingered as well, as she kept penetrating deeper into the cave, as time stretched into minutes, hours and more.

It was quite a distance. She had prepared for that, but the seemingly endless stretch still got to her. Hands curled into fists and she walked on. There were spots, giant spots, entire areas where torches had burned out and it turned almost pitch black, but she pressed on, and caught a glimmer of fire in the distance. Time lost meaning to her, even as she clung to it.

Voices echoed through the cave from distant places, but no more whispers.

She entered a large and wide part of the Path. It was both a giant hall and a wide field. When she stared at the ceiling she could glimpse stars and moons and the wide sky. There was a village by a cluster of trees. The entire tribe of fair-skinned people was awake and up, its members restless and scared beyond their wits. They saw her, as her dark glowing form appeared in the darkness, and exchanged loud words. She walked to them, easily breaking through the barrier to the other world. One large man was about to lift his spear against her, but lost his resolve and lowered it, before dropping it altogether. During the next few seconds all the warriors had done the same. Men, women and children dropped to their knees and lowered their eyes, trembling in fear before the visiting sorcerer.

Their effort was totally ignored and discarded, as the useless gesture it was. She went straight to the hut where two people, a man and a woman lay unmoving on their back. They stared, if that was the word at the ceiling. Janet bent down and touched them, and something passed from her to them. A semblance of intelligence returned to their eyes and they sat up, locking their attention on her. She walked back outside and they followed her.

The villagers expressed brief happiness when they spotted the two, but it faded quickly before really asserting itself, when they saw the emptiness still present in there.

– These are mine, Janet snarled. – You will never see them again. Next time, when you turn lax in your responsibilities, and let the torches burn out, I will take all of you, and you will suffer a living death a thousand times worse than these two.

The kneeling villagers tried fervently to speak, to assure her of their undying loyalty and servitude, but failed.

Janet of The Blue Flame left the village in tatters, like it had been when she had entered it. The man and the woman followed her, a little bit like dogs, a bit more like walking puppets. She returned to the realm she had left. A slight pressure in the air she passed through and it was done.

The cave turned narrow again, turning more and more into an ordinary cave. She spotted its opening just as it ran out of torches, and only the moonlight lit her remaining way.

– Not many know of this path, do they, Peter? My guess is that you did not, but now I do.

When she stopped momentarily outside, and looked back, into the dark hole, she was confident that most people finding the cave, and even walking inside would find nothing and see nothing but a wall blocking the path in there. There was no visible trail leading to the cave, no obvious signs that it was leading to other realms.

She headed east with her dogs in tow. It was not that far. The lights from the city, or at least one city were easily noticeable in the air. It came from her right. She realized before she reached the edge and saw the familiar twin cities of Talaho and Howell below that she was coming in from the north, from Lazoon, one of the lower mountains.

This was a resort area, with Roman baths and residents. She noticed before she passed the actual property. They had made a golf course up here, on this No Man's Land. Lazoon was seen as a fairly safe mountain, and not besieged by what many saw as the unexplainable deaths and mayhem on Torfu, the tallest peak.

– People are so stupid, are they not, Peter? They refuse to see the world as it is, and prefer to exist caught in their own paltry illusions.

The two following in her tracks did not react. They knew she was not talking to them, was not giving them a task to perform. The strange trio walked to the left of the estate, along the tall, northern wall. There was a road all the way down to the city, and also stairs for those who preferred walking without being bothered with the annoying presence of cars.

They hardly more than touched Talaho, the Old City, its southern point before crossing the bridge to Howell, the New City. They walked along the seaside, along the harbor, where lots of ships were lined up, to the quay where the ferry, the speedboat to The Island was about to take off.

The Island was big, reaching far out into the archipelago, its city Auburn covering most of its northern and western parts, what was closest to the mainland. The triple cities formed a sort of triangle, with three equally long sides. Janet did not need to strain herself in order to see it all from above, her perspective that of a flying bird, a giant eagle, Master of everything she surveyed.

One single streetlight added to the illumination provided by the seafaring vehicle. The speedboat's gate closed right after Janet and her two companions had walked through it. The engine roared and they were on their way, crossing the sea between the mainland and The Island.

People commented among themselves about the strange garb worn by her companions and about their bare feet, but not excessively so. She shrugged. It did not matter.

The boat was filled up. All the seats were taken, and many people had to stand. This was the night run, when everybody was on their way home, after having spent the evening on the mainland. Spending time there was different, a different flavor compared to going out in Auburn on The Island. People fond of variety changed venues often, and alternated between the triple cities when they wanted to have a good time out.

Her newfound awareness struck her in particularly powerful ways here on the boat, with all the people in close proximity. She did not look at Rosa and Toby, but knew they were there. They did not recognize her, even though they looked straight at her several times. *He* was there, with them. She looked at Peter Malone. The boy did not recognize her either. And she recognized nothing of the older Malone in him. This was only a bungling young boy, nothing or very little of the mighty sorcerer he would one day become. She had to work hard to hide her interest, her fascination when it came to him. He was an anomaly, a riddle of infinite magnitude. She sensed power, sensed potential in him, like his older self had done in her. Her beyond powerful awareness told her beyond doubt that this was the same man.

A drunk lost his balance and almost fell. He bumped into Rosa, and she, in turn bumped into Janet.

– «And so, even on this quiet sea», Janet quoted Stan Rodman, one of the century's great poets.

– You are so right, Rosa grinned. – Sorry about that.

– About what? Janet shrugged.

She waited, as the frown in Rosa's face turned apparent.

– You look very much like our friend over there.

– I do? Janet shrugged, very deliberately. – I had not noticed.

– Yes, you could be his older sister or something. PETER!

He turned and looked at them both across what to Janet was a ravine of two steps. His eyes, like those of Toby grew big and stunned.

– This is Peter, Rosa said. – Peter, this is…

– Cathy, Janet said quickly.

– I am so happy to meet you, Cathy, he said, the charmer, squeezing her hand lightly.

– And you two do not know each other? Toby said incredulous. – This is not an act, a joke on us?

– I have never seen her before in my life, Peter said.

– I guess it is not that far-fetched, Rosa said. – Our ancestors are few, after all. It is no wonder that a lot of us look alike.

Janet met his eyes and held on. She sensed no duplicity in him. He did not recognize her more than her friends did.

– Where have you been all my life? He wondered.

It was something a bungling teenager would say, attempting to charm young girls. She smiled sweetly to him.

– I have just moved here, she said, – and right now I am glad I did...

He reddened, such a cute boy.

– Here, of all places, in the whole realm, Toby marveled.

– Perhaps it was fate, Janet said.

The ferry boat docked on the other side of the strait. It was smooth, like it usually was, like the ride usually was. They disembarked, following the flow to the quay.

– I love your outfit, Rosa marveled. – Very alluring and mysterious.

– Thank you, Janet, or rather Cathy said, – it was a gift, and I certainly appreciate it.

She looked at them from under the hood, and she wondered if they could see her, truly see her, what she had become.

– You look like one of those sorcerers of old, Peter said.

There were quite a few drawings and paintings of them, and even a few early photographs.

She studied him without openly studying him, sensing his curiosity, his nascent, unfulfilled, yet not invoked abilities. He still looked innocent to her.

– It is a great fashion statement, Rosa grinned, filled with envy.

They reached the buses, most of them heading for Auburn's suburbs, at the island's opposite, eastern side.

– It was nice meeting you guys, Cathy said.

– Hey, where are you going? Peter said

– I am taking a cab. I can not stand buses.

– The Lady is in the money, Toby chuckled. – Please take me as your consort, madam.

Chuckles. Cathy smiled politely, though deliberately patronizing. She and her patronage left them and headed for the parking lot at the other side of the quay, not looking back a single time.

– Altram Hill House, Janet of the Blue Flame told the cab driver, sensing instantly how it bothered him, that he knew of the place and needed no further directions.

He nodded, mute as a fish. She and her servants sat down in the back seat, and he drove off, his trembling hands clutching the wheel. The urban landscape revealed itself to her as the car passed it. There were brief impressions of fairly untouched nature and then, after many turns and stretches the city of Auburn grew around her. The city was not really very auburn at all. She had always seen it as dark, and had always found comfort in that.

They passed her old learning house, a place that had never been able to teach her much, and then, in another part of the city they reached her house on the hill (a mound really) and its quiet neighborhood.

She paid the driver. His hands still trembled and he could not wait to drive off. She did not watch him as he did, but turned her attention to her home.

– It is waiting for me, is it not, Peter? It has always been waiting for me.

The sorcerer entered her home, her Place of Power, and they, her arms, her fingers, her nails followed her like the functions she had made them.

It welcomed her, as always, attuning itself to her moods, her needs.

– Prepare my evening meal, she bade them. – I Hunger so, after the Journey through the realms.

They bowed and curtseyed, and pulled back, towards the kitchen, where they would make her meal, not their own. There would be ample opportunity for them to add to its storage tomorrow. She chastised herself for her latter words, for attempting to justify herself to them.

The library, the shelves of books called to her again, as it always did. The tome of her ancestors felt warm and pleasant against her skin, as she slowly flipped its pages.

– I have learned so much, but there is still so much for me to digest. How could you stand it, Peter, the impatience driving you?

«Patience is a necessity, daughter of the Blue Flame, while dealing with the arts», her ancestor told her through the texts. «Preparation and meticulous study are needed before gaining major access to the arcane. Moving too fast can yield disastrous results, both for yourself and your Circle or clan».

Her thoughts went to the Orb, and she instantly felt its presence, its immediate surroundings. She had already done so much, and it felt like so little, a mere preparation for the feast to come. Excitement coursed through her.

The servants performed adequately already. She sensed them at work in the kitchen, practically saw them, as if they were standing right in front of her. The contact she had with them, her power over them was quite intoxicating. She made a deliberate shrug, playing it down.

They made dinner and set the table for her. She watched them. They were good at it, good at serving, even at this early stage. She looked pleased at them, as she sensed the changes within them, within herself.

The male pulled back her chair for her and the female put the plate, glass and everything before her, curtseying, awaiting her Lady's pleasure. They were bound to her, and could, to a certain degree read and anticipate her wishes and desires, understanding the modern community they were cast brutally into, because she did.

Janet enjoyed her meal, its purity as a meal, but in truth this was not purely a meal either, but yet another step on her path to glory and power beyond measure.

The wine, taken from Malone's private reserve touched her in such sweet ways. Among his other qualities he had equally good taste in wine.

She sat there afterwards, the wine and food burning in her stomach and veins, while her dedicated servants, her practically mindless slaves did the dishes. Hearing them was no problem. Seeing them through their eyes was easy. They were a part of her, an extension of her being.

In the quiet darkness of the living room afterwards she could hear them breathe.

– Sleep, she bade them.

Obeying instantly, they lay down on the floor. Their eyes closed and they slept. She marveled at the simplicity of it. The sensation of it echoed so pleasantly within her.

She probed them, curious. It was sleep, but one totally controlled by her. They would not wake up, or even stir, without her active participation.

Deciding against waking up her slave to pull out her chair she decided to do it herself. Movement was a flow, an instant act, one instigated by her mind, but continued effortlessly, a perfect interaction between her and her surroundings.

She walked outside, through the door, standing on the porch, studying the people passing by. There were a few of them. They did not speak to her or even look at her, except with quick, anxious glances, but hurried along. She looked amused at them.

A girl walked in a fast pace, obviously in a hurry.

– Hello, Janet called.

The girl turned her head, but kept walking.

– Yes, I am talking to you. Come up here, please.

Wavering eyes looked up and down the street. There was no one else there. She hesitated momentarily before obeying the pull of the other's will, torn between fear and society's conventions. Pushing herself forward she walked up the stairs to face the dark, imposing woman.

– Yes, may I help you?

– What is your name? Janet asked her amused.

– L-louise.

This was an older teenager, seventeen or eighteen, usually fairly confident, but now very much shaken.

Janet nodded to herself.

– Yes, I can use you. You have the right qualities I am looking for, and I would like you to join me, in my quest.

– But, I do not want to, Louise blurted out.

The dark woman put a finger on her lips.

– Hush, little one, it is not up to you. I have chosen you, and you will abide by my word.

The girl wanted to move, to run, to flee, but she could not move, could not make her legs obey her mind.

– You fell asleep earlier tonight, did you not? The sorcerer circled her, waiting for the cowed child to nod, grinning pleased when she did. – You dreamed about this house, dreamed about me…

– No, I…

– My guess is that it was all a jumble, difficult to make sense of, to recall vividly. But that is no longer the case, is it now? Now, you see it all with vivid clarity.

– Y-yes, Louise choked.

It played on and on in her mind. Janet saw it, experienced it, by just a light deliberation, like pushing a button.

– You will go home tonight, dream more, become even more suitable to me, go to learning tomorrow, return home from learning and then you will come to me, and then I will make you mine, tie you to me with a thousand strands of my web.

The sorcerer dismissed her.

Numb and with dull, dreary thoughts the girl pulled back and walked backwards down the stairs. She wanted to run, but could not, leaving at a normal pace.

Janet saw her fade away in the darkness.

I want you to teach me, she heard herself say. I want to be your apprentice. I want to learn all the secrets of the world.

I will do exactly that, Malone told her.

She stood there and searched for him for a while, with her mind and her magick, but he was still nowhere to be found, at least not anywhere she could reach him. Her hands rolled into fists, just a few moments, before she relented, and the roar in her ears faded, and the night had once again turned quiet and deep.

Chapter 8

She woke up the next morning, relaxed and rested, from a close to dreamless sleep.

They, the two below woke up the instant she did, so very attuned to her. She smiled and stretched on the bed, enjoying the moment, the sensation.

Her servants, her mindless, dedicated slaves prepared breakfast, while she enjoyed a shower, while she dried herself in slow, languished strokes.

– It is such a pleasure owning slaves, is it not, Peter, to know that they are yours to do with as you please, whatever your pleasure is.

She savored the sensation, the power.

They dressed her, and everything went so smooth. They managed to both do that and continue with preparing the breakfast. The male brought a chair and she sat down in front of the mirror, and the female combed her hair.

The table was set when she entered the dining hall. The food was ready, was tasty, delicious. She knew that before she sat down and began feeding.

It was just amazing how great it tasted, how the flavors melted on her tongue and spread from there, through her stomach to the rest of her body.

She soaked up the impressions of the room, of its many objects. It was like she could just focus on anything and read its content, and take its measure.

The statues on the table pulled her in and spoke to her. There was something about them, something she could not fathom, not even now.

Her meal, her feast ended, at least for now. The servants pulled back, leaving her alone, in tune with her desires. She sat there, enjoying, savoring the moment, the moments, as they were ticking slowly away.

– What is time, Peter? I think you know a bit about it. You traveled back in time to visit your younger self, to recruit me. What do you know about it, now?

She sat there, observing how every piece of Dust hit the floor, how it slipped slowly through her fingers, how it returned to normal speed and dust.

The kitchen was abandoned, fitting her desire. She brewed herself some spiced tea. It burned pleasantly within her, and enhanced her senses, her ability to perceive the corners and shadows of the world, as she returned to the living room. It was an age-old recipe, used by sorcerers for time immemorial to better glance beyond the veil.

There seemed to be no distance, no time between here and there, the kitchen and the library. She could not quite tell whether or not she had teleported, or if it was her perception playing tricks on her. Anger coursed through her fevered mind.

– You woke me up, Peter, she cried. – Woke me brutally from my slumber, but why? Did you see a purpose for me beyond your Ascension? You told me I would be your queen, but that could just be one more of your *lies*.

The various books lingered by her fingers. She immersed herself in the various scrolls and texts, virtually becoming the words, the spells, beyond memorizing, remembering, losing her sense of time, of herself.

When the bell rang, when she looked out through the wall and smiled in expectation it was well into the afternoon, into the longer and deeper shadows.

She walked into the hall and opened the door, just like she would an ordinary door.

Louise stood at the top of the stairs, vulnerable, curios and scared.

– H-hello, the girl said with numb lips. – You wanted me to come, and I came.

– I sure did, Janet grinned. – Your sure did. Come inside, child.

– You are not that much older than I am, are you? The girl asked stubbornly.

They would have attended the same class if they had been from the same area of town.

Janet ignored the question. Louise walked inside, scurrying in the shadow of the other woman. Janet closed the door behind them.

– What *is* this place? The girl wondered wide-eyed.

She yelped in pain, as the air itself seemed to slap her.

– What do the dreams tell you? Janet asked softly.

The girl's lips began shivering.

– T-that I am to be your s-servant.

– My devoted servant. The sorcerer nodded. – One doing what she is told, with no delusions of grandeur or independence.

– Y-yes, My L-lady.

The girl curtseyed clumsily, lowering her eyes.

The Lady smiled cruelly and the girl crumbled even more before her, her mind buzzing with instructions and modifications, slowly changing her.

– You are a bright girl, the Lady said pleased, – one that will be very good at what she does once she is properly trained and groomed. You are lucky I already have two groveling beasts in my house. I desire a little bit more from you.

She turned and returned to the living room, to her library and knew, with absolute certainty that the girl followed her there, trailed her like would a dog.

Though one which eyes were wavering here and there, one where curiosity was not quashed. That, too, pleased The Lady.

– What do the dreams tell you? She repeated and turned abruptly towards the girl.

– You are Janet of the Blue Flame, Louise replied eagerly, anxiously. – You are the Master of this place and your word and desire is Law. Your very thoughts become reality here. Everything within these walls becomes an extension of your being.

Janet found herself smiling, and the realization of that smile brought even more understanding and Power.

– Yes, she whispered. – You understand. Very good!

Cold laughter echoed between the vibrating walls.

Louise shook, and then shook even harder, before returning to a kind of paralyzing calm.

An image of a book appeared in her mind. She walked to the shelf and pulled it out. A sensation of her walking rose in her consciousness and a path was pointed out to her. She followed it, walked ahead of the Lady out of the living room, into the hall and down the stairs.

The Lady did not explain herself. She saw no need to do that to an underling, but knew that Louise was relentlessly fed information and instructions, was changed according to specifications. The spell surpassed her expectations.

The cellar, the cave welcomed her. The energies, more subtle, less potent were still there, more than sufficient for her task. Louise walked to the altar. She undressed, quickly, unhesitating and knelt on its cold glowing stone.

Janet removed the bracelets. They slipped off easily enough. Louise accepted them with an anxious glance, quickly fading in the throes of the overwhelming forces ravaging her mind.

– Put them on, Janet bid her. – They are mine, but I am glad to let you borrow them for your upcoming trials. Never let it be said that I am not a kind master.

The chilling laughter made the girl shrink further in her already subservient position. She put on the bracelets. They cut into her and made her gasp in pain.

– It hurts, she whimpered.

– Of course it does, Janet shrugged. – It is supposed to.

She drew the black blade, sensing instantly how it hungered, how its hunger grew, noticing how she responded to it, how the hunger echoed within her. The expectant smile playing on her lips widened.

One swing of the blade, and she made the first cut. Blood splashed on the stone and the area surrounding it. Louise screamed.

But she hardly moved beyond that. Frozen in place and with shivering lips, she stared at the wall.

The blood on the blade stayed there, as if being glued to the metal. Janet licked it off, taking her time, savoring the experience.

– I take your strength, she called. – I make it my own.

The spell came easy to her. The speaking of archaic words made the shimmer in the cave deepen and grow. She cut the blood sacrifice again. Louise screamed louder.

– Feel the pain. Let it burn your strength away.

Louise shook and kept shaking, but was unable to move, frozen like a fly in amber. Janet cut her again and again. The first wounds healed, closed up, as she watched and it was such a thrill. She felt power flow into her.

– I burn my mark on your back, to have you forever in my thrall.

She drew symbols, drawing circles around them. It was done in a casual way, with evident skill. She did not really have to think much about it. The wounds healed, the circles faded, but the engravings, the blackened lines and etchings on the skin remained.

Janet pulled back. Louise stopped screaming abruptly, gasped once and fell on the stone. She remained still for a while, her breathing slowly regaining its strength. Janet looked in contempt at her, feeling so very empowered and strong.

– Know that you are useful, little slave, and that you will continue to serve your master well.

Louise rose, stepped off the stone and knelt before the Lady with lowered eyes.

Janet grabbed her wrists and removed the bands and put them back on her own wrists. They buzzed and hummed so pleasantly.

– I can sense the Ascension, you know, just out of reach. One day it will open again.

The two of them, the Lady and her humble and eager servant left the lower base of the house and returned to the ground floor.

– You may clean yourself, now, the master of the house said distracted and patronizing.

She proceeded towards one of the showers, and hardly even noticed the other girl stumbling towards another.

The water burned as it hit her glowing skin and the sensation felt so good. She felt Louise when the girl rubbed herself in pain, and that made an even wider grin grow on her lower face. Every drop of nectar was a world in her mind, and she opened herself and her world further with each passing second. The warm rain was a pleasant wind playing with her hair and skin.

The sensation lasted for days and nights, staying with her, as she returned to the small, exclusive store to pick up her dress.

Louise followed her like a shadow, like the pale shadow she was, timid and attentive. She had become a constant, pleasant presence in Janet's life, marked skin and bone and soul, stamped and owned.

Even the singing birds and the people surrounding her in the narrow gateway moved to her moves.

– Is this power, Peter? If it is, why were not you content with that?

The people and the birds glanced cautiously at her. She paid them no heed.

She slipped into the store, and Louise did, too, pulled by the stream behind her.

Mary received her with honors and humility, as was right and proper.

– Good wishes on this beautiful day, My Lady, the young woman greeted the sorcerer.

– Good wishes, Mary, Janet generously returned the greeting. – I assume my dress is ready.

It was not a question, not even resembling one.

– It is, My Lady. It is merely awaiting your final approval.

The two maidens brought the dress. Janet placed herself in front of the mirror, and the three of them began working on her again. They undressed her, doing it in such an expert manner that it seemed like the clothes were flowing off her like mercury. Eventually, not many minutes later she stood there in her new dress, admiring herself in the mirrors surrounding her.

They had done as she told them, to ignore the remains of the big belly that had been there during her last visit and that was now completely gone. Janet ventured they were both familiar with sorcerers and that they were indeed taking orders well.

The three picked a bit here, fixed a little there, perfecting what was already perfect.

Louise moved around her, an extra pair of eyes confirming what Janet already knew.

– I will wear it immediately, she informed Mary.

– Very good, My Lady, the other nodded just as servile, just as useful. – We will need just a little longer before it is ready for you.

Good as her word, they were done long before Janet turned impatient. All formalities undone Janet saw the sisters stand together, as she left the store with Louise in tow, carrying the bag with her old clothes.

– I will be Cathy tonight, she told Louise. – Do you understand?

It was not strictly necessary to inform her directly like that, but Janet enjoyed doing it.

– I understand, My Lady. I will be your companion on your Journey through the night.

The night… Janet of the Blue Flame tasted the sensation it brought on her tongue and liked it.

They reentered the enclosed alley outside. The birds, seemingly tangled together in a massive string pattern, rose from the rooftops. They returned to the slightly secluded house at the edge of the neighborhood. Janet sort of enjoyed the walk back. Every single car passing them irritated her, but there were not that many. She ignored the cautious glances and malignant stares.

The scent of summer assaulted, almost overpowered her. It was not just that her enhanced senses made any sensation hit body and mind like a sledgehammer, but far more pronounced.

When a bird landed on a branch almost out of sight of normal vision… she felt it. When it rose from the branch and flapped its wings the vibrations flooded her. She found it hard to distinguish herself from the sniveling girl walking by her side.

– Power is good. She nodded, rolling her left hand into a fist. – I am power.

And Louise nodded and smiled in devotion.

– You are just a flee appearing in my orbit, of course, annoying with your buzz occasionally, but nothing more.

And Louise nodded and smiled in devotion.

The house loomed in front of them, making her heart skip a beat or two in happiness.

– It is my home, one surely befitting a future queen.

This time she did not watch Louise, but the house, able to observe so many of what to others were its invisible seams and details.

It spoke to her, whispered and shouted its secrets, tales of worries, warnings and power.

She studied herself before the mirror in the hallway. The mirror, too, spoke to her, spoke praise, admonishing and broken glass. The crack in the smooth surface looked deeper than the ocean to her. She almost drowned in it.

Louise did not look at herself. Janet was her mirror and nodded her approval.

– We both look great enough to devour, she told the girl.

And the girl glowed in gratitude.

She walked to the phone and called for a cab. Her well-modulated voice explained directions and instructions in a brief, steady manner. She put down the phone and returned to her master.

– Your carriage will be here shortly, My Lady.

She curtseyed deeply. Janet dismissed her with a nod.

Dark clouds greeted them when they walked outside. Janet bowed to them in acknowledgement and expectation. Louise crouched in her shadow with a smile on her lips.

The car arrived with hardly any wait at all. The sight of the approaching dark skies echoed pleasantly in her conscious mind.

The Auburn city center was at the north point of The Island. The urban landscape changed slightly into what was clearly a more densely populated area. They passed the place of learning. It was empty, now, deserted, also in Janet's heart. She heard briefly the faint toll of bells. The sound seemed familiar to her and made her frown, but she could not place it.

The driver chose the eastern coastline road on the final stretch north. The twin cities on the mainland could be glimpsed through the afternoon haze. They passed the ferry quay and moved further west. The archipelago opened up to the ocean beyond.

– I can see the Foggy Banks, Louise whispered.

Janet squelched the slight shudder down her spine. She knew the girl could not physically see the banks from here and she wondered if Louise saw it through the sharing of Janet's senses or if she saw it through her own in a way that Janet was unable or unwilling to do.

The teenagers gathered before Island Freeze, a smaller establishment owned by the same people owning Freeze on the mainland. Here, for some reason they did serve alcohol for minors. There were no laws against it in the triple cities, or in the land of Arcadia as a whole, just practices varying from tavern to tavern.

Janet heard mockingbirds cry, sensed the familiar flapping of their wings. It distracted her, as she and Louise departed from the carriage. A tall, well built boy and his entourage approached them and she did not notice before they were close. They handed out beverage to the new arrivals. She accepted the tribute and Louise, not really glancing at Janet in any way the boys could discern did the same.

– I have not seen you here before, he said, staring deliberately at the dark girl.

– I have not been here before, she replied, shrugging deliberately, calmly returning his stare.

Janet of the Blue Flame had not been here. The young, nascent woman she hardly remembered had come here often the last year or so of her life.

She drank. The beverage chilled and wet her dry throat. He kept meeting her stare, with some difficulty. She kept treating him with disdain and distance, something that was not unexpected to him. He studied her, her breasts and the shadowy curves of her body. She squelched the tiny ember of interest within.

He took her hand and she allowed it, allowed the somewhat mature boys to take her and her maid indoors.

– You are not from around here, are you?

– No, I am not.

– I thought so, he acknowledged pleased. – There is something wonderfully strange about you.

– Thank you, good sire, she grinned, granting him a smile, a shadow of a reward.

– Where are you from then? The South or the North or…

– I grew up on the mainland, she replied, – but I have recently returned from the Territories.

The way she phrased it, with the specific intonation it could mean anything, from the Far West to the distant, almost mythical Far Lands. It had the desired effect on him. He stared at her in awe.

– But you are from here, are you not, Lou? One of the other boys pushed himself at Louise.

– Born and bred here, she giggled.

Janet relaxed. Louise would do well.

They descended inside the dark rooms, the basement filled with shadows. Everything looked the same, yet different. Janet of the Blue Flame knew he was here, sensed Peter Malone, the sorcerer to be long before she saw him with her eyes. She had noticed his presence from far away, like a dark beacon of vibrations.

When her eyes spotted him, with those that once in a distant past had been her friends he looked no different.

This boy was an innocent, without the aura of confidence and menace and sophistication he would later emanate, the vast powers hidden within his frail form latent.

– I had the advantage of foresight. I knew your destiny, as well as my own from I was very young.

The both close and distant voice of Malone the Sorcerer echoed in her mind.

She allowed the tall, well-built boy to embrace her from behind and give her a kiss on the neck, giving him a sweet smile in return.

They found themselves a table fairly close to the bar. It was not difficult. This was a big place, an old storage facility abandoned by its previous owners. Most people could not see the wall at the far end of the building through the haze and shadows no matter how hard they tried.

She easily could.

Drinks were put on the table. They drank. The strong liquor burned in the throat of her present companions and made them cough.

It had no or little effect on her.

They swayed to the music. She did, too. Its waves burned pleasantly within her.

– So, a girl spoke up choked up with curiosity, – how is it out there, in the Territories?

As if on cue everybody at the table and also some passing by looked at Janet and listened hard.

– That depends, she replied, pondering the issue, not pretending to do so. – There is not one place or way out there, but many, an infinite number. I have only seen a tiny piece of it. I have been told by Travelers that it is both wonderful and horrible beyond imagining. There is a place called The Village, one of many, where Realms meet and part…

– The Village, another girl cried, – you have visited *The Village?* There is such a place?

– As stated, there are many such places, Janet the Sorcerer shrugged patronizing. – Yes, I visited The Village. I saw and heard The Bard and I experienced terrible and wonderful things, and lived to tell the tale. I escaped the cruel claws of Florence the Queen Goddess with no more time to spare.

They stared mesmerized at her, not necessarily believing her, but mesmerized no less. She did not care either way. It felt… good to talk about it, even the distilled part. She enjoyed herself in their company, benefited to a point surrounded by the haze of excited, innocent faces.

Later she would marvel at how she would be able to recall their faces, their features in immaculate detail, but not their names.

She lost herself in the music for a while, never allowing it to distract her beyond the moment.

– HI, CATHY! Rosa cried to her as she was on her way to the toilet.

Cathy waved to the group sitting by that other table.

She stepped into the large room with its toilet stalls, a fairly common arrangement in most public settings. The large wall mirror seemed to suck her in, spreading its mist and shadow across the room. There were several other girls here, coming and going, checking up on their mirror image. Janet did not do that, but went straight for the stalls. There was no queue. She found an available stall immediately.

It felt good to sit down and relieve herself. She did not see it as a distraction, but as one more step on the steady road of patience.

– I can wait forever, Peter, she shrugged, not raising her voice, – but I know

I do not have to.

She knew she spoke to him as if he was very close, and he was, sort of, no matter how far away he appeared to be.

Her piss burned, or she imagined it did.

– My body fluids are acid, she mumbled/chanted. – My spit is venom. Beware, my love.

The writing on the wall and door seemed to grow, spread into the air, becoming three-dimensional, becoming her spell. She smiled.

Everything opened up to her, even more so as she returned to the festivities. The waves in the air had become completely visible to her and she could pick and choose from them as she desired. She was not yet as powerful as she had been during the height of Malone's tutelage, but getting there.

There were no fixed points in the room, not to her. She was not fixed, but present on several spots simultaneously. The expectant chuckle rising from her throat was almost heard above the loud music.

Her heart skipped a beat when she caught sight of him between the people moving back and forth in the central hall and she scolded herself.

She was there, right in front of him a long time before she reached the table and he and her friends saw her appear from the crowded floor.

Peter, Toby, Eleanor and Rosa and the new tall and big girl welcomed her with excited and warm smiles. She sat down in the seat they had cleared for her, shrugging with deliberate indifference.

– I love your hair, Peter said startled.

– Thank you, Peter, she replied, granting him a smile.

She knew it moved like waves on a beach, in a way completely different from his, no matter how long it was.

– Do you want to dance?

He took the initiative from the start, suddenly very assertive. She had kind of expected that he would.

– I would love to, she heard herself say.

The dark, slow and hard music rocked everybody on the dance floor. That included the two raven-haired dancers. The drummer hammered the drums extra hard for a few seconds, hammered flesh and bone and receptive minds.

She spotted him from across the room. He was there and he was here, right in front of her, staring at her with his puppy look. Two minutes later, when they left the dance floor he was there, by her side.

He grabbed her and pushed her at the wall, giving her greedy kisses on the lips. She recognized his hunger. Laughter rose from her throat. She freed herself with little or no effort. He let go of her, still the innocent, the incomplete painting.

– You might want to ask for permission before you assault a girl like that, she said curtly, patronizingly, with the same indifference painting her face. – I am not your usual helpless victim, you know.

She did not hear his response, but returned to the table. He followed her like the panting dog he was.

He burned in her vision, even when she did not look directly at him, even when she looked away. Strands danced and stretched around him. His dreaded potential slowly emerged in her company, his powers resonating with hers.

– Cheers!

Eleanor raised her glass, and they had a toast.

– Nice brew, Toby commented. – They make it in the basement, do they not?

– Its stench is pervasive, Eleanor chuckled. – So, if it is not made nearby, it has some kick all right.

– It has, Peter insisted. – It has!

Beatrice, the new girl with the braids echoed his sentiment.

Janet drank some more. It had a sweet and strong taste. It did not really affect her much, but she enjoyed the sensation anyway.

She noticed that Peter did not drink much either. While the others eventually tipped over and became drunk, the two of them sat there holding hands. They did so, for a while, before leaving, before saying goodbye to the others and leaving, accompanied by many a cheerful and nasty comment.

Louise joined them, as they made their way out, hooking herself to the front train in a very casual manner.

– I promised her parents that I would make sure she would return home early, Janet whispered in Peter's ear.

He chuckled darkly, so honored by her trust, by being in her confidence.

His cock hardened, pushing at his pants. She noticed instantly. Expectation rose in her.

The air outside felt fresh and she pulled it into her in greedy breaths.

The cab approached, displaying a NOT AVAILABLE sign. Peter's frown turned deeper as suspicion turned to certainty. It was indeed headed for them.

They sat down in the comfortable seats, the expression of incredulity not quite leaving his face.

– How is it that the driver knew when we would… when he would be needed?

– Louise contacted the call center well in advance, Janet shrugged.

– *Louise?* But how did she…

He glanced at her, suddenly realizing that she was there, in the car with them and he clammed up.

– She has worked as my maid for some time, Janet shrugged again. – She has become increasingly perceptive to my needs.

And then, as he looked at the girl, at the haze in her eyes, it dawned on him that it did not matter that she was here.

Everything swelled within Janet when she saw the apprehension and growing interest in his opaque eyes.

She moved close and started kissing him in hard, demanding ways. The noise in her mind grew loud and deafening, obscuring everything else.

Her dark smile dazzled him, she knew it did. She pulled back a little, caressing his cheek, patronizing, like she would a pet.

He grabbed her and pulled her close, kissing her in very possessive and cruel ways, fondling her breasts.

– You are so big and beautiful, he mumbled with his mouth pushed at her neck, – so different from other girls.

– Thank you, she said breathless, – what a sweet thing to say.

His clumsy fumbling excited her, but she had been prepared for that. It did not drown the silent dark laughter and expectation, but augmented it.

You are exactly as I envisioned you, Peter. You carry no surprises for me.

– Do you have magickal powers? He asked excited. – Are you a sorcerer?

– Such a precocious boy, she grinned.

His skin color deepened in red some more.

– Yes, I have, she replied, staring deeply into his eyes, allowing him to experience more of her, of what was burning within. – Yes, I am.

He began shaking, not very hard, but noticeable to her.

Her wide grin exposed her fangs.

– Do not worry. I will not harm you… much.

– Very funny, he shuddered.

She put a hand on his thigh. He wanted to hide that his cock was pushing at the boundaries of his pants, but was unable to do so.

– Relax, she whispered in his ear. – Enjoy it. Savor the Hunger and anticipation.

He grabbed her again, just as the cab stopped in front of the manor.

She chuckled and returned his kisses as they stepped out of the car. Louise followed them in the same prevailing, disconnected daze.

The house towered over them.

– W-what is this t-tingling?

It pleased her to hear him stutter.

– It is the house, the Nexus welcoming us, she emphasized softly, –

welcoming powerful magick-users, those able and willing to receive and use of its bounty.

She listened to the drums rising from the ground, increasing the moment she stepped onto the hallway floor. They rattled her, shook her being to the core, and the rapture of expectation ravaged her. She reached out with her waves and pulled him close. Her lips ravaged his.

He grabbed her and returned her cruel affection with all the clumsiness of youth. The low chuckle rose in her throat.

His hands held hers, fondled them as breasts, the breasts so close to his red face. It felt very personal and intimate. She started breathing faster, inevitably and scolded herself, releasing a sigh of relief when he moved on to the bracelets.

– Nice, he acknowledged, a twinkle in his eyes.

– You like these, do you not? She said sweetly. – Would you like to try them on?

He nodded with big eyes.

– Then by all means, she shrugged. – Be my guest. I would love to see them around your strong wrists.

He was blushing. She started removing the first bracelet from her left wrist. Her strong hands grabbed his. He gasped when she squeezed and did his best to stifle the cry of pain. She put the bracelet from her left wrist on his right, and that from the right on his left.

– How does it feel? She whispered in his ear.

– It is tingling, he frowned. – *Tingling!*

She leaned closer to him, breathing on the skin of his neck.

– Wind and fire are blowing through us, she hissed.

A draft pulled at her from the cellar, from the cave. She smiled and stepped back, displaying herself to him. The draft played with her hair. She reached out a hand. He did, too. She took his and led him away, down the path of flickering shadows.

He was looking at her well displayed breasts again. She let him, in anticipation, in gathering triumph.

– I love your tattoos, he said hoarsely.

He was able to see them. The invisible markings glowed between the shadows dancing on her face. Expectation rose yet another notch.

It was inevitable that he noticed her interest. She shrugged. It did not matter.

– What? He exclaimed, like the young, inexperienced boy he was.

– You are coming into your power, she said softly, – becoming who you will be.

He blushed some more, torn between doubt and hope, unable to understand, making her feel equal amounts of rage and relief.

– Yes, she confirmed, – you are a sorcerer. When you are much older, many years from now, you will break free from your confines and wreak havoc in the nine realms and beyond.

– So, there are more? He practically shouted, eager like the immature kid he was.

– Nobody knows or will ever know how many there are. Humanity is far more numerous than the grains of sand on a beach.

She heard the echo in the cave, as if a thousand mouths breathed its delay.

Sounds reached her from pockets in the air around her. They descended once more the path to the cave that was sometimes a basement, Janet of the Blue Flame and he who would one day become Malone the Sorcerer.

– It welcomes us. Janet caught easily the sigh in the air. – It will always welcome us. It is our future and our past rolled into one.

She sensed how he was virtually drowning in her fire, totally unable to resist its lure.

– Stand on the stone before the altar, she commanded.

He grinned eagerly to her, practically jumping up on the stone.

She frowned, but then shook her head.

– You are just a silly young stud, are you not? She grinned curtly.

Expectation flooded her.

She readied herself, making the final preparations, reaching out with her arms and her mind.

– Eyes of the vast ocean of reality, serve me, she cried. – Come to me. Join me on my unending quest.

She repeated it, did so several times, as her speech turned guttural and incomprehensible in her ears and she slowly understood more.

– Join me... she exhaled.

It… began. She sensed it, at the tip of her fingers, by the charged air touching her skin.

She turned to the sacrificial lamb standing on the stone.

– Magick is easy, she told him. – There is nothing to it, really, beyond an initial willingness to do brutal acts and leave behind the illusion of compassion in the world. If you can do that, you can do anything.

He shook and froze to a statue, there, on the rock. His eyes turned misty and distant.

– To me, all blue flames. She shouted.

And they began dancing around her form, spreading from her hands to the rest of the body. The tattoos, the birthmarks turned visible to everybody.

– Tell me about yourself, she bade him sweetly, turning to him with a snarl backing up all her infernal power.

He faltered, but then began to speak.

– My name is Peter Malone, Pete among friends. I am seventeen years old...

A low sound of pain was working itself up from his throat.

– Tell me *everything*, she commanded, with a voice rising from a low point.

– I was born the fourth of six siblings, he said, he droned on. – I have always wanted to travel. The realm is still big, still have huge unexplored territories. I sat around a table close to the stage when the explorer Robert Townes visited the triple cities and told his fascinating tales. There is so much out there, so much to experience and discover, by boat, by airship and on foot. A man could spend his lifetime doing that. My first teacher was a real prick. I had a distaste for him I could hardly conceal. He pretended to teach us knowledge but taught only bias and intolerance and ignorance. I... My first teacher was... I disliked the man my older sister married. She behaved like a silly goose without an independent thought in her head. She...

– What is your name? Janet asked with a cruel smile.

He faltered, just looked at her, at nothing with a blank stare.

– Where were you born?

He shook his head and kept shaking it, until he stopped, until he froze solid.

There was a sound rising from the ground, a crack in the firmament. The bracelets began glowing. Janet felt a brushing on her shoulders, a rub on her back. She frowned...

And then it was as if a spear penetrated her, and she could not tell at what point. It seemed to be everywhere, at every single point of her body.

Her scream filled the room. The wretched pain filled her and her scream turned into a howl of infinite pain.

Louise howled, too, and the two on the floor above. Janet fell and they fell with her.

Blinding and deafening silent noise churned through her head, in her agonized mind. She hit the ground hard. The rest she hardly noticed, until she crouched there, shaking like a leaf, gasping like a fish on land.

He towered above her, the young boy, his scorn and contempt making her mind and body burn.

– He prepared me for you. I prepared me for you.

The voice was hardly a voice, but a sound like a saw blade on metal.

– You did not really think this through, did you, silly girl? You did not realize the obvious fact that time itself is stacked against you? Or if you did, you did not properly prepare to counter it.

He removed the bracelets, dropping them on the floor with a shrug. She did not hear them hitting the ground, but saw how they jumped up and down a few times, like a ball, before their movement stopped.

– I will clearly succeed with you, succeed beyond words, making you nothing but a leaf lurking in my shadow. I will enjoy that, I think.

He left. She noticed, in a way, in a distant, indifferent way. The place fell silent. Louise's whimpers did not really qualify as sound in Janet's ears. Time lost all meaning. She imagined she crumbled there on the floor that was also a ground for an eternity, that she was rotting inside and outside and nothing remained but dust and decay.

Sometimes, a timeless time later she was stumbling across the basement, fighting herself up to the ground floor. The walk to the next level felt like a monumental effort. She had to stop several times, to throw up and gather strength, what little of it there was left.

The mirror image slowly turned distinct and solidified before her. She had lost the darker hair and skin tone, the part of her that had been *him,* and looked at her old self, what she had been ages ago and hardly recalled.

Her dress was reduced to rags.

– Nothing left, she mumbled. – Nothing!

She reeked of blood and cold sweat and vomit and saliva. It dropped from her jaw and flowed between her thighs. She realized stunned that she had picked up the bracelets and wore them around her wrists. They healed her and comforted her. She choked and spat curses at the pathetic creature in the mirror.

There was a large hole in her memory. She stumbled along the road outside, putting one foot in front of the other, moving forward instead of backwards. Sometimes she fell and crouched there, sometimes on the road, sometimes in the soft and wet grass by the wayside. A while later she was up again, stumbling on.

It occurred to her that she encountered people on her way, but in her delirium she could not say for certain.

No matter how much she looked around her with wet, uncomprehending eyes.

She imagined she heard the sound of engines, of cars. If they were real, they did not come close to her. She walked in a stupor, without a conscious thought in her head. Indistinct images of houses and streets danced insanely in her vision. The noise in her ears finally eased. At least she imagined it did. She sniffed, unable to stop sniffing. Tears flooded her vision and her face, and the hands she used to wipe them off.

There was a fence she could lean on. Its texture hurt the skin on her palms. A prolonged wail rose from her throat. She cast her misery from her being and across the neighborhood.

A man and a woman entered her field of vision. They approached her cautiously.

– My Goddess, the man said stunned. – That is Myra's kid, is it not?

– M-myra.

Janet nodded

They grabbed her kindly, as if she was made of china.

– H-home, she whispered.

– Of course we will take you home, child, the woman said. – Where have you *been* all this time?

– Home, Janet repeated, Janet shouted her misery. – HOME

– Of course, the woman mumbled. – Do not worry, everything will be fine.

They supported her, dragged her with them. She let it happen, like a rag doll, totally unable to influence the direction, in any way.

– Poor girl, the woman whispered. – Poor girl.

She imagined they brought her to the right place, but she did not know. Fear haunted her and brought her waves of renewed panic attacks. They soothed her the best they could, or so it seemed.

Finally, after what felt like many nights, they reached the old house at the end of the road. And she was still not sure. The painting in her mind seemed blurry, so much out of focus that all its colors melted like hot metal, the horror burning her and torturing her. The young boy's wicked laughter faded only slowly in her abandoned thoughts.

– Mommy, she whimpered, – I want my mommy.

– Not long now, poor child, the man comforted her, or tried to, – not long at all.

And then she felt mommy's hands at her face, her scent in her nostrils and it felt true.

The almost unknown woman with the beyond shocked and horrified expression led her inside, inside the doll house, undressed her and put her to bed.

Drink, the woman said, putting a cup with a brew to her lips, and she drank.

– Mommy? The girl cried out distraught. – Is that you, mommy?

– I am here, mommy comforted her. – Sleep, now. Tomorrow everything will be better. Please, Janie, please.

And the unknown woman using the affectionate version of her name brought at least a semblance of peace to the shaking creature crouching under the thick, warm blanket.

– I can not *sleep,* she said, in both horror and contempt, a sick laughter erupting from her sore throat, finding its way between the clenched teeth and shivering lips.

But the brew was working, its gentle poison making its way through her body and already murky mind. Her hand fell down. She sighed in distress, writhing, writhing until writhing no more. Her eyes closed, and she fell asleep.

Falling, falling, floating away into the mists and shadows, even further into the wasteland of human consciousness, dreaming insane and horrifying dreams of yesterday and tomorrow.

Part Two: The Guys

Chapter 9

The young girl crouched on the bed and stared at the wall, blinded by the morning light.

She was tall and big, almost breaking the boundary of the seemingly fragile furniture.

A draft struck her when the door opened. She heard no sound or steps.

– You must eat something, the distant voice insisted.

The mere stench of food made her throw up what little slime she had left in her stomach.

– You must, the irritating voice insisted later, much later.

– He ravaged and raped me, mother, she said casually, – and then he ravaged and raped me again.

She heard the gasp and noticed that the stench of perfume faded from her attention.

Another night faded away. She noticed its passing.

A female health worker took a look at her, prodded her from head to toe. Janet answered the questions she hardly heard in a subdued and detached manner.

– I find no permanent damage. The pregnancy evidently proceeded… well. You are… seem, all in all remarkably… fit.

The woman left.

Myra sat with her, rubbing her head, singing her lullabies.

The young girl fed, devouring the soup, rushing to the bathroom to throw everything back up.

Janet showered. Each drop hitting her skin burned like acid. Janet dressed. The clothes did not fit her.

– They are too small for you, Myra said. – You have grown so tall and big… and strong.

The last word choired with a choke.

Joan and her partner Thomas were both tall and big magistrates, people clearly meant to instill comfort and a sense of security in her. Janet allowed Joan to sit close to her but not Thomas.

– Were there more than you, more… girls in captivity?

– Yes, more girls, she acknowledged.

– We found old remains of a child. Was that…

– It was mine, Janet confirmed.

– What happened to it?

– He… s-sacrificed it to his mighty god.

Joan faltered for a moment or two, before she managed to continue with the interview.

– The house was empty, even though we found traces of several people and blood types. We found no other girls and there was no sign of him. We can not find him. He has obviously fled the Triple Cities or he is in hiding somewhere within their borders. Do you know…

– I do not know where he is.

The snap cut the question short like a scissor. The man and the woman exchanged looks.

– We will guard you every single second of the day and night, the female magistrate stated hotly. – He will not be able to even watch you from afar before we are on to him.

There was a squeeze in the arm meant to be reassuring. The girl in the chair remained unmoving. The two magistrates left.

Time passed. She did not know how much. Days passed. She did not know how many. Her attention faded away to nothing and manifested itself only in glimpses.

The many-faced scent of the garden surrounded her. Various scents of pre-spices tickled her nostrils. She sat there unmoving, fumbling now and then with the bracelets on her wrists. Her fingers tingled and the rush of sensations overwhelmed her once more.

She ran to her room and removed the bracelets, throwing them into a drawer and slamming it shut. There was no mirror in the room, but she still saw herself from the outside. She shivered on the bed for hours before finally falling into a pitiful, unsettling slumber.

When she woke up she remained tired, as if she had not slept for days.

She returned to the garden, sought the blinding light of the daystar, even though it made more tears flow from her eyes.

Her friends visited her the next day, when she still sat unmoving in the garden. Rosa waved from the gate. Janet returned the wave, a move hardly visible. She did not raise her hand from her lap, but just moved it there, as if she did not have the strength to do more.

Rosa, Eleanor, Toby and Fran approached her cautiously. She forced a smile on her lips, greeting them with what was hardly more than a weak, shivering contraction. Rosa touched her face with an equally shivering hand.

– Poor baby, Rosa whispered, hardly audible.

They touched the crumbling girl, embraced her cautiously. When Toby wanted to do it, she pulled back.

– Sorry, she whimpered. – Sorry.

– It is all right, he said with a dull voice. – I understand. It is all right.

– We looked for you, Eleanor said exasperated. – Many people looked for you, but you were nowhere to be found. Did he keep you in that awful house all the time?

Janet nodded.

– And that woman… she was *in* on it, was she not?

Janet nodded.

Everybody fell silent. There were no more words, none she recalled, only a prevailing world of hurt.

The sun fell and vanished from the sky and Big Moon cast a soft light on them all.

Her eyes remained wet and sore.

2

– Come with us, Rosa said, today or tomorrow or the day after that. – Let us be with you, care for you.

Janet nodded. She felt the sensation in her legs as she stood up, in her upper body as she stepped forward.

She touched Toby and did not feel disgusted to her core.

They glanced at her, inadvertently, as the tall and big girl towered above them.

– You need… bigger clothes. Rosa said cautiously. – You were always tall and big, but now you are… taller and bigger.

Everything had become tight everywhere on her bigger and taller body. More skin showed. They giggled a bit and Janet giggled with them, making her friends breathe a sigh of relief.

She walked through the gate, and into the street, surrounded by her friends. The warm wind played with the exposed parts of her skin throughout the pleasant, brief and short walk to the bus stop. She spotted the girl waiting there immediately.

– Janet, this is Beatrice, Eleanor presented them to each other, – Beatrice, this is Janet.

Beatrice was slightly taller than Janet had become, with hard muscles and with moves like an animal. She still wore the light blonde hair in two braids.

– Hello, she grinned, reaching out a hand, – I have heard so much about you and it is so great that we finally meet.

– Hello, Janet returned the greeting, a little taken aback by the extensive word flow.

And because she looked into a face fairly similar to her own.

It had not really occurred to her before, when she had worn another face, but now the similarities between them had become obvious.

– I know, Beatrice grinned some more, – we are probably distant relatives or something. It struck me the moment I saw pictures of you, and even more, now, when I see you close up.

– Beatrice transferred to the school just after you… disappeared, Rosa said. – She is a great gal.

– I can imagine, Janet said, staring into the dark blue eyes.

– She is from a long line of demon hunters, Toby chuckled, clearly strained.

– Is she, now? Janet said pointedly.

– She has trained for the honor since early childhood, even though there are no demons left in our realm.

– We will be great friends, Beatrice stated firmly, staring at Janet, ignoring the boy.

– Yes, Janet heard herself say.

They caught the bus and it moved them forward. Everything seemed silent to Janet. She hardly heard the sound of the engine and certainly not that of the tires rolling on the shingle road. The others' small talk did not register in her mind. They attempted to not look at her, or doing it with such stealth that she would not notice.

But even in her numb state she easily did.

– Plain clothes, Janet mumbled, – I want plain clothes.

– And so you shall, Beatrice declared softly.

Janet glanced at her again, shyly and apprehensive. Beatrice returned her scrutiny with a teasing, but soft smile.

They did not speak much, any of them, during the ride. Others on the bus spoke, but Janet hardly heard them.

– Everything feels so *different,* Janet mused. – So strange and unfamiliar, as if I did not really grow up here and only visited during summers or something.

Her friends glanced at her with sympathy and concern and sadness in their eyes.

They noticed easily her reaction when new people entered the bus and passed her, how she squirmed and pulled away, even from her friends and their hugs and attempts at comfort, but they kept doing it until she let it happen and surrendered to their soft embrace.

Shadows filled her vision, even as the bright light hurt her eyes. She wanted to strike something, wanted to make fists with her weak hands, but could not bring more strength than a few twitches and shakes.

The bus stopped and they stepped off it, into Auburn's busy afternoon streets.

She crouched under people's condemning stare.

– They are not staring at you, Beatrice told her. – You are only imagining that, in your despair and shame, and even if you are not you should ignore them, hold your head high.

She did, straightening, strengthened by the might in her new friend's voice and pose.

There was something about the big girl Janet responded to, when she looked at her, when she caught her scent and glanced at her unobserved, not just the similarity of features.

This was an entirely different part of town from where that woman… the dark woman she had been had visited the tailor store, one where that woman would never venture. Janet relaxed some more.

They visited several tailors, two in Main Street and two off it, perusing the various prototypes of pants, jackets and dresses and matching clothes. Janet did not really do anything, leaving it to the others, to her friends to pick and choose.

– Do you like it here? Toby asked, concern evident in his voice and eyes. – Is it… okay?

– It feels kind of peaceful, she mumbled a reply. – Thank you, thank you for caring.

She choked.

The place where they ended up was quite different from where Cathy had visited, far more informal. The people there did not bow and act in servility faced with potential customers. These owners, though older were siblings, too.

That made Janet feel even more rattled, skittish.

She believed she spotted… puzzlement, suspicion in Eleanor's eyes. There was definitely a frown there when her friend looked at her. But she ignored that, like she ignored everything else unpleasant and went with the flow, allowing herself to be led, to be coddled and cared for.

The tailors spoke to her and she replied, but the queries and reply did not register in her conscious mind. She tried on new clothes and fits. It felt so pleasant when her fingers traced the line of the fabric.

She chose a plain gray tunic, equally non-descriptive shoes and matching pants. The look on the others' faces remained sad and sympathetic.

It made her want to say something, anything to break the silence, but she stayed silent.

She stood before the mirror, hardly seeing herself.

– I… like this, she said.

The others smiled in acknowledgment, but she could spot the doubt and worry behind their masks.

– It does not really suit you, Beatrice said, – but it will do… for now.

That made Janet smile. At least her new friend was being honest.

She could not quite hide her sullen look when she glanced at the others. Her dark, dank thoughts kept turning and turning in her ebon mind.

– I will wear it, she told the tailor.

The old man put her old clothes in a bag, and the others paid him. She allowed it with a shrug and a silent choke.

Her insides shook like leaves. The visit to the store had brought her no peace. Stepping out into the street brought none.

– Thank you, guys, she said, a bit hesitant, suspecting it sounded wrong, repeating it with a louder, stronger voice. – Thank you.

They tried their best to reach her, to see their old friend in light of what she had become. She easily spotted their insecurity, their dread.

They took a trip to the mainland, to Howell. The ferry waited for them as they reached the quay. They walked inside and walked upstairs, bathing in the white sunshine. The heat boiled Janet, made her cringe in the hot summer wind.

A man, one that probably could be mistaken for a young boy sat in the rear and beat a set of drums in a slow, deliberate, haunting rhythm. For some reason it made her cold as ice.

He sang, or rather hummed and chanted and for a few seconds it overwhelmed the sound of the engine in her ears and mind.

She did not want to dance, but did so reluctantly, as her body rose without her explicit permission and began swaying, moving on the confined deck.

Her body whirled and so did the realm caught in her vision, within her reach.

Then there was another body there, right in front of her, right by her side. She recognized Beatrice as if through a dream.

– You can feel it, can you not?

Feel it.

Like a snarl, a beast of happiness.

And suddenly all of it had become something different, unexpected.

The dance ended just before the trip across the sound ended. Janet experienced a slight nausea, but felt no need to vomit or anything. She glanced at the rear of the deck. The man had disappeared. She looked for him while they walked downstairs and off the ferry, but did not see him anywhere.

They went to Youth Freeze, the place not serving alcohol. Everybody had lemonade. Janet felt the cold fluid slide down her throat.

Joan, the magistrate was there, too, a shadow, a constant presence all day, at the edge of Janet's attention.

– There is not much action this early… Eleanor said.

– It is informal, calm and relaxed, Janet said. – I kind of like it.

She sounded so… adult and analytical. The catching in her throat did not go away and she scolded herself.

They left a couple hours later and she felt a great relief.

– This was a mistake, she choked.

Nobody commented on her words, but just looked at her with pity and that felt worse than anything.

She sat inside on the ferry on the way back, silent and timid. Her friends let her be. She caught their sad glances beyond the darkness enveloping her.

They followed her home, embraced her outside the gate, before she slipped away and walked inside the house and walked to her room, and fell down on the bed and crouched there, unmoving and with silent chokes constantly erupting from her throat.

The night arrived and the terrors with it. The girl writhed on the bed, mumbling and swearing and whimpering. She reached for dawn, but it remained far away. A big, big hole grew around her, expanding until she could hardly see its rim. She mumbled, swore and whimpered in the infinite darkness surrounding her.

Joan approached her with caution the next morning, making her presence known well in advance. She sat down by the dining table in the garden and studied the pale, timid girl before speaking.

– There was a woman, possibly a relative, possibly playing the game with him. Do you…

– I remember her.

The powerful light from the daystar did not seem to reach the girl. She remained in shadow.

– A girl, Louise was found wandering in the streets near the house in a catatonic state. We asked around and found that she had been in the company of the dark-haired, woman, this Cathy. People we spoke to, among them your buddies agree that she was clearly submissive and possibly even scared of the woman.

– She was there. She was not treated kindly either.

Joan drew her breath.

– We rather thought so. It is not pleasant to think about everything going on in that… house. Even more disturbing is it that none of the neighbors ever caught on to any of it.

– They were neither bright nor kind.

The adult woman easily picked up on the contempt in the weak voice.
– We experienced some major trouble getting in there, Joan mused. – We actually had to break through the wall. There was no door. How did you get in?
– He had his ways, Janet said, her voice hardly audible.
Joan understood. Janet easily saw that.
– He is not all powerful, you know, the magistrate insisted. – He is just a man, a horrible man.
Janet did not comment on that. She just sat there, with a frozen expression on her face, hardly moving at all.
– We can not find «Cathy» either. It is as if they both have disappeared, have fled into the territories or even the *Wasteland.*
There were anxiety and frustration in the big woman's voice and face, as if she feared some unseen force could hear her.
Janet remained silent.
Joan looked so helpless, so… lost.
Janet smiled.
She returned to Learning, to school the day after the next, after having suffered through a long, strenuous «conversation» with the principal. The principal asked her questions, treating her like china, and Janet answered them in a calm, relaxed pose.
– You have been away for a year and need to start at one level lower than your years, but as you know we place great emphasis on individual learning here. Higher Learning in other cities may favor horrible, force-fed teaching methods, but we do not do that. The students may learn at their own pace and desire, so do not feel you have to catch up or anything. You may still interact with your old friends during the free time and off school, of course, but you are also encouraged to seek new relations with students younger than you.
The ordeal ended with the parting words: «If there is anything I can do for you, do not hesitate to ask».
Janet walked through the yard towards the classroom, surrounded by open, flushed faces, feeling the stares stab her from every angle, striving to hold her head high. She sat down in the half moon facing the teacher.
The teacher, Gaia Ofolus wore a more or less traditional Roman robe, with certain colorful additions, something her father and some of his fellow council members and most of her kin most certainly would scorn her for.
Janet smiled at that, a shy, sad smile.
– We gather in this broken circle, the teacher greeted them, – the circle of Hecate, she who is chasing through the night, hunting all the knowledge of

the realms and sharing them with us, humanity as she sees fit.

– WE GATHER, the students cried. – HUNTING AND SHARING ALL KNOWLEDGE OF THE REALM AND BEYOND.

They were eager, even though they strived to not appear too eager. Deeper Learning was scoffed at among some students, and at some schools, but not here.

– We seek Learning and know that it is its own reward, a way of increasing our awareness of the Universe and ourselves.

– LEARNING IS ITS OWN REWARD.

Janet smiled with the others, momentarily forgetting the horror haunting her.

The class turned quiet. Everybody settled in their seats. Today's Learning began.

The teacher turned to one of the students.

– Tell us about The Great Mystery, Monique.

Monique stood up, slightly nervous, but eager and proud.

– Our society was founded by people fleeing the Roman Empire after the burning of the library of Alexandria and the brutal murder of Hypatia. They were persecuted and directly threatened by the supporters of the One God, and decided to flee as far away as possible, far beyond the borders of the Empire. These were fairly basic Roman citizens, but from quite a few subcultures and origins, a mix of the variety the Empire had to offer. They fled across the vast sea to reach these shores. After sailing through a storm to stagger all storms they reached the coast of the land Arcadia, in the realm of Montan, our land.

She drew her breath. Everybody listened in eerie anticipation and no one jibed the other student or anything. There was indeed a mystery here, one that somehow concerned them all.

– Several generations later some of the curious descendents of the firstcomers sailed the vast sea back east, aiming to return to Rome, in order to see what had become of it, but found nothing. There were no known landmarks to be found, no ruins to speak of, no massive population centers, nothing reminding them of the stories they had been told. They sailed across the entire realm, but Rome was, in short nowhere to be found. They eventually returned to Arcadia to relay their experiences and The Great Mystery was born. It has confounded scholars and all curious human beings ever since. Today, when communications are far superior to that faraway time, people have sailed and even flown across the realm, and the Great Mystery is more confounding than ever.

She looked like she wanted to say more, but did not and sat back down.

– Excellent, Monique, the teacher said.

Janet felt several jolts rock her softly, at uneven intervals. She wanted to join in on the discussion afterwards, but held her tongue. The mire of her thoughts and chaotic mind kept her from speaking out.

She joined with the guys after the day of learning ended. Their company felt kind of peaceful and comforting and even pleasant.

– «If there is anything I can do for you, do not hesitate to ask», Rosa declaimed in a great imitation of the principal.

Everybody laughed themselves silly.

It was as if the laughter did not reach Janet. She could only glimpse their radiant, open smiles through the thickest of mist. And behind Beatrice's smile she glimpsed the poised look.

They walked the short way to the local center, the cluster of shops and cafes. Fran rushed inside one to order, while the rest of them sat down by the tables outside. Janet felt it the moment her ass hit the seat, felt the air smothering her skin. They sat there, munching their lunch.

Beatrice looked at her again, studied her. Her uneven stare felt unnerving.

Janet turned away, doing her best to ignore the intense girl.

She spotted Joan not far away, by the restroom. The magistrate peeked at her from behind the corner, signaling for her to join her.

– Uh, I need to pee, Janet told her friends.

Beatrice looked patronizing at her.

The others merely nodded and tried to quell the burning uncertainty she wore outside like a sore thumb with their concerned smiles. The warm feeling of gratitude mixed with irritation within her.

Halfway to the corner she realized that she was glancing down, averting her eyes to everybody present staring at her. She straightened, forcing herself to do it, but the sense of shame persisted.

They were staring at her. Glares of accusation were very much there, in every pair of eyes she met.

Go away. I do not know you. I do not want to know you.

Joan waited behind the corner.

– It is not your fault, you know, she said softly. – Never believe it is your fault. You will. Every victim feels responsible and ashamed at some point.

Janet looked closer at her. Joan reddened, she actually reddened.

The adult hesitated, before rushing forward with her intensions.

– I know a little about it. I was… abused, too, by a teacher I trusted. There was not anything I would not do for her, and she took everything I could give and more.

Janet studied Joan's open, innocent face without revealing anything of her inner being.

– I just wanted to assure you that I am watching over you, wanted to let you know I am here for you. I work with your case full time and have even been given approval from my superior to do that, which is a tiny miracle in itself.

– That is great, Joan, thank you.

Janet smiled.

The restroom was in the back, a stretch to go around the fairly large building. There were a few people there, but it mostly looked deserted and peaceful to Janet.

She looked inside. There was one other young girl there, one from Janet's local house of Learning. Janet moved into one of the stalls and closed and locked the door. She pulled down her pants and panties and set down on the bowl, and she relieved herself.

There was a sound outside the door. It took a while, but eventually it dawned on her that what she heard was *breathing*. She shrunk on the bowl, unable to move much or act on the terror and rage flowing through her. There were spaces between the door and walls both by the floor and the ceiling. She watched them all with fast-moving, flickering eyes.

When she finally had completed her urgent errand and dressed herself and opened the door, there was no one there.

She wanted to use her powers, reach out with her enhanced senses…

A choke escaped between the shivering lips. The girl bowed her head. She wanted to shout insults at the pathetic creature in the mirror. She stood completely still, unable to move.

When she moved and walked through the door it did not actually felt like she was. The realm outside did not significantly remove her from the realm inside. She turned and suddenly a woman stood right in front of her. She recognized the fortuneteller from the carnival in a flash, in a flash of red, of crimson tide.

– You are a sorcerer, the woman hissed at her. – You reek of Magick. Its stain is all over you.

– What if I am? The girl heard herself respond.

Janet glanced around her in despair, searching for Joan, but Joan was not there, was nowhere to be seen. She forced herself to stare the woman down. The woman crumbled before her eyes and she could not say she did not feel triumph.

But then the woman rose from the mire of her madness again, once again becoming Janet's perceived menace.

– You are a wicked, WICKED girl and will get your just reward in the deepest, foulest boiling pits of Tartarus.

It did not take much, just a little push and the hag fell backwards and hit the ground hard.

– What? The wrinkled features twisted, changed into the mask of madness it truly was. – What did you DO, wicked girl?

– Stop this, you foolish old hag, the girl said. – Stop taking your troubles out on me.

– She pushed me, the woman screeched, a mist filling her eyes. – The wicked girl PUSHED me.

People gathered around the two. Janet felt it just as much as she saw it. They surrounded her. She wondered if they could see… yes, they could surely see the shame in her eyes. But more than anything she wondered if they could understand and interpret it, know what she was truly hiding.

To her it stood out, exposed her for the entire realm to see.

It looked like she would crumble before their wicked eyes, but then she straightened again, rebuilt herself from the dust at her feet.

– Good people, she cried, – This woman assaulted me with her bile. I did not do anything she did not deserve. Whatever happened to her she did to herself. She is a foul creature making me the focus of her deluded attention.

Dark laughter mocked her and she was falling, failing, slipping. The sky and everything below turned ebon and vile. Terror grabbed her, paralyzing mind and body, holding everything she was in its unbreakable grip.

Then Joan was there, placing herself between the girl and the mob.

– Are you okay, Janet? She asked, her voice and face clouded with worry. – Are you OKAY?

It took forever for the girl to reply.

– I am, Janet finally nodded.

Everything looked normal again. The crowd did not exactly surround her, did not glare at her with ugly eyes.

– You get away from here, Annie. Joan's voice shook, as she pointed a shaking finger at the woman on the ground. – And stay away from the girl. Or I swear I will find a way to make you *pay*.

– Goddess, a boy said. – It is the crazy hag from the carnival fair.

Janet did not recognize Toby or his voice at first and then only through another haze of gray and noise.

Suddenly her friends were all there, taking her into their protective embrace, and she felt like crying.

– Do you know this woman? Joan asked him.

– We know of her, Rosa nodded empathically. – She was harassing Janet at the fair not long before Janet disappeared.

Everybody turned towards Annie.

– Did you hear that? Joan asked her. – I certainly did, and you better hear me, too. Perhaps I have been too lenient with you for too long? Perhaps you are more than a crazy old hag intent on bothering people?

Annie hissed and groaned. Her lips moved, but there were no words. She crawled off, ran off when she finally managed to get on her feet, howling like the lost soul she was.

Howling, like a banshee in the night.

Janet felt kind of peaceful then, after a while, surrounded by her friends and big, strong Joan.

Everybody else pulled back and faded away. The silent dark laughter in the wind did not.

– It was not just Crazy Annie hassling you, was it? Beatrice said with contempt. – The others did, too, right?

And now some of the others did look ashamed.

– Yes, Janet admitted, and it felt like confessing something vile.

– You did stare at them with the contempt they deserve, did you not?

– I did, she nodded eagerly and gave everybody her best smile.

They returned to their table. It was still available. The rest of their food was as well. Janet sat down and started devouring it, as if she had not eaten anything for days. Once more she spotted relief in their eyes. Only Beatrice treated her somewhat normally and not like china.

– It is not bad to be down a little, for a while after what happened to you, the big girl stated passionately, – but you should not make a production of it. You are entitled to some despair, but you should not allow people, especially not anyone like those vermin we just encountered to bring you down.

It was such a refreshing approach that it prompted Janet to smile spontaneously and a chuckle to rise from her throat.

The rest of the meal turned out to be far more… pleasant. Taking their cue from Beatrice the guys refrained from tiptoeing around their friend.

– I would like to draw and paint you again, Rosa said. – Your ongoing portraits are a year behind the other guys, you know, and painting you and Bea together would be a great bonus. You are a great match and…

– Okay, Janet replied.

– Okay? Rosa blinked.

– Okay, Janet shrugged.

– Okay, Rosa nodded, – when? I can probably fit you in three days from now or so…

She stressed that she was kidding, still a little cautious.

– What about right now? Janet said lightly.

– Right now is excellent, Beatrice stated.
– Right now it is, Rosa grinned.
Everyone did.
They finished their meal, and eager beyond words, they were on their way.
Rosa's studio was just down the road. Before she knew it Janet found herself posing with Beatrice in the large hall brightened by the daystar light. Rosa worked with her canvas, clearly excited.
Janet could not help feeling that excitement, and glancing at the girl sitting by her side, she found herself echoing that girl's smile.
She found herself enjoying herself.
– Hold hands, Rosa directed them. – You are two sisters having found each other again after being years apart. – You are filled with sadness and happiness both.
– Sisters, Beatrice stated.
Janet nodded once, twice and they grabbed each other's hands.
Time flowed like a slow-moving river that afternoon in the studio, as the light changed from bright to golden, to blue, as Rosa drew sketches and painted with equal fervor.
She showed them her canvas from time to time, strangely eager to share her art with them. They and all the guys looked with their usual incredulity at the uncanny portraits.
– This is amazing, Bea whispered, – truly amazing.
Janet thought so, too, but could not quite articulate herself.
The drawings, the pencil art looked great in itself, but it was the brush paintings Rosa truly brought to life. Violet eyes twinkled just as much on the canvas as it did each time Janet looked hard at herself in a mirror.
– You do plan on exhibiting your work, do you not? She said.
– That has always been the plan, Rosa said embarrassed.
– You must, her friend insisted, unusually intense, even for her.
It felt like a compulsion just then. She held back, a little startled over her own reaction.
– You sound like it is a matter of life and death? Bea teased her.
– «Art is not just a matter of life and death», Toby declaimed. – «It is far more serious than that»
It felt so good to laugh, and to laugh with the guys, to join them in… in the concert of joy.
Janet pondered her own emotions when she walked home alone sometimes later, after having parted from her friends in a fairly high spirit. They looked at her with less concern in their eyes and allowed her to make the fairly short trip without escort. She sort of enjoyed the walk, the fairly long walk, the

feeling of not being in a hurry or anything.

Joan was there, of course, somewhere in the distance. Janet spotted her now and then and shook her head.

The house appeared in a gray, gray light on her right. She hurried inside.

Mother was home, ready with the dinner.

– Hi, mom, Janet greeted her brightly, disarming mother's concern.

She completed the entire heap of food and actually felt good about it. Mother rubbed her head.

– That magistrate is following you around, right, practically following you everywhere?

– I think she is, Janet acknowledged. – Sometimes I wonder if she ever sleeps.

– It must feel a little weird, Myra inquired.

– That is okay, mom, I actually like her and like that someone as strong and capable as her is bent on the sole task of my protection.

She stayed home and in her room the rest of the evening, but she made sure to convey to mother, when Myra cast her a concerned look, that she was not brooding.

– I just enjoy the peace and quiet, she said.

It started raining as darkness settled in the dark auburn streets. The light of the city lit up the gray urban landscape. After some hesitation she found a learning book, and stretching on her belly on the bed she started immersing herself in it or attempting to.

She yawned after a while and looked out the window, at the sky and the urban darkness. Goose bumps grew on the arm closest to the window. She bit her lip. Hesitation, indecision ruled her briefly before she stretched and looked under the bed. The book, her special book was not there. Of course it was not.

Janet crouched on her too small bed, eventually falling asleep, missing the evening meal.

She moaned in her sleep. Her mind and eyes moved outside her body, making it see itself, making her see herself. She saw Malone approach her with his winning detachment, his superiority, saw him cut her open with his surgical instruments, making her ripe for the taking. The sight and impression of another bed in the house of her training revisited her. She had felt like she was not really there, and she felt like that now as well. What she perceived to be her spirit wandered, stalked the night. One moment she was here, the next there. She attempted to stop it, to control it, but was helpless to do so. It just happened to her, like a dry leaf blowing in the powerful autumn wind.

Heartbeats thundered in her dream, as if she ran flat out and did not thrash about and squirm in her tiny bed. She moved, the sorcerer moved through the city on the Island, reached out at the tip of the land mass far from the mainland, far out at sea. The invisible force of nature called Jupiter's Cauldron revealed itself to her. It was not currently active, but she was still able to see it, see it whirling, whirling, whirling, sense its… its power. The formless form she had become bounced back and visited the two cities by the mountains, the twin cities of Howell and Talaho. The triangle the triple cities formed glowed at her. She studied it from the air both dispassionately and with a tangible exhilaration emanating from within.

At one level she was sleeping and knew she was. At another the leaf she had become blew in the wind.

Stop, she told herself, mouthed the word, but there was no conviction behind it. Ugly memories assaulted her every time she tried. The sight of Malone's twisted face and her own docile expression cut through her.

Random, involuntary thoughts guided her, steered her spirit through the wretched night.

A building glowed in the distance. Involuntary thought and action were one.

Suddenly she was there, in the room with the big girl, seeing her in a completely new light.

Everything looked different here, through the eyes of the mighty spirit Janet had become.

Beatrice turned and smiled, welcomed the visitor with badly hidden enthusiasm. Janet felt it all like a modest shock to the senses, her powerful senses, but nothing near what she could not handle. Excitement supplanted the shock in her flickering form.

– There you are. What took you so long?

And with that, left with a somewhat distinct impression of the place, she was pulled away, back to her bed, to her body and her slumbering state, unable to tell what was real and what was not.

She awoke next morning still sleeping, still in that blurry state of consciousness long after she had opened her eyes. The body sat up in the bed, practically on its own, without the will of the mind behind it. She rose and walked out of the room and down the stairs, through the house in a languid pace.

Her mother was out, had probably walked to her workplace down the road. The silence imposed itself on the young girl. She stood in the hall by the entrance. It felt like she was not quite present, neither in the house, nor in her own body. She recalled with a shudder her state of extreme and blurry awareness from the early stages of Malone's teaching. The memory just would not go away or even fade. The sense of power rattled her.

It was still here, if she had ever doubted that. She rolled her left hand into a fist and smiled.

Energy bounced back and forth between the walls, between the ceiling and the floor. It did so in a way that would hardly be noticeable to others.

But she noticed easily, sensed it flow from her body, sensed its reflection return to her, a pleasant wind scratching her itches.

It filled the room, the entire house. She filled it, realizing that this was the first time she had been alone here since her return. Mother had stayed home and nursed her back to health or its semblance. She and the guys had aided her in her reconstruction.

Alien thoughts kept haunting her, no matter how she wanted them to stay away.

She rolled her left hand into a fist again and smiled again.

There was a knock on the door. It sounded distant, not really here at all. She headed for the entrance, only a couple of steps away. Her hand reached forward to the handle and opened the door.

Beatrice stood on the doorstep with her grin and pretty smile.

Chapter 10

– Hi, she greeted the somber girl inside.

– Hi.

Janet found herself returning the grin.

– I thought I should stop by as myself, and not as one merely tailing the others.

– That is great, Janet heard herself say. – Enter then.

Beatrice entered the hall and the living room with the casual eyes of the hawk. Her clothes tightened around the big and supple body in a close to perfect fit. Her makeup was perfectly applied. She looked suave and sophisticated. Janet glanced at her in envy.

– You are a very interesting person, you know. I have wanted to meet you for so very long and I have to say that the real you exceed my expectations by *far*.

Janet reddened and looked down in embarrassment.

Beatrice walked to her and touched her jaw lightly.

– Never put yourself down, sweet witch, will you promise me that?

Janet nodded, not trusting her voice.

– And you should not be embarrassed by my praise. You are not one of those wearing a veil of false modesty, are you?

– No, Janet replied promptly. – Absolutely not! I loathe when people do not speak their mind, when they do not say what they truly mean. I have certainly seen enough of that, also when I was Malone's s-slave. Everybody in the neighborhood saw or at least suspected what was happening, even though they did not actually understand everything, but no one cared or could be bothered to interfere. Perhaps I was expecting too much, you know. Most people do have a limited understanding of reality, after all.

Beatrice slowly applauded, putting her palms together without making a sound.

She sat down in a chair. Even that simple act was so elegant, so supreme that it once again made envy rise in Janet hard and sore.

– Do you have any lemonade or anything?

– Sure, I will get some.

She hurried to the kitchen, rushing to do the queen's bidding.

The world outside the window opened up to her for a moment. She reached for the bottle in the drawer while looking at the garden and the road beyond it with her face locked in a distant expression. The image in the window looked more like a painting than something real and true.

She handed the glass of lemonade to the girl, the big, imposing girl in the chair.

– Thank you, you did not find anything to yourself?

Dumb cunt! Janet scolded herself and looked down once again.

She hurried back to the kitchen and found more lemonade, and returned with the glass in her hand.

– Sit.

Beatrice pointed to the other chair, as if it was she who lived in the house and Janet was the guest.

Janet did her bidding. The chairs were too small for them both. That made her feel a bit better.

– Tell me about it.

She knew what the other girl was asking, knew without clarification and it made her tremble inside.

– Exc-cuse me?

– Tell me what he did. I would like to hear about it.

Janet pulled back, literally.

– Come on, do not disappoint me, do not be shy or timid or *scared,* what do you remember?

Janet's hand shook so hard that she could not hold the glass properly. Slowly she clutched it, holding it so hard that her hand hurt.

– I am not certain what was real and what was not. He… fucked me over, to the point that I do not know where he ends and I begin.

Venom entered her voice and expression then, making Beatrice's eyes light up in excitement.

– Beatrice…

– Call me Bea, will you, will you do that for me.

Janet folded her hands in her lap, writhing in the uncomfortable chair.

– It is hard, Bea. He treated me so callously, as if I was not even worthy of his attention. But I knew he would, kind of. I had read about the complicated relations between a sorcerer and an apprentice. «The apprentice serves the sorcerer. The sorcerer can do whatever he or she wants with the apprentice». And he did. He treated me like *shit.* But I still got the impression that he… cared about me, that he wanted what was best for me. He was so clever, so damn clever. I feared he wanted my body, but he was far more devious than that. What he truly desired was my inheritance and my spawn, our spawn, to use in his mad venture. I was nothing more than a broodmare, a means to an end to him.

– But he taught you a lot, did he not? He granted you your devoirs, elevating you from student to teacher, from apprentice to sorcerer.

– Yes. Janet glared at her. – He gave me sufficient knowledge to fool me twice, to make me do his bidding two fucking times.
– I understand, sweetie, do not think I do. He raped you, not only physically, but also mentally, razing your very spirit, tearing it apart like he would a piece of paper, making you his creature, making you believe you were his equal… before showing you, showing you beyond doubt how utterly worthless you were. He raised you up and then he pulled you back into the mud, and it was all so easy, was it not, like he did nothing but snapping his fingers.
Janet shook, shook hard. She tried to stop herself from re-experiencing the last year, but was helpless to stop the sensations assaulting her. Small tears fell from her eyes.
– Go on.
Janet looked incredulous at her, her face suddenly twisted in fury.
– Why do you care? Do you enjoy listening to pathetic loser stories or what?
– You feel good, now, do you not, when you can return your suffering, unloading it on another poor, defenseless soul?
And Janet was once more overwhelmed with shame and regret.
– No, Bea, please forgive me. Please.
Bea's smile was strained, cold. Janet felt bad, really bad.
– I care, Bea whispered, after a prolonged moment of silence.
Janet wondered if she had spotted a storm of rage deep in those beautiful eyes.
Now, there was only concern, pity, and Janet felt even worse when she fought in vain to keep the catching from her voice when she continued her narrative.
– His opening gambit… He told me I was the child of a god, and that that made me incredibly powerful, but he also told me later, in not so many words that there are no gods. I guess he was quite an accomplished liar, adding to his other «qualities».
– Or… perhaps both statements are true, Bea said.
That made Janet look startled at her.
– It is to some extent a matter of… interpretation, Bea said, – a perception of some kind most people miss. You see, you are, like me a link back to an ancient power beyond any common cheap sorcerer. We were gods then and we can be so again. Malone was not talking about your mother or your father, but of far more distant relations. Your father and mother combined their individual lineage in you to make something unique and powerful, something beyond potent to rival and perhaps even *surpass* the Ancients,

something even stronger if we combine it.

Bea smiled and Janet echoed her smile, suddenly feeling better, much better. She did not need more prompting to go on. Unloading like this, telling the other girl what very few others could possible understand felt good, felt like a relief of beyond great magnitude.

– The power awoke within, like a storm, so terrifying and immense, undeniable. Everything my Master had told me was true. True! I felt excited, elated. The house, with its arcane library and old things had felt interesting right from the start, but now everything, my perception of everything changed, taking on a new and potent significance.

She rose from the chair, striking out with her hands, the onslaught they created shaking the air.

– He gave me basic teaching and then he took me on tour, displaying me to his fellow sorcerers, bringing me to various realms, showing me their wonders and horrors, leaving me wide open, ready for his further teaching and kindness.

More tiny tears jumped from her eyes.

She tried, tried hard to go on, but could not. Everything just… stopped inside of her.

– This is a good start of your story, Bea said softly, – but perhaps sufficient for now. I can wait.

She rose as well and took the other girl in her powerful embrace.

The silence and heat of the other body felt good. Janet dried her tears and they stopped coming. Bea put her back in the chair. Janet sat still for a while, hardly even breathing, but able to know a certain kind of peace.

Bea returned with another glass of lemonade and handed it to Janet. Janet accepted it and drank. The fluid felt chilled and pleasant as it made its way down her throat.

– You needed this, Bea stated, – needed catharsis. The others treated you like china, but you are tougher than that. Where others may crumble, you just pull yourself back up and stay there. A little stumbling does not change that

Something in her voice made Janet look closer at her.

Bea smiled, acknowledging her acute perception with a pleased nod.

– What is it? Janet asked, a little impatient. – Tell me!

It was a command, really. Bea did not let it faze her, even though she did comply.

– The player on the ferry that day…

Janet looked up startled.

– Did you hear him? Did you see him?

– I both saw him and heard him, of course.
– Do you know him?
– I know of him. He is known by many names…
– I know who he is.
Janet cut her off.
Bea studied her, bemused and with evident reverence.
– Al'rahan Amaro, the Bard of the Nine Realms is giving you his attention, singing your praise, she cried. – Are you aware how *rare* that is, what an unbridled honor he bestows upon you? Scripture tells of only a few such beings.
– I know. Janet shrugged. – What of it?
– Do you not see? Everybody else would have been beside themselves with equal parts excitement and terror, but you stay calm and centered, not nervous, not scared or excited. You accept it, accept his interest as a fact of life. I would have called it refreshing modesty… if it was not so *quaint*. You are not the timid gray mouse you have pretended to be lately and you know it. You have two faces, one you present to the world and one you keep hidden…
– How can you know that? The mouse whimpered.
– Because I sympathize. I approve. I know what it is like because I do that myself.
Beatrice told her softly, her expression clearly supporting her words.
Janet wanted to speak, to say something, anything, but everything stuck in her throat.
– As you have discovered, it is easy to deceive most people. Only those with the same or similar qualities can easily see through the weaving of such an elaborate illusion.
Janet nodded to herself, more than to her.
– Good, then we can move on to the true reason I came to visit my newfound and clever friend today.
She kept it light, but Janet noted easily the eager seriousness, anxiety beneath it, and knew that Bea did not really try to hide it either. Bea enjoyed the banter, the chitchat and keeping up a playful mood, but that was just a pretext.
Janet's eyes narrowed slightly and the other girl noticed, amazing Janet further with the distinct shiver passing through her.
– I, Beatrice Maximus Rosen, a mage in training have come seeking aid of the resident sorcerer, she stated formally, – and would be extremely grateful if she heard my plea, if she deemed me worthy of her attention.
Janet reddened. She had read the lore and was both startled and excited by

the girl's words.

And so had the blonde. It was not really surprising, given her origins, which her «newfound and clever friend» now understood so much better.

– Bea, she mumbled, – stop clowning around.

– But I am not, Beatrice Maximus Rosen countered with serious eyes. – I have come to the current Master of the Blue Flame to seek assistance in an urgent matter.

She fell on her knees and cast her eyes to the floor.

– Get up, Janet snapped. – Get up this instant!

The petitioner obeyed, in an instant, standing straight. Janet wondered astonished if there was a hint of fear in those big eyes.

– Have I done anything to offend the Master? My thousand pardons.

– You are close, very close, worm…

Janet managed, by an act of will to put an undercurrent of joking in her voice.

They both smiled then.

– Okay, Bea shrugged, – but I just wish you would not be such a sourpuss about it.

She visibly loosened up, but those big eyes stayed locked on the other one present.

– It is just a stupid tradition, Bea, Janet mumbled embarrassed.

– I understand where that statement is coming from, believe me, I do, Bea said, keeping up the casual fluctuation in her voice, – but do not scoff at tradition. Both the Maximus and Rosen clans are horse-mouths about tradition. I have heard repeatedly about the importance of tradition since I was very young. My mother was given away in an… *understanding* between them when she exchanged vows with my father. I am the foremost result of that arrangement, and they expect big things from me.

Janet sighed and decided to play along.

– Well, then, Beatrice Maximus Rosen, what is it you desire of the Master of the Blue Flame?

– See how easy it was? Bea grinned, letting her friend pay for her diligence.

Then she fell to her knees once again, lowering her eyes once more.

– This unworthy vessel, Beatrice Maximus Rosen needs a Samhain Blessing and subsequent full ceremonial Honors on the All Souls' Night, and she begs Janet of the Blue Flame to grant her its joy and delight. Beatrice is prepared to pay a substantial tithing and be the sorcerer's humble servant during the entire arrangement.

Janet felt power then. For a brief moment it did not feel like they were playacting at all.

– Janet of the Blue Flame is prepared to perform the Blessing, she heard herself say. – She will expect a high tithing and nosedive admiration during the entire Samhain and on All Souls' Night…

They giggled a bit. Bea signed for her to join her on the floor and Janet, after a brief hesitation did.

Bea drew something from her pocket and handed it to Janet.

– Your tithing, My Lady.

The last in the line of the Blue Flame suddenly had trouble breathing. She held an invitation in her hand.

Janet of the Blue Flame
Is hereby invited
To the Maximus Glory Guesthouse
On All Souls' Night
As the personal guest of the Rosen Clan

It was written in golden letters.

The Glory Guesthouse, the GG on the grapevine was also called Maximus' Folly and other less flattering names. It was a giant castle-like building halfway into the Territories, one where only the wealthy could stay, if someone less fortunate did not happen to have an invitation. There was no need to add anything to the five lines. The card and the words written on it was a value of the highest worth.

– And you expect me to…

Bea nodded eagerly.

– Please do not take this the wrong way, Janet said in the tiny voice she hated so much, – but I am not so sure I can do this. I wanted to put all sorcery and that kind of life behind me, you know.

– Well, that is too bad. That means I must accept one of the lousy sorcerers picked by the clans as my Guide, and they kind of suck, and will surely treat me badly.

Janet giggled with stars in her eyes.

– Okay.

Bea brightened.

– Okay? You will do it?

Janet nodded with her biggest eyes.

– That is *so* great. The big blonde embraced her. – You have saved me from a fate worse than *death*.

She looked and sounded very much like a child then, as if she truly meant it.

Janet felt a great catching in her throat.

– No. She shook her head. – What about the guys? I can not leave them.

Bea chuckled, grabbing her arms.

– You silly floss, I invited them along long before I invited you. You need them, need them around you. They are your friends, your childhood friends and will always have a special place in your heart.

Janet started crying then, abrupt and hard. She practically collapsed in the other's arms. Bea pulled her close and comforted her the best she could.

Sounds faded away again. The only thing the stricken girl could hear was the sound of her loud sobs. She dried her tears again, rubbing her eyes so hard that they turned swollen and sore.

– This is the last time, she swore. – The very last time I act like a crybaby.

– I believe so, too, Bea nodded.

Janet rose.

– The ceremony must be done today. I do not have my gear, but…

– It is alright, Bea said. – I have. You should check to make sure everything is there, but I did extensive shopping, with several alternatives, just to make sure.

She handed over her rucksack. Janet took it hesitantly, began checking its content hesitantly and it still felt right, did not felt awkward or wrong at all. She handled all the various ingredients as she checked them out, splitting them in viable and nonviable. It felt like the most natural thing in the realm.

– This is good, she acknowledged. – Not everything is here, but we can get the rest easily enough.

Bea looked at her. She noticed.

– What?

– Sorry. Another happy sound. – It is just so great to see you work, just like I have always imagined it would be.

Janet did not know how to respond to that. She signed for Bea to stay put and ran to her room. It was silent there and clammy. She opened the window, opened it wide. Her rucksack and the bracelets had been put nicely away in the closet. She put the bracelets on her wrists. They fit well and felt good, making her skin tingle and hum. She grabbed the rucksack and ran back down.

– They look good on you, Bea said.

– They are mine, Janet said.

She put all the relevant ingredients in her rucksack and the useless back in Bea's.

– Come on, let us…

– Can I call you Cathy?

Janet's heart jumped in her chest.

Beatrice chuckled.

– Please, do not look so shocked. Of course I recognized you. Some of us look beneath appearances, you know. I would have known even if I was not able to see or at least glimpse your invisible birth tattoos.
A strong hand caressed a shivering cheek.
– I like that name. Is it alright?
– I'guess, Janet mumbled.
– Do not fret. I will not use it while anyone is present. That might get my beautiful sorcerer in trouble and we certainly do not want that.
Bea grabbed her arms again.
– A bad man hurt you. No one will ever do that again.
Janet nodded.
The moment the decision, the final decision had been made they did not dawdle. Janet wrote a note to her mother, assuring her she would be fine, and that she would be back soon.
– The magistrate you met is following me, she said, as an afterthought, – following me *everywhere*. She is probably somewhere outside right now, and she most certainly saw you arrive.
– It is alright, Bea shrugged (again). – I do not mind. Everything will eventually be very public and a matter of much gossip anyway, so it is just an advantage, even prudent to have a qualified witness to it all.
They walked outside. The door closed quietly behind them.
– We could use the car, Bea offered, nodding at the luxury vehicle with the driver parked up the road. – Your pet magistrate will surely be able to follow you anyway.
– Thanks, Janet said, – but we need to walk, need to exert ourselves physically for the ritual.
– I knew that, Bea grinned. – We can run as fast as most cars, so it is no big deal.
They walked, both turning their head now and then, feeling the presence of Joan as an itch in their back.
– So, you are a mage, huh? Janet finally blurted out.
– A mage in *training,* Bea replied. – The lowest of the low on the magick pecking order. It is one task on a rather extensive list I have to carry out in order to complete my education, fulfill my age old obligations.
They walked, speeding up a little, making it harder for anyone without their level of physical prowess to keep up without running. To them it was no exertion to speak of.
The neighborhood had changed, or seemed very much changed from what Janet remembered before Malone had come for her. She saw that easily, now, when her eyes were not filled with tears.

– It seems so quaint, does it not? Her wise companion whispered in her ear. – You have moved beyond it and it does not truly concern you anymore.

The young sorcerer nodded to herself. That sounded so right, so very right.

There were quite a few people out and about at this hour, where most of them ended their workday. They walked and biked on their way home. Even the most insane painter or artist would have a hard time making anything out of this picture.

Janet rubbed her arm, rubbed her arm all the time.

She slowed down as they approached their temporary destination, one of the stations on their path. She did not notice until she realized that she walked several steps behind Bea.

The road rose to the low hill and the house in the quiet, eerily quiet neighborhood. They were about to pass the grocery store and she imagined that people stared at them, at her again.

– Are you coming? Bea asked casually.

She needed no further incentive and hurried to catch up with her friend.

– They stare, Bea, they stare all the time.

– At two giant amazons like us? Bea chuckled. – Why would they?

Janet tried, tried hard to contain the sudden burst of laughter, but failing miserably.

They know where we are heading, she thought, quickly sobering. They can tell by a glance.

The house towered above them. Janet stopped, and her companion did, too.

– It is palpable, is it not? Bea whispered, uncharacteristically caught in the mood of the moment.

It was a rhetorical question. Janet did not reply.

– Be prepared for anything. If Peter is in there, kill him on sight, do you hear me.

– He was such a wuzz, Bea said and shook her head. – I still have a hard time wrapping my mind around the image I have of him and how he turned out.

Janet looked at her one more time.

– Yes, her new friend said, very full of herself, - I know about that, too.

– I do not think he is in there, Janet mumbled, the house drawing her in once more. – I can not sense him.

– I will kill him, Bea acknowledged, – will eviscerate him slowly in order to honor you.

Janet hardly heard her. She moved forward in a daze. The magistrates or someone else had covered up the hole in the wall. There was no easily accessible way in anymore. Janet walked unhesitatingly up the stairs to the even wall at the top. She touched a particular place there, and the door appeared. The sound of Bea's hardly audible gasp reached her from behind. She walked inside. Bea hurried inside after her.

– Wow, she breathed. – I was clearly not wrong about you, Janet of the Blue Flame, not wrong at all.

The door closed behind them, and faded away, becoming a seamless part of the wall again, as if it did not exist at all. They stood there, in the entrance hall for a while, taking in the mood of the house.

– It has not changed, Janet decided. – One way or another it is exactly like it has always been.

– I guess it does not care who its occupants happen to be.

Janet frowned at that statement, pondering its validity.

She walked into the living room, to its Dust and tools.

– Goddess, Bea exclaimed, – my skin is *tingling*.

The Dust clung to them. It was like it was pulled to their exposed skin.

– My nipples are hardening, Bea cried incredulous.

Janet found the Book of Fate on the shelf and put it in her rucksack. She walked to the kitchen and found more ingredients, both in and out of the fridge.

– We still do not have everything we need, she told Bea, Bea staring at the mask on the wall and touching with reverence the statues on the table.

– There is a specialty shop not far from here, Bea said with a distant look in her eyes.

– I know exactly which one you are referring to, Janet said, feeling very good about that comment.

Bea turned with a grin.

– You are a veritable well of jokes, are you not?

Janet tried to make another witty reply, but was unable to do so. Once again, words stuck in her throat.

– At least you try.

The sorcerer returned to the entrance hall, followed by her colorful devotee.

– Will you not give Bea a tour, show her the sights in your castle, My Lady?

– Not particularly, no, the reply cut her off. – In any case, we do not have the time today, not if Beatrice Maximus Rosen, «the mage in training» wishes to complete the first part of her Samhain ritual at the right time and place this year.

– The Master of the Blue Flame makes such a compelling argument…

Janet sighed, but otherwise ignored her. She opened the door and walked back out, not bothering to look back to see if her companion followed. She did.

Standing on the stairs outside felt as strange as always. Janet half expected Joan to meet her there, but she did not. She scouted for the big magistrate, but did not see her.

There was a gathering crowd, though, fixing their ugly stare at the two on the stairs.

They were a rather disquieting bunch. A further study did not exactly alleviate the young sorcerer's fears.

When the two girls walked down the stairs they were immediately blocked from walking further. Janet stopped before they stopped her.

– Is there anything we can help you good people with? She asked quietly.

They stopped, suddenly not quite so convinced of the righteousness of their cause.

– We «good people», the woman in front said, – want to know what you did in that house.

– If you must know, Janet said, the catching in her throat noticeable, – I was held prisoner in that house for almost a year. The magistrates gave me permission to go inside and pick up a few private things.

The woman's face softened a bit, just a bit.

– My daughter Louise was also kept there. Not for as long as you were. But the people treating her fear she will never be *right* again.

Janet feared the chill trickling down her spine would be visible for all to see.

– I know that, she said. – I saw her. She was treated pretty badly. I was pretty much a basket case myself, but with the help of my family and friends I recovered.

– How come you were there a year and my Louise only a few days?

– Are you asking me to speculate on the motives of my kidnapper and rapist? The girl said icily.

They pulled back, literally. Janet took a step forward and they moved aside to accommodate her.

– How did you girls get in and out? A man asked in a very aggressive manner.

Suddenly Bea was there, in front of Janet, forming a protective shield with her body.

– Are you *good people* quite finished? Bea said sweetly. – If you are, we would like to be on our way.

It was amazing how fast the potential mob dissolved. They were fading away and gone between two blinks of an eye, or so it seemed.

– Thank you, Janet said quietly, bowing her head in despair.

– Think nothing of it and lighten up, my good girl.

– How can I? Janet whispered or hissed or whispered, almost shouting it out. – I did that to that girl and there is no excuse for it. None!

– Is there not? You were half out of your mind and the other half was not much better, and then young Malone came and put the icing on the cake of the wee girl's troubled mind.

Dry tears wet Janet's cheeks, but no wet ones. Bea embraced her and kissed her on the forehead. She held around her as they made their way further on their magickal walk.

– Better? Bea asked a while, a long while later.

Janet nodded energetic.

– I am, she insisted, rolling both hands into fists. – I will not let him win. I refuse to do that, the world be *damned*.

The warm glow within grew and blanketed everything else and it felt so good.

– That is the ticket, the Cathy I know and love, Bea said pleased.

Janet frowned and studied her, but there was nothing there, nothing to hold onto, and she relented and straightened and deliberately led on further down the road. She did not turn around to see if the potential mob followed them. They did not. She knew that without the use of her eyes. Joan followed them. The crowd faded away into nothing, in the terrain and in her mind.

– They are so small, are they not?

That was also a rhetorical question, but Bea answered it eagerly anyway.

– They are! She nodded.

Janet returned now, to the road Cathy had walked, and she felt her gut move and twist. They walked past the cluster of buildings where she had procured her dress, her beautiful dress, on the long walk to the city block stretching out in front of them, into an ominous alley dark in bright daylight.

Bea looked around her with her big eyes. It was not exactly her kind of area, but she moved with her usual flair, and basically ignored all the dubious characters studying them, as they made their way to their objective, their part-time goal for this rather tedious detour.

– This is so *exciting,* Bea said, almost cried out. – Have you been here often?

– This is the first time. Malone did not frequent these particular circles.

– Oh, Bea said, uncharacteristically apprehensive. – Oh, well, we will prevail. Between the two of us we can deal with virtually anyone, aside from a very experienced and cruel sorcerer, of course.

– Are you really like this, or is it a fucking act? Janet snarled.

– You wound me, oh, mighty sorcerer, Bea said piously.

The wicked laughter rising from the two of them drew even more scowling stares from the other strange characters visiting this shady spot of Auburn, a place unknown to almost everyone in the city. Janet consulted the Book of Fate cautiously, not removing it from the sack, but turning the pages carefully.

– The place we seek is in the book, is that old? Bea marveled.

– It certainly looks that way. Amazing, is it not?

The thought made Janet warm all over.

There was a store, one without a name or visible entrance at the dead end of the dark alley. Janet nodded, as much to herself as to her merry companion, a bit distracted, easily seeing what was hidden.

She walked down the alley easy enough, but Bea seemed to bump into something all the time.

– How do you…

– That is easy, silly girl, you just avoid the walls.

– Easy for you to say.

It was. Janet nodded to herself. There was a kind of maze obstructing the path, but as long as one could see it, and she could, there was no major trouble. She grabbed Bea's hand and led her through it, until they finally reached the door, feeling like they had walked far longer than the actual distance.

Reaching for the door handle felt like moving through a thick soup of mud. Janet curled her hand around the silver surface and opened the heavy door with little or no effort.

The inside of the building… revealed itself to her. There was no electric illumination, only lanterns with natural fires casting a soft light. She did not see only a room, but a space, one filled with sensations and objects, with display cases and magickal paraphernalia. To her eyes, perhaps, it resembled an ordinary store or rather shop, one clearly old-fashioned but twice interesting because of that.

A man stood behind the desk in the deepest part of the room. She approached him. Bea tailed her. Janet felt the nervous twitching in her hand.

– Good evening, she said sweetly.

– Good evening, the man said, glancing at the clock on the wall showing it was still afternoon. – Is there anything I can help you with?

– That would be my guess, she nodded. – When I look around in here, in your excellent store, I am pretty convinced that you can indeed help us procure professional Samhain supplies.

She stressed the end of the sentence slightly, cursing herself.

– Professional, you say?

– Indeed. You have the pleasure of talking to what is probably one of the youngest sorcerers in the nine realms. I guess a *dabbler,* even one giving off the right vibrations, could have stumbled his or her way in here, so know that I understand your slight skepticism, good sire…

– Professional Samhain supplies coming up, the not very old, but fairly experienced man coughed, dazzled by her smile. – Sorry about that.

– Oh, that is alright, she said graciously.

Bea giggled behind her, attempting to not be loud, failing miserably.

He moved to a locked cabinet and opened it with a large key, an old, definitely handmade key. There was a number of boxes in there. He grabbed one and put it on the desk.

– You will need a few more items, he said. – Excuse me.

– Do you mind if I open this? She asked it casually, politely. – There are certain specifics I need to check. We will not be able to return in time if something is not there, I am afraid.

– Not at all, he said, just as courteous.

It felt so good inside, all this. She strived to keep a big, big grin from manifesting itself.

It did not take much effort to open the box. It was made to be an efficient, not an elegant process. The ingredients had been arranged in neat little packages. She checked them out carefully with a practically visible gleam in her violet eyes.

She froze. He returned and stopped when he saw her cold stare.

– Is this a joke, or yet another attempt to weed out young, clumsy sorcerers? She asked icily.

He tried to speak, but failed to do so.

– You have not removed the fucking branches of the fucking Black Root. They are deadly, not merely poisonous.

He turned pale. She showed him.

– It is too late to remove them, now. The poison has spread to the entire root.

– I am afraid someone has made a terrible mistake, he said. – I did not pack this. I realize now that I should have. This is… this is… Is there anything I can do to make it up to you, My Lady? If this got out…

– Relax, I will not tell anyone about your slip up and ruin your precious reputation, at least not if you have the proper type of Black Root for us right now.

– *Useful* Black Root coming up, he said, and rushed off.

– That was a kind of funny remark on his part, Janet told Bea. – Do you not agree?

– I do, it was great gallows humor, *if* it was deliberate. If not it was very lame.

The embarrassed, flustered salesman returned, putting more Black Root on the desk for her inspection. She cast one glance at them and nodded curtly.

– Please, My Lady, accept these as a gift for my… for my blunder.

– That will be acceptable, she granted him.

He turned visibly relieved and put the rest of the additional ingredients on the table for her razor-sharp approval. She checked them against the description and drawings in the book. He leaned a bit forward, in order to see down in her sack, but relented without making an effort out of it.

– By the way, how did you… how did you know? He said, still both baffled and mortified. – Please do not be offended, but usually it takes a fairly trained eye.

– Janet of the Blue Flame sees such things, sees them *easily*.

She replied patronizingly, with visible pride.

He froze, visibly froze this time, and turned one more shade of gray.

– You are the heir to…

He turned downright *white,* he did, as understanding gripped him.

– Forgive me, I did not realize…

She looked at him and he fell silent, bowing his head. He did not fall on his knees, but he did lower his eyes, and it pleased her.

– These will be fine, she eventually said. – We will take them as they are, please.

– Put them on my account, Bea said. – My guess is that you know my credit is good anywhere in the realm.

– There is no need for that, he said hastily. – I would not demand payment from the Blue Flame.

He turned towards Janet, straightening.

– Please, My Lady, he said respectfully. – My name is Oliver Martens. Check me all you desire and you will find that I am trustworthy, that my word is my bond. If there is anything you need, anything at all, please do not hesitate to come to me.

He put everything in a paper bag and handed it to her.

– I will, she said. – Thank you.

Leaving was far easier than the arrival. They were back out in the sunshine in no time and without delays. Janet walked with a renewed sense of herself and with energy seemingly coursing through her.

– That was so cool, she cried. – In spite of his foul up, it felt so good to discuss the craft with him, to do that with someone.

– He practically groveled at your feet, Bea said with shiny eyes. – He was well aware of your stature, the Blue Flame's elevated standing in the scheme of things.

Janet turned her attention fully to her new friend with a pointed stare.

– And so are you, it seems.

Her new friend bounced off the pointed stare and the slightly agitated tone of voice with a bright shrug.

– Oh, yes, I am not the typical clueless young mage in training, you know…

In a stunning, daring move Janet jabbed her with the elbow.

– Well, then, I guess you are ready for the first part of your Samhain ritual.

– I am, Bea, insisted, suddenly acting almost like a pleading little girl.

Janet felt strangely good about that. It demonstrated to her that she was the dominating personality.

They made their way south, the mountain needle calling to them in the distance.

The two of them moved, moved forward. People watched them with both curious and suspicious eyes. The needle seemed no closer. Houses still surrounded them on all sides. Janet speeded up slightly, subconsciously. The initial smell of sweat turned into a stench. They were sweating hard. The number of houses finally dropped around them. They reached the open landscape between the town and the deeper wilderness. Janet spotted deer and wolves in the mountainside and felt a thrill grow from within. They reached the base of the mountain.

Janet stopped.

– Can you see the path? She asked her companion.

There was no visible trail up there.

Bea stopped, too. She did not look at her clever new friend, but at the steep terrain revealing itself to them. Her big, deep-blue eyes squinted themselves.

– I can, she said excited. – I can!

– Good, that means you have passed the first test, that Esteben the Mountain welcomes you, or at least accepts that you enter his domain. You go first.

Bea did, not giving in to the temptation of glancing back at her companion. She moved. Janet followed her with a casual stroll.

The invisible trail was steep and filled with hardship and hurdles. Bea moved forward at a steady pace and a determined look engraved on her face. She was clearly unprepared for what followed. It was as if the very air… moved. It slapped her cheek.

– Esteben the Mountain does not like you very much, though, Janet remarked unconcerned.

Another slap hit her other cheek. The girl yelped. Janet broke off a twig and in one, smooth continuation of that move she had given the girl in front of her a lash on a thigh. Bea sent her a look of disbelief and protest.

– If you stop or even stand still for more than a moment its hospitality will quickly take a turn for the worse, Janet shrugged.

Bea gritted her teeth and kept moving, set to ignore the occasional slap on the cheek, the strikes on her body.

Then, suddenly she received what looked like a beyond hard kick in the belly. She gasped and fell to her knees.

Janet was on her immediately, whipping her with vicious strokes.

– On your feet, trainee!

The whimpering girl jumped up and kept fighting herself through the invisible labyrinth.

– What are you doing? She mumbled, as she turned her head back and addressed the sorcerer. – What are you doing to me?

Janet kept whipping her, no longer giving her any pause.

– You called me Cathy. You baptized me cruel, setting the stage for the ritual. Such is magick. Reap thy reward, young mage to be.

The air chuckled with dark laughter. Janet shook as well, unable to tell if the sound originated with her or the very air around them, but it did not make her stop what she was doing. She did not give the girl any break.

Bea sniffed and choked as she fought herself further up the steep mountainside.

Janet saw Joan behind them, saw her far below without turning, grinning as the big woman reached the barrier, the barrier rejecting her, until she sat right down on the ground, frustrated and resigned.

Bea's makeup was no longer perfectly applied. It had spread all over her face. Her hair was in disarray and her eyes and skin puffy and unhealthy looking. She dried her sweat constantly. It did her no good. She could hardly see anything in front of her except the path. Janet knew she could do that. Janet felt very good and very bad.

High-pitched howls accompanied their walk on the path. Sounds both of the forest and not surrounded them. Bea hardly heard anything except the slaps and lashes, but Janet did. She looked around her in wonder, even as she kept punishing the big body in front of her.

There were sights as well, glimpses not of the forest, or at least not this forest. The wind picked up, hitting Bea straight in the face, making her gasp even harder for air.

She stumbled and fell. Unable to stand up, exhausted beyond words, she crawled forward on all fours. Janet kept punishing her, chuckling patronizingly, spitting cruel curses at her. Bea once again fought herself on her feet, unable to tell how many times she had done so. Her vision turned black, and there were only slow, painful glimpses of the terrain ahead.

Suddenly… silence reigned.

Janet stopped swinging the branch. Bea straightened, realizing that there was no more wind, no more punishment.

They had reached a plateau. Two big and flat standing, polished rocks appeared before them.

– Is this it? Bea wondered, while the air kept wheezing in and out of her strained lungs. – Please, My Lady, are we there?

– Just about, Janet replied softly. – The end of the path is through the portal.

Between the rocks.

Janet nodded encouragingly to her and she proceeded, hesitating a bit in front of the portal, before stepping through.

Nothing happened. There was no portal, no gateway to another place, just the two rocks. Janet caught up with her and they walked side by side into what appeared to be a small temple, one without ceiling and walls, but a pocket in the terrain clearly distinct from the surroundings and from the outer parts of the mountainside. Their eyes were instantly drawn to the altar at the center of the square floor and the spring fountain at the exit at the opposite side of where they had entered.

– The temple of Esteben, Bea breathed excitedly, swaying in her exhaustion, speaking with an effort through her swollen and bloody mouth, – the holy place in the needle piercing the sky, where sorcerers gather.

There was an unmistakable haze in the air and a kind of mist surrounding the shrine, making up what might have been walls.

– It does not look very impressive, Bea whispered. – But it is. It is!

– It is the place where you will receive your Blessing, Janet of the Blue Flame intoned, – where you will take one more step on your destined path.

– Yes, *yes,* the excited girl cried.

And then, seemingly catching herself.

– My Lady…

Janet removed the bracelets from her wrists and handed them to Bea.

– Put these on.

– They are beautiful…

Bea rubbed the smooth surface with her thumbs, admiring the shiny metal. She put them on. They fit her well. She looked startled at the sorcerer, as the initial sense of wellbeing manifested itself.

– They will heal you, make the Blessing slightly less unpleasant and make you look less like a meatball at your own All Soul's Eve Honors.

– That is amazing. Bea clapped her hands once. – Bea knew she would not regret her choice of Guide.

– I am sorry, Janet choked. – I knew it would be… brutal, but not…

Bea put a hand on her cheek.

– Janet of the Blue Flame should not apologize. Bea knew what awaited her. She was ready and is even more ready now.

– Very well.

Janet became colder, businesslike again, forcing it on herself.

– Kneel on the altar.

The command sounded far harsher than she had intended and wished for. Bea rushed to obey. Janet opened her rucksack. She began preparing the ingredients, putting them on the ground in a pre-arranged pattern.

– Does Bea hear voices?

– She does, Janet confirmed. – She is not the only one who has sought this place tonight. Quite a few come here for their Blessing and for other reasons during Samhain. There are many temples on this mountain.

– And no unworthy vessel may find mercy in the cruel eyes of Esteben the Mountain, Bea stated proudly. – And we do not worship him, anyway, but come to this High Place to give prayers to Samhain, Lord of the Underworld.

Janet put the five small black candles on another pre-arranged pattern on the floor. She began crushing the Black Root into a powder, into dust falling into the chalice.

– Strange, is it not? But this does feel like a dungeon of sorts…

– Shhh. Janet raised the left index finger to her lips. – The girl seeking her Blessing will be quiet or suffer the consequences.

And Bea obeyed. She knelt on the sacrificial altar and lowered her eyes like a good, polite girl.

Janet brought the chalice to the height of her jaw and breathed the Dust floating in and around it. It stung in her nostrils. Then she pushed it at Bea's face. Bea breathed hard and deep, and gasped as the initial workings of the Black Root started ravaging her.

– The girl will now undress.

Bea did, in rushed moves, a little clumsy and unsteady, noticeably reddening as she displayed herself before the sorcerer. Janet felt inevitable heat as she forced herself to study the sturdy but supple and curvy body.

She started mixing the potion. The initial effect of the Dust they had breathed was not pronounced, but still noticeable. When it moved in the chalice and mixed with the herbs and ointment and poisons she saw it, sensed it, downright felt it. She mumbled her spell, and it came easy to her and the effects of the ritual in its infancy became even more pronounced.

– O'Samhain, god of the mountain, Lord of the Underworld and all spirits roaming in-between, please look with favor at Janet of the Blue Flame and her Blessing of the child kneeling before your throne.
The five candles lit themselves. There were two, three, four heartbeats and the fire spread and formed a pentagram. None of the candles melted, even as the flames licked and caressed them. The potion started liquidating in the chalice.
She stopped the chanting. A loud crack rocked the mountain and the creature of flesh and blood on the altar.
– The girl will now give me her hand.
The girl did. Janet cut her wrist. Blood flowed into the chalice. Janet let go of the arm. It fell right back in the previous position. Janet cut her own wrist. More blood dropped into the chalice, joining what was already there. The mixed liquid started boiling, rising to fill the chalice.
– Beatrice Maximus Rosen, is it your intention to Come of Age?
– It is! Bea replied.
– Well, then, are you ready to receive your Blessing?
– I am!
– Then drink the blood of the gods and be recreated in their image.
She put the tip of the chalice at Bea's lips, and tilted it, and Bea drank. She coughed once, twice. Janet drank the remaining half. The potion itched and burned in her throat, and the itching and burning spread, slowly reaching her entire body, filling her mind and her body, and the mind and Shadow, in turn filled the room, filled the flesh and bone and mind kneeling before her. Bea began breathing faster, deeper. Her nipples hardened and she turned wet below. Janet felt it, too, not that pronounced.
– You want this, do you not, the sorcerer said softly, – want it more than anything?
– I *do!*
– *Rise,* then!
She did, with visible difficulties. She stood straight, shaking under the onslaught of the magick ravaging her.
Whispers, spells, chants and curses once again spilled from the sorcerer's throat and mouth, her lips moving fast and furry.
– The light is gone, the dark is here, blessing us with its presence. We are here, in this forest, in this heaven to probe the unknown depths of existence. In the hidden, non-existing corners of the realms, we find ourselves.
O'Mighty Samhain, deity of the mountain, Lord of the Condemned, I give you this sacrifice, condemning her, knowing that she will be yours forever.
There was a sound of something tearing, the air, the flesh or something else,

Janet could not tell. Bea rose in the air, until she hung suspended half of her length above the ground. Something smothered her, squeezed her from all sides. She moaned in pain and excitement.

The sorcerer fell silent, studying the sacrificial lamb hovering before her with predator eyes.

– The girl is close, now. Can the girl taste it, taste the great spices in her mouth?

– She can, Bea replied, hardly able to speak.

– Do you foreswear the wretched light of day and embrace the hot, inspiring darkness, binding yourself to it forever?

– I do!

Blood flowed from her nostrils. Her features twisted in pain.

– Beatrice Maximus Rosen, I grant you your Blessing. Know that from this moment on, and until the completion of your All Souls' Night Honors, you do not exist.

The scream shook flesh and bone and rock alike. A blinding darkness briefly filled the ether. Reality blinked. Beatrice Maximus Rosen fell on the flat, horizontal rock, collapsing on a surface covered with warm sweat and blood.

The chalice slipped from Janet's grip. The sound of the metal hitting the rock roused her from the trance. Bea began moving, writhing on the altar, slowly regaining herself.

Janet stepped forward, holding an unlocked collar in her hand.

– Others may be collared with metal. Know that this is mere leather. It does not actually do anything, except exposing your low standing for all to see. All with knowledge and understanding will know what a pitiful creature you are. It is a necessary part of the ritual, a single step lasting forever of your transformation from dependent girl to independent woman and mage

She put the collar around the girl's neck.

Bea sniffed and choked.

Janet reached out a hand.

– You may rise, Beatrice Maximus Rosen. Know that tonight's trials are at an end and that you are blessed and forgotten.

Bea fought herself on her feet, aided by the sorcerer's helping hand and left the altar weak and dizzy. She embraced Janet with tear-filled eyes.

– Thank you, she sobbed. – Thank you!

Janet found herself holding her, comforting her.

The mist and haze surrounding them faded, like all impression faded. They stood there enjoying each other's closeness until the world finally returned to that small dungeon at the top of the tall mountain.

Chapter 11

The two of them drank from the fountain, wetting parched throats, suppressing the burning taste of spices in their mouths. Bea cleaned her face of blood and shit and makeup and dressed herself in her now very dirty and torn clothes.

– Do you like me better now? She asked sheepishly. – Now, when I look like the lowest commoner and not a haughty high-born Lady?

– I always like you, Bea, Janet replied.

They left the temple through the exit portal. The path back down was no path, only an ordinary mountainside terrain. They spotted Joan down there.

– Ah, your pet magistrate. She is really taking her duty a step beyond, is she not? You know she can not join you during the Festivities, right?

– It does not worry me, Janet shrugged. – She may be useful in certain situations, but I can take care of myself.

– You sure can…

They reached the base of the mountain. Joan was not there, was not visible. Janet looked for Bea's car at the parking lot, but it was not there.

They returned to the town in the manner they had left it, on foot.

– The streets seem darker, so much more distinct in my vision.

– Your eyes have been wrested open, and so have your wits. You are a vessel, now, for the sorcerer to use as she sees fit.

– This girl knows that, Bea said humbly, – knows she is only a maiden, fit only to serve, to grovel at the sorcerer's feet.

– That sounds so good… Janet grinned wickedly.

– The sorcerer feels… good? The mage in training offered.

– She does, Janet nodded, adding a frown to her expression of pride, – but she is also guarding against the arrogance that felled her.

– The girl is so happy for her.

– Thank you, Bea, Janet momentarily fell out of the role playing, – thank you so much.

She stopped, embracing the other in a powerful grip.

– You should not thank the girl, the other said softly. – The sorcerer did only what the sorcerer is born to do and would eventually have done so without encouragement.

The words created a thrill within Janet of the Blue Flame, making her blood sing.

– This collar has no chain…

Beatrice Maximus Rosen said sheepishly.

– The sorcerer does not need that to keep her pet on a leash, Janet said cheerfully.

The chuckle echoed in the night and followed her the next few days and nights, to the dawn of the big day.

Mother looked at her at the breakfast table. The teachers and the other students at learning looked at her in and out of the classroom. She ignored them all with a studied shrug, masking her gathering euphoria.

The guys could share it with her, of course, even though they could not share the most important part, not yet.

But by the end of the day they would know. Anxiety and excitement kept warring within her.

The dark, classy car picked them up outside their homes right after learning. The lot of them shared bubble-water in the big backseat, looking at each other with shiny eyes.

– I do not know about you, guys, Rosa giggled, – but this is a big deal to me. No one in my line has ever been invited to either the Maximus or Rosen soirées, not to any of them, and certainly not to an All Souls' Night.

– Where is Bea? Todd wondered. – I expected her to be here, with us, really.

They realized that they were on their way to the harbor, leaving the Rosen estate farther behind with each turn of the wheels without them ever catching a glimpse of their friend.

– Hey, James, how about it? He asked the driver.

– Miss Rosen will not be joining us today, the driver replied.

– That can not be right, Fran insisted. – She said she would. She has spoken about this shit for weeks, hardly spoken about anything else.

– Miss Rosen has already departed for the resort, James explained, the very picture of calm. – She will be there to meet you.

– She told you that? Janet asked him lightly.

– That was what I was told, James explained.

– Okay, then, thank you, James, Janet said, just as pleasant.

And that made everybody look at her.

– It is no big deal, she shrugged.

They arrived at the harbor, a private, secluded part of it. They recognized another Rosen employee before he waved to them and called attention to himself.

The boat made its way across the sound. They were its only passengers. Waves struck its side in a pleasant low hum. The big airship already filled their vision. It hovered above the ground on the mainland, securely tied to the landing site. Lots of people were already walking up the landing bridge to its vast interior.

– This is the social event of the year, Eleanor sighed in delight. – I never thought I would even be able to see the outside of the GG, far less its inside.

There was a small harbor not far from the landing site. They disembarked the boat without taking their eyes off the giant airship hovering above them.

Big men and women guarded the entrance to the landing area. There were those who had to show their invitation, but most did not have to.

A woman approached and stopped before Janet and the guys.

– Greetings, Janet of the Blue Flame, she curtseyed. – This woman's name is Maria. She will be your guide and council on this trip and during your stay at the Glory Guesthouse, if you allow her the honor.

– That will be acceptable, Janet responded good-humored.

The others, Eleanor in particular looked startled at her.

– The man in that house was a sorcerer, she told them curtly. – He desired for me to learn lots of arcane skills to benefit him, and I was a good student, a good apprentice, until he gave me his devoirs and left me in tatters.

– You are… you are serious, Todd gaped.

She did not bother with a reply and felt good about it.

And they grew even more astounded.

– Please follow Maria, the woman said.

Janet and the others did. Maria brought them through the checkpoints without the hassle many others experienced and they boarded the airship. Its interiors appeared to them as if in a dream. It was not really that luxurious. This was a rented commercial airliner after all. But the teenagers' eyes still grew wide.

A feeling that only grew when they were given a window spot in the upper section. Janet pretty much knew their thoughts. They wondered if that was due to Janet or their friendship with Bea.

Janet briefly scouted for Bea, until she no longer found it worth her time.

There was a thug, as the moorings were let go. The airship rose, free from its constraints, the city of Talaho and later Howell and Auburn shrinking in her view.

She half closed her eyes and enjoyed the trip, turning off the guys' excited chatter.

The oblong balloon with its comparatively small passenger section rose above the mountains, its engines moving it inland, leaving all the triple cities behind. A vast mountain plain revealed itself.

– You should have told us, Rosa said, with what was clearly a subtext of hurt in her voice.

– I know, Janet said subdued, – but it is hard, hard to even think about it, about what he did to me, inside and out. He made me his creature, but I can not help feel that he also did me a favor. He showed me a hidden, precious part of myself. The horrible way he treated me aside: he opened the world to me. I know what I am, now, and I love it, just love it.

The features of her friends softened. Everybody rose and embraced her and comforted her the best they could, knowing that it would never be enough, all of it very transparent to Janet, and she fought off the sense of contempt threatening to spill over her full glass.

– Hey, this is fantastic, Todd cried out, loud enough to turn heads. – We actually have both a demon hunter and an honest to Goddess sorcerer in our circle.

They waited until Janet started laughing and then joined her. Everybody stopped after a while, as if on cue.

Rosa rubbed her cheek with wet eyes.

– It is all right, Janet told her, told them. – I am okay, now. A bad man hurt me. No one will ever do that again.

The fear for her, instead of the fear of her kept dominating their features and bearings. Janet swallowed hard.

A waiter served drinks, served pearly, bubbly wine.

– It feels good, Janet insisted. – It feels great.

The others knew she did not mean the wine. She had not tasted it yet. They raised their glasses in a toast to her.

– To the mighty sorcerer, Rosa cried.

– TO THE MIGHTY SORCERER, the rest of the rascals choired.

Janet giggled and drank with them.

The wine tasted so pleasant in her mouth, in her throat and stomach. It spread like spices and magick in her veins. She wanted to drink more, to drink much, but contained herself.

People stared at them, at her. She raised her glass in defiance to them all.

The guys noticed and glanced at each other, at her with pity, uncertainty and the inevitable touch of fear. It did not faze her. Even Bea had done that.

Others stared harder at her. She recognized that look and fought to meet those intense eyes with a casual interest.

The woman rose and approached her, her, not her companions.

She stopped at what could be described as a modest distance from the sitting young sorcerer.

– Well met, Janet of the Blue Flame, she said, not unfriendly.

Janet waited, not saying anything, studying the other somewhat composed.

– My name is Illandra. I am of the Inlands, what you call the Territories. I am also of the clan Josbari, of the Bone People.

Janet eyed her. She did not look old, only ageless. Janet blinked. There was

something about the tall woman, something she did not quite get.
– Well met, Illandra the Inlander, Janet returned her greeting.
– Your great grandfather was my mentor. He told me about you.
– Oh, Janet said, fighting to conceal her emotions, – which great grandfather was that?
– One of those you have never met, Illandra confirmed her suspicion. – Your great grandfather was not a Seer himself, but his great grandfather was, and he told my mentor a lot about you.
– What did he say? Janet asked hoarsely.
– You have his eyes, Illandra said curtly. – But yours is darker. He knew they would be, knew you would not be only of his line, but also of another, equally powerful. And added to that would be a third. He said that most sorcerers are only born twice, but that you are born thrice.
Illandra had long, black hair and a strange, dark complexion. Janet could not take his eyes off her and she was unable to speak.
– Your trainee… is she with you today?
– No, she is…
– Of course not.
Illandra cut her off with a smile that could chill the hottest summer.
Janet noticed that the older, experienced sorcerer also traveled without her trainee.
– We will meet again, heir to the Blue Flame, Illandra breathed her parting words.
– We will meet again, Inlander, Janet confirmed curtly.
She glared at the other woman as she returned to her seat at the other side of the hall.
Her friends looked at her, even more incredulous than minutes ago.
– Wow, that was intense, Toby said.
– I guess it was, Janet shrugged, making a production out of it.
– She acknowledged you as her equal, Eleanor stated with admiration and longing in her voice and entire demeanor.
Janet studied her friend closer, but did not say anything.
– I thought the Bone People did not travel beyond the confines of their home, Eleanor said.
– This one obviously does, Fran said in a hushed voice. – This one does so in abundance. The Inlands, the Territories are far away from everywhere.
– She claimed that a man dead several generations before you were born had prophesized your birth, Rosa said incredulous. – That is… preposterous!
– It is quite funny.
Something distracted Janet. Visibly preoccupied she rose and walked closer

to a window, drawn there, looking down on the landscape below, at the vast valley revealing itself.

– It does look a little like a gap, a boy said.

She felt like it did, like it reached for her, closed itself around her, teeth and all.

– Look at the unicorns, mom, the boy cried excited.

– They are horses, dear, his mother sighed.

The ship rose further towards the sky, in order to escape the even taller mountains at the other side of the valley. They towered above it for a long time, until the big balloon with its cargo climbed high enough to make even those peaks seem like they were far below.

The Glory Guesthouse, the giant hotel building appeared through the window in front. Most of the travelers flocked there. It grew like a mirage in the late afternoon golden light.

The passengers saw how the area was flooded with activity. The two other airships from the other triple cities in the south and north had already arrived. An even stream of people flowed from the landing spot to the guesthouse entrance.

The third airship joined its siblings at the dock. There was wind, a little bit of it, but it did not impede on the docking in any discernible way.

People disembarked in a fairly orderly manner, both excited talk and cautious reserve present in the crowd.

– Please come with me, Maria bade them politely.

They followed her down the landing bridge and to a secluded area outside the guesthouse.

– Please wait here. Maria will check if your rooms are ready and make sure everything is in order.

She hurried off, disappearing into the vast shadow of the building.

– I do not like this servant crap, Toby swore.

– Neither do I, Janet said.

They glanced at her.

– It is tradition, she added to her earlier statement, – but I am not particularly fond of tradition.

– Thank the Goddess, Eleanor said.

Activity picked up even more around them. The Glory Guesthouse hectic nervousness rose to yet another level. Something touched Janet's consciousness, something she could not fathom.

She turned and then she saw it, saw her, the creature in hood and robe. Janet recognized Bea through a dim light. She walked to her. Bea stood there, making every attempt to hide herself from her surroundings.

– We missed you, Janet said softly, containing her anger. – We all missed you when you were not there. Why did you not travel with us?
Bea looked up cautiously. Janet realized startled that her friend only reluctantly met her eyes, her gaze drifting off constantly.
– Tell me! Janet urged her, commanded her.
Bea looked sullenly at the ground. The stench of body juices and dirt and unwashed skin emanated from her, filling Janet's nostrils.
– You said it yourself, she practically mumbled, – told me I did not exist and was forgotten. Father took one look at the collar around my neck and stopped acknowledging me, and thus everybody else in the clans did as well.
– He takes it that seriously?
– Of course he does. From the moment I entered Esteben the Mountain I knew I would be lost. I did not have access to my home or any funds. I could not travel with the airship and can not get inside this wretched castle except in your company. I am yours now, to do with as you please.
– Come with me, then, Janet forced a shrug and turned around, not bothering with looking back.
They returned to the others.
– Bea has run all the way here, she conveyed to the guys. – It is part of her initiation ceremony.
– That is so cool, Fran marveled.
She reached out to touch the other girl, but Bea evaded her touch and Fran relented with hurt eyes.
Maria returned, clearly out of breath.
She stopped in front of Janet, waiting for the sorcerer to acknowledge her. Janet did with a nod.
– Maria is happy to report that everything is in order and she will be delighted if the Blue Flame and her entourage will follow her into the humble guesthouse.
– We will, Janet said. – Lead on.
– «The Blue Flame and her entourage», Toby snickered.
Janet did her best to ignore him.
– «The humble guesthouse», Toby snickered louder.
That made Janet smile.
They approached the entrance. She could not help noticing the big women and men standing there, potentially blocking the way for the unworthy. Bea sought closer to Janet. The two and the rest of the guys walked past the sentries, breathing in relief. Janet sensed that Bea remained tense by her side.
The lush insides of the place revealed itself to them. Janet and the guys gaped in wonder. The reception area looked like a foreign, strange land to

them. Bea, still looking at the floor, sought Janet's hand and clutched it in a hard, shaky grip. Janet squeezed the hand reassuringly.

The guys walked up the stairs, a group rather standing out among the guests and also among the children present. Maria walked elegantly ahead, like a doll or a puppet. Janet saw several others doing that as well. Something, a sudden familiar pressure in her frontal lobe, a sense of recognition caught her, unaware at first, then she realized the why of it.

Far from all, but a few of those being shown to their rooms were sorcerers, sorcerers not dressed up. She focused on ignoring them, and as long as she avoided meeting them face to face, she succeeded. They reached the room. Each of the youths was given their own dwelling. Bea stopped outside Janet's and did not walk inside until Janet had given her a deliberate permission to enter.

– You are home free, now, you know, Janet sighed. – There is no need to act cowed anymore. Take a shower, relax and change clothes.

– As My Lady wishes, the girl curtseyed.

She dropped her dirty clothes on the floor as she rushed to the shower.

Maria appeared in the open door. Janet acknowledged her.

– Does My Lady need Maria anymore?

– Not for the moment, no, Janet replied distracted, listening to the sound of the shower and studying the drifting clouds outside. – Grab those rags, will you and remove them from my presence.

Maria did so, clearly eager to perform her duties.

– Then Maria will be on her way. If My Lady needs Maria she can only ring the bell and Maria or another equally dedicated to My Lady's welfare will come.

– Thank you, Maria, the sorcerer dismissed her.

Maria curtseyed and the door closed. Janet kept studying the drifting clouds. They drifted like her thoughts, not solidifying or stopping long enough for her to catch them or to freeze their image.

Bea emerged from the shower, very clean and much rubbed, and she kept rubbing herself with the towel.

– You will sleep on the floor tonight, of course, Janet heard herself say casually, as if she had just discussed the weather with someone. – Tomorrow is your big day. Today and tonight will belong to me.

– Yes, My Lady, Bea replied tonelessly. – Of course, My Lady.

– That is a good girl. You may dress, now. We will take a stroll through the castle before dinner.

She giggled darkly, unable to help herself. Not even conjuring up the image of herself crawling on the floor before young Peter, the memory of her second and worse humiliation stopped the triumphant joy she felt from expressing itself, from rearing its ugly head.

Bea dressed, picking the fabrics from her rucksack. The clothes were clean and nice, but rather crude compared to her usual standards, more in tune with her current low stature.

They were still far more elegant and expensive compared to Janet's. Janet shrugged.

The smile in the air mirror made the pleasant shudder pass through her again.

– Come, my servant, let us travel these wretched halls with impunity.

Bea rushed forward and opened the door well before the sorcerer reached it. Janet walked through it very casually, her jaw set in a firm mold.

The hallway was empty of people. Lush paintings covered the walls and expensive carpets the floor, but there were no people.

– Show me the tower, the sorcerer commanded.

– The stairs to the right in the next intersection will take us there, My Lady.

Janet walked first, following the simple directions and they were there. A spiral staircase led upwards. They walked it, round and round and round. Janet stood in the tower room, turning slowly looking out of the four windows, enjoying the view of the vast plains of untouched wilderness surrounding Maximus' Folly.

– There is something about this place, she speculated, – something I can not grasp. I noticed it the moment we arrived. Something...

She noticed that Bea listened attentively. She shook her head, dismissing it.

– I just wanted to see the view, she said embarrassed.

Bea did not notice, or did not seem to notice, remaining in her mage-in-training and servant mode.

Janet walked to each of the windows in turn and took another look.

– The landscape is beautiful, she acknowledged, – and so different from the triple cities.

– Beautiful, Bea echoed.

And the temptation to treat the meek and almost child-like girl badly surfaced again. Janet shook her head, shook it decisively.

She led on back down. Bea tailed her, the loyal and obedient companion.

The bell sounded, its deep sound reverberating through the building, signaling that the festivities were about to begin. The two of them moved down to the ground floor with the flow of guests and participants. They met up with the guys on the last stairwell.

– There you are, Rosa cried. – We looked everywhere for you.

– Not everywhere, Janet said lightly.

They still approached her with caution and embarrassment, even if they made an effort at fighting it.

Eleanor's approach was completely different. Speculation and interest hid in her eyes.

Janet, opened wide had no trouble reading any of them.

They reached the reception area. It was filled with people going in both, practically all directions. Janet spotted Justin Rosen by the desk. He was rubbing his hands in expectation and gratification. She studied him as they passed him. There was no sign at all of him greeting his daughter, or even acknowledging her existence. Bea made no attempt at getting his attention.

Janet felt strange before they stepped into the great hall. She just saw it through the fairly small door, but her senses began tingling. The moment she stepped inside a dark chuckle bubbled in her throat, one she was unable to contain.

– What is it that amuses the lady? Toby wondered, keeping a light tone.

– Nothing important, she replied, striving to sound convincing. – A private, personal joke.

She saw the place empty and in moonlight, and when she turned Peter Malone was at her side.

– It is empty, *now,* he cried in her mind and memory. – But it will be mine, my castle, my Place of Power when I return from the Beyond, and you… you will be my Queen.

The sight and event faded in her eyes, but lingered in her consciousness.

– A very private, personal joke then, Toby said, slightly caustic, – since we do not know about it.

She bent forward and kissed him on the lips, to the guys' amusement.

A man followed by a shadow, an older man followed by a young boy approached her. She froze, instantly recognizing him.

– Well met, Blue Flame, he greeted her.

– Well met, Grayson, she returned the greeting, fighting, fighting hard to keep her voice and pose even.

His ward, his mage in training did not say anything and was not acknowledged in any way.

He left and the boy followed him. They walked to seats not that far off from theirs.

– He also acknowledged you as… Eleanor said incredulous.

And then stating, with visible insight in her voice and stance:

– You really are the Blue Flame.

And the mere fact that Eleanor knew the name's true significance told Janet everything she needed to know about her friend's strangeness the last few years, what she had been hiding.

– Yes, I am, fellow magick-wielder, she said softly, not able to hide her spite.

And Toby and Rosa shook their head in mute amazement.

– Suddenly I feel like I am in a minority, he said, and to Eleanor: – Why did you not tell us?

– Yes, fellow magick-wielder, Janet said, – why did you not tell us?

– I felt… embarrassed, Eleanor said, – and every time I tried to tell you, you just joked about it. You used to be embarrassed, too!

Her accusation hit Janet, as she instantly acknowledged the truth of it.

– I guess you both felt insecure in your nascent steps, Rosa said softly. – I can understand that.

Toby nodded.

– You guys had it easy, Bea snorted.

There were smiles and Janet felt the hard spot inside melt a little.

They do understand, or at least they accept.

She chuckled, another harder, accentuated laughter differing from the smiles.

They turned towards her as one being.

– A crown for your thoughts? Toby wondered and this time she knew he wanted an answer.

– For just a brief moment in time, really, since I returned to your excellent company after the regaining of my freedom from cruel incarceration, I denied who I truly am, no longer than that.

She could tell by a glance that they knew, understood what she meant, what her words signified.

All the guests sat down by the tables, and they joined them.

Dinner was served. Spices and meat drowned in wine. There were loud cheers and cries, as the outside turned dark and all fires and candles were lit inside.

A musician played a harp somewhere, warm, brittle tones, hardly sounding like a harp at all. Its waves resonated with those flowing from Janet, from her hands, feet and skin.

– Look at you, Eleanor said darkly. – Look at you1

Janet acknowledged her friend's accusing stare with an amused nod.

Justin Rosen struck a spoon at the glass in front of him, sending more waves into Janet's ears.

– Welcome to the modest start of our gathering, he declared, his voice jarring in Janet's mind. – A gathering focusing on transition, on time-honored traditions…

He spoke a lot. She did not really listen, and neither, she noticed did Bea.

Most of the people present pretended to listen, pretended to be attentive of his golden words, but Janet, with her enhanced awareness had no trouble looking through their masks.

– People will speak about these nights forever, Justin boasted, ended his speech.

Jugglers and fire-breathers entertained the assembly, adding to the music, the blood flowing through people's veins. The Blue Flame had more wine, practically feeling how it mixed with her blood, her blue flame.

Grayson remained at the center of Janet's attention, no matter how hard she attempted to make him stay away. She spilled some wine as she took another sip, the cold fluid chilling the skin on her jaw.

– If My Lady wishes for her interest in Grayson the Sorcerer to be less obvious, perhaps she should not try so hard? Bea offered.

Janet looked at her both amused and furious, the sore pain in her gut persisting.

She forced herself to rise somewhat slowly.

– I need to pee, she declared with an intoxicated individual's typical panache.

She rushed off, hardly even noticing that Bea followed her. Turning the first corner did not hide her from anyone. She rushed towards the next, and finally there, she trembled in rage.

Bea spoke to her in a strangely normal, disaffected and suddenly informal tone.

– You want to kill him, want to disintegrate the very Dust of his bones do you not?

– Do you know, know what he did, what he and other sorcerers *do?*

Janet remembered, suddenly remembered vividly, with images and sensations that would not let go.

– It is not unknown to me. The clans have not reached their level or influence by being ignorant in matters of true power. Say the word and I will disintegrate him in thy honor, My Lady.

Bea looked at her with her huge and intense eyes.

A welcomed calm settled in Janet's mind.

– That will not be necessary, at least not yet. Besides, it would not reflect well on the Festivities…

– My Lady is so funny, Bea giggled.

It felt good to laugh together, so very good.

They made their way to the lavatories, did what they needed to do and returned to the table. The Festivities continued. There were lots of drinking and eating, and more than one guest puked his or her guts out on the floor.

Janet sipped more wine now and then, but kept herself at a distance to the surroundings. The alcohol and spices did not truly diminish her faculties. She imagined, in glimpses the place, not as it was now, but a while after… after Malone's return. She saw him sit on his throne, and on the throne by his side… she saw herself. Anticipation and terror held her in their grip. Her hand tightened around the knife she held.

Most of the guests returned to their rooms eventually. Others, too drunk to move would have to be carried back. Janet and her guys stumbled up the stairs with bottles and glasses in their hands.

She heard the music all the time. The alcohol did not dilute her experience of it at all. The new chuckle did not come from her throat, but from the very air around her.

– Good night, guys, Rosa cried from her open door. – We are on the quest of a lifetime.

– I see all the treasure I need right in front of me, Toby told her with a hungry smile.

She returned an expression filled with promises. They disappeared into the room, behind the closed door.

– Showoffs! Eleanor mumbled.

Janet and Bea were alone in the room.

– You can sleep on the bed if you want, Janet sighed. – Of course you can. It certainly is more than big enough.

A kind of relief shadowed her face, the face of Cathy in the mirror reflection.

– I would be honored to share your bed, Bea said, – but only as your equal, and you, Cathy of the Blue Flame is so high above me right now. Your master was correct. Apprentices and their like belong on the floor.

Janet wanted to argue, but cat (or alcohol) got her tongue.

Shouts of enjoyment echoed through the giant building. She heard them in their muted form. She devoured another gulp of wine. The room turned dark, or partly dark. Bea blew out the candles and quelled the torches in the water-filled buckets. The stench of ash faded through the open window.

Janet rested on her back on the bed.

– Grayson better not fuck with his charge tomorrow, she mumbled, half into sleep.

And then Bea's voice clear as cold spring water.

– He better not, or he will answer to the Lady of Vengeance chasing his tail, she declared.

The thunder drums and sensations of the vast plains outside haunted Janet's dreams. Black four-legged creatures paced the night, making a cold draft blow from the farthest corner. The old graveyard outside seemed different, more sinister, somehow. It imposed itself on Janet. And so did the featureless gray faces staring at her. The morning seemed to come faster than a blink. Janet opened her eyes. The room, everywhere around her, bathed in light.

Bea offered her a tray of delicious breakfast.

– Fresh from the kitchen, My Lady.

The sandwiches flowed into Janet's mouth. They melted on her tongue.

– It feels good, does it not? Bea said. – To let go?

– No, it does not! Janet replied empathically. – I tried that and it did not work. You know what happened.

– A minor mishap, Bea sniffed unconcerned. – You were entitled.

– You have such a casual… perspective on life, my good girl, Janet tipped her hat with a thoroughly solemn expression on her face, – I love that!

And she imagined that Bea actually blushed with pride.

The halls and hallways filled up with people, both guests and employees. It was a building seething with activity and anxious action, and it did not settle, but increased as the day turned to evening and night.

They walked around, drifted around during the day, doing the tour several times, the two and the guys. Excitement and the brittle, poignant mood struck the sorcerer and the mage in training and the guys both. Janet felt it all flow through her.

– I do not get you, she told Bea in a moment where both the irritation and her curiosity got the best of her.

– Me, My Lady? Your humble servant is not difficult to understand. Her ambitions are modest and her goal not far fetched. When tradition is served she will be free to follow her desires and achieve wonders.

They walked through a hallway, a bridge between one part of the building and the other. A haze caught their eyes where the daystar rays fell from the window ceiling in a small intersection hall.

– The entire building feels like a place of… of worship, Toby breathed, caught in the moment.

– That is because it is, My Lord, Bea said humbly. – It is an ancient burial ground and that is precisely why this one's clans raised this temple to their vanity here.

He was blushing, while pondering her words.

The girls poked him and teased him lightly before getting distracted by further wonders.

Eleanor walked with her head tilted for a while before nodding.

– Your servant is correct, she told Janet pointedly. – This is a cathedral raised on vanity's altar.

They walked outside. The bright daystar light hit them head on.
– And the entire place is a burial ground, she continued with a shiver in her voice.
Janet knew her friend to be correct. It was what she had felt since she arrived.
- Not just a burial ground, she said, frost in her voice, – one of sacrifice and slaughter. The deaths happened here, not far away.
Eleanor turned pale, as she grew aware of thc significance of the Blue Flame's words.
Janet spotted Illandra far out there, in the field. She moved in a strange manner. Her body language spoke to the young girl, somehow. Janet did not see anyone, but when she studied Illandra it looked like the sorcerer, the way she acted was surrounded by people. She moved her lips, smiled, communicated with what resembled nothing but open air.
And then, in the blink of an eye they appeared to approach and face each other.
– Well met, Janet, the voiceless voice hissed.
Janet did not voice a reply, but stood her ground. The apparition faded. Once again the woman walked alone in the far field.
Bea and Eleanor glanced at her. It made her smile. Everybody looked curious at her and clearly wanted an explanation, but she was not accommodating.
– Your clans have… big plans, have they not? She asked Bea casually.
– They have, My Lady, the other big girl replied unresistingly.
– I could have asked you to explain yourself further and in detail, Janet said, – but that is not really necessary, is it?
It was a rhetorical question. Bea stayed silent.
The trumpets sounded, very medieval and solemn, the first signal to herald the upcoming night's festivities. Bea straightened, brightening, a weak light returning to her eyes. Janet touched her cheek lightly, in an attempt to encourage her.
– You are practically shaking in apprehension, in abject *fright,* Janet said. – I would like to roast your entire family over open fire for doing this to you.
Bea jumped forward and embraced her, unable to speak, to voice her sick, sick gratitude.
They were drawn inside, with the other guests. It had become a warm and moist place to Janet, like a mouth. Maria showed up, practically from nowhere, curtseying before the sorcerer, waiting to be acknowledged. Janet felt an abrupt nausea grip her and present itself in her throat. She acknowledged the servant with an irritated shaking of her head and knew

well that her anger terrified the other girl.

– Refreshments are ready for My Lady and those accompanying her. If My Lady so desires, this girl will lead her to the modest afternoon dining hall.

– You may do so, Janet nodded, striving to keep her anger from being directed at the girl.

The afternoon dining area was in the opposite direction from the giant hall where the Festivities would begin in earnest later. Maria brought them to one of several minor halls, to an isolated table, a quiet corner in the busy and humming guest house. A bountiful display of food greeted them.

– A dinner before dinner, Toby murmured. – No wonder members of the «upper class» tend to be… chubby.

– You, sir are a laugh riot, Rosa chided him.

They delighted in picking and choosing from the generous variety of food put before them. The wine felt pleasant on buds, throat and stomach alike. Glasses met at the center of the table, accompanied by loud cheers. They drank again, and it felt more potent than less than a minute earlier.

Janet focused on Eleanor with large, lupine eyes.

– So, fellow magick-wielder, show me your worth.

Eleanor reddened under the powerful, penetrating stare. She pulled herself together, concentrating on breathing evenly. Her hands formed a globe in the air above her plate. She visibly strained herself, her fingers trembling slightly, the furrow on her forehead deep. The green vegetables on her plate stirred, one moment, two, before rising in the air, forming a circle fitting the perceived globe. The green shifted, blurring and glowing briefly, before returning to the plate.

Toby and Rosa watched with big eyes. Bea yawned unimpressed.

– Not bad, Janet acknowledged. – We may make a decent sorcerer of you yet.

The patronizing tone made Eleanor glare at her. Janet kept staring at the girl until she lowered her eyes. Janet smiled, her lips a thin, thin line.

They sat there for a while, relaxing, not making haste, smiling more, less tense as the afternoon and the meal continued. The knot in Janet's stomach loosened somewhat. The muscles stayed taut, hard to use. She rocked on her chair while devouring a heap of strawberries. Bea hardly spoke and only in something akin to a whisper.

She kept sipping wine. Janet watched how she turned ever more intoxicated. A comforting touch on the girl's cheek brought no visible comfort. There was more laughter, loose and light, but Bea did not laugh.

The afternoon passed and evening approached. Their «brief» meal ended. The bells chimed. The signal hit all cold bones and shimmering flesh. They made their way to the great hall.

Everything shimmered there, and burned. Janet of the Blue Flame nodded pleased to herself. She did so long before they found their designated seats with name and all, and before she realized that Bea did not have any.

It did surprise her… and then it did not.

The hall moved around her. Its every angle was hers to enjoy. She sat down and watched from behind as Bea placed herself behind her, as everybody watched as Beatrice Maximus Rosen behaved like the lowest of servants.

Maria placed herself behind Janet as well and waited for her to acknowledge her. Janet turned around.

– If the sorcerer will follow Maria, the girl will lead her to the preparation room.

– Lead on.

Janet rose and followed Maria. Bea trailed them both.

The preparation rooms were a glorified wardrobe section of the hall, really, located by the left and right side of the stage. Maria opened the door. Janet and Bea walked through it. Maria closed the door behind them. Silence suddenly surrounded them.

Sets of hood, robe and suit hung displayed on hooks on the right side of the room. The left side prominently featured a large mirror. A soft light shimmered from some undisclosed location in a manner that was quite striking.

– The houses Rosen and Maximus would be honored if the sorcerer would deign one of these worthy of wearing.

Janet studied them closer, tested them by touch only at first, before choosing one. It was wide and would fit outside her clothes. Janet handed it to Maria and the girl began fitting it on the big girl's body in a cautious but effective manner. Not long afterwards the sorcerer stood there transformed, no longer a young girl, but a creature drawn from the deepest cautionary tale. The smile felt strange on Janet's lips.

– With the sorcerer's permission I will now take the girl, Maria said.

She held up a chain for Janet to see. The Blue Flame nodded. Maria attached the chain to Bea's collar.

– The girl will now accompany Maria, Maria declared.

Bea did not say anything or react in any visible manner, but when Maria tugged the chain Bea followed her without protest.

The door closed behind them. Janet stood alone in the room, filling it to the brim, filling the realm in the mirror, breathing it all. The sorcerer smiled in the shadow under the hood.

She heard it from the distance, all the pretty words, saw Justin Rosen speak about «the initiation into precious adulthood» while his daughter and the other daughters and sons of both prominent and less prominent people knelt collared and leashed by his feet. It was not even hard. She hardly had to close her eyes. The entire spectacle made belch rise in her throat. It felt like a pregnancy.

The waves brought all good and bad things to her. She knew that Maria was on her way back long before she showed up in the door.

– Maria is known to be well versed in the arcane arts. She is trained from birth to aid sorcerers and will act as support for the Blue Flame during the Festivities, if that is Blue Flame's wish.

It was like Janet had surmised. The girl was raised to act as a servant of the truly powerful, not the likes of the Rosen and Maximus clans.

The warm, low-keyed feeling within Janet persisted.

– You will suffice, Janet stated, visibly indifferent.

A change came over the girl. She stepped into the sorcerer's shadow in earnest.

– Your mask, My Lady…

There was just the smallest suggestion of a movement, and she had directed Janet's attention to the leather cloth on the wall, a startling representation of the Horned God. Janet put it on. She turned towards the girl. Maria curtseyed deeply. Janet lingered a moment in order to study herself in the mirror. She did not truly need to, seeing herself fairly well through the servant's doe eyes, but her curiosity got the best of her, and suddenly she felt a little breathless as well. The Horned God, both the God and the Goddess of the Hunt had a long tradition in human life.

She followed the servant, returning to the great hall. It looked different, now, somehow, through her new eyes. The stylized horns sticking up from the mask pushed at her forehead. They became her ears. She heard the whispers, the excitement and apprehension through a strange, distorted quality. The mask, the mask was…

It was alive.

It was like with the knife and the bracelets Malone had given her. They had been forged with a piece of long dead sorcerers.

But this was different. Here the mind, or a semblance of it, had been engraved into the object as well. The voice was faint, but Janet heard it, heard it far more distinct than she heard other whispers, other spirits.

The stage revealed itself to her, through the currently narrow chinks she looked at the world. She was the last to arrive, as custom dictated. The other sorcerers nodded to her or ignored her. She returned the nod.

– It is a stage, you know, Illandra the Inlander told her casually. – The spectators gather us here and elsewhere, paying our dues, in the vain hope that it will give them control over us. Ignore them.

The buzz from the hall faded to insignificance in the young sorcerer's ears. Only the floating masks surrounding her looked real through her bewitched eyes.

She glanced down at the creatures kneeling before them. They hardly seemed real to her.

– They look so lost do they not? Illandra said, looking even more enigmatic to Janet. – You wonder if they are worthy of our attention at all.

Janet blinked. The masks were not faces, were not movable flesh, but they certainly looked the part, looked like they had become life-like features and flesh of those wearing them.

All of them, assisted by a personal servant began mixing potions. They were nine, nine sorcerers, nine servants and nine on the floor.

Illandra turned around, facing the crowd, creating a stir among them. They saw her, even though they did not. Janet, drawing breath certainly did.

– Behold the flower, she cried. – It opens wide, revealing its beauty. We have nine potential flowers with us tonight.

Both her voice and appearance had turned dark, changing the hall and the mood, creating one more of the prerequisites for the Festivities.

– We have gathered here to honor Samhain, she said, suddenly speaking softly. – On this night, this very hour he, the god of the underworld gathers to him the condemned, giving them one more shot at life.

The mere mention of the name brought a chill to the hall and to those gathered there. Janet felt something touch her, something unfathomable, alien. Even the incessant voice the mask brought to her awareness fell silent.

It was as if… as if it had turned afraid.

The mere mention of that name had done that.

Illandra turned towards the altar again. She placed the cup with potion on the floor in front of the boy chained before her. The other sorcerers repeated the act in front of their respective charge. Janet managed to follow the actions of her older and more experienced colleagues without being too clumsy, revealing too much of her inexperience. She had read in detail about the ceremony, but even though she could recall every detail about it at will, she still had trouble executing it all properly. Maria was there when needed, discreetly offering her aid. When Illandra spoke her brief spell and the others choired it with her, the youngster was half a heartbeat late. When the potions burst into flames the ninth did so notably later.

The nine leashed youths breathed in the smoke of the burning potion in front of them and coughed every time they succeeded in drawing breath.

Faces turned red and tears flooded their eyes.

– Yes, suffer, Illandra shouted. – Being born hurts.

Janet voiced it, repeated it soundlessly.

She studied the kneeling boys and girls. There was not so much fear there, as a kind of resigned and numb quality she recognized, the conviction that there was not anything one could do in order to affect one's own fate.

The smoke seemed to… stick to the chained youths. Every time they drew breath they pulled a concentrated dosage of it into themselves. Their agitation and writhing temporarily gained intensity, but then their body turned slack and their eyes dazed. They knelt there, hardly aware of what was happening anymore.

– Jezidan Matthews, do you want to be baptized? Illandra asked the boy. – Do you want to be a free and independent human being?

He strived with responding, opening his mouth several times without succeeding.

– I do, he gasped. – I DO!

Illandra bent down then and grabbed the cup of fire. She emptied a small part of its content in her palm. It kept burning there. Janet admired the casual way she handled it, as if she was making toast in the morning. The fire in her palm did not seem to bother her at all. The still burning cup, with its remains she handed to her aide.

She smeared the blazing content in her palm on the boy's forehead. The skin hissed and burned.

– So cold, he whimpered.

– You are now a mage, Jezidan Matthews, Illandra declared. – You are no longer forgotten and exist in the world, able to take the next step further on your Path.

He… swelled, Becoming right there, before everyone. His fingers fumbled a bit with the collar before he removed it with a simple pull. He rose and stepped down from the stage, met by jubilant members of his family.

Illandra stepped back. The next sorcerer stepped forward and began his recital, his liberation of the youth shivering in excitement and fear before him. Janet disconnected partly from it all, well aware that she was the last, that there were seven more before she was up.

But there was an itch, one she could not scratch and did not go away, as the ceremony, the «Festivities» progressed. She forced herself to stay in this place, keeping her thoughts and consciousness from drifting.

The second sorcerer was done and had «freed» his charge. It was Grayson's turn. Janet visualized him, as he stood two spots from Illandra, the indifferent visage of the old man. He did not move. Janet realized it well before the rest of the assembly did. There was slight unrest, but nothing pronounced. Grayson's charge either did not realize what was happening or he had fallen completely and forever into the stupor of his mind.

The seconds passed away. Janet pretty much knew the time frame. Hearts started beating faster. Grayson kept standing still, unmovable like a statue. One loud shout of despair sounded from the hall. A few more moments passed. Then the fourth sorcerer stepped forward. The moment - and the collared boy on the floor - was lost.

The fourth sorcerer did his chore, as if nothing ordinary had happened and then pulled back, but the fifth, Dasek looked like she was not going anywhere, and Janet knew she would not. The woman appeared much more like a spectator than a participant and she was clearly comfortable with that.

Janet felt a stirring, a rising growl inside. She moved discreetly, but without hiding her intention behind the line of sorcerers until she reached Illandra.

The soundless bell rang once again, and yet another collared youth slumped disowned on the floor. The girl released a tiny groan.

– What will happen to them? Janet asked Illandra, speaking low and fast.

The older sorcerer looked patronizingly at her.

– You know what will happen to them. One way or another they will be lost. Their former parents will not and can not acknowledge them and society will mostly shun them as well. Even if not everybody follows the old traditions anymore, old habits die hard. They belong to the sorcerers from now on.

– Not yet, Janet stated.

Illandra studied her with amusement in her cold eyes.

– Others can do what Dasek and Grayson refused to do.

Illandra looked very bemused at her.

– Is that not so? Janet persisted.

She was now very happy that she had read the lore thoroughly.

– That is so, but according to tradition one sorcerer can only do one extra candidate.

– Then I will do one and you, Illandra of the Bone People the other.

One heartbeat, two passed.

– Very well, but does the young sorcerer happen to know their names?

– She does not, but that is…

She had hardly raised a hand when Maria appeared by her side.

– We, the two of us request the names of the candidates, Janet informed her.

– I have them right here, My Lady, the servant replied.

She handed the youngest sorcerer a sheet. It was a very formal, elaborate description of the names and what had to be the entire family tree of everyone involved. Janet accepted it and held it up for Illandra to scan, before putting it away, knowing it would be useful later.

Grayson and Dasek's eyes were on her, on them, even though they appeared just as indifferent. That brought some modicum of satisfaction, made more of the sizzling and pleasant rage rise within the young sorcerer.

She held her breath while the ceremony proceeded. The other sorcerers did their chore. She released her breath.

Janet of the Blue Flame walked to the number three in the row.

– Velodor Azmedus, do you want to be baptized? She asked the boy. – Do you want to be a free and independent human being?

He fought with himself, with his desperate response, with hope beyond hope, opening his mouth countless times without succeeding. She waited patiently, but did nothing more to encourage him.

– I do, he gasped. – I DO!

She bent down and grabbed the cup of fire, putting the embers in her palm, surrendering the cup to Maria's trusted care and smeared the volcanic-like content of her palm on the boy's forehead.

– You are now a mage, Velodor Azmedus, she declared. – You are no longer forgotten and exist in the world, able to take the next step further on your Path.

He tore off his collar and rose. She knew he wanted to embrace her, to kneel down before her, but he did not. He fought off that impulse and stumbled down on the floor, where his suddenly ecstatic kin received him.

Illandra walked to the girl, repeating the ritual with her.

Then Janet walked to Bea. The big girl seemed even more lost to the world than the two almost-unfortunates had done.

– Beatrice Maximus Rosen, do you want to rise above your circumstances? Janet asked.

– I do, Bea replied, – thank you, great sorcerer for your boon.

An amused, nervous laughter rippled through the hall. A more or less shocked assembly waited for more.

It almost felt like an anti-climax when Janet bent down and grabbed the fire, as she made it twist and burn in her hand, as she practically slapped it on Bea's forehead, her free hand holding on to the cup.

– You are now the greatest of mages, Beatrice Maximus Rosen, she declared with a happy smile. – You are no longer forgotten and exist in the world, able to take the next jump further on your Path. Congratulations!

Bea removed the collar and practically jumped on her feet and kissed Janet on the lips, embracing her in the strongest of grips, while the loud, audible bell chimed. Janet felt how the mind cleared, how the fire rose within, returning from where it had been misplaced, an endless echo of her own, jubilant mood.

Chapter 12

They stepped down from the stage together. Bea held on to her and would not let go. The Rosen and Maximus clans were first in the «row» of happy faces. Bea embraced her father. He was not that much bigger than her. She squealed in joy.

She is not that tough, Janet thought.

He turned towards her, his blue eyes catching hers.

– You have our thanks, Janet, he said, deliberately personalizing it. – Our clans owe you.

– It was a pleasure... Justin, she responded casually.

She removed her mask and handed it to Maria. The servant gracefully accepted it.

The world once more flooded Janet's senses.

Their friends arrived, with further best wishes and embraces. Janet noticed how Bea stiffened when her father did not approve of her closeness with the commoners.

– Will you join us at our table, Janet? Justin offered, as they moved towards the various sections of the hall.

– Thank you, Justin, she replied, – I think I will!

The two girls waved with regret to their friends. Their friends waved back, carefree, even though Janet noticed Toby's toxic stare.

The banquet began. Bea led Janet to her seat, sharing the glory with her, back to being the enigmatic teenager Janet had first gotten to know. They were the natural center of the conversation. Janet found herself enjoying herself. All the bright lights did not blind her.

She scanned for Grayson and Dasek, but did not spot them and eventually allowed herself to relax somewhat. Bea raised her glass and Janet joined her. They toasted with each other.

– Cheers! Bea said softly with twinkle in her eyes. – Good cheers!

– Good cheers! Janet choked, attempting to swallow the catching in her throat.

Glasses met and parted. The two drank.

The taste lingered in Janet's mouth.

– C'mon, beautiful witch. Bea jumped on her feet. – Dance with me!

Janet obliged, reaching out a hand. Bea took it and pulled her up. They ran to the dance floor in a whirl of motion.

A tangible uplifted mood ruled in the hall and twice so between the two young women dancing tight and slow. They moved between the other couples and solitary dancers, ruling the floor. Everybody watched them with both badly concealed and open attention and desire.

Little Moon shone through one large window and Big Moon through the other, bathing the entire open space in silver shadow, playing on sweaty skin with the shimmering fire from the million candles.

Bea kissed Janet on the lips, a lingering, smothering kiss sending shockwaves through them both. She kissed her on the neck and on the lips again. Janet responded, suddenly just as passionate, just as eager. They both sighed content and in expectation of what they knew would come.

– You were so sexy up there, in that dreadful mask and that fantastic outfit, the now adult girl whispered in the Blue Flame's ear. – I could not take my eyes off you.

Janet hardly heard anything but her voice and the noise of her own breathing.

One dance ended, one in a row of thousands. Janet could not tell its number.

– I am thirsty, Bea declared.

So am I, Janet thought, unable to speak.

There were queues in spite of the numerous punch outlets. So busy with each other, the two of them did not care and almost lost their place several times.

– Look at them, Bea chuckled. – How they can not take their eyes off us, how they stare with envious eyes.

Janet did, and happiness surged through her being.

They reached the punchbowl. Bea filled two of the largest glasses to the brim. They drank.

– It is spiked, Beatrice Maximus Rosen giggled. – It always is.

They emptied the first glasses fast, without moving away from the bowl and filled them up anew.

A group approached them as they made their way out of the hall. Janet, through a slightly hazy vision easily recognized Velodor Azmedus and his clan.

The two young women and the other group stopped simultaneously, as if on cue. A man, an older man stepped forward.

– Greetings Janet of the Blue Flame, he said and bowed. – Greetings Beatrice Maximus Rosen.

– Greetings, Asalor Azmedus, Janet slurred.

Bea mumbled something incomprehensible but somewhat polite.

The older man grabbed Janet's hands, a startling breach of etiquette. She looked stunned at him.

– It is a great thing you did for us, he stated, he choked. – One that can not be underestimated.

She wanted to say something polite, casual, but ended up saying nothing.

– She is a Goddess, Bea declared. – One that has descended to the mortal plane to bring happiness and joy to us lower beings.

– Yes, she is, Velodor said with puppy eyes.

Janet strived to ignore him, making an effort to not look aloof.

– Others may not remember you with fondness, but we always will, Asalor, said. – Ask anything of us, now, or years, generations from now and it will be granted.

– I will consider the matter most carefully, Asalor Azmedus, Janet slurred.

Her happy smile blinded them, made them crouch before her person.

– Thank you so much for your kind words, Asalor Azmedus, Bea bowed. – We must take our leave, now. Be well!

– Be well, the man echoed.

They left. When they turned in the doorway they saw how he still watched them. They giggled and waved to him. He slowly raised his hand and returned the wave.

The silence of the reception hall greeted them. There were others there, but they hardly noticed them.

– He acknowledged, accepted the debt, Bea said. – They are yours, now, to do with as you please.

The words registered somewhat in Janet feverish mind, but did not really take hold.

She pushed the other at a pillar and began kissing and caressing and fondling her.

– My, oh, my, thou are so forward, madam, Bea breathed. – I love it so much!

They moved against each other, rubbed against the other as if there was no tomorrow. Janet moved her head constantly, sometimes mouth and eyes buried in soft skin, sometimes glimpsing the world beyond that lovely state of affairs.

She frowned, unable at first to understand why she was frowning.

Illandra stood right there, left of the pillar.

– You made a choice tonight, always remember that.

Illandra told her.

Janet did not think Bea could see or hear her, no matter where she turned her head.

Then brief thought and vision-like experience dwindled once again, as the two kept enjoying each other, each other's skin, scent and touch.

– Come, Bea whispered. – Come…

They moved up the stairs, as if floating. There was no sense of them moving. Only their closeness mattered, nothing else. They danced, hand holding hand down an unknown hallway, a foreign path they could not name.

The door before them had been placed ajar. Bea pushed it open and they stepped inside. This was the suite, the dwelling worthy of the heir to the Rosen and Maximus riches.

– This is not worthy of Cathy of the Blue Flame, Bea said hoarsely. – Thou are my goddess and I will place the world at thy feet.

Janet blushed, blushed hard and an even more powerful visceral reaction passed through her.

– It is adequate, she nodded, – yes, adequate.

They began moving before each other, undressing in slow, languishing moves, taking their time.

– We are sluts put on display, Bea called, – sluts performing for our master in the biggest, most prestigious pleasure dome in the realm.

– We are, Janet agreed. – Our master is strict, expecting the best possible performance.

Mirror images moved, every motion an echo of the other. Janet pulled the robe over her head, revealing nothing but more fabric, pushing the tip of her tongue between her lips, enticing the other. Bea unbuttoned her blouse, half revealing the already swelling breasts. Mirror images circled each other. They did not remove the fabric covering them. No hands touched it. It removed itself. They saw no hands, only clothing fading away on burning skin.

Janet bit her lip, giving up quickly, letting go of her lip, releasing a throaty sound. Bea stepped close. Suddenly they were close, touching again, and there was nothing between them.

Bea fondled Janet's breasts, squeezing the nipples. Janet shouted short and sharp.

– Lovely, lovely…

The bed revealed itself to them, suddenly, from nowhere. They knelt on it, had knelt on it forever, pushing against the other. Bea sucked on a nipple. Janet felt it, felt teeth and tongue and lips. She caressed the other's head. A forceful hand sought between thighs.

– Wet, wet, wet, Bea grinned.

Janet's loud moan filled both their ears, filled all the space between and around them. She grabbed Bea's hand and pulled it back out. Bea resisted. They wrestled a bit, neither giving ground. Then Janet pushed and pulled, and suddenly she had Bea stretched out on the bed, at her mercy, her hands

held behind her back and her feet locked in an unbreakable grip.
Bea gasped, in shock and awe.
– The Goddess is so strong.
– The Goddess' knight is impertinent, Cathy snapped.
She slapped the butt in front of her. Bea snorted in stark surprise. Janet slapped the butt again, slapped it hard, slapped it several times. Bea stopped resisting, the powerful body turning limp in Janet's hands and feet, a few tears falling from the wide open big eyes.
– That is so much better, Cathy grinned wickedly.
She held the arms with one hand and moved the other between wet thighs. It flowed like a river there. She let go of the hold she had of the body beneath her. The other young woman did not move.
Then she began moving, began writhing, as invasive hands made her move. One touch brought one sound, the next one completely different. Bea stretched her powerful body out in all its length. Janet pushed a hand at her groin. Bea pushed her groin at the hand.
She grabbed the hands in a sudden move and threw the other at her back, climbing on top of her. Janet let her, with badly concealed anticipation. Bea kissed her greedily on her lips, on her long since sore lips.
– The two women are so evenly matched, Bea declared. – This woman rather thought they would be.
Janet wanted to bit her lip, but was unable to do so. Her lips just kept moving, kept attempting in vain to connect. The loud, horny snort rocked them both. They began pushing against each other, letting go of any restraint. One level of restraint had faded long ago, another long before that and a thousand others they could no longer recall.
Hands clutched hands, hips pushed at hips. Lips devoured lips. One body turned, the constant touch never letting up. Both heads rested sideways on hips. They had their heads between each other's thighs, their mouths buried deep in the wet, wet hole flowing like a river.
– Such a tasty snack, Bea mumbled.
– SNACK, SNACK, SNACK! Janet shouted, practically screamed.
Hands clutched hands, hips pushed at hips again. Light blue fire burned around wrists. Bea shouted in pain and ecstasy, and Janet echoed her simultaneously, an immeasurable time span later. Movement turned faster, more brutal, losing all semblance of control. Wild, savage howls shook flesh, bone and walls, making the air itself shimmer and burn.
Bodies turned rigid. All sounds stopped. The larynx in their throat froze. They collapsed on the rumpled bed, their bodies slack like rag dolls, their breath still a loud wheeze in their beyond sensitive ears.

They relaxed in each other's arms, feeling how sleep came, sensing how this would be the only time tonight, yet content beyond words.

– … love my goddess, Bea mumbled, – love, love, love…

Janet caressed her cheek, kissed her brow, the burn on the forehead, blinking, blinking slow. Bea yawned, a beyond happy smile brightening her face. Shadows overwhelmed Janet. She let them. The dancing flames of the torches and candles faded in her vision. She let them, surrendering with a smile on her face. Bea slept. Janet noticed that as an afterthought, just before she joined her lover. The happy smile haunted them into the depths of their dreams.

She opened her eyes not that many hours later, wide awake. Bea already was. She rested her head on her palm and her elbow on the bed, studying Janet with her huge, twinkling eyes.

– Hi, Bea said.

– Hi, yourself…

They kissed, their lips lingering, playing with each other's tongue.

Both entangled and left the bed simultaneously. They walked towards the shower hand in hand. The bathroom was big, far bigger than in Janet's room. They stepped into the shower. Bea turned on the water. It hit and rinsed them from two different hoses. They began soaping each other in.

– It was good, was it not? Bea stated.

– It was good, Janet agreed.

Bea's hand on her cheek softened the rigid expression on her face.

– The Blue Flame has things on her mind. That is alright. Know that her lover, her consort supports that, like everything else she might decide.

The catching in Janet's throat grew so hard that there was no way she could voice her response.

They washed each other, using soft, pleasant cloths and hands and teasing fingers. Bea smiled, a slight warning before she once more began getting pushy.

– I love it when you spank me. Will you spank me, sweet witch?

– Sure, Janet snorted. – Why not? You are a naughty bitch very deserving of punishment.

She grabbed the other big girl and pushed her front at the wall. Then, without hesitation she smacked her on the butt, smacked her hard. Bea gasped. Another followed, even harder. Janet did not hold back. Tears jumped from Bea's eyes, joining with the hard-hitting water from the hoses. Hands pushed at the wall moved like flickering candles in the shadows.

The punishment continued unrelenting. Bea turned rigid briefly, but then she gave up fighting or resisting entirely and just stood there, the sobs reaching Janet's ever more feverish mind.

With the wicked grin in place her hand began wander on the inflamed skin before her.

– Now, let us see…

She practically slapped several of her fingers at the hot and wet place between Bea's thighs. Bea's mouth stayed open, unable to keep the water from flowing into it.

Janet kissed her in the neck, biting it just a little, enough to taste blood. The sensation caught her off guard, making her muscles turn to rubber. She growled in the other's ear.

– Naughty bitch, she mumbled, – naughty bitch, naughty bitch…

Bea turned around, the grin very much present. The mutual caressing and fondling began, quickly turning eager and intense. Something both a shout and a moan rose from both open mouths. Weak legs gave way and they fell hard on the tiled floor. Hands kept reaching for hot skin, kept moving on its own accord. Lips, tongues and limbs writhed and pushed against each other. Dazed eyes focused both close and distant.

They had to clean themselves again. A timeless time of touches later they stood on the bathroom floor and dried each other, enjoying each other's closeness and lingering pleasure.

– Tell me, sweet witch, what would you have done if yet another unfortunate trainee had needed saving from a cruel sorcerer?

– I would have saved the unfortunate trainee, of course, Janet snorted, – and kept Beatrice Maximus Rosen as a pet. She is a cute pet.

Bea bowed her head, her cheeks turning red in even more excitement.

– She is your cute pet, My Queen…

Quiet hallways moved around them as they moved through them. Most of the revelers had withdrawn from the celebration by now, even though the two night birds encountered the occasional stragglers.

The door in front of them stood ajar. To Janet it seemed wide open. She and her companion walked inside.

Illandra sat in the chair by the bed. She had not undressed. Her dark eyes burned Janet.

– I suspected that the Blue Flame and I had more to talk about, she said.

– The Blue Flame suspected that as well, Janet said dryly.

– So, what brings my young colleague here on this fine night?

– I want to charge the sorcerers Grayson and Dasek with grave misconduct before a council of sorcerers.

– You will not get anywhere with it, the older woman pointed out instantly.

– I know, Janet said. – I just want to make my displeasure known, want it to be on *record.*

Illandra kept her face impassive, as she looked closer at the seemingly calm young woman in front of her.

– Then I must ask why you are involving me in this. I must commend you. It is an interesting move, but why me?

There was a draft, a chill, a warm, warm breath of air.

– The Bone People have an abundance of invisible birth «tattoos» on their face. I could not see yours at first, but then I saw them, and found that my suspicions about you were correct: they are almost identical to mine. You are Illandra Caldwell of the clan Josbari of the Bone People, my father's mother.

Now, Illandra did shake, just a little. There was a frown, a very visible frown.

Janet's own tattoos showed, or at least were glimpsed. A little focus on the young sorcerer's part was all it took.

– I am afraid, poignant as that is, it is not sufficient in this case. I can not involve myself directly, at least not yet. According to the laws of the People you are not yet an adult and…

– Yes, I am! Janet said empathically, – and I am ready, ready to face my ancestors.

Illandra raised a brow.

– Okay, then, I suspect you have actually thought of everything, but then you also know that your lovely companion will not be able to accompany you, one yet not accepted by the ancestors to such a gathering.

– I know and I accept that. I put myself in your hands, grandmother.

Illandra rose, chuckling darkly.

– You are such a sly bitch. It pleases me that you are more like me than you are your dumb father.

Janet fought back the anger rising in her sore throat, knowing that Illandra had deliberately provoked her and could read her like an open book.

– Oh, well, you should say goodbye to your companion then. The two of you will never meet again.

– I will, Janet said respectfully. – Thank you, grandmother.

She turned towards Bea and touched her jaw.

– Will you be well?

– I will! Bea replied, somewhat calm and fairly undisturbed, not fuming too much over the fact that she had been practically ignored since they entered the room. – But will you?

– Trust me? Janet said.

– I trust you, Bea said. – And I know this is important to you, and I am looking *so* much forward to help you in your endeavor when the time goes.

A warm trickle flowed inside Janet.

– Wait for me, then.

– I will wait for you.

All three left the room. Two went left in the hallway and the third went right.

Two walked down the empty hallways, down the stairs where no people roamed.

– Your mother hid you from us, Illandra said. – Her magick is strong. We could find no trace of you, not until Malone had made you a sorcerer and you had earned your own place in the world.

– My mother was wise.

– You do not instantly bow down to authority, Illandra commented. – That makes me proud.

Janet felt good about that acknowledgment, no matter how hard she strived to mask her feelings.

– But do not forget that even the hardest nut is soft within its shell.

– There is very little chance of me forgetting that, thank you, the girl flared.

– You are understandably upset, Illandra said.

They walked in silence. Janet still heard the whispers. They entered the reception area. The whispers picked up. She imagined she saw wicked grins form and dissolve in the air. Waves moved around them. She had a sense of herself and the older woman as they purposely walked towards the entrance and left the building, the big, big shrine surrounding them.

Illandra studied her. Janet sensed that easily. She hardly had to make an effort in order to sense it. After merely a few steps outside her sense of being watched multiplied. It felt like a thousand needles pricked her skin, but she did not bleed. They entered the field, crossing it diagonally towards both a distinct and fleeting spot at its center. Illandra turned and so did Janet, until they stood face to face in the swaying tall grass.

Deep eyes met and held. Silence prevailed between them. Illandra studied her. Janet waited. She wanted very much to say something, anything, but held her tongue.

– Welcome, young maiden of the Bone People, Illandra cried, – to this place of your ancestors.

A shiver passed through Janet.

– Thank you, mother of my father, she replied formally.

– Is it your intention to become an adult, to know where all bones are buried?

– It is! Janet confirmed.

The whispers rose to a choir. The night turned even a bit darker. The light from the sky and from the modern structure not that far away vanished. The tall grass faded away. The surroundings changed, transformed and Janet realized startled that they were not in the same place anymore.

She wanted to ask the older woman more questions, wanted to gawk in her presence, but masked her feelings carefully.

– Yes, I can do this that easily, Illandra confirmed, – under certain circumstances.

And Janet felt chastised.

She sensed the wall, the cave rising around them.

She knew that the torches burned and that people approached before she actually saw them.

First there was the field, then there was nothing, then there was the cave and the gathering of people with painted faces, the assembly forming a circle around Illandra and Janet.

– This girl of our tribe has become before us seeking Confirmation, Illandra confirmed.

– She is not of our tribe, a man stated.

There was a pause, one, two, three heartbeats. Everybody stared at the girl. Janet did not say anything.

– She is, Illandra insisted. – Surely you recognize her tattoos?

– The question is moot, a woman with a face painted white said. – She has not completed the Offering.

– Like father, like daughter, the man snorted.

Illandra opened her mouth to speak. Janet stopped her with a raised hand and index finger. Illandra stepped back.

– I have! Janet stated, aggression audible in her voice.

Everybody stared at her.

– I killed my son and his sire, or at the very least caused their deaths.

She waited and stared at the man and woman facing her. She grinned wolfishly when they held their tongue.

– That is correct, she chuckled. – I may not have killed my mate, but I sent him to the Kal Chek, the Ascension, which amounts to the same thing. He may not be dead, but he is clearly lost to this world.

They turned, as if to leave.

– I demand a ruling, she growled. – It is my right. Your precious laws say so.

She spat the last sentence, as if something vile crossed her lips. The elders froze. They glanced at Illandra. She seemed completely indifferent. They exchanged a few words. It was in the ancient tongue. Janet did not understand it.

They turned back to her.
– The blood of your brood and your mate are indeed on your hands, the man declared. – The ancestors accept your Offering, Janet of the Blue Flame and the Bone People and are ready to grant you Confirmation.
The burning heat warmed Janet's blood.
The man and the woman walked to her, stopped in front of her.
– Undress, the man ordered her. – Stand nude before your betters.
His potent will sent shivers into Janet's mind. She obeyed instantly. When she spoke it was as if her voice did not belong to her anymore.
– I wear my father and grandmother and ancestor's tribal markings and I have grown my own. I put myself in your hands, my tribe.
They fondled her with cruel, invasive hands. She felt them touch her mind with their vile thoughts.
– She is a healthy and sturdy mare, the woman cackled. – She will bring us many and fierce children.
Janet shook her head, or attempted to, but failed, defiance denied her.
– Dance, insolent girl, dance your blood hot and strong.
She felt it, felt it coming before it began. Drums began beating, instantly stirring her mind, each beat rocking her, rocking her hard. She began swaying, her feet moving slowly up and down, hitting the ground in an even, potent rhythm. It had begun and could not be stopped. She let it proceed.
Then her feet hammered the ground, and there was no transference, no sense of time from one moment to the next.
Dance, dance, dance the chant repeated in her mind, and she obeyed its irresistible call. There was a big campfire and she circled it, facing it, turned away from it, from the dancing flame. Between blinks of eyes it turned light blue, dark blue and loud gasps reached her from her surroundings. Loud, euphoric laughter erupted from her open mouth. She danced harder, her breasts jumping up and down. Skin drawn tight on hard muscles shone in the golden and blue light.
The drums picked up pace, she danced faster. The drums slowed down their pace, she danced slower, like a puppet. The spirits, both corporal and not around her… entered her, filled her up. She felt bloated, ready to pop.
The choir pushed at her inside, made her burst, her walls cracking in a million pieces. The drums stopped abruptly. She gasped and fell to her knees, remaining there, heaving for breath.
Illandra towered above her. The older woman's lips moved, but there was no sound. Janet knew she was speaking, that she was casting spells, but there was no sound. Illandra spoke the silent tongue of the beyond ancient ancestors.

Janet moved her lips as well, speaking aloud, startled realizing that she echoed the other's words.

– Do you swear to serve us with all your power and everything you are? Illandra asked in English.

– I swear to serve thc tribe with all my power and everything I am, Janet stated.

A shiver passed through her, a triumphant grin shadowed her face, as she realized, along with everyone present what had just transpired.

– Present your hands! Illandra bade her.

With the defiant grin in place Janet obeyed. She stretched her hands out in front of her, displaying them to her kin. Illandra grabbed them, hard, sending waves of pain through the young sorcerer. Cold sweat broke on Janet's forehead. She stared with burning eyes up at her father's mother.

Illandra produced a tiny knife from her pocket. She made two small incisions into each wrist. And then Janet felt true pain again. It surged through her body in inverted waves. She screamed and rolled her hands into fists. Blood red like fire, like blue flame merely flowing at first, burst into the air as straight and curved lines, splashing Illandra and everyone standing close. It burned and hissed whatever surface it struck and had contact with. Janet's tattoos, her usually invisible birthmarks appeared in full. A hole opened up in the very air. Janet stared straight at Bea, into the room where the two of them had spent the earlier part of the night. Bea stared at her, absolutely stunned, frozen in place. Janet reached out a hand to her. Something dawned on Bea and she started charging forward. There was a loud crack and the nascent, temporary portal closed.

Silence reigned. Illandra, after a brief hesitation put a hand at her granddaughter's forehead.

– You are now an adult, Janet of the Blue Flame and the Bone People. Rise and take your place in your tribe as our equal.

When she spoke, when the words left the space between her lips other, incomprehensible syllables accompanied them, and even as Janet frowned, even more excitement ravaged her.

Illandra took one step back and reached out a hand. Janet rejected it. The tattoos faded back into obscurity. She dried the blood from her lips and rose without aid. The older woman's hand fell. Janet picked up her clothes and dressed. Her wounds kept burning as if they were actually burning. She imagined she saw flames.

– You killed my father, or made him kill himself, which amounts to thc same thing, she told them with her pointed stare. – Unyielding tradition supported by its unyielding servants destroyed him and my mother. That will never happen to me.

The wall, the entire cave-like surroundings and the ancestors faded away. Only she and Illandra remained.

Silence and darkness once more ruled the night. The stars in the sky and light from the giant structure reappeared. The wind had stopped blowing and the tall grass was no longer swaying.

She walked to Illandra and bowed.

– Thank you, grandmother, for repaying the first part of the debt you owe.

Illandra chuckled.

– You are everything your great grandfather told me you would be, she said. – I suspect, if anything he was not quite accurate. You are clearly far more than we dared hope for. It was and will be a pleasure, grown maiden.

Janet turned and walked away.

She knew Illandra did not follow her, that the older sorcerer did not move and remained in the field, but it seemed like she was close, that she walked by Janet's side and always would.

The return to the shrine seemed short, like a flash in a pan. The reception area stayed empty of flesh and blood. One blink and she caught all the Wasteland stares. One more blink and they were all gone. She still felt their presence.

Bea brightened visibly when Janet walked into the room where they had spent the night together and rushed into her arms. The sultry kiss made Janet instantly breathless.

– How was it? Bea asked in her childish voice. – You kicked ass, I trust?

– I kicked ass, Janet responded. – You bet I did!

– I knew you did, Bea bristled. – I felt it and…

– You *felt* it???

– I did, Bea nodded with her big, big eyes, – and then…

She held up an index finger and rushed to the bed.

– Then I saw you and wanted to go to you, but you disappeared before I could reach you.

– And then? Janet sighed.

Bea made a sweep over the bed with her hand, and it… turned transparent for a moment, and there was a display of energy. Janet turned cold, turned warm.

She squinted her eyes slightly, and then she easily saw it, something very distinct and easily recognizable. It was as if there was a hole in the air… a leak.

– You made this, did you not? Bea said excited.

– I guess I did, Janet admitted, both embarrassed and thrilled. – I did not

mean to. I thought about you and it sort of got away from me.
– You made a scratch in the fabric of reality without meaning to? Bea shook her head in amazement. – You made a fucking hole leading to the Wasteland without consciously willing it?
Suddenly she was right there, in front of Janet, close to Janet again.
– That is *fantastic!*
She grabbed Janet's head and kissed her on the lips. Janet found herself responding heartily.
They fondled each other with increasing fervor while moving towards the large bed, where the Wasteland shadow was visible to them both. Chuckles rose and met, like their bodies, as they undressed each other. A small frown manifested on Janet's brow.
– But should we not fix it?
– Do not bother. Let *them* deal with it…
Dark giggles rose and met, like their puckered lips. Sounds, ghostly wails and distant howls reached them. Touching turned more intense again. Gasps echoed in the void.
– You are so sweet, Bea whispered. – Such a beautiful doll…
Hands squeezed Janet's butt, bringing on more pleasant sensations.
– Use your powers, Bea whispered. – Bathe me in your kindness.
Janet hesitated a bit, before getting on with it. She had to make several attempts. Focusing proved difficult. She rubbed Bea's forehead.
– I do not want to hurt you.
– You will not hurt me, Bea snorted. – I am made of sturdier stuff than most people, remember?
The waves flowed from Janet's hands, from her very body, from the tongue probing her lover's skin. Bea shouted short and sharp, a delighted smile cracking her face.
– That is it. That is it, lovely, lovely, lovely, lovely mighty witch.
Bea grabbed her head and pulled her close, and when their tongues touched this time, a beyond pleasant shock shot through them both.
Janet hardly recalled anything beyond that.
There were flashes of light long before the night ended and flashes of dark long before the day came to an end.
The airship floated slowly through the sky. The two of them stood on deck and looked down at the distant ground. There were only the two of them holding hands, looking at the shadows of the clouds on the land below. Only in glimpses were the guys and the rest of the passengers present.
During learning the next day they sat in the yard, still hardly seeing the world around them.

– What are you thinking? Bea asked.
– That it feels strange returning here, to a somewhat ordinary life, Janet mused.
– You are right, Bea shrugged. – It does not really matter. It is immaterial to our true life beyond the veil.
They kissed, kissed yet again.
– Do they come up for air at all? Someone wondered somewhere.
That brought more grins, more exchanges of long, deep and pleasant perusals. Those huge eyes hardly closed when their attention was at each other and that felt like all the time.
They rejoined the guys eventually, when the most powerful infatuation had taken a backseat to a lingering, prevailing passion. Hands kept seeking hands, lips kept seeking lips.
Janet of the Blue Flame and her companion and friends walk through the Auburn streets. They look around them with bright eyes, enjoying every moment, every step. Janet knows Joan is somewhere behind them, but right now she does not care. The moment is with her and the moment does not let go.
Toby declaimed with a loud voice, bringing hearty laughter from those walking with him:

Now
Now, the evening begins
In the heart of life
People meet
On the edge of the night
Celebrating life
In all its forms
We are human beings
We are forgotten fire
We are the essence
Of what was lost
Of what is

Bea kissed him on the cheek.
– You stir my blood, good sire, stir it to no end.
They enjoyed each other's company on Tenrec, a coffee shop in the northern point of the city and the Island. Coffee beans dissolved in hot water found its way down their throats, along with tasty cakes containing chocolate and marihuana.
– It is happening, Eleanor giggled. – I can feel it.
Rosa was the only one smoking it. The sweet scent lingered in the others'

nostrils. Frances coughed and kept coughing.

– You do not have to smoke it, you know, she pointed out the obvious to her friend. – Even if we have to put more in our cake or in our dinner it is still inexpensive.

– I enjoy smoking it, Rosa shrugged.

– What do you think? Bea asked Janet.

– It is quite mild compared to the… stuff I am used to, Janet replied with very little chagrin in her voice. – But I still enjoy its mellow quality.

It made it easy to laugh. The giggles rose unresisting from her throat. She floated away on a mellow cloud.

– You want strong? Eleanor asked, a little pointed.

– Well… yes, Janet nodded.

Everybody slowly turned their attention in the same direction.

Eleanor revealed quite a few pieces of paper with a purple spot at its center resting in her palms. Gasps rose from everybody gathered around the table.

– You have got Deep Purple drops? Toby exclaimed incredulous.

– You better believe it! Eleanor said, hardly able to contain her pride.

– But the seeds only grow…

– On the north islands. Yes, until recently that was true, but it no longer is. I do not know if this is a mutation or if something else has happened, but they have spread to the mainland and are now far more available, or will be soon, when the secret is out.

She rose with a wicked grin.

– Stick out your tongue, seekers.

They did, eager like dogs in heat. She put two pieces of paper on each tongue.

– One drop is enough, she hummed. – Two drops are better and three will not harm you.

Janet felt the tiny pinprick taste on her tongue. She pulled her protruded flesh back inside, flooding it in spittle and swallowed the paper with the spot of purple fluid.

They kept eating cake and smoking weed.

– I do not feel different, Frances mused.

– It takes almost two hours for it to start working, Toby said.

– It has been so helpful to me, Eleanor said passionately, – opening up so much within. Even if there comes a day when I will not need it anymore, I will keep using it.

– I always paint better and more after I have used it, Rosa said with a dreamy expression in her eyes. – We in the art community have been granted special consideration by the Deep Purple guild for years. I have always seen them as pricks, though. It does not displease me that they have lost their advantage.

The smoke sizzled in the air. It hissed when Rosa blew it from her mouth. Candles flickered in the wind of the quiet room. It had turned dark outside.

– Time flies so slow, Frances complained, – so very slow.

– Nothing is happening, Bea cried. – Why is not anything happening?

She looked at her watch for the tenth time in less than a minute. At least that was what it felt like to Janet, who was watching her.

– This joint lasts forever, Rosa said puzzled.

Then, when she blew the smoke, there was a whooshing sound. Janet, taking one glance at the candles realized that they were *flickering*. The shadows cast by the candles moved fast like lightning on the floor, on the far, far walls. Frances' giggle sounded like dark, dark laughter.

They ran through the street, through the night slow as turtles.

– The colors, Rosa giggled. – The colors are fucking *floating*.

They had chocolate, real chocolate and it felt like they had never had chocolate before. Janet tasted it, like she had never tasted it before. Every tiny sensation seemed different.

– I cast a spell, she shouted. – One of night and fire, unbinding the illusion of the world, opening wiiiide the eyes of the world.

Her voice distorted itself, shaking her surroundings. And the air shook, truly shook, at least to her senses.

– Careful there, sorcerer, Toby shouted carefree.

His laughter had never sounded so… full. She blew him a kiss.

– Perception is reality, Bea mumbled and mumbled and mumbled.

Colors mixed and split, into an unrelenting pattern constantly changing.

Janet gasped and stopped, bending over and something seemed to be slipping from her open mouth, as if it was being born.

– Look at it, up there, Frances marveled. – The fucking Milky Way Galaxy.

– Hera's milk, Eleanor mused, – the fucking *Ocean* of Mankind.

Up there, Janet thought. Down here. I am up there, up there, up

She lost the thread.

They entered an unknown place, a huuuge apartment. The slamming of the door seemed to last forever.

– This is it, Bea chuckled. – Daddy's fucking present to moi, my gift for entering adulthood.

– It is so biiig, Toby said slowly.

Slow-ly, Janet thought. Slow-ly.

– It belongs to us all, Bea choked, moved beyond reason.

All all all.

Black was the sky, one brief moment, before it turned into the brightest of skies.

– The Universe, Rosa muttered. – That was one universe. And then, with a snap of my fingers it is No More. Then it is me, a tiny part of the giant universe I have become.

– Fast, fast is the carol tree, someone mumbled.

Janet could never, ever tell who.

They sat in the big chairs, swinging round and round and round, falling, falling into the deep of those vast worlds. Janet and Bea rested in each other's arms, and then everybody else was there as well. They touched and caressed and fondled body and mind, and it felt so good, good, good.

– Good, good, good, Janet mumbled, mumbled, mumbled.

They danced, danced to the music coming from everywhere and nowhere.

Turning, turning, turning in the circle dance.

The Milky Way Galaxy was down there, with them. They were swimming its pleasant currents, drifting aimlessly in its warm, warm water.

A chill colder than any ice spread from Janet's spine to her flesh, to her very hair and toes.

And then they were riding the fast onslaught train and all impressions faded, all sensations hitting them simultaneously, and Janet could not fathom how she could bear it.

– This is it, Eleanor gasped elated, – the ten minutes of eternity scaring the living bear shit out of those afraid of the world.

Everything… assaulted them, and no matter how hard they tried, they could not close their eyes to it, could not avoid its beyond brutal currents. Their existence turned into one single unending gasp.

– Everything, Bea shouted. – I am EVERYTHING.

Every angle, every viewpoint ever experienced. Janet gasped and could not stop gasping.

And then they were falling, rising slowly into the pleasant afterglow of the ride.

And they forgot, and they kept remembering everything they slowly forgot.

Their bodies were thrown like garments across furniture and carpets and floors, and the big, big bed embracing them where skin touched and kept touching.

They wandered forever through the pale darkness.

Their spirits kept soaring infinite treks.

Chapter 13

The sound of clashing wands echoed through the terrain. The two tall and big females went at each other with something strongly resembling hostility.

All the others, who had also been sparring with each other stopped and watched and stared.

Bea had found the wands after breakfast the next morning, a quiet, exalted morning, a breakfast of a thousand tastes. Each new flavor brought further enjoyment and delight.

– This is great, Toby stated. – This is such a great meal.

– It is an exotic dish, Bea shrugged. – You guys are just not used to those.

– But each piece brings multiple flavors, Eleanor said.

– That is what good food does, Bea said. – It brings variety and change to our lives.

Janet looked lovesick at her. The two of them grabbed and held hands.

They had all set out south, to the terrain surrounding Esteben the Mountain, its vast plains.

The daystar burned behind the small continent of people. Little Moon, with its strangely powerful and eerie shine glowed in front of them, creating a strange shimmer in the air. Janet felt it almost like something physical in her gut.

They reached the clearing, the fighting circle in the field, one distinctly marked after centuries of use, just as the daystar passed behind the mountain and everything surrounding them was cast in Shadow, and the shimmer turned even more eerie.

– We did a few tryouts before you returned, Bea told Janet, – but it never amounted to much. I am a lousy teacher and my skills surpassed the others with a considerable margin. I rather expect you will offer better resistance.

– I am confident that that is a safe bet, Janet responded brightly.

– I imagine you do…

She pulled a collar from her jacket. Janet instantly understood its purpose.

– But first we need to neutralize those pesky powers of yours, even their subconscious use, or you will quickly make mincemeat of me and the value of our exercise will be quite negligible.

– You think of everything, do you not? Janet said, the subtext of anger noticeable in her voice.

– I try.

She slipped the collar around Janet's neck and gave her a gentle, comforting kiss.

Janet noticed it quickly, the way the collar worked, dampening, diminishing the outpour of waves from her body, effectively crippling her. Her knuckles whitened around the wand.

– You are trying to goad me, are you not, to make me angry? She smiled brightly again. – You are such a sweet, conceited bitch…

She made a few swings, a few tryouts, reaching for murky memories, into a past she could not remember clearly. It surprised her how accessible everything was.

Bea picked up her wand and walked into the fighting circle, where a waterfall of both sweat and blood had been spilled during the years.

They rushed at each other. Their wands made contact with a loud CRACK. Everybody present jumped in their tracks.

– You are a bit rusty, I guess, Bea cried.

– It is just like swimming or riding a bike, Janet cried back.

Ducking and avoiding a hard swing did indeed feel easy. She countered with a brutal swing of her own.

It… returned to her, if it could be said to have been gone at all. Her body remembered and her mind caught up quickly.

She blocked an attack, but did not counterstrike, did not leave herself open for the trap Bea had prepared for her. The grin felt good on her lips. She stepped aside and then she struck out, hitting Bea on her mouth. Blood flowed into the hot air.

Bea responded in anger and hit Janet on the side of the head with a somewhat ineffective, but still hard strike. Both stood there facing each other, shaking their heads, attempting to clear their vision.

Janet's instinct was to use her powers. When she was unable to do that, it disrupted her concentration, leaving her open for attack. And then there were the flashes of memory assaulting her, interfering even more with her defense and offense.

She focused. The voice of her teacher, her teachers became her voice. She had fought the man with the wand on one level as well, since he, like her was able to move through the air.

Bea stayed focused on her. Janet sensed her frustration. She was not used to striving in order to win. It had always come easy to her.

They kept going at each other. Sometimes, when the wands collided instead of touching, there was a crack of thunder. After a few minutes they were both bleeding from both mouth and nostrils, and had several lacerations and swellings on face and body.

Bea intensified her attack. Janet caught it in glimpses, how her eyes narrowed like slits and her abused mouth turned into a thin, thin line. The wand hammered her opponent's defenses. Janet's instinct was to jump back, to retreat, but she stood her ground. She struck out with her wand. There was a loud crack. Bea staggered backwards. Janet pressed her advantage. Bea stopped with a stubborn expression frozen on her faze. She swung her wand. Janet avoided it and struck her friend and opponent in her midsection. Bea doubled over. Janet struck her neck. Bea went down. Janet struck her again. Bea stopped moving.

Janet stood there, heaving for breath, with pride coursing through her. She removed the collar and felt the active part of her power return. It swelled within her.

Bea groaned, slowly, slowly regaining consciousness, fighting to rise, leaving the wand on the ground, acknowledging her defeat, signaling it in countless small and big ways.

The others approached, visibly awestruck.

– That was… amazing, Rosa said, looking at them both.

Eleanor looked at Janet, a fixed, sullen stare.

– How could you do it? Bea has been a seemingly inaccessible reach above the rest of us, totally unbeatable.

Bea looked at her, at them, at them all. She spoke calmly, remarkably clear through her swollen mouth.

– She learned the hard way and so shall we all.

She bent down and picked up her wand.

– Now, you, she told them. – You will go at each other as if you were enemies and vanquish your opponent. Then, children, My Lady and I might teach you some moves.

Cracks and blood and cries of pain and triumph decorated the vast field, resonating in the air above it. Eleanor and Toby fought, and Rosa and Frances.

– Look at them, Bea said to her lover. – Look at them *go*.

Then she giggled darkly.

Janet saw blood flow, flow like the blue flame itself.

– The Deep Purple is still affecting me. Bea's giggle took on a hysterical quality. – It is weaving my vision and my thoughts.

Janet spotted the waves in the air without trying. She watched as Eleanor struck Toby, as her wand left its imprint on the very air it moved through. She struck him again and again, until he stopped moving by her feet

Frances overwhelmed Rosa, made her fall unconscious to the ground.

– Do as we do, Janet instructed them later. – Move as we move.

The two lovers moved and the others did their best to imitate and emulate them. One step forward, one step back, two steps forward, a thrust with the wand.

– The enemy is in front of you, Bea cried, clearly inspired. – Attack until he, she or it no longer moves.

Her words stirred something within them. They started charging the invisible target in front of them with something at least resembling fierce movement.

The fast expenditure of power tired them quickly. They stopped and glanced at the two instructors.

– Do it again, Janet commanded. – Do not hold back!

They obeyed, her directions penetrating deep within them. Janet sensed it, sensed how her words made them increase their efforts even further.

– Again, she snapped. – *Again!*

The word echoed across the field, recast from the mountain.

Big Moon rose, well before the daystar set in the western horizon, slowly turning on its glow as the sky turned dark, and both fairly close celestial objects did their joint dance on the night sky.

They set the long course home, bathing in the shine from Little Moon slowly changing to silver and Big Moon with its pale but distinct colors and the dancing flame of the torches and ghostly gaslight they passed. The walk seemed endless, until Bea's cozy apartment welcomed them.

– My home is your home, she told them all, not just Janet, making that very clear, walking to each in turn and grabbing their hands. – We are bound from now on, beyond death and the Wasteland.

Her oath touched them, moving and shaking their insides.

She found glasses and a bottle of red wine.

– Drink the blood, she breathed. – Feed on its vast fragrant.

They had a toast, and they drank, drank deep.

– It hurts, Frances complained. – It hurts even when I do not breathe.

And the laughter made their sore and bruised skin hurt even more.

The alcohol numbed them, numbed the pain. Janet felt herself floating, floating away on a nice cloud until she found herself writhing with the other warm, warm bodies on the big, big bed, falling into the pleasant haze of sleep.

– Kiss me, Bea implored her. – Please, kiss me.

Eleanor rode Toby. Frances and Rosa were enticing him, spurring him on from both sides somewhere else on the vast plain the bed had become. The kissing hurt at first, but as the pleasure intensified it no longer mattered.

Janet found herself writhing on the soft bed, surrounded by soft and enticing bodies. She slept, but was still awake. The two moons made their dance in the sky. Big Moon turned red and transformed the sky and landscape below. She found herself in unfamiliar streets, bathing in the blood-red air. When she looked down on her hands she saw that she held a sword and that both it and she were covered in blood.

The dream seemed endless and she was tempted to believe it was not a dream, but that she was actually experiencing all this right now, these surroundings of red haze and indistinct impressions.

It was later in the night. She woke up and walked to the window and stared into the city streets. Big Moon hung full in the sky, but it was not red.

She stood there, not noticing the passing of time, studying the streets below. Sounds reached her from afar. The images and sensations from her dream superimposed itself on her vision.

Bea slipped up behind her, grabbing her shoulders, kissing and caressing sensitive skin.

– I was convinced Big Moon had turned red, Janet said. – It must have been a dream, but it felt so real, as if I was awake and only imagined I was asleep. It was as if Big Moon… called out to me.

– I am convinced your dreams are real, Bea said, – or that they will be.

A warm, warm trickle rose from Janet's depths. She turned and started returning Bea's affections.

– We are distant cousins, she whispered in her ear. – We are perfect for each other.

They smelled each other, breathed each other, enjoying the moment.

It was low-level and did not grow beyond that this time. Janet stopped after a while and rubbed her temples.

– My head hurts, she said with regret. – Looks like you hit the mark, after all.

– Then use the bracelets, Bea shrugged unconcerned. – They will heal you in no time.

– No. Janet shook her head decisively. – I will not do that. Pain is a good teacher.

The words echoed from the past, into the future.

They tried starting up again the next afternoon, but their heads hurt and their skin and bodies hurt all over, and after a while they had to use the bracelets in order to continue. It just was not possible to keep it up without them.

– This is a good thing, Bea stated with a shrug. – We clearly did a very good job of fighting each other.

– Only you can turn something like this into an advantage, Eleanor glared at her.

Janet put the bracelets on first, demonstrating their effectiveness to her friends.

Wounds healed. Bruises faded. Health returned. Once again, she observed the wonder in the guys' eyes. They could hardly wait to try on the magick metal.

It took time and patience for everyone to be healed, though.

When fighting finally resumed they went at each other even harder, and learned faster.

– Do be advised that you can not be healed from death, Bea cautioned them. – Remain alert.

And then the two companions withheld the healing from them. Janet threw the bracelets far away, out of reach, daring them to overcome her in order to fetch the magick health. They did not make the attempt, but even though Janet saw resentment in their eyes, she also spotted understanding and further determination.

After a few more days more potential recruits approached them, asking for lessons, and even if most of them were quickly discouraged and left, their circle grew steadily. Yet a few more joined now and then, as the rumor spread.

A couple of dozens applicants stood before Bea, doing their best to look tough before her invasive scrutiny.

– Most of you, perhaps all of you will fail, she spat at them. – But one or two may be made of sturdier material.

Toby, Rosa, Frances and Eleanor took part in the teaching now as well. Cries of pain and rage filled the air. Some just could not take it and practically ran from the arena.

– Yes, flee, you unworthy vessels, Bea, cried after them with glee in those big eyes.

One of the boys failing the initiation looked at Janet with a pained look in his eyes, or at least she imagined he did. He looked downright out of it, as he stumbled off.

The six sat by the breakfast table at Bea's place days later. The mood was high, even exuberant. They laughed and enjoyed themselves while feeding to their heart's content.

– I feel so… fit, Rosa said.

– I feel like I can eat a horse… or a unicorn, Toby chuckled.

– Do not say that, Eleanor grumbled.

But the laughter found them all easy.

– They are sentient beings, Eleanor insisted. – And they have been gravely wronged in the past.

– And that has also made them very grumpy, the way I have heard it, Toby shrugged unconcerned. – They would probably have *us* for breakfast…

All six kept their light mood and easy-going manners.

They walked to Learning. There was a considerable distance from here to there, but not really that far, not for people with their stamina and strength.

Janet tried listening to the teacher, to what went on in the classroom, but found it difficult. Big Moon, with its indistinct face called out to her even there. She realized that she had been humming without being aware of it. The melody sounded eerily familiar, but she could not place it. She shook her head.

The others in Learning glanced at her, most of them with curiosity, but a few with spite in their eyes.

Bea, sitting by her side during free time, rubbed her cheek in a comforting gesture.

– Do not concern yourself with them, she whispered in her ear. – They are beneath you.

They were quite a pair, where they sat and walked together. Bea had fixed her hair, made it like Janet's. It became apparent that they were fairly close blood relatives.

The two of them spent most of the free time between classes together, and the guys joined them most of the time. Most of the others kept their distance.

Janet stood alone in the yard, on the same spot where Malone had first approached her. She reached out with her senses, but there was nothing there, nothing she could point at to say that he was in any way present.

Bea walked to her, rejoined her, followed by the guys. They surrounded her with a presence that felt like an embrace.

– You were lonely, Eleanor said. – We failed to notice that and thus we failed you.

– But you will never be lonely again, Bea stated firmly. – And if you should need some space, we will give you that, too.

They got to her and she was unable to speak, to even voice a choking reply.

– I know, it is all sickeningly sentimental, Toby smirked.

She embraced him, and held on to him for dear life.

They stayed by her side. During Learning, when she was in one class and they in another, when they were not there, she quickly grew aware of their absence. But when the free time returned and they returned as well, it was as if they had never been gone.

Music from one of the distant practice rooms sounded near in her ears. The wind and the waves brought it to her without her even trying.

And then the wind and the waves shifted in the air, and another type of music altogether filled her ears. She froze and stared straight forward, searching in vain for its point of origin.

– What do you sense? Bea asked her, as casual, as intense as ever.

Janet shook her head, smiling apologetically, replying, not replying.

Eleanor stared at her as well. Janet included her and also the guys in the smile.

They left the place of learning together and returned to Bea's apartment, to… their place.

Bea served them more wine and they drank. It wet their parched throats. Laughter filled the small space around them.

– I see things, now, Eleanor said, – things that were always hidden.

Everybody nodded solemnly and had more wine. Another pleasant glow filled their perception.

– I always saw them, I guess, she continued, – but I feared they were not real.

She refilled her glass. They all did, refilled it numerous times.

They sat there, enjoying themselves, as time passed slowly and their world expanded.

– I am afraid that you all need to go home tonight, Bea said just as the darkness had settled. – Or your parents will be livid. They are probably at the end of their ropes, and Janet's mother has good reason to be worried. It is regrettable, but there will be lots of opportunities for us to enjoy each other's company later.

She had that rare gift to get her point across quietly and forcefully. They found themselves nodding in their drunkenness.

That thought brought a smile to Janet's lips while she stumbled home later and relived the memory.

Drunk, drunk, drunk, she droned on in her mind.

She was still far from home, and was not really very successful when she attempted to speed up either. The intoxication made her stagger from one side of the broad road to another. She sat down on the road, dumping down on her ass, giggling, relieved that she had not fallen harder and injured herself. A timeless time passed while she sat there. Air whirled around her in the night, totally beyond her control. She giggled some more, imagining she saw clusters of light ahead, a sight signaling that she was not that far away from home.

And then she heard the music, the guitar strings vibrating in the night. She listened for the voice, but did not hear it and that brought a frown to her brow. Before she knew it, she was on her feet, chasing the vibrations in the night.

Three men approached her around the next corner. Their expressions turned lewd and filled with cruel expectation.

– Greetings, fair maiden, one of them called to her.

They stopped before her, blocking her path.

– Greetings, she mumbled.

– You are out here alone?

– I always walk home, she replied shyly. – It is no big deal.

– You are a child of the night.

The man nodded to himself.

That sounded so right to her. She found herself nodding, nodding empathically.

– And so very desirable…

He touched her jaw, appraising her.

She grabbed his hand and squeezed. He yelped in pain.

– Boys should not pretend to be men, she giggled darkly.

They pulled back, unblocking her path. She walked on and forgot about them, sobering up somewhat, as she approached the cluster of streets ahead.

It was Firewind, one of the «suburbs» of Auburn, a place filled with stores and entertainment establishments and hidden spaces, an area where the haunted and the lost sought and stayed. Janet sensed the hidden spaces. They stood out to her like open wounds and sore skin. Everything looked gray here, but not to her.

She spotted him on a corner, one of the many crossroads. He did not carry his guitar. He did not sing. She walked closer, approaching him apprehensively.

He turned towards her and she froze, froze completely, unable to even blink.

– Hello, he greeted her.

– Hello, she replied absolutely stunned.

– I would very much like to entertain you tonight. What do you say, fair maiden?

– I would like that very much, she heard herself say.

His voice sounded completely casual… normal. Nothing separated it from that of an ordinary male.

He grabbed her arm lightly and they walked down the street side by side. She glanced shyly at him, but quickly looked away when he turned his head to meet her eyes.

He was tall, taller than her, but not with more than half a head. It was hard for her to get a grip on him, as if he was not really there, but he was. She felt his presence, subtle but still an overwhelming push at all parts of her.

They entered a tavern on the north side. It was a quiet and nice place. A troubadour played a guitar and sang on a low stage. She hardly heard him or his playing.

– I was on my way to buy some… supplies, she said.

– They will still be there tomorrow, hc pointed out.

– Yes, My Lord, she mumbled.

She straightened, inadvertently posing for him, displaying herself in her inevitable awe.

He walked to the bar. She walked with him, pulled into his slipstream.

He bought ale, two large glasses of dark ale.

She could hardly contain her excitement and curiosity when they sat down by a table in the deep section of the room.

– They can… see you, interact with you?

– When I wish it, he shrugged.

Even that was such a powerful movement. She shuddered under its relentless force.

– Cheers! He raised his glass.

– Cheers! She mumbled, still not able to fight off the embarrassing sense of inferiority.

They drank.

He put down the glass. She did, too.

– I am Jason, he said, – Jason Gallagher.

– I am…

– I know who you are, Cathy, he stated calmly.

– Of course you do, she mumbled.

The name he had given her just slipped away, faded from her consciousness.

He studied her with his open stare, his fireeyes. They burned her. She blushed and darkened to ashes under that relentless stare.

– You probably wonder what this is about, he said.

– Yes, very much so.

She nodded, knowing that she had not given it a single thought.

– I wanted to show you something, he said, – and get to know you better. You are an interesting person.

If anyone else had said that she would have perceived it to be very condescending, but he was clearly not. There was a certain aloofness to him, but not that.

– I see, she said caustically, before being able to stop herself. – You were no longer content with observing me from a distance. You wanted to get up close and personal.

She turned a deep shade of red when it dawned on her what she had actually said.

He did not say anything, just kept studying her with bemusement in his eyes.

She wanted to hide, to fall between the cracks in the floor and never rise again.

The eyes were his face. She turned dizzy and practically fell into them, their dark well.

And then she heard the sound of buzzing wasps, or something similar.

And not long after that found herself a part of a vast open space, briefly before he closed her out. It was as if her gut made a jump inside her body. She frowned.

– What was that? She gasped, blinking tears from her eyes.

– I will tell you everything, he said, – if you truly want to know and is able to take it.

She nodded, giving him a strained, sweet smile.

– Cheers! She raised her glass.

Glasses met and parted.

They drank. The taste of the ale played with the buds on her tongue. It spread through her body like waves, the waves bouncing off him as if he wore armor, as if he was totally impenetrable. And then, the next moment they passed straight through him, as if he was not there.

He bought more rounds, and they drank.

– Are you trying to get me drunk? She smiled, swimming in the haze of her mind. – There is no need. I am already dead drunk.

The music from the low stage turned darker and the troubadour a little less ridiculous. She heard it, now, as it imposed itself on her, and she started shivering.

– Is that running water?

There was a sound, but no reply from him.

There were a dozen replies, all of them contradicting each other.

The music moved her, making her move.

– You want me, do you not? I can tell…

Behind everything she felt his desire, his potent need making her dizzy beyond belief.

She smiled as she rose, as she began moving, began dancing to the myriad of various music tunes surrounding her. Her body flowed across the floor. The discord moved her like never before.

The tavern floor was not too extensive. She could not move too much back and forth before she faced the constrictions of her surroundings, but it did not look like and did not feel like she was constricted at all.

– I have been sweating all day, she hummed. – Can you smell it, smell the burned out alcohol, the ashes of my body and spirit?

– I can smell dust from miles away, he said dryly.

There was nothing dry about him.

She crawled onto his lap, kissing him, smothering him in wet kisses, rubbing her sultry body against his, barely touching the edge of the true him.

– Do not worry, I want you, too, she said sheepishly. – You rattle me, sire, rattle my very bones.

– You will go deep within yourself and fetch power, he said.

She shuddered, shuddered hot.

– You should not grovel in my presence.

– I am not, she assured him.

Thinking better off it and relenting.

– I guess I am, but you are so far above me, or rather *beyond* us all that I can think of nothing else. You are a presence, casting your shadow everywhere. The first time I encountered you I could not discern what you are and I still can not, but now I have the beginning of an inkling at least. Why do you interact with ants under your heel?

– My reasons are my own, he said. – But as I said I will tell you everything in due time, if you still desire it.

– Testing this girl, are you, High Lord? You want something from her. A god wants something from this speck of dust. What is it?

She could hardly believe herself, the bold, shameless thing she had become.

They walked. It was a long time ago they had left the cozy tavern and now they walked through a gray light in a remote landscape without end.

– One snap of your fingers and you move. I thought my former master's ability to move through realms was impressive, but he is just a gnat compared to you.

She looked at him, at the giant thundering at her side. Every time he took a step it diminished her. It was incorrect to say that his waves overwhelmed hers. Hers did not exist compared to his.

They walked towards a cabin on the heath. Which heath she did not know.

– This is my place, he said. – It will still stand in the morning. I had it made long ago. When gods make love realms shake and shatter. Feel it, Cathy of the Blue Flame, feel the Ocean of Mankind.

Hera's milk glowed and flowed across the sky. She could sense all the countless specks of light floating up there, down there.

– The souls of the dead, she whispered, – they cry out like banshees in the night.

They walked inside. She felt it. She…

– Your need is…
She turned deaf and mute. He grabbed her clothes. It was like he touched her skin. When he removed her clothes patiently and methodically it was like he ripped her flesh from her bones, her burning, burning bones.
– I wanted you to experience this, somewhat safely, he said gently.
She almost laughed out loud.
– This girl is not made of china, sire, she giggled. – She can take rough, knows rough intimately.
He touched her arm. She stood there with her mouth wide open. The loud moan rising from her already sore throat was like a scream. He pulled her closer, holding her up like candy. When he kissed her she suffered an instant arousal.
– Ah.
She breathed fast, could not believe how fast she breathed.
– Ah…
He undressed. She helped him, unable to not touch him, touch him constantly, with no reprieve.
– AH!
He surrounded her, outside, inside, everywhere.
He stood on his knees above her. They were in bed. She writhed impatiently and beyond need below him. A hand struck her butt. It was her hand. She struck herself again, and kept doing so. A very pleasant feeling spread from her sore skin. A million moments passed as he studied her with his cruel eyes.
The bed was sturdy, well built, made of iron and woven in hard, hard ropes.
– Thy touch… she gasped. – I had no idea my skin could be so s-sensitive. I am burning up, nothing but a toy in thy hand. Play with thy t-toy, good sire, please… please…
He lowered himself on her and then he penetrated her. She moved under him. They moved together, a wonderful fit. The Ocean of Mankind set fire to all the pieces of their skin. She heard his growl, his growl shaking worlds. Her wide open eyes caught stray waves from him and it inflamed her further, terrifying her, exciting her. Nameless ecstasy shook her, shook her hard. And then she screamed. Every piece of flesh and bone on her body caught fire.
They rested in bed afterwards. She crouched by his side, playing with his so very ordinary looking cock.
– Thou have picked up such great tricks in thy ageless existence, have thou not?
She looked at him, totally mesmerized, but still herself. Her teasing smile affected him, she knew it did. She crawled on top of him, on top of his hard

cock and began riding him, and everything just went away for her again. Her recall had been reduced to bits and pieces, because that was «all» she could process. Blue flames began licking her body, completely surrounding it, and she knew startled that that was her, not him. His fire still burned her, both his fireeyes and the other dark fire consuming her, turning everything she was to ashes.

The morning light reached them. Her eyes opened. He looked at her as she woke up from her slumber. She displayed herself to him while smiling content.

– Hi, she said and she had never grinned wider before.

– Hi, he said. – Good morning.

– It is such a great morning, is it not?

She spoke and behaved like the worst kind of slut, as if she had been trained in a pleasure dome for years. The pleasures from the long, long night lingered in her, erupting in fleeting moments to remind her of the all-encompassing joy she had experienced.

– You have not slept, have you? She stated softly.

– I never sleep, he said.

She pushed herself at him, becoming even more a part of his shadow. Everything went away again.

They sat by the breakfast table. She glanced through the window at the heath, the vast heath. Everything seemed uncannily bright, a specter of gray and color so deep that she could not fathom it. The food tasted better than she could have possibly imagined.

– No one can resist you, can they? She said subdued and thrilled. – I certainly can not.

She stared at him with awe beyond awe.

– What are you? She whispered. It pushed itself from her, very much like a cancer. – I want it. You do not have to be afraid that I do not want it. Show me, please show me, I want to know, please show me…

She kept it going for minutes, droning on like a mantra, until she trailed off and left only the begging puppy eyes.

– I will show you, he finally said. – You will never rest until you know. I will show you a tiny glimpse. It will drive you insane, but it will not kill you. Thus, it will serve my purpose.

Her face cracked in an expectant smile. She frowned. His words registered in her mind, but they did not seem terribly important. He put his hand on her forehead. She frowned. The whisper in the wind made her frown, frown, frown. And

Then

Then…

She experienced it all, his entire being. In one blink was *eternity times infinity squared.* She had believed him vast. How silly of her. She had had no idea what vast was. The Ocean of Mankind was nothing but a tiny pond at his feet, at the nail of his little toe. And then, after another blink she truly began experiencing his being. A billion bells tolled. There was no end to him. Every piece of him was like… like…

The scream began and did not end

She stumbled down the road, as if drunk, humming a melody, a childhood rhyme. The walk, the stumble seemed unending. Her feet grew beyond sore. That had been a very long time ago.

The bench in the garden felt so pleasant. She sat there and did not move from there for ages. Her eyes stared straight ahead, empty and dull.

Bea stood in front of her. At one level she was aware of the sweet girl speaking to her, beseeching her. But the overwhelming, prevalent impression was that she was far, far away and out of reach, that she was just a mirage, a long forgotten memory from a lost age.

– We are just dust to him, she whispered, hardly hearing her own voice.

Bea caressed her face, her eyes filled with concern and need and love.

The guys had joined her as well, and mother.

– He took me dancing. We shared ale, shared everything. He shared everything with me. I begged him like a petulant child until he granted me his precious gift. I am open, now, and I am his, forever his, which I was, which we all are anyway.

– Who? Bea took her head in her big hands. – Who, my love?

And then her eyes widened, her skin paled, and she shook her head in denial, in distress and a dawning delight.

The others looked at Janet. She returned their inquiry with a triumphant smile.

– I saw myself, saw my face in a thousand mirrors. It looked different every time, but they were all me. I have died and lived a million times. I will never die.

Her laughter sounded totally off compared to how they had learned to know her. Her face looked like a jigsaw puzzle of disjointed pieces. Insanity ruled in the slowly comprehending eyes.

– He wanted to show me life in a dish of death, but I do not think he knows what it is himself, that he has not for a long time. I try to focus on what he revealed to me, but every time I try I end up in a loony bin with a sick, sick smile painted on my face.

She tore at her hair, tore it from her scalp.

– Dump, dump, dump, she hummed. – Sighs the old, old house filled, filled, filled with rotting, rotting bodies.

They took her hands gently and held them, held her, soothing her, making an effort at it. She recalled glimpses of the next days, years, ages. They spoon-fed her like they would a baby. She accepted their kindness with a *big*, excited and grateful smile.

She sat on the bench in the garden. She walked through the streets of Auburn, surrounded by her friends.

– I hear the sound of buzzing wasps, she said, not really speaking to them. – They are big and angry, not like buzzing wasps at all.

The next moment she found herself alone with Bea and she had no idea what had happened in the meantime.

Two girls walked hand in hand down a remote road.

One moment she was perfectly fine, then she could zone out or the chilling cackle could erupt from her throat.

– I begged him to show me the sights, she wailed. – He wanted to, but would not have done it if I had not wanted it, had not desired it with everything I am, the dumb, dumb fuck that I am.

Bea dried her forehead with a warm cloth. It felt wonderful. Janet kissed the girl in gratitude, in longing and desire.

A transparent man stared at Janet from five steps, an infinite distance away. She froze. The girl noticed and turned and looked where she looked and saw nothing.

– My father stands there, Janet stated.

A violent shiver rocked her. He faded to nothing and only the warm sunshine and the kind girl remained.

Her ability to see spirits, living or dead had increased tenfold, at least in moments of clarity and confusion. She saw or glimpsed them on many spots, as she and the girl held hands and walked to the Auburn city center a sizzling warm afternoon.

Joan sat clearly distressed by a table on a sidewalk cafeteria. She made no effort at approaching them, just sat there waiting, drinking. Janet and Bea walked to her, sat down with her on the other side of the table.

– I can not protect you, she muttered. – One moment you and that man were there, the next you were gone.

– You did nothing wrong, Janet said softly. – I wanted to go with that man. I will follow him wherever he wants me to follow.

– You may stay with us, anyway, Bea said, very condescending. – We would love to have a good, capable servant around.

And Janet observed how Joan crumbled and bowed her head.

– Shall we put our pet on a leash? Bea inquired.

Janet heard only her own mad laughter.

She shook her head.

– Okay by me. Bea shrugged. – She does not require any visible proof of her servitude, anyway.

Bea kissed Janet. Janet returned the affection with a happy sigh.

Joan was drinking, drinking hard. She had hardly finished one glass before she started on another.

– I could not protect you, she mumbled. – I am useless.

– No, you must not think like that, Janet protested.

– She saw two people disappear in open air, Bea said unconcerned, – and she can not handle it.

And when Janet, startled looked at Joan again, she realized that this was the truth.

She rose, determined.

– Come, let us leave this place, she stated, looking decisively at the intoxicated woman. – You will come with us.

Joan did not protest when the taller and stronger girl dragged her on her feet. They continued down the road. Joan stumbled and fell several times. She crouched by the roadside more than once and unloaded her burden. Her helpless coughing sounded strangely mute in the quiet neighborhood.

The two girls supported her. Both turned their heads several times. There were sounds in the night. They did not see anything, but felt the spirits whisper around them. It was impossible not to.

They tucked her in on the large bed later. She fell into a stupor almost immediately, almost asleep already.

– She is just having a one-time party to drown her sorrows from having reality brought down on her, Bea said. – Do not worry about it.

– You see so clearly, Janet said, kissing her.

– Oh, I do not know about that, Bea grinned. – We have given our bed to our servant and have no place to sleep tonight.

– Let us use the sofa, Janet shrugged unconcerned. – It is more than big enough, anyway.

They returned to the living room. It was a nice sofa, far more than a mere couch, one more distinct sign of Rosen and Maximus wealth.

Janet walked to the eastern window. Bea followed her. Janet looked at the streets, at the distant mountain peak. Bea studied her closely.

– Something has changed, Janet said. – I feel like he ran me through a thousand mazes of pleasure and pain. Something has changed in me.

– He prepared you, Bea said. – Toughened you up for what is to come. He

has chosen you as his representative, his messenger in the age to be.
– But why, to what purpose?
Bea looked at her, both subdued and pointed.
– Who are we to question the actions of a being such as he?
Janet frowned without quite knowing why.
– If you ask me I do not believe he wants a woman that does not seek her own council.
– I think that is very much correct, Bea said softly, touching her cheek.
Janet grabbed her hand and kissed it fiercely.
They stood there coddling a bit, before disengaging, sighing content, the other's close presence creating a pleasant valve in them both.
– Or perhaps there is no particular reason, except that he fancies you and took you as his consort on a god's whim…
Bea shrugged, giving off a teasing grin.
Something made Janet turn back to the world outside the window. She saw the mist form, out there at sea, beyond the archipelago, where water and sky became one, saw it reach for the triple cities, like a claw.
– What is it? Her companion asked impatiently. – Tell Bea.
– It is the Cauldron, Janet said surprised. – It moves and dances. Can you not feel it?
Bea shook her head.
– Nope! You are my superior in all things, My Lady. You were even before The Wanderer touched you.
– I can, Janet stated with a dreamy expression in the violet eyes, distracted, not quite catching Bea's banter. – It speaks to me tonight. At least it whispers. But I can not understand what it is saying, not a single word, if words there are.
– Perhaps there is only… noise? Bea suggested.
– No, no. Janet shook her head. – There is more to it, I know that! I almost get it, but it keeps eluding me.
They return, arm in arm to the deeper, safe section of the room.
It is late at night. They stretch out on the big sofa. Janet is asleep. Bea is awake. She stares at Janet. Her attention is locked on the other's peaceful face.
– We are bound, bound by blood, Bea stated. – We are One!
Janet stirs, but does not wake. Bea mumbles a minor spell, casting it with her lips and tiny hand movement and makes Janet fall into a deep sleep.
Bea's smile is a thing of beauty, her girlish eagerness brightening the room.
– I *can* hear it, she concedes, glancing out the window at the gathering mist, the velvet rain. – But it is not speaking or whispering to me. It is

weeping. It is a shriek haunting all my nights and days.

She turns back to the girl sleeping soundly.

– We belong together, she whispered. – We always will.

She leaned back, putting her head on the pillow. Her eyes closed slowly. They dreamed while still awake.

– You will see! You will see everything!

With that the two sleeping beauties writhed side by side, sometimes sleeping quietly, sometimes with visible unrest. The mist danced outside the window. An indistinct face formed there, one twisted in hatred. Janet glimpsed it, and fought to wake up, but could not do it. She moaned in distress.

When she woke up later at night, in Bea's arms it was gone. There was nothing there, no matter how long she looked, how hard she stared and recalled the nightmarish ghoul from her dreams. She sighed and relaxed, stretching on the pleasant cot. Her eyes closed and she slipped back into sleep, doing so as easy as breathing.

The night had turned quiet and calm and pleasant and sweet and all great flavors.

Chapter 14

The day broke, bright and harsh. Janet could not help slipping into the crazy laughter and it brought harsh looks from her fellow students. The harsh looks only made her laugh harder.

– They all look like paper dolls to me, she giggled in the presence of the guys, – as if they are not moving at all.

Bea rubbed her cheek and was her usual supportive self. Sometimes it helped and sometimes it did not.

Janet felt like she was floating away on that distant, close Ocean of Mankind, on the vast black undercurrent the eternal wanderer had displayed to her. There was nothing to hold onto, nothing to grab hold of, except the girl by her side and the more ephemeral insignificant shadows behind her.

She waited alone for the guys to join her in the free time. It did not truly bother her much. She hardly acknowledged the condescending and poisonous stares directed at her. Others from the wider circle of wand-fighters and trainees sought her out and surrounded her and helped her block the unpleasant presence of the majority of the students. She included them in her grateful embrace.

Harley, Harley Corcoran looked at her as if he wanted more. He had been among those «failing» Bea's rather disagreeable initiation stipulations.

– What happened? He asked.

– Nothing happened, she replied. – Nothing much.

– You look… look so *down.*

She smiled at his bad attempt at comforting her.

– You misunderstand then, she shrugged. – I am just preoccupied, that is all.

– You are not *here,* are you?

– I am here, she assured him.

– It is so cool seeing you touch the firmament without effort, a girl giggled. – I want to learn everything I possibly can from you.

The others circling her nodded in solemn agreement and with stars in their eyes.

Bea and the guys entered the yard at its distant point, and the others made room for them. There were more caresses and warm greetings, almost too much of it. The catching in Janet's throat grew almost too big.

– You guys do this in all the breaks? A boy cried, both incredulous and envious.

They chuckled a bit, but mostly ignored him, and most of the rest.

But no one could ignore the Blue Flame and her knights. Janet would have seen and known that truth easily, even without her spatial ability to perceive countless angles.

– Look at us, she mused. – We have become the center stage of the circus.

– The dominant force wherever we stride, Bea said. – People of Arcadia have not seen our kind for centuries, and they know it.

Janet and Bea were picked up by James by the gate just after Learning, yet another event in their lives, where everyone present and those watching the car as it made its way towards its destination had a first-row seat.

James drove them directly to the Rosen mansion. The car stopped in front of the lavish courtyard, the big doors decorated with intricate patterns. They spoke to her, but Janet could not understand their language, even as they repeated themselves, echoed in her mind.

– The Rosen clan does have a long and proud history, Bea remarked curtly, clearly perceiving the effort the other girl made. – Too bad it is not reflected in the present…

Servants opened the doors to the car. Others opened the big doors leading into the luxurious house. Janet hesitated before putting her foot down on the polished floor for the first time. It was a reflex, one she was unable to stop. Bea noticed with a patronizing grin.

– You must rid yourself of such ridiculous notions of inferiority, sweetie, she said. – You are soon to be a member of the family, now, and must know how to conduct yourself.

Her words made Janet redden in further awkwardness, discomfort and joy. They brought heat and shame and everything in-between.

It did not matter that there was a notable dichotomy in Bea's words and stance. Janet still fought with herself to get rid of the sense of inadequacy riding her.

– You should have worn your attire, your hood and robe. Now, you hardly look like much more than an ordinary girl in the eyes of the clans. They will not see you as I see you.

– But we wanted them to see me, not the powerful sorcerer, Janet reminded her.

– Of course, Bea mumbled. – It is just frustrating, that is all.

They squeezed hands and gave each other affectionate kisses.

Janet could not help but stare as they made their way through the entrance hall and the hallways. Polished surfaces flashed at them from all sides.

– The servants are busy keeping everything shiny, I imagine?

– Hush!

Bea placed an index finger on her lips.

They entered the dining room. The family sat in the sofa.

– The two most important attendees have arrived, Bea said lightly. – Dinner may commence.

The four on the sofa, Justin Rosen, Madge Maximus Rosen, John Maximus Rosen and Turner Maximus rose. Justin greeted Janet with an outstretched hand.

– It is so good to see you again, Janet, he said. – Welcome to our home and our modest meal.

She noticed that Bea stared sullenly at him, but paid no visible attention to it.

– Thank you, Justin, she replied graciously. – It is nice to be here.

– Dinner will be served shortly, Madge offered pleasantly. – A light snack and beverage will be served while we wait.

Janet had to strive in order to contain her laughter, but she managed.

They sat down in the sofa and deep chairs around the smaller table.

Wine and sandwiches were served quickly, almost before they had settled down. The servants were quiet and efficient, almost to the point that it was hard to even notice that they were present. Janet mused quite a bit over that.

– Good cheers, John said and raised his glass.

– Good cheers, everybody echoed his words.

He looked at Janet fairly openly. It was obvious that he did not even attempt to hide his interest. He was a couple of years younger than Bea and differed from her physical appearance and personality in various ways. There was the solid build, but he was not as tall and made less of an impression. Janet returned his interest with a calm, direct gaze, not looking away, but not making a point of staring either.

But then, in a flash of madness she did stare, studying him from top to bottom, unnerving him to no end. She knew he could not stop hearing her silent giggle, no matter how hard he tried.

The servants were done setting the dinner table. The hosts and the guests moved there. Rosen pulled out Janet's chair. She gave him the sweetest of smiles and sat down.

The group had dinner. The servants kept whirling in their surroundings, imposing discreetly on their space, making sure they were all taken well care of. Janet kept her wicked laughter contained. She had the wine and the veal, and more of what the table had to offer.

Rosen kept his eyes on her, more or less ignoring his daughter. Janet's wicked laughter stuck in her throat.

– As stated I was very impressed with your performance, Janet, he said. – You and your paternal grandmother stole the show, so to speak.

That did rock her. He had obviously researched the matter.
– Thank you, Janet said, striving to keep up the politeness. – We made an effort to make it something special.
– You will pursue your career in the magickal arts, I gather?
He was totally casual about it. There was no doubt or awkwardness there and that told her more about him.
– I will! She shrugged.
– We see this pretty much as a homecoming, you know, Madge said. – You are, after all a long lost piece of the family. Your great grandmother, Jenny was one of us, until she ran away with a savage.
Madge, born a Maximus had apparently vigorously accepted her role as a Rosen.
– That is not unknown to me, Janet stated calmly.
– It was a great scandal at the time, John said.
– You and dear Beatrice are far removed cousins, Madge said, as if to rub it in.
Janet refrained from speaking.
– Do not worry about it, Turner said. – The Rosens are and have been about good breeding for generations, and inbreeding with a drop or so of foreign blood is quite their stock in trade.
There was enmity here, thinly veiled, and obviously not directed at the guest of honor. That made Janet send him an involuntary smile.
– I have been studying you young people for a while, Justin confessed, as if revealing some great secret. – Your activities are both interesting and impressive. The wand training and what goes with it is of particular significance to me.
– Oh, why is that, Justin?
– You are building a squad, eventually even a militia. I can use that. You are a great and cruel leader. I see endless future possibilities. You are a rare treasure, Janet of the Blue Flame.
She was blushing, unable to help herself. Pride coursed through her.
The wine… worked on her, making her dizzy and lightheaded and hot. The candles in the room took on a pleasant glow.
The dark, unmistakable undercurrents got to her. She bathed in their flow.
– It is as if a Rosen left and returned better off, John said. – You will fit well in here, I believe.
She could not quite tell whether or not he was serious or hassling her. She frowned. Sister and brother stared hard at each other. She noticed that, too.
Dinner ended. The visit ended. The sense of breakup became evident long before it became obvious.

– Are you sure you will not stay a little longer? Madge asked.
– Dinner was great, mother, Bea replied, – but we must be on our way. Duty calls.
– What duty? John snorted.
He received no reply.
They left the house. Mother just waved goodbye and returned to the pleasant shade of the building. They left the estate on foot. Janet waited a bit before she spoke.
– That went well, do you not think?
She recognized the irritated pull at the edge of the mouth of the other girl, in the face she had learned to know so well.
– They just want a sorcerer, a sorcerer's blood in the family. They have worked for it for generations. Many of their friends, or rather associates, do have mighty blood in their clans or at least pets with such. It is an issue of great concern to them.
Bea waved her hand in a dismissive gesture. Janet looked at her with humor and puzzlement.
– But it is just as well that you are not put off anymore. It makes everything easier.
The callous remark made Janet study her even closer.
Bea turned away, hiding her face from her. Janet grabbed her and stopped her, stopped them both.
– What is the matter? She asked softly.
Bea kept staring down, her brave front crumbling. The shaking of the lower lip turned evident.
– Look at me.
Bea did, with a stubborn look in her moist eyes and angry face.
– He gets to you, does he not?
Bea nodded.
– I knew it, Janet cried. – He keeps nagging you and nothing you do will ever be good enough for him.
Janet grabbed her upper arms, holding on to her as gently as she could.
– This place is not good for you. He is not good for you. Why should we return here?
– Because our future is here, Bea pointed out. – Because everything that is his shall be ours.
The cruel confidence and callousness returned to her voice and stance. Janet shook her head in sadness and bewilderment. She touched the other's cheek and the caress was instantly and spontaneously returned.
They held hands again as they crossed the town, doing small and

affectionate and passionate talk.

– Mother does not count, Bea said. – She has settled long ago in her role as father's furniture and hardly even that. Turner is merely visiting, hardly more than the Maximus clan's glorified observer. John is jealous because I am the chosen one and not him. Yes, there was hostility in his voice when he spoke to you. He dislikes you, even as he is taken with you because I like you. Pay him no more heed than you must. He will do his duty when the time comes.

Janet chuckled.

– What? Bea asked instantly, needling her when she did not reply immediately. – What?

– I just love it when you go obscure on me…

They kissed, stopped on the spot for a while, enjoying each other closeness, not caring about those watching.

Taking their time they walked to the small house at the end of the road, where Janet's mother had another meal ready for them. This was a quiet room, a quiet house. They noticed it in countless small ways they had not noticed before.

Bea leaned back for a moment, taking a break from the eager feeding.

– This is such great food, Myra, she said, with a dreamy expression in her eyes. – You grow it in the garden, do you not?

– Most of it, yes, Myra replied, clearly pleased by the praise.

– We get the chicken from the nearest farms, Janet rushed to point out. – The animals there enjoy a somewhat full life, at least until their heads are chopped off.

They returned to the tasty meal. Janet found to her amazement that she was still hungry, hungry as a wolf. She reddened embarrassed when she realized that the other two studied her.

– I was never this hungry, she giggled. – In fact I used to eat like a bird.

– You practically starved yourself, Myra said with regret in her voice and features.

– You are bigger and stronger, now, Bea stated. – You can not deny who you truly are anymore.

The awkward silence after that particular exchange of words could not obstruct or even frustrate the pleasant mood in the room and house and between the three of them.

Not much was said. Not really. They sat there and enjoyed each other's company. But they did not actually talk much. Conversation was low-keyed and fairly relaxed, or not too uneasy.

– You should not ask about that, mother, Janet said to a question she was unable to recall.

There were more awkward glances.

– I hid you for so long, Myra said, – but it still was not enough. I could not protect you from the threats I did not know, and now you are so empowered and mature, powerful in your own right, no longer taking shit from anyone.

There was something callous in mother's voice that Janet had not noticed before. The woman had always been there, like another piece of furniture, and that thought would not go away, no matter how hard Janet tried making it.

And now it was like Myra appeared like a creature of flesh and blood and emotion and independent thought, stepping forward from the background where Janet had always seen her.

– Do not trust Illandra, Myra said. – She has her own agenda, and is more than happy to lead you around in a chain of your own making.

There was anger there, slow burning but intense. The daughter saw a different side of the mother.

– I am not, Janet said. – I know.

She noticed her own self-conscious smile and demeanor. The smile widened.

The dinner proceeded in a slow, pleasant manner. Bea burst into laughter after a somewhat funny remark from Myra, and it was go unexpected that Janet felt an instant catching in her throat.

People passed by outside, casting long, fearful and angry looks at the house. Janet sensed them, but they did not really bother her. She enjoyed herself in the company of the two women in a way that felt strange, alien to her.

The self-conscious smile from earlier changed into something else and different.

– What do you see when you look up at the sky at night? Myra asked abruptly, after yet another exchange of words Janet did not recall.

– THE OCEAN OF MANKIND, the girls choired instantly.

Then, just like that, they were there again, floating in its pervasive embrace. The warm, warm feeling inside Janet grew even more pronounced. She still noticed how pleased, how smug Myra looked.

The two girls were about to leave. Myra put a hand on Janet's shoulder. Janet studied her, the smile not leaving her face.

– I have got something for you, she said quietly.

Myra walked to a drawer. She mumbled something, archaic words the two girls did not catch.

A spell, Janet thought stunned.

The drawer opened. Myra reached into it with her left hand, picking up an amulet in a necklace. The older woman returned to the two curious and suddenly excited youngsters.

– Your great grandfather gave this to me to keep, she said. – It waited, he said, waited for you.

Janet looked stunned at her.

– Not the one I knew, I presume, not your grandfather, but *the* great grandfather on father's side of the family, the great sorcerer of the Bone People?

– The very same, Myra confirmed.

– You *knew* him?

– Not really, but he seemed to know me… and you. He was a very impressive man. I could tell, even though I only met him a few times.

– He died fairly young then?

– No, Jonas Caldwell was fairly old when he mated with the woman giving him the son that mated with Illandra and was the father of your father. He was over hundred, at least that, when he died. Some said he had waited for the young mother of his son his entire life.

She put the necklace around Janet's neck. The amulet rested on the girl's chest.

Janet grabbed it and studied it, studied its violet jewel. She wanted to embrace Myra, but could not make herself do it.

– It matches your eyes perfectly, Bea breathed.

– It does, Myra agreed.

They said their goodbyes.

– Thank you, Myra, Bea said. – Dinner was great and the host is an example for others to follow.

– You are making me blush, girl, Myra said.

Janet looked at, studied them both. Understanding did not illuminate her mind.

Bea and Janet entered the garden, entered the streets.

– Your mother is cool, Bea said. – That was quite different from the snotty meal we had at the mansion, do you not think?

– I do, Janet replied.

– You do not seem sure? Bea teased her. – Perhaps Myra also has her secrets?

– I feel like she is always watching me, Janet said frustrated. – And she is absolutely hiding stuff from me. As you just saw. She has always had secrets, never truly opening up to me. Even though she has mentioned our heritage occasionally, she has rarely elaborated, and she still does not. This…

She touched the amulet, rubbed the violet jewel.

– … is hardly more than an appeasement, a way of pretending to good will.

It twinkled between her fingers as she rubbed it, not in light, but in waves.

– It is so pretty, Bea marveled. – Like your eyes.

Janet let go of it. It returned to its position on her chest. The twinkle faded. She glanced shyly at Bea. Eyes met eyes.

They stopped between two streetlights, facing each other on a spot between two clusters of buildings. Skin on blushing faces flashed in the shadows.

Bea grabbed Janet's hands.

– I like you, Cathy, Bea said softly. – I like you a lot.

– Thank you, Bea, Janet replied hotly. – I like you a lot, too.

– I like you so much that I want us to exchange wows, Bea said.

The heat rose within Janet and filled her to the brim. She felt faint and failed to voice a reply.

– Will you? Bea squeezed her hands harder with a solemn smile. – Will you agree to be my Companion?

– Yes, Bea, Janet replied happily. – I will be happy to Share life and experience with you. I would love for us to be Companions.

They kissed. Lips held on to lips. There was arousal, but mostly a pleasant, eager calm.

– Come! Bea urged her, holding on to her hand.

The two of them walked down the shadowy road stuck in an ongoing sideways embrace.

– It will be fun, Bea declared. – We will enjoy ourselves beyond joy in full public view, even as we disregard everybody present to share our happiness.

Janet could not help but pick up on the subtext of her words, the venom not expressed explicitly.

– What is it? Janet asked her quietly.

Bea hesitated.

– Please tell me, Companion to be, she implored the other softly. – We should not hide anything from each other, right.

Bea nodded, then nodded again.

– You have probably guessed that I am not particularly fond of the ensuing public spectacle my clans will make of our happiness.

– Guessed, yes, Janet grinned, attempting levity.

– There is a small matter we should discuss… before we make it official, I mean.

Now, she was clearly awkward, even touching on embarrassment.

– Small? Janet joked, this time not attempting to keep the edge from her voice, to ease the other's tension.

Bea stopped, averting her eyes briefly, before looking back stubbornly.

– They would want us to breed.

Janet looked amused at her, not puzzled or baffled or put off, but she still looked at her upcoming Companion with inquiring and not exactly kind eyes.

– As stated, the Rosens have been crafty breeders for generations, and they want us to become one bloodline.

Janet touched her cheek, calming the other's turmoil.

– There is no need for you to be ashamed or anything, Janet assured her. – I would love to have children with you.

– You will? Bea said, becoming excited when she read the acceptance in Janet's eyes. – That is wonderful!

They stood there for a while, breathing in the other's scent and presence.

Bea became the practical and arrogant one again, regaining her composure.

– I will pick your mate and you will pick mine. The children will be ours and ours alone, of course. Our chosen mates will have to agree to that, to swear on it in blood.

Janet nodded, both to Bea and to herself. This was a fairly well known and accepted custom and arrangement.

Suddenly Bea fell on her knees, with her eyes cast to the ground.

Janet frowned and looked irritated at her.

Then a trickle touched her spine in more than one place.

– Oh, she said, as the impact of the situation dawned on her.

She turned and stood face to face with the Wanderer.

Suddenly it was as if a horrible sight came into focus for her.

– Come with me, he told her.

It was not exactly a command, not in her ears, but he clearly did not expect rejection. She did not hesitate, but walked to him without a second look at the kneeling, humble creature she left behind. Soon, in whiffs of movement and change Janet could no longer see that creature when she turned and looked back, and she stopped trying.

He filled her being with his essence. His close proximity alone did that. And when he focused on her, even the slightest she could hardly sense anything but him. Every piece of their surroundings just faded away.

The man and the woman walked on the desolate road. The question burned in the woman's throat.

– Why did she kneel for you, now, and not the other times she has seen you?

His answers were unsatisfying like an icy wind.

– I did not fully disclose myself to her or to you then. I was just the shadow most people perceive me to be. This time she also experienced me fully manifested, though not anywhere near the way you briefly did.

He caught her in his shadows, doing so without even the slightest visible effort, not allowing her to move either closer or further away. She wanted to, wanted both, unable to do either.

They walked on. He moved forward, a quiet, unending storm, followed by the dry leaf caught in his slipstream. She lost sense of time and the surroundings and herself, and the feet attached to her body. They passed a mountain on the right, on a stretch without houses or buildings of any kind. She did not recognize it or any of the landmarks, in any direction. The valley was not the first. She did not recall what number it was. The road seemed endless, the wilderness they walked through without end. She stumbled, but managed to stay on her feet.

– You do not care much for us, do you? She asked him with a subdued look.

– I care for you, he said. – Give me one reason why I should care for the others.

She straightened herself, sniffed, but straightened herself, searching for a strength that was not there, but that she none the less needed in order to go on.

– You need to toughen up, he added, after some pondering. – You need to be prepared for the place we are going. It is more unrelenting than you have ever experienced or imagined.

– You are… testing me? She realized weary and stunned. – For a task?

He did not reply, or even acknowledge her words.

The skies changed above them. If that was the first or tenth time it had done so since he had come and fetched her so long ago she did not know. There were not two moons anymore, but five, no, not five, nine, they were nine.

Nine globes dancing in a circle, a wheel.

She studied him with hard, unrelenting eyes that did not seem to be a part of her body, probing him in ways she could hardly believe.

Each push returned a force thousand times stronger. She persevered.

He stopped at the edge of a forest that looked like nothing she had ever seen before. There were two trees that looked like a gate there. They were pulsing and glowing. Something resembling fireflies, but not quite that lit up a path further on and revealed a mist-like area where she glimpsed movement, glimpsed just about anything strange and chilling.

Birds sounding like some kind of mammal, like something completely different cried wolf. Yet another shiver passed through her.

She swayed and had trouble staying on her feet. He handed her a bottle of water. She drank, drank deep.

– How do you feel? He asked her.

– I feel fine! She replied fiercely.

The violet eyes burned at him. He flashed his fangs in delight and a warm trickle flowed down her spine.

– So, this is the place where it is easiest to take us where we are going? She mused.

– It is easiest on you, he shrugged.

He grabbed her. She felt the potent charge when he did.

This felt different, was different. They moved in a way, but drifted more than moved, and the Wanderer did not drift, but move. Dizziness overwhelmed her, as he brought them through nothing. She realized startled that it was very familiar to her. It felt exactly like the remote sense of it she had experienced when she had borne witness to Malone's rise into the spheres. Blood left her and filled her up again, far more potent than before.

She was burning, burning in blue. It consumed her, but did not devour her. Every licking flame brought a new sensation, yet another set of experiences she could not quite grasp.

Then she turned up elsewhere, by Jason's side. She had major difficulties standing. He held her a few moments before he let her go, and she stood straight on her own. Her wide open eyes had trouble making anything out of their surroundings. There was air of a kind, even though she could not be certain she was actually breathing. There was ground to stand on, even though she could not decide whether or not it was actually solid, was matter.

She chuckled in a more powerful elation and stared at him in stronger awe.

He had brought her to a different realm, one vastly different from anywhere she had previously visited. It spoke to her in a roar of whispers, its quiet waves being tall as houses.

– Where are we? She wondered wide-eyed and timid.

– One of the «high realms», he replied. – You feel its seething energies, do you not?

She nodded preoccupied. The very «air» here seemed to touch and burn her skin.

– The «high realm» designation is mostly bullshit, of course, he shrugged. – Only unimaginative beings place confidence in such labels. It is not totally without merit in this case, though. Call it the Heights, if you will.

Her eyes cleared or the air, the ether did. She could not tell which. Pellets reminding her of angry wasps swarmed around them.

She spotted the long row of… statues not far away, so far away she could not imagine the distance. Then, by that very thought they closed in on them in one single moment. She gasped and gasped again.

– What are they?

– You know, he replied.
She did. They spoke to her, as if they were alive. And… and…
They were!
She knew, long before she recognized the man at the end of the line.
– Do not touch them, Jason admonished her. – If you do, you become part of their reality, become like them.
She almost did. Thought and reality were the same here. She tried almost all the old meditation techniques before she succeeded in disciplining herself sufficiently in order to resist the omnipresent lure.
Hot and cold ether, mist and time flowed through her. She recognized Malone the Sorcerer, studied apprehensive and pleased his frozen face.
– This is the Ascension, she stated stunned.
She turned towards him, forcing herself to look at The Wanderer, and not lowering her eyes, not fall on her knees before him like a slave.
– You did this? She heard herself say.
– I did! He confirmed.
– You brought us here, to a place powerful sorcerers have sought for millennia and it was only a casual act to you. You trapped them here, everybody fulfilling the Ascension, like you would swat a fly.
– I did. They would have become quite bothersome if they had been allowed to complete the cycle.
He swatted the flies coming too close in a burst of irritation. They fell inert to the ground.
Another landed on her arm and her local skin turned numb. The numbness began spreading instantly from that point. He grabbed it and healed it, just like that.
She stared at him in renewed awe.
– What are you? She whispered.
But she knew, not exactly what he was, but everything he was not.
The tiny moment he had revealed himself to her the last time they had met kept bouncing through her consciousness, creating havoc and strife there. She just stood there frozen for ages, almost becoming a statue herself.
Slowly, she tore herself free from her stupor. She raised her eyes, her head, and looked at Malone. She recognized the substance covering his face. It was the wasps, the flies transformed into something similar to amber. Malone's… coating was quite recent. It had not properly settled yet. He was still moving a little. She felt bits of what he felt, numb, frozen, comatose, but aware, trapped. It was a far worse punishment than she could ever have devised for him. Terror and delight warred within her.
Spittle worked its way into her mouth. She allowed it to fill the cavity

before releasing it. It splashed at the statue in front of her, mingling with it, joining it.

– I want you to know, she spat. – I will be with you, like you are with me.

She left him, turned her back to him and walked down the row, studying the others in impassionate ways.

Their coating was thicker, thicker the longer she walked, and after a while it was covered by another layer of a substance with dust-like properties. Men and women of different ages, wearing many different kinds of garments paraded before her flashing violet eyes.

She stopped before a woman almost at the end of the row. This one pulled her in even more than the others. Janet wanted to become familiar with her, to know more, but resisted the lure once more and pride riddled her.

Janet of the Blue Flame walked away and rejoined The Wanderer on his hill, where he surveyed his great work.

– You have given me such a beyond precious gift, My Lord, she said humble and elated. – Thank you.

She bowed deep, presenting her eager expression, displaying herself to him, the dust making a ridiculous effort to entice the wind.

It was later, much later when she walked the dark road alone. She could not tell how much later it was, in her mind filled with bliss and delight. The recent days and nights just faded away into one, continuous flow in the haze of her thoughts.

People passed her in all directions. She ignored them, hardly even noticing them.

The fairly nondescript building in busy city streets pointed itself out to her. She allowed it to pull her, to draw her close, and suddenly she was there, in front of the door. She opened it and walked inside.

Bea and the guys waited inside, more than a little anxious, brightening visibly when they saw who it was. They rose and greeted her. She and Bea embraced. Janet kissed her softly.

– Oh, baby, I am so happy to see you again, Bea said.

– We all are, Toby said.

– And I am so happy so see all of you.

Janet and Bea stood there, on the spot, kissing and fondling each other.

– He did you and us all an honor by choosing you, Bea said, – but in my weakness I still feared that he would take you away from us forever.

– Come, Eleanor said kindly, – you are just in time for dinner, for food and wine.

Janet sent her, sent all of them a grateful smile. She joined them at the table.

The clicking of glasses and the sound of food being devoured echoed in her ears, in her acute senses. She reddened under the others' scrutiny.

– I am so hungry, she munched, – and so thirsty, and…

– And so everything.

More soft sounds echoed in her ears and mind.

Bea raised her glass.

– To our sweet wanderer, she said softly, – to her long walks on remote paths and in distant realms.

– TO OUR SWEET WANDERER

Glasses met and parted. They drank. Janet blushed.

– You bring back even more joy and knowledge to our coven, Eleanor said.

Then she kissed her on the cheek.

They walked through the streets of the town not long after that, visibly enjoying every step, making others cast long looks at them.

All in the happy party kept drinking as they walked, from glasses and sometimes directly from the bottle.

– There is reason to celebrate, is it not? Bea asked her.

– There is, Janet nodded, a flash darkening the violet eyes and the stone resting on the sorcerer's chest.

The darkness persisted with the smile as they sat down by a table at the outdoors tavern of Raven Bird at Rowan Park. This was a place where nature was very much present. This was not unusual in the triple cities, but this establishment had succeeded better than most with integrating the building and the furniture in its wild surroundings.

Janet had more wine. She smiled some more, even as she felt the curiosity in her companions, the way they all, perhaps without being conscious of it directed their attention at her, doing so like one single curious beast.

Her chuckle had that dark taint she did not care to hide.

– He did many things, for various unfathomable reasons, among them granting me one particular precious boon… He threw his faithful bitch a bone.

– What was it? Bea breathed. – Tell me what it was.

– He brought me to the Ascension, and it was like nothing to him.

Bea and Eleanor gasped, and the others looked astonished as well.

– It is a sham, a trap instigated by him thousands of years ago in order for him to easily rid himself of bothersome sorcerers, potential competitors. Every single one ends up like a statue trapped in amber, alive, not alive, an unending, horrible existence.

They sat there, in the midst of people and what at least resembled wild nature and it was the buildings and furniture that did not seem real or true.

They heard animals, heard birds cry in the night and they imagined they were surrounded by forest.

And behind it all, on a deeper level the sorcerer's words, her story became reality.

A raven landed on the table in front of Janet, an event making her companions stare even harder, and also catching the attention of the other revelers.

It moved back and forth, staring at her with its dark eyes, squeaking repeatedly, before taking off, creating a storm flapping its mighty wings, its waves touching everyone present, all over the establishment and even on the street beyond it.

The storm faded slowly to a kind breeze and then to nothing.

– Malone was there, at the end of the line, displayed like the rest, and it gave me such great pleasure to look at him and know that he ended up as nothing more than a plaything to a far greater power, a helpless display object in its museum.

Her friends noticed the distress evident in her voice beneath the bravado and triumphant snarl, and gave her comforting squeezes and rubs.

The evening proceeded like a rush of wind, a slow breeze.

The campfire in the middle of the yard, between two heartbeats grew and in Janet's mind became both deep red and blue/violet, shifting constantly between those two extremes.

A man danced, danced nude on a table. The crowd cheered. The cheers rose even more as his cock hardened and dangled between his thighs as the dance turned wilder. Two women joined in. But that was it. In spite of the cheers and the good mood, the celebration never quite took off.

Janet writhed uncomfortably on her seat and knew she was not alone in doing that. Most of those present, of both sexes were quite adversely affected by the three's table performance.

– Come, sit in my lap, Bea told Janet. – Come!

She patted her thigh. The direct, potent stare made Janet hot and queasy in an instant. She glanced around her, pondering the issue.

The move took her only an instant. The big girl sat down in the other big girl's lap.

– That is my sweet girl…

Bea rubbed her cheek with the back of her hand, touched her lips with sensitive, teasing fingers. Janet crouched in her lap. Bea kissed her softly on the lips. They made out for a while, enjoying the low-keyed arousal, like the rest of the guests watching the threesome show on the tables.

Janet saw it as if through shadow, heard it as if through water, experienced it through filters enhancing her perception, not lessening it. Shadows danced beyond the shadows, revealing the hidden realms to her.

The extraordinary occurrences grew more pronounced, not less.

– You see, now, do you not? Eleanor asked/stated. – You see more!

I do, Janet nodded.

– You see the Higher Realms, feel them in your… your…

– The Wanderer does not exactly subscribe to such definitions, Janet shrugged. – And if he does not, why should we?

She spotted the waves, in ways she had never before done, as they flowed from a central point, from countless central points. The three-headed beast on the table burned, as they grunted and moaned and screamed in pain and joy, and a pleasure unheard of, and the cheers rose like embers into the night, beyond the tall trees of the endless forest still very much present even between these buildings of dead wood and stone.

Eleanor's face lit up in an even stronger glow.

– I can… sense your might. She attempted to express her deep-felt thoughts and emotions. – It draws me to it. I can not resist it and I do not want to. I do not!

Janet pulled back a little, in order to give the other room, knowing it did little or no good.

She raised her glass. Everybody else did as well, also Eleanor.

– A la vida, the Blue Flame cried softly.

– A LA VIDA! The others choired.

They drank. The water of life burned in her throat.

She and Bea's lips met and parted.

The Blue Flame and the Guys ventured the dark streets and alleys of the city night, drunk, but not drunk, sober, but not sober. Sounds and sensations bathed Janet from all sides, but did not bother her. They toasted and drank as they walked, their laughter easy and loud.

She sent a brief thought of spite at the statue in the land of the Ascension and chuckled pleased to herself.

You did not get me, Peter. I got you! Your action against me brought your downfall.

They did not intend to, or perhaps they did, but no matter, they ended up outside town, at a stone circle. There were no houses nearby, none at all.

– There are several such circles throughout Arcadia, is there not? Fran wondered. – What is this one called?

– It has no name, Eleanor replied. – Most of the others do, but not this one. Let us call it the Nameless Circle.

Janet and Bea looked stunned at each other and eventually nodded and studied their friend with penetrating eyes.

– The Nameless Circle it is, Bea confirmed.

Everybody stopped, if not in awe, then clearly taken by the moment and the place. They walked inside the elaborate arrangement of stones and markings. There was a subtle stir in the air as they crossed the threshold. Janet felt it, and she noticed without even looking at the two of them that Eleanor and Bea felt it as well.

My skin tingles and burns, Bea cried excitedly. – I have been here before, but did not feel anything tangible then.

Eleanor closed and opened her eyes.

– It is remarkable, she half whispered. – I feel like I have just opened a window in a house filled with clammy air and am able to breathe for the very first time.

She turned towards Janet, her eyes fixed on the other girl.

– I would like to be your apprentice, Eleanor stated.

Janet practically ignored her or at least did not voice any reply.

– Please make me your apprentice, Eleanor implored her. – Please!

– Are you aware of what we are talking about here? Janet asked her anxiously. – You will become nothing but my whim, dust of my desire, lower than a slave. My mind will overwhelm yours, yours hardly more than an extension of mine.

Eleanor lowered her eyes, rushing forward, placing herself in front of the sorcerer, her entire posture speaking of humility and submission.

Janet gave her a wicked, fixed stare far more penetrating than her old friend had given her.

– Perhaps you require a demonstration, a lesson in the facts of life as they pertain to an apprentice?

She slapped her on the cheek. Eleanor cried out in shock and pain.

– Yes, it is arbitrary, is it not?

She slapped her on the other cheek.

The others looked frozen and horrified at the spectacle.

Eleanor choked and fell on her knees.

– You look like a slave already! Janet said softly.

The snarl in the voice turned pronounced and nasty.

– You disgust me!

Janet turned and walked off, stopping right outside the circle, shaking in uncontrollable fury.

Sometime later, when time and space once again returned to her, she felt a soft hand on her shoulder, one she recognized without turning, without conscious thought. Bea nuzzled her neck with her lips, rubbing her back,

comforting her in ways no one else could.
They stood there for a while, for time without time, and enjoyed each other's company.
– Sorry for acting up, Janet mumbled. – My temper again.
– I love your temper, Bea whispered. – I love it every time your passion burns me.
Soft lips met. There was a bench nearby. They sat down on it, not letting go of each other's hands, hands seemingly burning the air touching them.
There was no talk. Silence spoke volumes. Janet felt peace enter her. The wind was blowing around them.
– Perhaps you should reconsider?
Janet turned and stared hard and incredulous at her.
– I think you should teach her. You have the experience of far older sorcerers. She will benefit greatly from your teaching, and we will benefit equally great from her once she has liberated herself from being your shadow.
The big girl shrugged, ignoring the other's scolding glare.
– It is not about her, anyway, but about you, you know that. You fear you will not be worthy of her trust. The rest of us, though, will always be there to tell you that you are wrong.
Janet strived to speak, to clear her throat of the choking almost overwhelming her.
– How do you know me so well?
– You know why. Another elaborate shrug. – We are twin souls, destined to do great things together.
Janet nodded slowly, a movement hardly noticeable.
They returned to the others. Janet let go and pulled Eleanor into her grasp.
– Well, then, but know that we will not be playacting, will not pretend. The moment you submit to me there is no going back. You will obey me without question, without resistance, willfulness or pride. Do you understand, Eleanor of the Golden Bowl?
Eleanor nodded and a shiver passed through her.
– I… Eleanor understands and she will strive to be worthy of the beyond great honor Janet of the Blue Flame bestows upon her.
She fell on her knees again.
– Eleanor submits herself, her very self to the mighty sorcerer before her, begging her to teach her the secrets of life and death and everything outside and within.
– The sorcerer accepts. It is done!
And just like that, it was.
The kneeling girl shook.

Then she froze and knelt unmoving before the regal creature towering above her.

The Blue Flame turned and looked curtly at the others.

– The rest of you should not address her. If you do she will not reply to you or even acknowledge you. The sorcerer is her entire world, her entire focus and will be for some time, until she is once again able to assert herself.

The voice cut into them, making them look apprehensive at the two unknown girls in front of them.

Bea stepped forward, touching her Companion-to-be on the cheek.

– We will of course heed thy words, sorcerer, she said softly.

– Of course, the sorcerer snorted, looking at her with eyes of glass, glass.

The hand fell.

– Rise, my apprentice, Janet of the Blue Flame commanded. – Serve your master!

Eleanor obeyed, her eyes attentive, but cast to the ground.

– Was this how Malone treated you? Rosa asked, not hiding her resentment.

The sorcerer looked at her with her eyes of glass. It was enough to make her old friend tremble.

– Certainly not, Janet snorted. – He chose a far more informal approach. It stands to reason that his methods should not be mine. Rest assured that I will follow the age-old protocols to the latter.

Most of her attention was on the apprentice, too. The deeper exchange and communication of thoughts and emotions had already begun.

– Come, my apprentice. Follow thy Master!

A curtly nod to the rest. Then she took her leave and the apprentice trailed her like a dog down the trail towards the town.

Chapter 15

The sorcerer returned to the small house at the end of the road with her apprentice in tow.

She noticed that Myra noticed the moment they stepped inside.

– You did not? Myra said. – Tell me you did not.

It was a rhetorical question. Her daughter shrugged it off.

– I most certainly did, Janet said haughtily. – She practically begged me, the little tramp, and I found it in my heart to hear her prayers.

She started ascending the stairs, stopped briefly on the second step, a smile touching her lips.

– She will do all the chores in the house for a while. Rest assured it will shine on every single spot.

The bedroom looked different, somehow, even though she could not put her finger on anything and state categorically that it had changed.

She watched it with four eyes, now. Even though the impression through the second pair was muted, it was distinct and irrefutable in her mind.

– You may undress me, now.

Eleanor rushed forward to obey the command, never raising her eyes from the floor.

It was a pleasant sensation to have a maid again, to have her at her beck and call. The sorcerer smiled.

The servant removed her jacket, putting it away in the closet. She removed shoes and pants, and her underwear, the clothes snuggling her skin, placing it neatly below and on the chair.

– You will sleep on the floor.

The bed smelled nice. Janet savored the sensation of that and a thousand others. She stretched out on it and put her head on the pillow and closed her eyes.

The sensations grew stronger. She experienced more of Eleanor's past and present life.

Eleanor whimpered as she experienced what was her master, her revered sorcerer, her terrors and dark joy.

Janet saw Eleanor grow up, feeling her emotions, her antagonism towards her mother and father.

She was aware of how the process grew more powerful and even more so as they slipped into sleep and dream.

Malone felt closer again. He never strayed far from her thoughts, and thus not far from Eleanor's either, making the innocent youngling whimper some more. Janet quickly grew consciously aware of the obvious: He had been more experienced when he had taken her as his apprentice and could control the process to a greater degree. She knew he had held back because he needed her to grow powerful while she was still the apprentice. There was no need for her to do that with her apprentice.

She was sleeping and sleeping soundly, but it still felt like she was awake the entire night, invigorated by the process, sensing without straining herself how her knowledge and power of will imposed itself on the whimpering creature writhing on the floor.

The sun shone on her face the next morning. Her eyes opened without strain. She felt wide awake and empowered, ready for the day.

Eleanor knelt on the floor, her eyes cast down.

Janet ignored her, until she emerged from the shower. Then she signed for her to rise and act. The servant dried her with a huge towel and pleasant moves. Then she dressed her. Janet felt pampered and lazy.

– I can get used to this, she chuckled and spoke in a very patronizing manner. – It is quite enjoyable. No wonder some sorcerers hesitate to let go of their pets.

She did not speak to the girl, but just spoke.

Eleanor set the table and served breakfast. Myra knew better than to protest. She knew the age-old rites of passage well, like any full-fledged sorcerer.

The two girls walked side by side down the road later, even though the smaller walked with her eyes constantly lowered, but it did not bring any attention. Most people did not know the significance of what they witnessed.

Janet realized startled that Joan was not there, keeping an eye on her. The realization alone was quite disconcerting.

She shrugged and walked on. It was a really long walk, as she brought the girl with her to the hidden store in the hidden street, where only those that could find their way walked.

Eleanor bumped into the walls of the invisible maze several times. She was practically shaken apart by its brutal environment. Janet ignored that and her and kept charging forward casually.

This time, when she reached for the handle it felt like a handle and was no more difficult to push than any other. The door opened and they emerged into the illustrious space of the magick store.

– Fair morning, she greeted the man behind the counter.

– Fair morning, Oliver Martens returned her greeting.

He was slightly nervous, but she also read anticipation, read interest behind his fairly calm surface. It was not hard for her. That was easy for her as well.

– I am pleased to be in need of your services again, Oliver, she dazzled him with her smile and alluring personality.

– What can I help the Blue Flame with on this fine day? He asked with a fluttering voice.

– I need a discipline collar, she informed him.

He did not look at Eleanor. That would have been impolite, a breach of etiquette, an insult to the sorcerer. But he could not stop himself from doing a casual glance. Janet knew then that her first impression of him had been correct: he had not been a caretaker of this place for long.

– I believe I have several in my possession that could prove useful to you, he replied. – A moment, please.

She excelled further by the distinct reddening of his skin.

He returned with several collars hanging from leather chains, doing his utmost in order to not touch any of them.

She did, measuring one by one as they made themselves known to her, threatening, cajoling and attempting to impose their will on her.

– This one, she stated.

Her hand squeezed the metal.

– Hello, Karmak, she mumbled with a distant, spiteful grin.

He, the spirit bonded with the collar responded to her with a subdued snarl, quickly realizing that she was no pushover, that she could not be easily conquered.

She turned towards the girl. The apprentice bared her neck and Janet slipped the collar on her, scratching the skin on her left cheek with a nail, drawing blood, rubbing some of it on the metal.

The whispers began almost immediately. Janet heard more of it, too, through the girl. Eleanor shook in a moment's defiance. The current flowed through her instantly. She screamed and fell to the floor. Janet studied the effect with keen interest.

The punishment finally let up, after a series of moments Janet knew that Eleanor had imagined was forever. She looked at the sorcerer through a veil of tears.

– You need to learn proper discipline, a certain set of conduct. This will aid in that crucial process. If you do right nothing will happen or you may be rewarded. If you do wrong you will be punished. The stern teacher, the wicked, wicked man embodying this pretty necklace will teach you to be a good girl.

Eleanor remained unmoving on the floor, making no attempt at drying her tears.

– You have my thanks, Oliver, Janet told him.

He tried replying, but was unable to do so.

She turned and headed for the exit. The apprentice fought herself on her feet and followed her.

They walked on what were familiar roads to them both, the grounds they had played on since childhood. The daystar shone hard on the ground, on their flesh, seemingly disintegrating them both. Janet felt herself slipping away like melting ice.

The familiar house appeared in her vision detailed and true. Janet opened the door and walked inside without knocking.

A man and a woman having breakfast in the kitchen looked startled at them, at the sorcerer and at the girl with lowered eyes.

– Your daughter is yours no longer, the sorcerer declared. – She will never return to you. I have taken her as mine. Her life is forfeit. She is my dust to do with as I will.

They knew, well aware of the rules governing the relation between a sorcerer and an apprentice. One glance would have told Janet that, even if she had not known.

The woman rose, visibly shaking.

– El? She said. – El?

There was no response. The girl kept her entire attention on her Master.

The woman grabbed the girl, doing her best to embrace her and coddle her, to no avail. It was like touching wood. The woman choked in distress.

– Answer your mother, apprentice, Janet commanded casually.

Awareness, somewhat returned to the girl's eyes. She straightened.

– Janet of the Blue Flame speaks the truth, mother. She claimed this girl and made her her apprentice, her devoted servant, and through kindness and cruelty, if it is her will, she may make her a sorcerer.

The man and the woman wanted to speak and spit harsh words, but cat got their tongue.

– You will not seek her out, not search for her or make any attempt at reclaiming her.

The chill in the sorcerer's voice froze them, made them unable to move.

– I require your family heirloom, Janet stated, – your Book of Shadows, your Grimoire, all of them, if more than one there are, from both sides of your progeny's line.

She rubbed it in, kept doing so long after the dim light of understanding was lit in the mother's eyes and slower, incredulous in the father's. The mother walked to the shelf in the darker parts of the living room. She found two leather-bound books and brought them to Janet.

– You carry them, apprentice, the sorcerer said casually, poignant to the girl.

– They are your burden to bear.
Eleanor rushed forward to receive her inheritance from her mother. The mother held on to them for a moment, as if being reluctant to let them go.
Eleanor stood there, practically embracing the books, holding them close to her chest.
– Does that not make you feel better? Janet said to the mother with a cruel grin.
The sorcerer left and the apprentice followed, not looking back for a moment.
The Blue Flame started speaking, started burning as they passed through the gate.
– You wanted this, she said, with spite dripping from her voice like poison, – wanted it more than anything, so much that you discarded everything you were before, thereby making exactly the same mistake I did. It is almost funny.
The apprentice shook under the onslaught of the sorcerer's venom.
Eleanor wanted to reply. She opened her mouth to speak, but a sharp pain in her throat kept her from speaking, and she was assaulted by the sensation of a huge man standing behind her with a large whip in his hand.
– Listen to Karmak, apprentice. Karmak will teach you exactly what you need to hear in order to become a good, attentive servant. Karmak died with those instructions engraved into what is left of his mind. Do you understand, servant?
– Eleanor understands, Master, the girl whispered, bowing her head in further subservience.
They returned once again to the small house at the end of the road, to its wild garden. Janet found two wands in the shed. She threw one hard at the apprentice. Eleanor caught it, embittered, defiant.
– We will now start exploring thy potential, apprentice. We will identify and explore thy active power and how we can best utilize it. Thou think the previous exercise and wand fighting was tough? If then I pity thee.
The formal language came easy to her. She did not have to think before she spoke.
– The infant wants to climb the mountain, but it must master walking before it can run.
Janet raised her wand, signaling that she was about to start the lesson. Eleanor dropped the books on the ground, raising her wand in defense just in time. Janet's wand hit hers hard, making her stagger. The sorcerer struck again. Once again, Eleanor managed to block the strike. Janet moved, moved fast on her feet and with her weapon in a coordinated multi-part attack. The

tip of the wand hit the apprentice on the side of the head, hit her hard. She went down. The wand slipped from her weak hands.

– On your feet! Janet struck her thigh, making the girl cry out in pain. – Make your stand, weakling!

Resentment, respect, fear and hatred coursed through Eleanor as she fought herself up. The reclaimed wand shook in her hands.

– You move constantly. Your feet and you never stand still, not for a single moment. You are a whirl of motion, a living weapon.

Janet moved and Eleanor looked like she was standing still.

– You defend yourself with the strong part of the wand or the sword, what is closest to your hands. You attack with the point or points, you maim and kill with it. A sorcerer is whatever he or she chooses to be.

Eleanor shook when Janet's wand hit hers.

– You know something is missing, do you not, apprentice.

– YES! The girl shouted. – This girl knows, but she does not know what it is.

Tears glimmered in her eyes.

The cracks of wand hitting wand, screams of pain and frustration and words snarled echoed through the garden. People passing by on the road speeded up visibly. Neither the sorcerer nor the apprentice paid them any heed.

Janet struck her down again, and kept striking her while she was down.

Eleanor collapsed on the ground, practically shaking herself apart.

Janet turned her back to her and set course for the house entrance. Once again the apprentice forced herself on her feet and stumbled after the regal woman she obeyed in all things.

Cathy's dark laughter shook them both.

Eleanor scrubbed the floor, doing so meticulously, totally focused on her task, unable to tell how long she had been doing it, the timelessness of the outside joining that on the inside. She began in the kitchen below and slowly moved on from there, up the stairs and every single inch of the house. The memory of the hard and harsh wand training kept replaying itself in her dull mind.

Janet saw everything through her eyes, imagined she was able to feel every sensation, the numbness in her fingers because of them being exposed to water and soap for so long, each breath as she drew air into her wheezing lungs.

She sat at the top of the stairs, hardly smelling the stench from the bucket filled with dirty water by her side, fighting off exhaustion, still breathing hard, cocking her ears in order to hear Karmak's voice, but he was silent, and she felt base relief at the very thought.

Janet casually made her way up the stairs.

– My, oh, my, you have certainly been busy.

The sorcerer petted her servant, and the girl practically purred in joy.

Janet moved on. The cruel smile touched her lips and she kicked the filled bucket. Some of the water landed directly on Eleanor, but most of it spread across the room, as the bucket made its erratic way down the stairs.

Eleanor cried out in misery. She collapsed in tears. The chokes filled the house with the stench from the water.

– Busy, but quite lax, obviously, as your work is far from done.

Eleanor kept washing and polishing, rubbing, rubbing, rubbing every single point. In her total exhaustion, it felt like her work would never be done.

– Do you want me to move out, mother? Janet asked the woman appearing from the living room. – I can move back into my house, where I am queen.

– Why should I want that? Myra responded with equal poison. – You are doing exactly what you are supposed to be doing.

The mother's words stung and stunned the daughter.

She was quite good at the game of pointers and needles, Janet realized.

– I… enjoy it too much, she told Bea at the dawn of a day when Big Moon rose in the sky. – Peter never did. He just saw my training as a necessity and acted casually according to that.

– You are good at it, Bea stated quietly. – Be content with that.

They snuggled a bit, low-keyed arousal slowly building.

– And it can clearly be useful. In fact, my father's idea of a growing squad is not bad at all. We can train an entire cadre of young sorcerers, adding them easily to our already devoted trainees.

– Young sorcerers that will be ours to command? Janet said pointedly.

– Of course, Bea replied unconcerned. – They need direction, you know that. And once the word goes around that the Blue Flame has returned to the game, there will be a rush of recruits.

Janet found herself nodding. The smile broke on Bea's face.

There was a knock on the door, forceful, impatient. Expectation brightened Janet's eyes. She rose and walked, somewhat dignified into the hall. Bea followed her.

Janet opened the door. Illandra stood there, her usual haughty and aloof self.

– Everything is set, she said without small talk. – Are you ready, Janet, scion of the Bone People?

– I am! Janet stated firmly. – We have been awaiting your arrival with eager anticipation and will be ready to leave momentarily.

– Good, good, Illandra grunted.
She finally turned to Bea, acknowledging her.
– Greetings, Honored Grandmother, the girl said and curtseyed.
– Greetings, betrothed of my granddaughter and mage of demons, the woman said, not too patronizing.
Eleanor rushed down the stairs from the attic, carrying bags on both shoulders, creating more than a bit of noise. She had her eyes cast down and knelt the moment she reached Illandra's sphere. Illandra nodded imperceptibly and Eleanor rose again, slipping back into the background of their attention, practically fading from their view.
Myra appeared in the kitchen door.
– Illandra, she said curtly.
– Myra, Illandra said curtly.
And that was that.
It was a strange entourage that made its way down the road some time later. The four of them did not look that much different, but people still noticed, doing so beyond appearances, beyond their superficial, mainstream views on existence. The three teenagers and the considerably older woman enjoyed a casual stroll on a fairly empty road, and very few observing them were any wiser.
– We could have had a pleasant ride in a car. Bea said, frowning, as if pondering her statement, not really complaining.
– I sympathize with your preferences, Illandra said. – Do not think I do not. I have become used to the finer things in life myself. You may look at this as a quest or walkabout of sorts, though, and long walks are a good thing on such ventures.
They walked and quickly began sweating in the shine of the hot morning daystar. Eleanor strived harder than the others, as she was carrying most of the gear. Janet strained her eyes in an effort to spot Joan, but the magistrate was not there, was not anywhere near them, she just was not.
They stopped at the same tavern the youths had visited late at night not so long ago. It gave off an entirely different feeling compared to then, but the sense of familiarity could not be denied and the girls re-experienced the evening and night in poignant flashes and glimpses.
Janet and Bea held hands, sitting close, exchanging kisses and caresses. The sorcerer felt a catching form in her throat, momentarily overwhelmed by a worry she could not name. She kissed her betrothed in a sudden, potent, desperate longing, as if it was the last time.
– You do approve of this, all this, do you not?
Bea looked at her with her usual ambiguity, with both her overbearing and

soft self.

– Of course, I would have strongly suggested it, if you had not realized it on your own, realized your potential to teach, to lead. You will be a legend among sorcerers and humans alike, and I will be right there, by your side.

Janet blushed hard, and the catching in her throat grew. She glanced at Illandra, but her grandmother seemed very preoccupied with her food and drink, hardly interested at all.

They reached the quay, where the ferry was about to disembark. It closed its doors just a few seconds after they stepped inside. Janet looked astonished at the goose bumps on her arm.

She studied her surroundings with flashing, anxious eyes, but there was nothing there, nothing to grab or hold onto. It was only yet another mundane trip across the bay.

Illandra studied her, measured her. Janet felt a flare of irritation.

– You have so much to teach me, grandmother, so many stories to tell.

She did not attempt to hide the slight sarcasm when she named their relation, even as she failed to conceal her interest, her needs beneath the veneer of casual talk and spite.

– And I will! Illandra stated calmly.

Her words played so pleasantly in Janet's ears. Expectation rattled her.

– You are part of a proud tradition, so many proud traditions, in fact that you are almost unique. The Blue Flame has burned for thousands of years, so long that no one alive knows its origin. The Bone People began before the settlers from Rome arrived here. They mixed with them, strengthening their blood, like the Romans themselves did. The bone tattoos and the flame have mixed in you, like they have mixed with too many to be counted other lines of sorcerers throughout time and the Ocean of Mankind. Your Great Grandfather knew about you and what you would become. Your task is quite simply to join with the prophecy, to meet its challenge and embrace its potential. You have already survived its first trial, thriving and growing more powerful in its wake. Your decision to become involved in sorcerer politics is certainly a good move. You will present yourself at the stage of power and stake your claim on its domain. Know that I, your paternal grandmother am proud of you.

Janet wanted to speak, wanted to express herself, but found herself unable to do so, the unpleasant memories revisiting her with a vengeance. Bea squeezed her hand in support and enthusiasm.

The ferry reached the mainland, docking at the western quay at the south point of Howell. It remained a sunny day. Shadows kept clouding the bright air. The door slid open. They and all other passengers crossed the landing bridge. The quartet walked along the seaside, along the harbor, where lots of ships were lined up, to the bridge crossing over to the Old City, hardly more than touching it before making their way up the hillside of Lazoon, the flat mountain.

Janet had no trouble sensing the interest their walk roused among a selection of the people currently occupying the resort area beyond the tall wall. Sudden irritation filled her.

– You will teach me everything you know, she snapped, – all your knowledge and understanding of the lore and more, and you will hold back nothing.

– Of course, Keeper of the Blue Flame, Illandra said, accompanying her reply with a humble bow.

This time Janet's temper did not worry her, but strengthened her. It felt good and right, and the prevailing doubt about herself and whether or not Illandra was mocking her could not counter that.

Do you see, Peter? Are you proud as well?

The last remnants of the city faded behind them. The wilderness, the massive, untouched nature surrounded them and isolated them, cut them off from the urban landscape they had just left.

– This always appears like a different realm to me, Bea shuddered with longing in her voice. – I want to paint it, paint it all.

They headed west, the short, long walk to the cave. They reached it. Janet had no trouble locating it, even though the memories of walking here were not altogether clear in her mind. They stepped inside. Its murky dark embraced them, devoured them.

– This is a good thing for you as well, apprentice, Janet told Eleanor. – You need to experience other realms and other resources of teaching skills and mystical knowledge. Rest assured that I will take you on any perilous journey necessary in order to complete your education.

You snotty, patronizing bitch! She told herself glumly.

The dark revealed itself to sensitive eyes and minds. The opening leading to the trail appeared, even as it seemed to be only the wall there. Janet spotted the torches just as the dark threatened to overwhelm even their senses. They walked through the narrow cave with confident steps. Its walls seemed to shake and boil, the rock, if rock there was, never staying still for a moment.

The cave turned wider. They breached the slight pressure in the air and walked on the wide field with the village. Activity picked up between the huts almost immediately. All the inhabitants rushed outside, towards the four travelers. They knelt about halfway between them and the huts, timid, terrified and eager to please.

Janet walked on without acknowledging them and the three others followed her. The villagers remained in their position, their eyes cast to the ground. They still knelt unmoving, when the four returned to the path. Torches lit every spot on the cave. There was not a single trek of darkness anywhere. Janet nodded smug to herself.

– This is your doing, is it not? Bea said in awe. – You informed the villagers of your desires?

– I did indeed, Janet replied pleased. – They followed my instructions to the latter.

They took a break again. Eleanor dutifully arranged the lunch table, spreading the blanket on the ground and made the delicious sandwiches. She took care of everything, not once looking up or even displaying a need to do so. Janet nodded to herself, and then nodding to the apprentice, giving her permission to join in on the pleasant feast.

The cave walls and ceiling felt close, felt both comforting and disquieting. Sounds, including loud cries signifying activity reached them from some indefinite point, but they grew neither closer nor farther away and the four did not become too worried.

– It is like it is coming from the very walls, Bea said, both excited and alarmed.

– There are ancient legends about this cave, Illandra said, not unkind, – about how its entire length is potential gateways to different realms. Many have become lost in here, and never found their way back to the path.

Eleanor packed their gear again, just as efficient and skilled, and they moved on. The new torches burned fresh and tall on the walls, the old sputtered and their fire slowly faded. They were really old, as if they had burned there forever. The people of the field had clearly tended this path for generations.

The four reached the spot where Malone had brought her, where she later had brought herself. There were voices, but they quickly backed off and left them alone. Janet could practically see it. It made her smile. Illandra studied her. Janet pretended not to notice.

The music was still there, surrounding them, embracing them.

– Can you hear it? Janet asked Eleanor.

– I can not hear anything, Master, Eleanor replied, frowning at her.

– Neither can I, Bea said. – What is it?

– It is music, Illandra stated. – We can not hear it, but the current Blue Flame can.

Bea looked at Janet.

– I can, Janet confirmed.

– It is a test, of sorts, Illandra said.
– A test of power, then, Bea stated with confidence.
She looked at her betrothed with love in her eyes.
They walked on towards the exit. The color of the torches shifted from ordinary fire to blue, until they no longer hung on walls, no longer were torches, but dark lights levitating in the air, in the thick mist.
She and also the other three heard what sounded like ordinary voices, even though it was impossible to make out where they were coming from. The ground began shaking the moment it was no longer ground, but the bridge.
– Whatever happens, do not move outside the lights, Janet cautioned them.
– A good advice, Illandra nodded.
The older woman was visibly tense, but Janet found herself strangely calm. She had not been frightened the last time she had walked on the bridge and was not now either. Few sorcerers had stepped outside the lights, off the path… but she had, and not only survived, but thrived.
She felt the volatile forces down there, their ebb and flow. They invaded her, even more than they usually did.
Bea studied her again, as always very sensitive to the tide within her.
– It is the Dark River, Janet said with a hollow voice. – It flows towards the ocean, and keeps flowing below it, never truly gone.
And Bea's smile cracked in an excited grin.
There was a shadow by the river bank as the mist temporarily cleared. She could barely make out its outline, as if whatever or whoever was there had become one with the air. As they reached solid ground, reached the road with the flat stones, both apprehension and excitement touched her. The numbing chill and scorching heat did not let go.
A few more steps and the small township resembling a medieval village grew out of the mist.
– We have arrived, Illandra informed them. – Welcome to the Village, the place where sorcerers gather.
Janet did not see or hear the bard anywhere. There was no one playing music in these streets today or tonight, in this eternal twilight.
The building appearing around them was different. She noticed it without doubt. This was not Florence's house, not her eminent domain. Janet felt a sickening relief.
People seemed to appear around them from open air, fade in like from a dream.
Then, as many of them stared hard at her they felt very real.
Bea squeezed her hand and she felt better, felt much improved in an instant.

Insecurity and bravery charged through her like cold, like heat.

Anger, the fist closing so hard that it hurt replaced both. Her waves got away from her. She let them. Her three companions and also others in the hall started breathing faster. Fear and anticipation flashed in sorcerers' eyes.

– Fetch ale, my apprentice, she snapped, – and be quick about it.

Eleanor rushed forward, joining other prospective sorcerers on their way to the bar. Janet noted to her satisfaction that she was quick on her feet and resourceful, and was among the first reaching the men and women behind the desk accepting funds for ale.

They found a table in a deep corner of the room. Illandra led them there. Janet found no fault with her precautionary measures. The young sorcerer sat down, very aware that she had the best possible view of the hall.

– Look at the man over there, Illandra spoke in her ear.

She did not really have to point to him. Janet spotted easily the man with authority written all over him, in the very manner he moved.

– That is the Speaker, Illandra said. – He enjoys an elevated position at this gathering and others.

The young sorcerer watched him, and those surrounding him, how they swarmed around his person like flies.

Her eyes moved. Practically by themselves, as she kept studying the room and the others present. She saw an older woman that also had a significant number of followers around her person. There was a lot to study and take in and she sucked it up like a sponge.

– It feels so good to be here, she declared, – to return here.

– Here? Bea queried, clearly curious.

– The Village. Janet shrugged. – It is all The Village here. It is where sorcerers meet and parley.

Bea looked at her with the deep, deep all-consuming love.

– I love the way you speak, love the very punctuations and nuances you make.

Janet feared she would blush, but she did not, and felt even better. She turned her attention to the older woman in their midst with calm eyes.

– You did the right thing from the very first moment here. Illandra praised her. – It is good tactics to take the measure of your potential opponents.

The young sorcerer turned away from her kin and her betrothed and the apprentice, aware of them on some level, but focusing on the rest of the gathering. She recognized some of the sorcerers she had met as Malone's protégé, but most of them were unknown to her, at least in appearance.

Their predilections and desires were not, not in any significant manner.

Bea comforted her with light touches and sympathetic smiles, calming, somewhat the raging storm. Janet squeezed her hand in gratitude.

There was movement somewhere. Janet did sense it. A draft, a drift in the wind. Her waves, easily expanding to the entire room registered the miniscule disturbance in the ether.

– It is such a small thing, really, she mumbled, Cathy mumbled.

– What was that? Bea asked.

– Nothing, Janet smiled, – nothing important.

She petted the other girl on the cheek.

A door, a portal opened somewhere. Two sorcerers arrived. Janet knew they were Grayson and Dasek before they appeared to her eyes. Hot expectation and cold rage flowed through her.

– Do they know? She asked Illandra.

– No! The older woman shook her head. – Why should they? They are probably aware of your antagonism, unless they are *completely* insensitive, but sorcerers' dislike of each other is not exactly news. They loathe your popularity among the younger guard, though.

– My popularity…?

– Yes, have you not noticed?

She did notice, now, as she looked around again and saw young faces turned towards her in admiration and even awe.

– It is a classic tale. You were sold into slavery by a cruel man, and returned with a vengeance. You have survived the Kal Chek. Why should they not favor you?

– Indeed, Bea marveled. – They see you as a living embodiment of the prophecies. The actuality of what they observe tells them that vague, ancient stories may have a foundation in real life.

– You are aware, I trust, of how many have claimed to be an embodiment of ancient culture, Janet sniffed, – and failed utterly to meet its standards.

– Of course, Bea shrugged unconcerned.

– But we did prepare for your coming, Illandra pointed out, – generations before you were born.

There was something there, that Janet both understood and not, or at least glimpsed, of the woman's motivations and intent.

– Thank you, grandmother, Janet snorted, – for being so concerned with my well being…

She turned her head, a little distracted. Some of those belonging to the younger guard approached her, cautiously, but resolute. It was pretty easy spotting the pattern of their migrations.

A young man, cocky, but still serious-minded walked ahead of the procession. He stopped in front of the older sorcerer.

– Well met, Illandra, High Priestess of the Bone People, he greeted her.
– Well met, Dane of the Deep Purple, she replied, evidently pleased with his manners.

He turned towards the girl.

– Well met, Janet of the Bluc Flame, he stated calmly.

She repeated Illandra's words, bathing in the lukewarm, pleasant eagerness of his eyes.

Others stepped forward, and the process repeated itself several times. The formality of it all made a giggle form in Janet's throat, but she kept her cool. She noticed easily how the older sorcerers looked with disdain at the spectacle and felt even better for it.

– That went well, Bea said afterwards. – They adore you and fear you. They will become excellent squad members.

– In your father's «squad»?

– In ours, My Lady, Bea said softly and eagerly. – In ours!

– And you staked your claim in the community, Illandra remarked casually, very casually, – doing so without even trying, a feat not to be underestimated.

This time Janet turned towards her with a pointed stare.

– Explain yourself!

– That is easy enough, daughter of my son, the older sorcerer shrugged. – You are the first of the Bone People in many generations to have taken an active part in the affairs of others, in the larger society surrounding us. The fact that you are also of other, equally powerful heritages only adds significance to that.

The bugle that perhaps no one was blowing sounded from an undetermined point in the hall. A few seconds passed and a large crack of thunder added itself to the horn. A considerable part of the wall slid aside. Dark light flooded everybody's eyes.

Everybody filed into the darker hallway. It felt like they floated or flowed instead of walked. The corridor, neither narrow nor wide opened to the other room.

They entered a special place. Janet sensed that without trying. She saw that Bea and Eleanor did as well. Everyone present reacted to their surroundings in similar ways.

Nothing but torches, natural fires provided lighting. All bodies cast multiple shadows, creating an eerie mood impossible to cast off.

Then, as the giant door that was more like a wall closed, orange shifted to blue and torches were no longer torches, but lamps with flickering flames levitating in the air. Mist drifted in from nowhere, and they appeared to be outside. The walls were no longer walls, but the thick mist surrounding them.

The lamps formed a circle in the air, with one sorcerer below each lamp. Those accompanying them stood behind their backs. Janet heard the whispers, both those coming from the air and from parched throats. One man, the Speaker stepped forward with a very solemn expression on his face. He held a wand, a talking stick in his right hand. Janet stifled a giggle.

– Sorcerers sought a secluded place to meet, he stated. – They found this place long ago. Sorcerers have met here since. This is one far land where sorcerers gather.

His speech was pompous to be sure, but there was also a justified pride and authority there Janet could not help but being affected by. He had certainly become speaker because of his ability to convey that better than others. She resisted its influence, knowing it was yet another part of the general scenery designed to make the younger sorcerers fall in line. This was a circle, but she easily noticed that those closer to him were mostly elders, with a few strays of younger supporters. Most of it was obvious. She did not need Illandra, with her small pointers and suggestions to show her that.

I know power, Peter, I know how it works.

The elder spokesman ended his speech. The true deliberation, if there was such at all began.

The next sorcerer, a woman began talking. She did not exactly make a speech like the man before her had done, but kept speaking in generalities. Janet noticed, again without trying that many of those present stifled yawns and would have wanted to sit down, if there had been chairs to sit on.

– I am pleased to say there have been few disputes within our assembly lately, the woman concluded. – We are pretty much a uniformed group without many and serious grievances between us.

Janet curled her lips in contempt and did not care if others noticed.

They did. There was little doubt about that. Everything between fear and interest and anger showed in faces illuminated by lights and shadows. She realized startled, when she spotted Illandra and Bea's approval, and the glances from the occasional sorcerer throughout the place that she had suddenly taken a step further away from anonymity.

All that, by practically doing nothing. The contempt changed into a triumphant grin.

Bea shook in awe. Janet reached out to her and touched her cheek in what was meant as a comforting gesture.

Others spoke. There was a more or less obvious pecking order of sorts. Janet shrugged indifferently, and she knew that more of those present picked up on that.

Then Grayson and Dasek looked at her and that look more than told her that they more than suspected, now, her motive for coming here. The waves of the space, and the pattern they wove suddenly hammered her. She could not stop herself from tensing, and Bea and Eleanor could not either.

Illandra stayed cool and relaxed, and the three girls, studying her, taking their cue from her turned calmer, too.

Those speaking, now, lower on the pecking order or first time visitors not necessary known to the regulars of this particular assembly stated their name and heritage before speaking. It was pretty much like Janet had read in the lore. They were all, in one way or another presented or witnessed by relatives or friends or acquaintances and thereby vetted by the assembly before being allowed to speak, or speak much.

There was still a considerable time to wait. The «queue» «lined up» before Janet seemed endless to her. She performed internal exercises and meditation in an effort to slow down the waves within.

They kept manifesting themselves, and everybody noticed.

One more sorcerer serving platitudes was about to finish his plate. The next made himself ready for his spot.

A loud sound, more like a whine penetrated the air and eardrums of everyone present. Everybody looked up. They sensed a draft, and a chill down the spine. A loud scream, more like a screech made everybody jump out of their skin. They all knew what this was well before they heard the flapping of wings.

A creature, one resembling a man entered the «sacred» space of the sorcerers. It dived and clipped a few of them. They threw themselves on the floor in panic. It floated effortlessly upwards again with more loud shrieks. A few took a shot at it with their powers, but did not even come close at hitting the mark. The creature was so skilled at maneuvering that it seemed like it could foresee the path of the energy beams and the various attacks.

It dawned on Janet that perhaps it could. She studied it with endless fascination. It dived again, faster than she could register it. There was a brush of wind, a wing brushing against her waves, not her flesh, and a loud yelp.

Bea jumped high, and caught the creature's neck in a steel grip. She dragged the creature down and it hit the floor hard. It attempted to strike her with its wings, but she was too close to its body. There was one loud crack, and scream. Then another loud crack and scream. Bea rose, holding on to the beast with a cold smile. She struck it, struck it several times, quickly pacifying it further. Janet realized startled that Bea had broken its wings.

Bea dragged it with her, as she approached Janet, bowing deeply.

– Thy prize, My Lady.

She threw the creature at Janet's feet. It did not move, but shook in pain and fright.

Bea opened her purse and pulled up a collar, a red band of metal and a strange substance reminding Janet of leather.

– Combined with the spell of Kordar, you may use this to bind him to you. It will make him even more cordial, and open to your instructions.

Janet accepted the band. She surveyed the pathetic creature a bit, and then she put the band around its neck. It glimmered a bit. She spoke the curse. The band tightened and settled around the broad neck. The dull look in the beast's eyes turned even more pronounced.

– Congratulations, My Lady, you are now the proud owner of an already housebroken pet.

Janet studied it. Its large, half erected cock made her a little uneasy, but no more than looking at a horse or another animal did. She rubbed its skin. It looked at her with love in its eyes.

She turned away from it. It did not move, but stayed on the spot where she had placed it. She stepped forward, claiming the turn of the other sorcerer, long before her time. Everyone froze. They had stared, but now they froze. She sensed a well of emotions and sensations touching her waves.

– I am Janet, Master of the Blue Flame, scion of the Bone People, she greeted them.

Both her words and the reactions to them surged through the hall without walls.

– Surely an excessive claim…

A fairly young sorcerer commented.

Then, and only then she pushed herself, making visible what had been concealed. Both the tattoos and the blue flame danced on her powerful frame, mixing, actually mixing, interacting with the floating lights, making several of those present gasp involuntarily in wonder and sudden fright.

She voiced no vocal response.

– I wish to be heard, she stated calmly, – in matters of importance and not.

– The gathering acknowledges the heir to the Blue Flame, the woman, the perceived «second in command» stated on behalf of the man, making it unnecessary for him to say anything, to directly involve himself.

The man, the Speaker let go of the wand. It drifted slowly into Janet's left hand.

She struck it at the ground, and the echoes of those waves shook the air surrounding everyone present.

– This is my first time here, she grinned. – I am very happy about it. It appears to be a great place, filled with magick and untapped energies.

The gathering could not possibly miss the fine-tuned irony in her voice and expression. It was there, very evident in every little move she made. The present youngsters giggled without bothering to hide it, using the opportunity to show off their disrespect for the elders.

– Let it be known that I hereby charge the sorcerers Grayson and Dasek with grave misconduct.

That made them all shut up that very instant. The entire gathering stared at her in what was akin to shock.

Grayson turned red, his wrinkled face distorted in anger. Dasek's sweet features twisted themselves in the poisonous expression dominating it. Grayson opened his mouth to speak, and he did so, but not a single sound reached attentive ears, not even his own.

Janet grinned. She held the talking stick. She decided who would be heard.

Everybody looked speechless at her.

– They have moved far beyond their rights, abusing their duties at every turn. They are not the only ones doing so, but are clearly at the forefront of it all. Young, aspiring sorcerers and mages to be come to them, and instead of aiding them in their transformation, scoundrels like Grayson and Dasek keep them as pets, eventually discarding them as garbage or selling them off like collateral as part of some deal or another.

She spat the last words like she would vile things.

– I will also chastise everyone taking part in Florence's «education program» and similar. That is clearly an integrated part of this. It is a vile practice that has to stop. Its only purpose is to narrow the field of emerging sorcerers and make elders fat and their lives easy and comfortable. It is one of several elements in and outside our community slowly obliterating our kind. There are very few of us left. Let us fight our extinction, instead of eagerly supporting it… like Grayson and Dasek, and their «equals» are doing.

Half of those present stared at her with hatred in their eyes, close to the other half in bewilderment.

She held on to the wand, to the spotlight far longer than she was entitled to, forcing them to keep their attention on her.

Then, she let go. The wand slipped from her hand and returned to the Speaker.

The ruckus, the loud, angry yapping began. The Speaker did nothing to prevent it. Janet stood there, grinning at the angry mob, spitting at the angry words directed at her, bathing in it all, openly enjoying it, and slowly, only slowly it dawned on her detractors that she was feeding off their rage, that all the rampant emotions charging through the air actually strengthened her.

It faded like a punctured balloon. She kept swaying in sweet pleasure long after it had ended, as the hall fell completely silent.

She spoke again, and was heard, heard loud and clear, in spite of her not holding the talking stick.

– I charge the sorcerers Grayson and Dasek with grave misconduct. They should be censored and never be allowed to walk these halls again. The others, their collaborators and supporters will get an extension, a chance to improve themselves, but they should not become idle or their chance at redemption will quickly be forfeit. Thus speaks the Master of the Blue Flame, the Scion of the Bone People.

The silence turned deafening.

Chapter 16

Those gathering around her afterwards had grown in number and fervor compared to those who had done so before the meeting.

– That was such an excellent deliberation, Janet, Dane of the Deep Purple told her, while fighting to keep his most extreme excitement contained, to not go completely overboard and leaving behind any semblance of formality.

They, the various factions came to her for many reasons, and far from all had honest intentions, but she felt convinced that he had. She found herself blushing under the stare of his huge purple eyes and chastised herself.

– You said what needed to be said, Livy of Lambruia stated, – what should have been stated plainly *ages* ago.

Livy's dishonesty was quite evident to Janet.

– And even though it did not bring the intended and desired results at this juncture, Jess of the Orchards said with regret, – it might at a near future date, thanks to you.

And there were others, making their voices heard.

She watched them, how they were practically fawning in her presence.

– Thank you, Janet replied, giving them her best smile. – Thank you all.

– Would it be an imposition if we kept you company on your path back? Dane asked.

– No imposition at all, she assured him and took his hand.

The whirl of motion did distract her. She scouted for Grayson and Dasek and others that she knew positively had taken part in Florence's schemes.

One man she was not confident that she recognized scurried out of there in the shadow of the considerable crowd leaving the premises.

– They have all fled, Bea told her. – Yellow cowards worried about what a young girl of an upstart sorcerer might do to them if she should feel so inclined.

Bea kissed her on the lips, clearly aroused. As always the girl's passion affected Janet, awoke her own desire.

– And let me also congratulate you with how well you handle Dane of the pompous Deep Purple. You twist him around your little finger as easily as thin rope.

– Thank you, I think…

Janet giggled, her good mood improving further.

A little ashamed she cast the boy a glance, wondering if he had overheard the conversation. Apparently he had not, no matter how little Bea had bothered with lowering her voice.

– Yes, Bea whispered in her ears. – I am jealous and vengeful and you are entirely to blame, my too delicious to devour betrothed witch.

The extended traveling party took their leave from the Village. They were not merely four, but twelve emerging from the houses and into the unending mist surrounding them. In close proximity as they left, they remained thus.

The river appeared before them, and just for a moment there, it seemed like there was no bridge. Janet, strangely unworried studied the dancing foggy banks, the gray shifting into red, into faces unknown and captivating.

They crossed the bridge. An orb floated in the ether, constantly speaking in Janet's ears, directly to her feverish mind, making her smile, making her lips twist in expectation.

Illandra walked by her side. The older, experienced woman sought her out, not the other way around.

– You have involved yourself in sorcerer politics with a bang, her grandmother cautioned her. – Today was one thing, so was the scenery at the Guesthouse, but sooner or later, you will need to back up your preferences and desires… with acts of power, not merely demonstrating it.

Her words created a lingering sense of anticipation in the young sorcerer.

Her curiosity, when she studied the older magick-wielder did not exactly wane.

They returned to the cave, where blue fire slowly turned red and orange. The voices there still spoke to her, but with humility and respect, very much like the winged creature crouching in its walk by her side.

– I trust you can find your way alone, until I call for you, she commanded casually.

It growled its response, its confirmation.

– Scat, then, until I do find some modest use for you.

It flapped its recently healed wings, and was off. The ensuing wind hitting her hardly fazed her at all.

The others, the eight that had joined the four at the Village glanced at her.

– You look like you are… listening, Jess of the Orchards wondered.

– I am! She gave him a relaxed smile. – Can you not hear it, hear the music?

– I can hear *something*, he frowned.

He did. It was faint in his ears, but there. She nodded to herself, not giving anything away.

They walked the long path back through the tunnel, crossing several narrow rock bridges across vast depths and daring dark passages making the first-timers shrink a bit in their tracks. The eight cast uncertain glances at her and each other. Bea looked so smug that Janet wanted to chastise her. Bea noticed and behaved with a sweet smile. They reached the open space, briefly touching what was clearly another realm. Eight pair of eyes widened when the villagers rushed forward and knelt with their head bowed.

– That is correct, Bea grinned in triumph, unable to hold back. – They worship the current Master of the Blue Flame here. They dedicate themselves to a life in her service.

Janet fought the treacherous whisper of pride, but it still asserted itself. Bea's words stirred her, made her warm all over. She squeezed softly the other girl's hand and Bea squeezed back. They exchanged affectionate smiles.

The travelers moved on through the tunnel. The glances and open stares the other young sorcerers sent Janet did not grow less admiring.

– This is a magickal shortcut, is it not? Dane of the Deep Purple cried excited. – One not generally known.

– It is not, Janet replied roguishly, – not even to many older sorcerers. I know for a fact that my master did not know of it.

She had debated with herself whether or not she would reveal it to them, but had decided to not bother with keeping this particular knowledge from her extended entourage.

– Then you have given us yet another valuable gift this day, Livy said humbly.

Janet suddenly found herself regretting her indifference…

– It is called the Cave of Spirits, she said, clearly smug, – for obvious reasons.

– I think I know what you mean, Jess of the Orchards mused. – Sometimes, when I squint my eyes, I can imagine, at least that the walls are not truly here, and that this is a piece of the Wasteland made manifest somehow.

Yes, Janet closed her eyes halfway, the Wasteland, a tiny piece of its vast stretch. She recoiled and smiled as her vision briefly shifted into the blue, ultraviolet specter.

Time stretched out, becoming harder to measure. The twelve moving together through the cave made this different from the previous times Janet had walked here. Twelve magickal beings in close proximity made it all more volatile. Janet felt it, and she had to focus when she feared a fork appeared on the path. It, if it had ever been there in the first place disappeared quickly, but the air kept shimmering in all directions and the effect intensified several times.

– Everything around us feels alive, totally animated, Dane said amazed. – I want to paint every single texture I encounter.

– You would want to exchange words with a good friend of ours, Bea told him, good-humored.

Janet sensed the textures, as they shifted and burned in her consciousness.

They practically called to her. Everyone continued to look around amazed, until they reached the opening, at least that long.

They emerged into bright sunlight. It warmed them, even as it gave them trouble with watering eyes. Suffering from sudden, unexplainable panic Janet made certain that the tears evaporated fast.

She wondered what she had seen or glimpsed, if anything, and became more than irritated when glancing at Livy's smug smile. Bea's presence calmed her down, as it always did.

The landscape seemed different compared to Janet previous perception of it, somehow. She wondered if it was her or the landscape that had changed.

They moved through it. Jess and others that had never walked this path before looked around them with curious eyes.

– It resembles the territories, he mused. – Are you certain the triple cities are close?

He was of the Orchards, but aside from that he had evidently not set his foot outside the middle triple cities much.

– You will soon be able to confirm that for yourself, Bea shrugged, practically ignoring him.

Janet was not so sure. She suspected that the cave had moved, that it had not stayed in the same position in the terrain. Even the daystar seemed to be in the wrong position. The very air ahead shifted and stirred.

– What is it? Illandra asked her lightly, as ever cleverly attuned to her moods and impressions.

– I… do not know.

They both stopped and the rest did as well.

Illandra took, grabbed her hand. Janet felt how their shared power surged. She glimpsed more details in the air before her, but she could not identify it. When the older sorcerer mumbled a spell, she felt its potency, but could not identify it or its purpose either.

It, whatever it was faded away, until air was just air again. When she looked around, the distortions she had noticed had also disappeared. Everything had returned to how she remembered it. Illandra let go of her hand. Janet frowned and studied closer the inscrutable face. She relented quickly and turned away and walked on.

They kept walking eastward, towards the coast and the cities.

– I understand you have walked here before? Dane said.

– Enough to find my way.

– That is comforting, he said with obvious relief.

She grinned.

– You are not afraid of getting lost are you, a big strong boy like you?

He reddened, and she felt good about it.

Little Moon reflected its golden light at the edge of Lazoon, where the resident and resort area began. Janet still occasionally glimpsed it in the wrong place in the sky when she blinked. They passed along the tall northern wall. A sign glowed on it. It warmed her, madc her hot and queasy. She could not read the sign. It was no language or symbol she had come across before or even similar to one. She frowned, unable to know what to make of it.

It faded as they passed by. Janet briefly entertained the desire to make a closer inspection of the now unblemished wall, but let it go as Bea took her hand in a comforting gesture. They smiled to each other.

The two tall girls walked hand in hand in front of the other travelers in twilight. They walked down the slope towards the triple cities and the sea.

Talaho surrounded them. They experienced it as a very poignant sense of being swallowed. Something was off, and this time Janet felt edgy, and the fairly short walk across the narrow piece of land seemed to take far longer than usual.

Illandra slowed down, to a point where she was falling behind. Janet kissed Bea on the cheek and joined her grandmother.

– Something is happening, is it not?

– Something, Illandra acknowledged. – I can not pinpoint all of it, though.

– What *can* you pinpoint? Janet raised her voice.

Illandra only smiled to her, easily disarming her aggression.

– What are you to me? Janet asked.

– I am your guide, your advisor… whatever you desire me to be.

The older, experienced woman's words echoed so pleasantly within the girl. She nodded pleased to herself.

– So, what was that on the moor, the twisted reality, in my advisor's opinion?

– It was exactly what you suspect it to be, Illandra shrugged, – a sweep and catch spell. Your experienced advisor recognized it for what it was and grabbed your hand. There was no time to confer, so I acted in order to prevent the sinister intention of the spell. Our combined power rendered it ineffective.

The Blue Flame cast her eyes to the sky, at the dark clouds.

– Yes, Illandra confirmed, – the spell, unable to pinpoint an exact location or details about you sought you, sought the heir to the Blue Flame or something similar, known or obscure, localized or not. Somewhere out there someone knows you or someone like you as the threat you are. Through their Seers or other methods of divination they have been warned of your ascension and seek effective preventive measures in order to stop you early in your… your flight.

They reached the quay. The ferry was about to disembark. The four and eight stopped, waiting among the others waiting to take the afternoon voyage across the bay. Janet studied everybody present carefully, not caring if they found her interest offensive. There was nothing, nothing specific, nothing standing out with any of them. Everybody looked totally unremarkable.

The ferry hit the shore. Its doors opened. Its passengers emerged onto the quay, flooding it like a wave. Janet tensed, preparing for trouble, for the danger chiming off and on in her mind. She used her waves on them, taking their measure, like a bat would do with sound. Nothing in particular revealed itself to her casual and close scrutiny.

A few did react, sensitive enough to notice that something was going on, but unable to identify the source of their unease.

There was something tugging at her consciousness, something tangible. She turned in a rush, and at the other side of the quay she spotted the dark figure. He was dressed in a traditional robe and hood. She recognized him instantly.

– Peter, she snarled.

One blink, ten tears filling her eyes, and he was gone.

– Are you certain? Eleanor was by her side in an instant, worry filling her voice, momentarily forgetting herself, being the friend more than the apprentice.

Janet shook her head in dismay, chuckling darkly.

– I would recognize him anywhere.

– Of course, Eleanor mumbled, supporting her friend as she stumbled onboard the ferry.

– Was it Malone the Sorcerer or the young boy? Illandra wondered casually.

– I do not… know…

There had been only a flash, the figure she had glimpsed hardly being anything but a ghost.

The ferry left the quay, its doors closing.

Eleanor and Bea held her hands. She straightened, somewhat gently pulling free from their comforting gestures, forcing herself to give them smiles of gratitude.

She kept releasing her waves, gauging the room and everyone in it. There was nothing raising her suspicion further. These were mostly commuters on their way home from work. Jess, Livy and Dane and the others looked curiously and slightly shocked at her, but she would have been surprised if they had not.

She saw him again, through her inner eye, just the flash, the ghost. It did something to her, returned all her insecurities and sizzling hatred. Bea's hand squeezing hers felt so good, so comforting.

She pictured the statue standing on the pedestal in the realm of the Ascension, and a relative calm settled her insides yet again.

They reached the Island, and a tingling spread from her feet touching its ground and to her entire body. She sensed the far away needle mountain, felt it gut her. The house without visible doors called out to its master. A well of sensations touched her. Eleanor looked concerned at her crouching form.

Janet straightened. She knew she had everybody's attention.

– We will gather on the fields beneath the needle, she stated, relaying to them all the sensations of the place she had carried within, – and begin our training in earnest.

– Good idea, Jess beamed. – I just need to go home and…

– We will do so immediately, she stated firmly.

He sagged, like a balloon losing its air.

Janet turned to Eleanor.

– Fetch the trainees, she commanded. – Fetch everybody.

– Yes, Master, the apprentice acknowledged eagerly, and was off in a rush of movement.

Bea looked at her with boundless admiration and love, casting the boy a patronizing and triumphant snarl.

– It is a good thing we are weary, Livy said eagerly, – we will need to dig even deeper into ourselves in order to learn, and thereby learn better the Blue Flame's lessons.

She displayed herself, placing herself at attention. This time Janet could almost imagine that she saw a true flash of admiration in the young woman's eyes. Livy of Lambruia bowed down before the person she recognized as the dominant force present.

The people of the procession, individually and as a group, before, during and after their walk through Auburn attracted attention everywhere they tread. Heads turned and eyes burned at them. Janet felt it all, the dynamics and both attraction and repulsion cast in their direction.

– The natives are restless, Livy remarked, before giving off a patronizing shrug. – They always are, it seems. It is certainly no different from my homeland.

And Janet gained insight into what made her tick. She found herself nodding and she realized startled that the two of them had something in common after all.

Esteben the Mountain towered above them long before they reached the fields that were at the base of its rise. Everybody's attention was drawn to it and the city streets faded from their view while they still moved through them. Janet looked at its peak. It always seemed to be cast in mist and shadow in her eyes.

They emerged onto the southern fields, spreading out like they would if there was an upcoming battle. Janet studied them, Illandra, the strangers and Bea all. Illandra had checked out the area from a distance, and she kept doing so.

She seemed attuned to Janet in a way rivaling even what Janet shared with both Eleanor and Bea. Janet blinked, feeling it in an almost physical manner, unable to hide her astonishment.

– Why so surprised, Scion of the Bone People? The older woman said. – I prepared myself for your coming long before your birth, remember.

Janet found herself nodding again, while still fighting against the treacherous feeling of pride growing within.

The guys and the rest, led by Eleanor appeared not long afterwards, bringing extra wands and fighting gear. Eleanor waved. Janet sighed.

The eager apprentice stopped in front of her master, bowing in reverence. She handed over a wand. Janet accepted it.

– The Time of Change is upon you, apprentice, she stated with a steady stare. – You are ready for the next step of your evolution.

Eleanor curtseyed happily and pulled back. Janet raised the wand above her head and turned towards the others present.

– Transformation seeks us all, she cried, – and the aware is always prepared for its pain and joy. Be prepared here, now.

She began swinging the wand, began moving among and at her charges, attacking them in a relaxed, but clearly vicious manner.

– Everybody, she growled, – fight for real.

Bea smiled to her.

– Congratulations, she said sweetly, – you sound pretty much as if you stand for election to the city council already.

Janet struck at her, aghast. Bea deflected the attack easily. The counterattack grazed Janet's jaw and made blood flow from her mouth.

– I struck a nerve there, did I not, beloved?

Everybody moved around them in disorganized, but still fluid movements. The whirl of motion turned everything indistinct in their eyes and to all their senses, physical and not.

Janet struck Bea, struck her hard. The brutality of it made those glancing at them while doing their battles gasp. Bea stumbled backwards, blocking the next brutal attack. The next swing of the wand brought its tip straight at her head. Bea fell and remained on the ground, too stunned to rise.

– You did, Janet grinned wickedly. – Congratulations…

She extended a hand and Bea took it, and Janet pulled her up. They kissed. It brought pain and joy in equal measure.

The exercise hardly paused during their brief touch. They flowed towards each other and just a moment afterwards they parted again, and continued the training with other partners.

Janet, even as she fought and instructed Eleanor kept an eye on Illandra. The older woman's handling of the wand was just phenomenal. She moved with it like a flash of lightning, and just as cruel. Opponents were left bloody and beaten in the dirt wherever she turned.

Faces flowed in front of Janet. Eleanor's, briefly viewed in blood and bruises, was supplanted with Jess's somewhat unblemished features.

She made sure it did not last long.

He gave her his best smile. She did not return it.

There was a wounded expression in his face when he not long after that crouched in pain on the ground. She ignored it, casually turning her back to him. It did not stir her one way or another. She kept whirling round and round in the pleasant storm of flesh and wands surrounding her. A… discord reached her ears and eyes.

Blood flowed. Cries of pain filled her ears.

She fought Illandra. They were the only ones left standing. She recalled catching her eyes, recalled charging her. They went at each other.

Illandra caught her strike, deflecting it with the strong part of her wand, until all its power faded away. Illandra returned the strike only a moment later. Janet managed to deflect it only with great difficulty. They circled one another, striking, deflecting, striking, striking, striking. Then, only seconds later they were rising into the air and continuing the fight there, the fact that Illandra was able to do that hardly surprising her granddaughter.

They did not speak. No words, harsh or soft fell. Janet still felt like Illandra taunted her with the tiny smile hiding on her lips, the flash in her hard eyes. Rage flooded the young sorcerer. She fought to not let it distract her from the fight, using the seething anger in every strike, in every big or small attack she made.

There was an energy field around Illandra's body, so much stronger, now, when she was fighting. Janet could not quite get a grip on it. It actually proved elusive to her waves and interfered with them in a way making it harder for her to properly utilize them.

Farrell's words and harsh teaching about not letting the anger get the best of you coursed through her. The mere thought made her even angrier. Blood started flowing even faster through her veins.

She deflected an attack with difficulty, feeling shame because her knuckles turned white as she clutched the wand. A second, hardly more than a moment later she had counterattacked. The tip of the wood graced Illandra's jaw, but not hard enough to make blood flow from her mouth.

The older woman struck back almost instantly, the wood of her wand hitting the meaty part of Janet's shoulder, making its muscle turn numb.

She shook her head, fighting against the spreading numbness, clutching the right hand holding the wand, striking back, hitting Illandra in the head with a brutal blow. The older woman was practically struck unconscious in an instant. Janet caught her in her waves. It acted like a cushion, slowing down her fall, keeping her from hitting the ground too hard.

Janet lowered herself to the ground. Illandra did not move.

She was breathing. Janet noted that the chest moved regularly up and down. She cleaned the tip of the wand by rubbing it at the ground. There was blood on it.

Illandra began stirring, moving. Janet felt her dizziness and disorientation. Illandra attempted to sit up, but failed. The second time she managed, somewhat. She shook her head in an effort to clear it, in vain. Blood trickled down her cheek. Janet sat down on her heels and grabbed the older woman around the jaw.

– Can you see me? She asked curtly.

Eyes tried to focus, but did not quite make it. Her speech sounded more like a mumble than actual words. Janet let go of her jaw.

– Of course, I am alright, Illandra mumbled indignant.

She fell back.

– Carry her, Janet ordered. – We are done for now.

Eleanor grabbed her feet and Jess grabbed her upper body under the arms and lifted her up. Bea began cleaning her wound.

Janet walked off and everyone tailed her. She felt strong and triumphant.

– Your education is still lacking, Illandra stated, – still far from complete. You should have vanquished me considerably faster.

She sounded strong and forceful and just as patronizing again.

– I did not want to harm you… too much, Janet shrugged deliberately.

Illandra wrestled out of Eleanor and Jess's grip and rose, and walked, fairly steady. She allowed Bea to tie a bandage around her head. Eleanor began treating the others for minor wounds.

Livy stepped up by Janet's side, her awestruck smile and sycophancy very much visible. Janet ignored her, knowing fully well that the other girl expected that.

The group attracted the usual attention as they made their way back to tighter populated areas. If anything it had grown compared to previous walks.

– Sorcerers stay mostly in the shadows, keeping out of sight from most people, Livy said. – Generations and even centuries may pass between each time our kind draw mundane attention. It has always been a significant mark of things to come each time we reveal ourselves to the public.

– You certainly do not seem to mind much, Toby said, not attempting to hide the sarcasm.

– I do not, Livy beamed. – Our time has come. I am proud to stand by the Blue Flame's side at this fateful moment in history.

There was... a rhythm to their walk that certainly stood out from others. Janet sensed it, both in herself, her «charges» and the surroundings. She did not close her eyes, but each blink felt like she did, the sensations lingering in what seemed like an eternity.

And sometime during one of those blinks... fear, unidentifiable and timeless touched her.

Haunted eyes sought the surroundings for something tangible, anything to focus on, in vain.

– You are a... history buff? She abruptly asked Livy.

– I am, Honored One, Livy replied humbly. – I enjoyed an extended education at the Art and Antiquity Higher Learning House in Howell. I am well versed in political and social relations of the ages, and can aid the Blue Flame greatly as she blazes her trail of blood and power.

Fear and excitement in equal parts touched Janet.

She turned to Toby, calling his attention.

– I agree, he said cheerfully. – Advisors are sorely needed, *lots* of advisors...

She chuckled, giving him a relieved and grateful look. He certainly did not bow down to «Her Majesty».

They walked through well-lit streets, dark streets and well-lit streets again. Somewhere between those two extremes Janet stopped and froze. Her eyes caught a dark, featureless shape standing on the opposite corner.

Bea, sensing her distress was at her side in an instant.

– What is it? She wondered. – What do you see?

Janet shook her head.

– Nothing, she replied. – Nothing at all.

When she looked again the shape was not there, was nowhere to be seen.

Eleanor stood at her other side, sensing the same unrest that Bea had sensed. Janet rubbed their cheeks, comforting them, instead of the other way around.

The shape stayed in her vision, slowly turning solid, gaining texture. She knew it was not physically there anymore, but she still saw it.

– As your power grows, your sensitivity will as well, Illandra told her, instructed her, returning to her side. – The realms and their Abyss will open up to you as if you were a hot knife slicing butter.

Janet nodded, pondered grandmother's words and nodded again, determination brightening violet eyes. That, in turn brought more awe to the mundane faces surrounding her. A pleased, silent snarl worked itself up her throat.

They reached a fork in the road, an intersection, a crossroad. There was a road going right. She knew well where that led. The image of the house without doors imposed itself on her. She did not stop or visibly hesitate, but walked straight forward, immediately sensing the others' disappointment.

– It will wait for you, Illandra stated calmly. – It will wait forever.

Everyone knew what she was talking about. The decision to not go there added to the Blue Flame's stature, not the other way around.

They crossed a stretch of road without houses or with fewer houses and no streetlights. Only distant lights illuminated dim and dark faces. Janet usually had her eyes on Illandra, pondering her often cryptic statements. Even her plain words sounded cryptic in context.

Janet could not help but ponder, analyze and study the scenario, her companions and the entire crowd moving in her…

Her sphere.

A thrill fired itself from an undisclosed point in her body and spread through veins, bone and flesh. She turned towards Bea, grabbed her hand and pulled her close. They kissed lips to lips, chuckling throatily.

Bea pushed herself at her, so hard that it seemed that she was attempting to push herself into the other body. Janet could not help but feel a little detached, still experiencing it from all angles, through all the eyes staring at them. Bea's eyes twinkled in boundless affection.

– Such a lovesick puppy, Livy said with scorn in her voice.

They finally disentangled, both breathless, still holding hands as they walked on.

There were no streetlights nearby, but the path still seemed lit to the Blue Flame, illuminated like a crest, a river of violet and azure fire. It looked like a mirror image. On the flat road burned and sizzled a bed of inverted flames without a visible source. All of it appeared muted, as if it was not real, or at least not there, with them.

– I get goose bumps, Livy said with a shaky voice, sounding completely different from when she had spoken her previous sentence.

A face materialized in the dancing inferno. Janet shook. The flames vanished in an instant and the road was once again just a road.

Bea comforted Janet with little kisses and gentle rubbing. Janet looked at her with deep-felt affection and gratitude.

– The Blue Flame sees more than others, Dane said solemnly, – with a vision so powerful that she can make others share her experience.

They feel my fear.

Eleanor clearly did. She had turned pale and sweaty. Janet pulled her close and kissed her on the brow, focusing on comforting her as best as she was able.

A dozen paths revealed themselves to her, each new step bringing on yet another fork in the road, even as the walkers in the night continued down the single road in darkness.

They approached Myra's house. Janet saw it as a very distinct shape among all the others surrounding it. She also spotted the tiny movement by the fence closest to them, just a tiny variance, texture in the shadow but There.

The wind and the waves brought the burning stench of alcohol. The stage revealed itself fully to Janet, and she felt both shame and relief.

Joan sat there, with her back against the fence. Her face seemed featureless, dissolved. She chuckled to herself and did not seem to be aware of those approaching. The chuckle was continuous, uncontrolled. It sounded more like crying or rather sobbing in Janet's ears.

Janet looked into empty eyes. She felt like she was sucked into them, into their abyss. A very pronounced sense of dread touched her.

– She is drunk, Bea said with contempt in her voice. – Dead drunk.

– Looks like she has been for quite some time, too, Livy agreed.

It was an obviously correct statement. Joan looked like she had been binge drinking for days. The woman attempting to focus her eyes on Janet was clearly totally out of it.

Janet bent down and shook her, shook her hard. First there seemed to be no reaction, but after several attempts an expression of recognition was finally lit in Joan's eyes. A dull, warped facsimile of an excited smile found its way to her face.

– Hi, Janet, she grinned, – how is it hanging?

That was it, really, all she managed before collapsing on the ground, puking her guts out, practically bathing in her own vomit. Everybody stood there, watching, feeling immensely bad about the sight before them.

– I am so fucked up, the woman mumbled, sobbing uncontrollably, – so totally fucked up. I was supposed to guard you, to protect you, but I could not, could not, could not…

Janet pulled back, almost unnoticed, away from the circle of familiars and supporters, unable to witness the onslaught of the other's mental collapse any longer.

She felt like she stood there forever in the shadows before Bea joined her with her leveled head and support.

– You should not grieve for her, Bea said quietly, petting the other's cheek gently.

Janet almost screamed it out, in her distress.

– She seemed so strong, so confident in herself and her abilities.

– She was not, Bea pointed out, dismissing it all. – It was just a pretense. Commoners are not very good at handling events conflicting with their view on reality, you know that. She is just yet more driftwood floating down the Dark River.

Janet nodded, pondering her own reaction and nodded again.

– Good girl!

Bea kissed her cheek. They returned to the others, to the closeness of the circle.

– You and your apprentice will certainly appreciate an opportunity to spend the night in your house, in somewhat secluded premises. We will meet up again tomorrow, continue our venture and take it one step or ten further with ease and elegance.

Janet nodded firmly and looked grateful at her Companion to be.

Bea picked up Joan, doing so as if the heavyset body was a feather. She put it on her shoulder, carrying it off, away from Janet's sore eyes.

She turned after a while and waved. So did most of the others, not really questioning the course of action decided upon. Janet returned the wave, putting up a brave front, unable to quite shake off the bad feeling in her gut, to even explain it to herself.

– Joan could not guard me because she could not keep up with me, she spat, – and she could not handle it. Bea hit it on the nail.

She watched her own distress unfolding. It was very visible in the apprentice, the flickering eyes, the shivering lower lip and general condition.

– What do I care? She is not exactly my friend or anything.

– That is so very true, Janet, Eleanor echoed her sentiment. – You should not care at all.

And Janet did not, not when she saw the way her bad mood rocked the apprentice either.

They walked inside, the sorcerer first and the apprentice tailing her.

Janet did not sense Myra anywhere in the house, except as a general, lingering presence. It was quiet or should be. Janet still felt the noise beneath the surface, a sound she could not stop herself from noticing.

Eleanor rushed to the kitchen and began preparing the late evening meal. Janet envisioned her out there, the eager servant. She curled her lips in contempt.

The apprentice set the table, served the big sandwiches, put two big plates of them on the table, and stood there, waiting for Janet to acknowledge her. The sorcerer sat down. She grabbed one of the sandwiches in front of her and took the first bite. Then, after a deliberate, very visible delay she signed for the apprentice to join her. Eleanor sat down and began feeding, wolfing down the food and the drink.

Both of them did, hungry beyond hungry, synchronized, thoughts and emotions flowing constantly back and forth.

A loud crack made them both jump in their seats.

– Is that you, Myra?

She knew it was not Myra.

Her waves filled the room, all the rooms in the house instantly accessible to her, and that was most of them. She sensed nothing, no one threatening or even present.

There was no one else in the house.

– There is something wrong here, Janet cried out to Eleanor, mumbled to herself, – but I can not grasp it, can not catch its…

She grabbed the other's arm, digging her claws deep into the skin, making them both cry out in pain, and the bad feeling inside multiplied.

They finished their meal in silence.

– The bad stuff will always be there, will always be a part of my life.

Janet froze when Eleanor spoke with rigid features in a voice very similar to Janet's own.

– What is wrong with me? Eleanor asked with Janet's voice.

Janet shook her head, wanting to scream at the other girl, knowing there was no point, that it would be like screaming at herself.

Her fingers formed like claws, and she wanted to scratch her face until blood flowed like water, her reason fading like twilight.

She realized she was tired, physically and mentally. A grueling «day» had lasted far beyond the time sleep was normally required, and all her defenses were down. Images, sensations assaulted her. The past kept swatting her as if she was a fly.

Eleanor removed the plates from the table and began cleaning them. It did not take long. Her time at the kitchen sink did not drag out. She rushed back to her master, awaiting her word.

Janet did not speak. She walked up the stairs to her bedroom, and her shadow followed. The room was at the end of the hallway. It felt like an impossibly long distance to cover and seemed to grow longer for each new step she took. A shaking hand reached forward, finally, after something resembling an eternity making contact with the handle. She opened the door and stepped inside…

Memories flooded her. They rose within her like a wound. Her stretched out on the sacrificial altar and Malone standing above her frozen body with a wicked triumph etched on every single feature. Her brutal time at Florence's castle. The trap sprung by young Peter and the horrible pain he had inflicted on her. Her childhood before, during and after her father's death.

The vast darkness outside, outside everything invaded her, sucking all life out of her.

Everything just filled her in a moment, and shook her like a rag doll.

An assault. Someone *did* this to her. The weak thought hardly reached the surface. She rolled her hands into fists and her nails drew blood, and it worked, making the spell and its results fade, making a modicum of sanity and balance return to her world.

Eleanor writhed on the floor in horror, helpless to resist the brutal onslaught of the sinister spell. She recovered as well, but slowly, so slowly.

Janet sat down on the bed. She just sat there without having any idea how much time had passed. Her mind tried wrapping itself around what had happened, in vain. There was just too much wool up there to make deeper, analytical thought likely. Her body eventually fell over. She pulled herself the final stretch onto the bed, until her entire big and tall frame was stretched out on the soft, tiny surface.

Eleanor crouched on the floor. Neither had undressed.

Janet mumbled a spell, spat curses, in an effort to protect the two of them from further attacks, totally unable to tell whether or not she was successful or to put any will behind it. She curled up in bed, and kept sniffing while tears, scared, angry tears wet her cheeks. The apprentice echoed all of that on the carpet. The flow back and forth cut the sorcerer like the sharpest of blades. She cried herself to sleep.

Chapter 17

She awoke in a state of dread. It seemed to stick to every single part of her body without ever fading. Base relief flooded her and rivaled the bad feeling, when she opened her eyes and saw that nothing bad had happened, that she and Eleanor were safe, for now. She glanced around her, at every angle, so hard that her eyes hurt. There was no one here, nothing immediate threatening them.

Eleanor opened her eyes. She rolled her body and rose to her knees, her eyes cast down before her master.

Janet smiled. She rose and undressed as she walked to the shower. Her skin felt sticky all over. She studied herself through Eleanor's eyes. Everything looked fine. There was the haunted expression in her eyes, but she had grown used to that.

Water rinsed her body, her big and strong and lethal body.

– Transformation seeks us all, she mumbled. – The strong embraces it, seeking it out.

She struck the wall in a deliberate, controlled move. The entire house vibrated in its wake. She smiled.

Eleanor had not moved when she returned to the bedroom.

– You may clean yourself, now, the sorcerer told the apprentice exactly in the offhand, casual tone of voice expected of her.

The apprentice rushed to obey her master.

Janet stood nude by the window, looking out at the garden, a peaceful scene calming her anxieties. The wet towel slipped from her hand and silently hit the floor.

There was a distant hammering she could not avoid hearing. She knew they did some repair-work two houses down the road. It did disturb her peace, inevitably, but she did not allow it to faze her.

She dressed slowly, taking her time in front of the mirror in order to get it right.

They had breakfast, enjoying somewhat the heat and light from the daystar filling the room. Janet kept getting the chills. She was unable to put a stop to it.

Eleanor did not seem to notice that much of it anymore, though. She seemed upbeat, almost euphoric.

The sorcerer noticed that she desired to be heard and nodded her approval.

– Allow this apprentice to thank her master, the girl said humbly. – Eleanor had expectations, but did not imagine they would be fulfilled to such a degree.

Janet frowned.

– Janet is teaching her far more than she ever hoped for.

– It is not exactly a walk in the park, Janet said lightly, probing the other carefully.

– But that is just the point, master, the girl said excited. – The Blue Flame is not only teaching this girl magick, but to be strong as well.

Now, Janet understood. The girl believed that the sorcerer was testing her, doing so constantly and relentlessly, far more than Janet was actually doing.

The bond was strong, but not that strong, not powerful enough for Eleanor to realize the truth.

– You are just a blue-eyed, innocent waif, Janet snorted.

– Yes, master, Eleanor acknowledged and bowed her head.

– Are you not the respectful apprentice, being so to such a degree that the teacher you are wearing around your neck hardly has seen it necessary to punish you?

– Yes, master. This apprentice acknowledges that even though she and the sorcerer are of the same age, the sorcerer is ages ahead of her in experience.

A door slammed open somewhere. They both saw it, heard it, felt it. It interrupted their line of thoughts and stopped Janet from saying whatever she had intended to say. Both jumped up and rushed to the entrance hall.

There was no one there. The door was closed.

They glanced bewildered at each other.

Janet frowned again, deeper this time. Eleanor looked at her, wondering why, what it was about.

– It is probably the fucking hammering, Janet shrugged. – A clumsy worker must have lost something, something big. I wish they would finish their slow work soon. It makes me uneasy. It never lets up.

– It sounded like a door slamming in the wind, Eleanor pondered, – but it was just once and so loud that there would be nothing left of the door.

They both looked at the undamaged door in front of them.

Then, they heard the sound again, much louder, almost deafening, one loud crack like thunder.

Janet sensed something, something potent making the very air shiver everywhere they looked. She was about to send out her waves, project them and pull them back, in order to probe and assess even deeper her surroundings, but before she managed to do that something slammed into her, into them both. There was nothing solid about it, nothing pushing at their bodies. Powerful, uncontrollable sensations invaded them both and rocked them hard. Images, sounds, emotions of events spilled into their minds.

Suddenly Janet found herself back on the coach, or a coach, similar to the one she had traveled with Malone. He was not there, but Eleanor was. It lasted only a moment and then it was gone, but flashes of reality kept revealing themselves to them. Whether or not that happened within or without they could not say or possibly discern. To them, right now, it was one and the same.

They saw, experienced a remote, desolate landscape filled with dark, ghostly lightning. Dark towers hovered in what seemed like a featureless void. One single house in the wilderness shifted constantly in form and size, making it impossible to get a proper view on either.

A thousand more flashes, most of them impossible to recall flared in their extended consciousness.

Janet had her attention fixed on the driveway outside.

The shapeless shape took form.

A man appeared outside. She saw him clear enough, but still like a shimmer in her vision. He had horns on his forehead and pale, cruel eyes. She stared at him through the window. He looked straight at her with a twisted grin on his face. It looked like he was standing right in front of her.

– The door will slam in your face, he hissed at her.

She saw him move his lips, but the sound came from behind her. She turned in a whirl, but there was no one there, not Eleanor, not anyone. Pearls of cold sweat formed on her forehead. When she turned back and looked through the window he stood on the same spot.

– Florence is coming for you, he spat. – And she is not the only one. You feared you were being attacked and you were right.

The chilling laughter practically emanated from him and made a chill more than touch her spine.

– Everyone is coming for you. Your wicked grandmother is absolutely correct. Vast forces you can not comprehend seek your utter destruction.

She watched him turn and walk away. Her desire to follow him never manifested in her legs. She just stood there, frozen and weak like an infant. The image of his face not a face remained solidly implanted behind her eyelids. She turned and Eleanor had returned, as if she had never been gone at all. The apprentice looked anxious at her. Janet grabbed her, squeezed her arm. She hardly heard the moan of pain. When she turned back and once again stared through the big window, the man was gone.

The house seemed quiet, empty again. Janet and Eleanor returned to the living room. Two pairs of feet moved of their own volition, pacing the floor and carpet endlessly back and forth.

Janet sat still on the couch. Eleanor crouched by her side, with her head in her lap. Janet petted the girl with a distant look in her eyes. They both went away for a while. Time itself seemed to dissolve into nothing.

The door to the hall opened and steps Janet feared were made with an invisible body closed in on her. Janet looked up, into Bea's calm face. Bea noticed instantly her distressed state of mind.

Janet hesitated, but then, with a light prompting she began speaking with a brittle, whiny voice.

– A… man visited me, haunted me. I… recognize him from my childhood. He told me then that my father would die. He looked no older, now.

She looked down again and was unable to look back up. Bea sat down by her side. Her comforting presence and caresses calmed her betrothed somewhat, enough for her to keep speaking in a fairly calm manner.

– He told me that F-florence and «vast forces» are coming for me.

Silence held her for so long, as she slowly fell apart.

– This is good news, Bea told her.

Janet looked up startled.

– Do you not see? There is a reason you are eagerly sought. They believe as I do that you are indeed the power prophesized, the one spoken of by many a fearful voice throughout the centuries. Well, we will give them reason to fear.

Growing awareness touched Janet's features. She nodded eagerly and empathically. Bea smiled and gave her a gentle kiss.

Eleanor looked better, too. She discovered that both of them were looking at her and sat up, clearly embarrassed. Janet shook her head in equal mortification.

– I do not know what happened, what came over me. It was like I was almost paralyzed, as if I was scared out of my wits. Worse! The very sight of him filled me with f-fear.

– I guess he made an impression on the four year-old girl you once were, Bea shrugged. – Stuff like that will haunt you, will linger long after that girl has turned into a powerful and confident adult taking shit from nobody.

Janet chuckled then, looking grateful and affectionate at the girl on her right.

– He will not find me unprepared next time he shows up, she declared. – No matter what agenda he is pursuing he will find me, find us ready for him.

Violet eyes flashed in smoldering anger.

The rage helped her, made her regain the shaken center.

– I love it when you talk like that, baby, Bea smooched.

They smooched a little more, both relaxing, quickly calming down. Janet realized that Bea had been upset, too. Of course she had been and was.

Three young girls walked on the road to central Auburn later that day. They were not exactly that dissimilar from others, even though their clothing did draw stares from those currently sharing the road with them. There was not first and foremost the clothing that separated them from the crowd, but their behavior, the way they moved and conducted themselves.

– You were right when you suggested we did not ride the bus, Janet said. – I needed this.

She pondered it, probing herself and what she experienced.

– It is as if… I was purified, as if the fear and strong emotions I experienced have made me more powerful.

– «What does not kill you or turn you into a zombie makes you stronger», Bea said exalted. – It is a well known theorem, and we both know you have yet to truly tap into your potential. That man, that loathsome man, though he certainly did not intend it, did you a favor.

Bea's words rang very true in Janet's ears. She rolled her hands into fists, opening and closing them several times, sensing, feeling, touching herself within. She deliberately called forth the memory of the man. Fear and rage filled her and her waves grew to become potent charges, like those that had shattered the mirror.

– I think you are right, the Blue Flame said. – He made me dig deep into myself, made me pull myself from my deep, deep self, to hide No More.

She grabbed the other tall and big girl and kissed her hard on the lips, treating her like a puppet, laughing throatily and pleased, quickly changing from one emotional extreme to the other.

– What did he look like? Bea wondered, with an always present curiosity that could not be denied.

– Like a… demon, Janet said hesitatingly. – I know that they are not real, are only part of the folklore, but he had the horns and did not look like any creature of the Wasteland I have ever seen.

The inhabitants of the Wasteland had often been mistaken for demons and were generally seen as one of the origins of the myth of demons and the various hells in the mythologies of the nine realms.

They both turned to Eleanor.

– I never saw him, she replied to the unspoken question, – except as an indistinct figure.

She paused a bit, the memory itself making her shrink in her tracks.

– There was a sense of menace and horror about him, though, one that can not be denied. He was… spooky, very, very spooky.

– I will thank him handsomely for the great service he rendered the next time I encounter him, Janet swore, comforting her apprentice with soft

touches and caresses.
– That is my girl, Bea purred.
The chuckles rose easily between them. Eleanor joined in as well, remaining apprehensive.
The apprehension stayed within all three, Janet knew it did, the deep chill never fading completely.
On one level the warm light from the daystar could not touch them.
They reached the central part of the city, with its tighter building configuration and different architecture. There were several distinct differentiations compared to the more chaotic variations of the suburbs. The shifting patterns drew themselves in Janet's mind. They closed in on Bea's apartment. The very notion made a sense of expectation dance in the empty spaces between Janet's thoughts.
Bea opened the outer door and they stepped inside.
– I took the liberty of putting up our foreign charges at the nearest modest guesthouse. I assumed you did not want them permanently at our sweet abode.
– You assumed correctly, Janet said haughtily.
Bea locked them in. There was a fairly long hallway before they reached the living room. Janet heard distinct sounds and was not really surprised when she spotted Joan doing her thorough scrubbing of the floor.
– I put her to work, Bea said casually. – Menial work is all she is good for, really.
Joan kept scrubbing, as if she had not heard Bea, heard them arrive at all.
Janet looked with contempt at the pitiful creature on the floor.
– You are obviously correct again, my love, and the poor thing needs something to do, in order to feel that she is contributing. Anything would do, I suppose.
She turned to Eleanor.
– You may start on the dinner, now, apprentice.
They had dinner, enjoyed dinner, the three of them. Joan kept scrubbing. The open windows brought in the sounds from the streets. Janet did not find them noisy. They became part of the background sound stage, her whirling waves.
The waves had long since become a part of her surroundings, a part of her. She could not quite recall the moment that had happened, but now they felt like a comfortable coat.
She enjoyed the food, too. It brought such a pleasant sensation on her tongue and in her stomach.
– My compliments, apprentice, she said. – You are actually an excellent

cook.

– Thank you, master, Eleanor blushed.

– Any witch and would-be witch is, by default, Bea pointed out. – It is in our blood.

Eleanor sagged on her spot.

Music reached them from one of the open windows. It was distant, but easily audible. Bea danced slowly on her chair, moving closer to Janet.

– They are playing our song.

She frowned.

– Strange, is it not? It is such a silly little tune.

Janet started laughing. Bea looked at her.

– What?

– You are so deep, so complex, Janet chuckled. – I never know where I have you. It is so great. You will always keep things interesting, I think.

– You are such a sweet witch.

Bea cooed and grabbed her hand.

– And things are looking up for us. The… clans approve of our plans. So, now, all is on your wicked grandmother.

– I guess it is, then, Janet said, feigning indifference. – So the clans approve, do they?

She failed in her half hearted attempt to keep the sarcasm from manifesting in her voice.

– It is as I pointed out, Bea said. – They firmly believe you are an excellent addition to the bloodline. They could not care less about the rest, the more important things you and I care about.

She kissed her betrothed and all irritation faded from Janet's mind.

Thought itself faded from her surface consciousness, everything but the pleasant closeness of the girl.

Bea whispered sweet words in her ear.

– Dance for me. Perform to your heart's content.

Janet smiled and rose.

The swaying and dancing came easily to her, without conscious effort. She did not necessarily look at Bea all the time, but she was very aware of the fact that she was always there and always would be. The thought made a pleasant chill pass down her spine.

She moved on the fairly big open space between the furniture. Her body turned round and round and round. The heat between her thighs grew. She used her waves to heighten her moves, making them more potent and accentuating.

– You are good, Bea whispered. – You are really good.

– All witches can dance, Janet responded with closed eyes. – It is in our blood.

The whirl and light steps of the dance kept going, seemingly by itself.

– You are mine, Bea kept whispering. – Say that you are mine!

Janet opened her eyes, frowning.

– I will not! She said emphatically. – I do not belong to anyone!

She stopped dancing, embracing herself with her arms, rubbing her shoulders.

The soft, enticing voice reached her, seemingly from afar.

– But if you belonged to anyone it would be me, right?

Uncertainty revealed itself in Janet's eyes.

Bea walked to her and grabbed her, staring at her with her big eyes.

– Say it, she whispered.

– Yes, Janet breathed, – if I belonged to anyone I would belong to you.

Bea smiled. Her smile grew wide and ecstatic.

– Yes, you are my betrothed and we will paint Arcadia and the Ocean of Mankind with colors strong as blood.

– We will!

They did a high five.

Twin smiles grew wide as an abyss.

The other girl's words echoed within Janet and stirred her to no end.

The four took to the streets again later, Joan practically unrecognizable in the hood and robe Bea had purchased for her.

– What do you think? Bea asked Janet, while they both measured the magistrate or former magistrate up and down.

– It looks good on her, Janet shrugged, – and not the least expensive.

– Only the best is good enough for Bea and Janet's maid, Bea shrugged even harder.

They walked through the streets as if they owned it, an act very unusual for sorcerers, especially in the middle of the bright day and huge afternoon crowds. The tradition was to keep to the shadows.

They did not hide, but displayed themselves proudly. It made Janet's skin and innards tingle pleasantly and constantly. She and Bea did not hide their affection either. Though open display of emotion and passion was common in Arcadia, theirs was perhaps a notch or two above even that.

As if to confirm that, people mostly kept their eyes on them, not so much on other couples or groups displaying their affection and desire openly.

– Those gals are *hot,* a girl cried from the side, with just the right type of enthusiasm.

That alone made Janet feel even hotter. She wished the two of them were home in bed.

Bea chuckled. She clearly did not mind the attention.

They visited the market on Wayward Plaza. It was busy and crowded, but that did not truly faze them either. They slipped through the crowd without effort, not making haste, but enjoying the moment, the many moments slipping through their fingers. Clouds moved across the sky. Once in a while they covered the daystar and shadows crossed people's faces. It formed a pattern, one Janet, in the emptiness between moments, imagined she could read.

There was an enclosed space between nine buildings nearby. They walked there, to the tavern Circle of Nine, its name prominently displayed on the wall. Another powerful shiver passed through them. They entered the place through one of nine passages, dark and narrow alleys all guests had to pass through.

– The owner actually dares calling it Circle of Nine, Eleanor shivered pleasantly. – Such a well known and feared name. Playing with fire like that is commendable, I suppose.

The other three nodded in acknowledgment.

– We still have files on them, Joan said shyly, as the other three focused their attention on her, – on the actual cult, I mean. They are frequently used as studies at the academy.

The name was very ambiguous, with both very mundane and sinister origins. On one hand the use of the number nine was quite common in Arcadia and on the other it was forever associated with the Cult of the Nine, an ancient, downright mythic organization that had supposedly existed for thousands of years. It had not been heard of in centuries, but some persisted in the claim that it still existed.

– This is a new and enlightened age, Bea said, – one filled with promise. I guess the owner or owners in question just want to play with fire a little, create some interest for the establishment, drawing in the interesting crowd.

– And she, he or they succeeded, Janet said.

She spontaneously kissed Bea again.

Looking around, Janet saw that the crowd was indeed different, not exactly the typical sample found on a given street or gathering at any given moment. The place was not as huge as Freeze, but still big. The haze in the air made it difficult to see from one end of the circle to another. There was a constant flow of people entering and leaving.

– I think I will take up painting again, Bea mused. – Rosa's example sort of inspired me.

– Sort of? Janet joked lightly.

– Indeed. The muses work in mysterious ways, or so I have heard.

Janet spotted Rosa and the guys entering from a passage to the left. Rosa waved. Janet returned the wave, very consciously of the fact that her waving created almost visible waves in the air.

Their newest recruits entered from the right. Livy waved enthusiastically. Janet returned her wave as well.

The three groups met at the center and instantly engaged in a hearty welcome, embracing and cuddling each other.

– Honored One… Livy greeted her respectfully, grabbing both her hands.

But as soon as that was over and done with, she proceeded to everyone else.

There was no lack of tables this early. They found two with nine seats each close to the southern passage. Janet realized startled that it «pointed» right at Esteben the Mountain. She imagined she could feel its energies, its Chaos, as it spread outward from one single point at its peak.

A team chose itself by brief glances and meeting of eyes. Livy, Dane, Rosa and Toby braved the path to the bar. It did not take too long before they, with great skill, balanced eighteen glasses in their grip and brought back ale for everybody. Eighteen raised their glass, raised it high and had a toast, a cheer loud enough to fill the hall and be heard by everyone present.

They drank. Janet drank. She felt how the ale flowed down her throat, how it whet her appetite for more.

There was nothing overtly sinister with the place, nothing she or her waves caught. She tried a bit harder, and still did not sense anything overt. The clientele was mostly dabblers, hardly more than playing at the task of being sorcerers or magick-wielders.

The Blue Flame and her followers stand out even here, she thought self-consciously and ironically.

They were dining later, eating hot food and sipping wine at a pleasant pace. Time flowed slowly. The barkeeps were clearly experienced in their job, easily keeping up with the many demands as the busy afternoon turned to evening.

Livy danced with Toby. They heard her trilling laughter. Everyone looked puzzled at each other.

– She has really shown… progress, has she not? Rosa mused.

– Perhaps her initial arrogance was not that at all, Dane acknowledged, – but a shell she used to protect herself when faced with new and uncertain circumstances. Rampant insecurities can get the best of us all, I guess.

There was a touch of wickedness in his voice, but not more than that it could easily be interpreted as playacting. They heard no malice.

Livy clung to Toby. She practically pushed herself at him and kept doing so relentlessly, making no secret of her intentions.

The obvious finally dawned on him, and he began returning her affection.

Janet made yet another attempt at deep-sensing her surroundings. The others inevitably noticed.

– There is something, she admitted, – something I still can not grasp.

– My guess is that there is still a lot of that, Bea said lightly. – Rest assured that it will come to you.

Bea's confidence in her, as always felt very reassuring and pleasant.

– It will all come to you, Bea added.

They exchanged one more set of heated glances. It went back and forth for several moments, until the others' laughter shook them out of it.

– You guys are so right for each other, Eleanor said spontaneously. – It is so great to behold.

The two of them blushed deeply and grabbed each other's hands, looking grateful at the apprentice.

The good mood persisted and grew as the evening progressed. The warm, pleasant feeling within dominated to such a degree that the anxiety Janet could not quite discard was reduced to a tiny blob in the molten sea filling her.

Bea was clearly moved when she at some point stood up, her usual bluster and rough edges almost completely absent.

– Thank you, all of you, she said with a catching in her throat, – for sharing our happiness. My betrothed and I both thank you.

Janet stood up as well. They stood there bathing in the affection of those gathered around the two tables. Hand grabbed hand, and they rushed to the dance floor not that far away.

The two of them danced, not touching much, but still moving like one person out there, on the vast, ebony floor. Lips touched and burned. Moist palms clasped and held.

They disengaged, flustered and happy.

– Time for my tenth visit tonight to the piss and shit bowl, Janet apologized with a grin.

– That is alright, Bea said lightly, – I can actually manage without your glorious company for a few minutes.

Janet floated on the giggles and laughter on her way to the backrooms. Her bladder was full, so full that she had trouble keeping it from leaking, especially in her intoxicated state. She stumbled a bit the last few steps to the nearest stall and toilet bowl.

She sat there, relieving herself. It felt good, felt twice as good as other times she could recall. She chuckled to herself, the many pleasant memories of the evening replaying themselves in her mind.

A draft, real or imagined caught her the moment she stepped back into the hallway. She turned and discovered the open door. Someone had just stepped through it and into the backyard. She crouched slightly, preparing herself and walked outside.

Harley sat on the worn bench, looking kind of worn himself. She relaxed a bit, but remained tense, casting quick glances around her. There was no one else close.

– I thought I heard someone call out to me, she said.

– I called you, he said. – It is my power.

– Your… power? She frowned. – How did you discover that?

– On my own, he shrugged.

She studied closer the stranger sitting there.

– You look different, she said, frowning, pondering her own words and conclusion.

– You, too, he said. – I hardly recognize you.

She nodded to herself. He did not tell her anything she did not know or had not discovered for herself.

– I am not certain I… recognize myself anymore, Harley.

She recalled herself, found herself with the other kids in the yard at Learning, just before Malone had come and fetched her. The memory had turned dim, but awareness about it still burned bright. There had been other incidents before that, she knew that. He had not truly brought it all upon her, only awakened her, put her on her… on her predestined path.

The smile shadowed her face. A cloud covered the daystar. Another chill passed through her.

– And now you are betrothed, about to be wed to the heir to yet another ancient power, he remarked casually. – Congratulations!

– Thank you, she replied, ignoring the implied, imperceptible irony in his voice.

– Bea is not good for you, he said angrily, suddenly letting go of all pretense.

– She is good for me, she countered quietly.

– You do not know her.

– And you do?

He hesitated.

– I know of her.

She smiled, rebuffing him without effort.

– You lack even the most basic awareness, she told him, deliberately patronizing. – There was a reason you flunked in the selection process, a process fairly impartial, leaving little or nothing in the way of decision-making to me or any other teacher.

– I should not be easily rebuffed, he stated. – I have the potential of both you and Eleanor, if you just let me show you.

– You flunked yourself, she shrugged, – and would most certainly have failed the one, major initiation later, the one that would have stuck you in the Wasteland forever. The clumsiest apprentice has more skill and will than you. I did you a favor.

He shrunk under her scorn, her scathing contempt.

She turned and left him, left him to rot.

A warm, warm draft caught her the moment she stepped inside. She felt like she was floating on it on her walk back to the great hall. The guys welcomed her as she returned to them, to the two tables.

Bea grabbed her arm and looked worried at her.

– Are you alright, my love?

– It is sweet of you to be concerned, Janet replied. – But there is no reason to be. I just met up with Harley and he insisted on projecting his rampant insecurities onto me. He did not succeed.

– Of course not, Bea shrugged. – He is beneath us, hardly even worthy of being called a fiend.

She still insisted on fussing, and Janet, easily won over allowed herself to be fussed. Bea pulled her down in her lap. Hands and lips and soft touches made Janet's life feel even more pleasant and pleasurable. She rocked slowly in her beloved's lap to music and rhythms both heard and unheard.

Half closed eyes slowly opened. A previously hazy vision burned with clarity. She easily spotted Illandra standing in one of the northern passages. The distinct shape caught her attention, like it always did.

Bea noticed not long after she did.

Janet slipped down on the floor. Bea rose. Both walked a little unsteady towards the older woman. They did not explain themselves or even offered a word to the others gathered around the two tables, but just left.

Illandra turned and returned to the dark passage. They followed her outside, into the quiet night. She turned and faced them after a brief walk, at a point where even the loud choir of voices from the tavern had grown distant. A double-decker bus covering a streetlight cast a large shadow on the three of them.

– Everything is ready, she said. – The elders have agreed to your request, allowing you to appear before them, to be weighed and judged in their presence.

– That is good news, grandmother, Bea said softly. – Thank you!

– Your bleeding is fairly synchronized?

– Yes, Janet replied, – we were only a few hours off the last moon.
– And I presume you have not enjoyed pleasures with a male since then?
She was telling them, not asking. Janet quelled the sudden burst of irritation.
– We have not.
Illandra raised a hand. Both girls felt like they were being grabbed and held.
– Listen to me and listen carefully then. Once it has been set in motion it can not be stopped. From the moment you bleed and the High Priestess has accepted you, you will not leave until the deed is done and proven to be effective. Do you understand?
Janet felt the power emanating from her relative like never before.
– I understand.
– You will need to submit to the elders' will and will be treated like broodmares and become the purpose of the spell.
– I understand. Janet shrugged.
– I understand, Bea assured her.
– Then, as your elder, from this very moment I become your guardian and you my wards. You will not leave my attention until the ceremony is complete and its purpose has been fully implemented. You will not talk back to me or contradict me in any way, but obey me unconditionally. Do you understand?
– Yes, grandmother, they choired.
The response was instantaneous, practically automatic. They felt like they were floating, as if their mind had become wool.
Janet fought off, shook off the pervasive influence and she sensed that Bea did as well. They both needed to struggle in order to do so, and it made them even more determined to keep doing it.
The three of them returned to the tavern, to the Circle of Nine. The letters on the wall above the passages danced in their vision.
Janet easily sensed the excitement surging through the sixteen at the two tables when they spotted Illandra.
– The fun is over, Bea declared, giggling feverishly. – The fun is about to begin.
The burgeoning excitement grew to full-fledged exhilaration. It was visible in all the faces swimming before Blue Flame.
– We are actually going to do it? Livy wondered in awe. – We will be accepted at a festival of the fabled Bone People, as candidates for its initiation?
– It is no big deal.
Janet shrugged, deliberately downplaying it all.

– But it is, Livy assured her. – To us, her devoted followers it is a great honor and the Blue Flame will finally gain a piece of her childhood lost, and be that much closer to her birthright, to power unheard of.

Her words prompted visions. Janet could practically see it, see it unfold.

– We have two maids, Illandra stated brusquely.

Eleanor and Joan rose at her light prompting.

– We will need two more.

Livy rose instantly, displaying herself with a proud smile. Rosa, after some hesitation rose as well.

Janet scrutinized her, with dispassionate eyes. Rosa reddened.

– Someone must protect you, she half mumbled, half joked.

Janet's expression softened.

She noticed without trying the attention they drew from their surroundings, from the entire crowd gathered at the tavern tonight. Some in that crowd had evidently known of them, caught their conversation, and become envious and stunned and interested. It did not truly faze her, and with that single thought more pride coursed through her.

– It is time for the heir to the Blue Flame and her consort to leave this wretched place, she declared as snotty as she could possibly make it, drawing lovesick giggles from Bea and solemn acknowledgment from Illandra.

They did, they all did. The buzz from the crowd faded slowly, only slowly in her ears and from her mind.

Nineteen made their way on darkened roads. Two tall and dark females led the way. Illandra, as was often the case spoke to her granddaughter as if the others were not there.

– Your apprentice is making nice progress…

– Thank you, Illandra of the Bone People, Janet replied politely, ironically.

– But to make further progress, to move beyond a given critical point she will need access to a Way Station, where she with less danger can find her name or at least go on a Spirit Quest worthy of being called that.

– My… master took his apprentice to such a place, Janet said, – but only to display her before his astounded peers, and he used manners of travels she is not privy to.

– There are other, harder ways to reach it, Illandra said casually, ignoring the catching in the teenager's voice. – Paths that are practically initiations in themselves.

A cold, sudden wind hit the girl. She froze and began shaking in an instant.

Illandra grabbed her with a sick, triumphant smile.

– Yes, you feel it, feel it in your very bones. You are indeed a worthy scion of the Bone People.

Janet felt her waves flare. She made them, striking at the monster with every erg of power she could muster. Blood flowed from Illandra nostrils. She was pushed backwards, into the air, several times her own body length up, until she eventually stopped, made herself stop, and levitated there, the close to ecstatic smile never leaving her face.

– I *knew* that your rage would be something to behold, a thing of beauty, but I had in truth no idea of its true potential. Know that this is nothing compared to what it one night will become.

She lowered herself back to the ground with total control of the process. The others had stopped and watched the spectacle with huge, opaque eyes. She cleaned the blood from her face and put cotton in her nostrils. Bea rushed forward to clean what was left. There was no more visible bleeding. The respect she commanded among the group had not exactly diminished.

They were walking again, and after a while all of it almost felt like a distant memory, as if it had not even happened. Almost.

A group of people followed them. They had done so since they left the tavern. The chatter among them had picked up. Janet would guess that they, at the very least had glimpsed Illandra's brief flight and could not quite dismiss the sight as a trick of their imagination.

– Allow me to confirm to you that Joan is a fairly good choice for servant. Illandra continued her dialogue as if nothing of consequence had happened. – She is strong and sturdy and will perhaps even survive your fits and rages without serious injury.

Janet gave her the look, the one she now knew impressed everybody so much.

– Did you know that her line has served yours for centuries? She is not really properly trained for it, though, not like they used to be. It is fortunate that she has a niece that can be trained from an early age.

– Explain yourself! The words came easy, flowing from Janet's mouth like water.

– It means we need to take one final detour.

Janet nodded. She knew or had a strong suspicion where they were headed.

She walked in front, not content to let Illandra lead, to the fairly large settlement by the sea. Seen from the air it formed a nine-point star. She could easily see that with the smallest use of her waves. She did not need to do it, any of it in order to know what she was looking at.

It burned in her open and closed eyes.

– What does the symbol mean, grandmother? She wondered.

– It is their clan's crest, I guess, Illandra shrugged. – Many clans use variations of nine in their standard, do they not?

She walked through the gate. It opened without her touching it. Janet and the others followed her. She stopped a considerable distance from the door to the first house.

– There are protective wards here, Janet said. – Very vicious and aggressive. They are all over the place.

– There are, Illandra confirmed. – If the wrong kind of people had entered through that gate, they would have felt their full force.

It was true. They hurt, but did not harm the two of them or any in their company. Janet sensed that by a slight focus of her power. The spells were very specific, meant only for those perceived as enemies of those inside.

Joan stepped forward, with love and devotion, despair and resentment both in her eyes, as she bowed down before Janet.

– By your leave, she declared humbly.

Janet nodded absentmindedly, dismissing her servant, hardly even acknowledging her.

Joan walked into the house without knocking on the door or announcing her presence in any way.

Janet studied everything around her, making no secret of it. She saw more symbols wherever she turned, variations of the nine-point stars and others. They all made her skin tingle, in one way or another.

A man and a little girl appeared on the heels of Joan returning to those she served.

The man, one generation removed from Joan resembled very much both Joan and the girl. He had something about him, something Janet could not help but pick up on.

She saw that something in his eyes, too, a sense of recognition, of simultaneous awe and fear. It lingered there, never truly going away.

He glanced at her. In fact he could not take his eyes off her. She knew he felt drawn to her. That was visible in every small move he made.

The girl moved forward, transfixed and with her entire attention focused on Janet. She stopped before her. Janet acknowledged her presence with a stiff smile.

– Hi, Janet said, – what is your name?

– My name is Caroline Tsjekov, the girl replied brightly. – What is yours?

– I am Janet Kathryn Caldwell of the Blue Flame, scion of the Bone People, Janet heard herself say.

Shock and fear and awe all manifested in the girl's face, as she curtseyed and lowered her eyes, humbling herself for the regal woman.

– My life for you, Honored One, she cried out with a loud, thin voice.

She began shaking and kept doing it. Janet touched her cautiously, attempting to comfort her.

– Be at ease, young one, she said softly.

The girl finally looked up, looked at her with dedication and loyalty burning in her wet eyes. Janet felt a catching in her throat.

– The girl evidently knows her place, Livy remarked.

Illandra stepped forward, halting before the older man. He straightened visibly.

– Rafael Tsjekov, Illandra said, – do you still honor the age-old arrangements?

– We do.

He swallowed hard.

– Then you better make sure the girl receives the proper training, or there will be hell to pay.

– It will be done, he assured her, and Janet and everyone present. – As the gods are my witnesses.

Illandra and Janet turned and walked away as one being, and the other seventeen wanderers in darkness followed them. Rafael and Caroline remained, standing unmoving, as the group left the Tsjekov land and resumed their long walk.

Bea walked by Janet's side with shiny eyes.

– Now, Bea stated. – Now, it begins!

And Janet felt it, felt the truth of that statement in every nerve and nerve ending, as they made their way further down the darkened road.

Part three: The Tribe of Bones

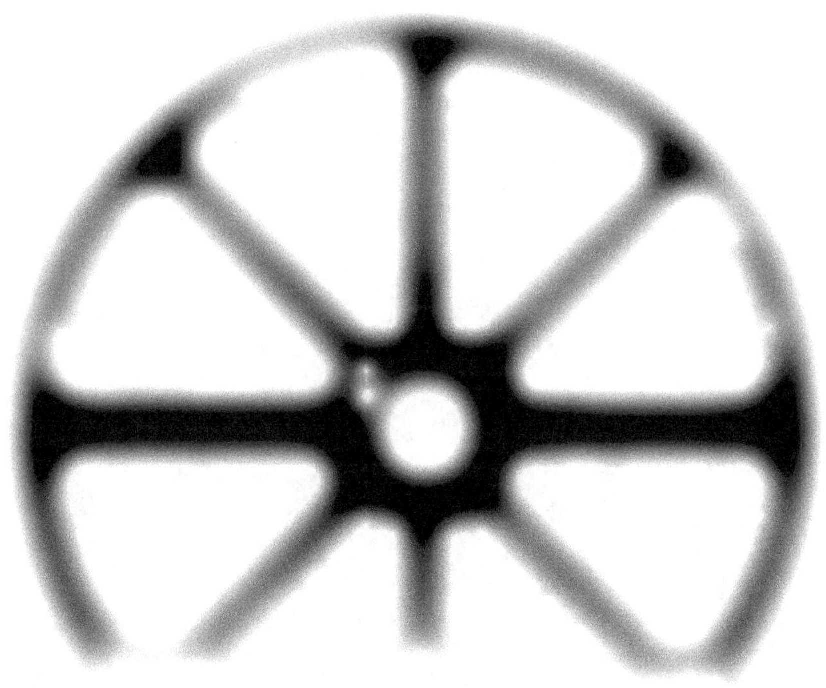

Chapter 18

A curious crowd had gathered outside the Rosen estate. More people that had followed Janet and the others at a distance all the way from the tavern joined up.

She ignored them, as she led her people through the gate, where the curious crowd could not follow, making her feel twice good about it.

They reached the lavish courtyard and the big doors decorated with intricate patterns. The servants opened the doors just before they reached them, in exactly the right moment. The wanderers walked down the hallway with the polished floor, ceiling and walls.

Janet recalled without effort the awkward, insecure and nervous girl she had been the last time she had passed these hallways and visited these halls. The very thought made her smile.

An older servant stared, stared... Janet realized that he was staring at Illandra, at both of them, as they walked side by side and Janet instantly knew why.

– We are Rosens, are we not? Janet stated.

– We are of the Rosen line, yes, of the Rosen line as well.

They, the entire big group entered the living room. The same four people sat on the sofa.

Justin rose, with a stunned, almost happy expression on his face.

– You are Jenny's daughter, are you not, he asked Illandra.

– I am, she confirmed.

She was completely relaxed, unexcited.

– Welcome home, he said.

– Thank you, she said.

Bea walked to John and stopped in front of him. He rose.

– Everything is set, she stated. – Come with us.

– I will, the boy said, striving to sound indifferent. – I am looking forward to it, to all of it.

He turned towards Janet and looked at her with something very similar to a sleazy grin, staring at her half exposed breasts. She returned his kindness, studying him from head to toe, making him blush hard. His inexperience pleased her.

He was, when she bothered to ponder the issue actually fairly tall for his age, and quite muscular, quite capable, well suited for the task Bea had chosen him for.

– I expect everything to be ready with our return, Illandra said, very formal.

– It will be, Justin assured her. – It will be an event remembered in Arcadia for a thousand years.

– I am confident that it will be, Illandra agreed. – If we return.

– What will happen if you do not? Madge wondered, fidgeting nervously.

– Then you will never see either your son or daughter again.

Turner did not say anything. He just studied the spectacle with a spiteful look.

The wanderers' number had increased to twenty when they returned to the night, a fact not lost on some of the spectators gathered outside. Newshounds pointed and moved forward. Illandra mumbled simple curses and their forward momentum stopped abruptly and brutally. Fear struck them.

The road of those following the twenty suddenly seemed beyond dark and fraught with hurdles. Only a few held out the relentless hammering of forces. They could not tell what made them afraid, only that something beyond their reach did.

The wicked laughter echoed in their ears and timid minds.

Nineteen youths studied Illandra of the Bone People with deep-felt admiration and glee.

The lights from the airship brightened a large area. They spotted it long before getting close. It arrived from the north with passengers and goods, and would make a stop here, before continuing to the southern triple cities.

This was a different, bigger ship compared to the one they had flown to the Maximus Guesthouse. It was better equipped without and within and could handle more passengers. It blocked the light from Little Moon and cast a big shadow on the ground. A shiver Janet could not prevent coursed through her.

– This is huge, Dane said excited. – This is a moment in time that will rest forever in infamy, mark my words.

Janet nodded to herself and could not decide how to feel about it.

The few remaining newshounds and the curious kept trailing them, even though they kept their distance, never imposing or getting close.

– All of this, their version of it will be accessible for people in the papers tomorrow, Bea snarled, unusually agitated.

She gave Janet an apologetic smile, a stiff version of what was usually blinding and radiant.

– Look ahead, betrothed of my grandchild. The sickly curious may have some limited power up here, but down there, in the turning wheel they dare not even venture.

They had ventured down there on occasion, but had either returned with nothing to show for themselves… or not at all. For the wrong kind of traveler the southern triple cities were a vast, black hole.

– I will. Bea sniffed. – Thank you, grandmother.

The wanderers climbed the broad landing bridge. It felt to some degree as if they were floating. Janet felt the pull of both the ship and the future. It imposed itself even stronger on her as they entered the hovering craft. The bright lights of the hull faded to a normal, warm glow, as they emerged into the entrance hall.

People stared and studied them all the time. It still unnerved Janet, even though she had started getting used to it.

– Do get used to it, Illandra advised her. – You will get assessed, judged, condemned. It is the way of all realms and societies.

They entered the lounge. It was slightly below half filled by the time they sat down in the comfortable chairs and slightly above half filled when the time of departure approached.

– It is ridiculous, is it not? Frances said. – Less people travel at these late hours, fearing the darkness. They do not realize that the night is our home.

The others found themselves nodding without being consciously aware of it at first.

Sounds reached them from the inside and outside as the moorings were released from the ground and the airship rose into the air in one fluid, smooth movement. The low-noise engine pushed the giant balloon and its far smaller attachment south.

The crew served wine. Not all the passengers had any, but all in Janet and Bea's group did. The chilled «white» fluid, the pale wine flowed down their throats.

– This is quality wine, Bea brightened, subsequently frowning, as if the very idea was foreign to her.

– What is it, beloved, Janet teased her, – did you not think commoners could make fine wine?

Bea clearly pondered the issue, before responding.

– Now that you mention it, no, she replied. – It is a pleasant surprise.

Her arrogance clearly showed. Janet giggled cheerfully, unable to keep it contained any longer. Bea's expression softened.

Janet delayed her walk to the toilet room purposely for minutes, before rising and giving the others a sweet smile, seeking the solitude of the darkened hallways.

She walked through them, drawing on their solemn mood in order to calm herself. The jittery she could not quite discard did rest a little.

She did go to the toilet room, even though she did not strictly need to do so yet. Her feet moved and sought out the nearest stall and bowl. She pulled down her pants and underwear, and sat down. It did feel good to release her load, emptying both her bladder and her lower cavity. It distracted her from her troubling thoughts.

They kept dancing on the wall before her and behind closed and open eyelids.

Bea waited for her outside, a patronizing smile very evident in her expression.

– I saw right through you, of course, right through your brave act. You are as transparent as glass, beloved.

– Congratulations, Janet said in an equally mocking tone, – you are wise beyond words.

Bea was close to her in an instant. Both were shaking as they grabbed hold of each other and touched.

– Forgive me, beloved, Bea whispered in regret. – I was being mean and presumptuous. Forgive me?

– Of course, Janet said softly. – I am sorry, too.

They stood there for an untold time, comforting each other.

– Let us take a walk on the balcony, Bea whispered, – just the two of us.

Unable to give voice to her emotions Janet kissed her in affirmation, and they crossed most of the ship, walking through more modestly populated hallways to the front. They emerged onto the large balcony. There was no one else there. The vast southern marches revealed themselves to them. Big Moon lit up fields and rises below the slowly floating ship.

– It is so beautiful, Janet breathed.

– And so different from the north, Bea marveled.

– Yes, you have been there, have you not, Janet said, visibly envious. – You get to travel a lot.

– Yes, I do, Bea emphasized, – and now, or at least not far ahead in time everything that is mine is yours.

A catching in the Blue Flame's throat once more made it impossible for her to speak.

Bea made a quick trip to the cupboard by one of the exits and brought out a bottle of chilled pale wine and two glasses.

– Some more quality wine, My Lady?

– Thank you, that would be lovely, Janet replied, dazzled by the other's twinkling and so very pretty eyes.

Bea gave her one of the glasses and filled both.

– Cheers! She said.

– Cheers! Janet said.

Glasses met and parted, and the sound very similar to a tuning fork filled the space between them. These were quality glasses as well.

They drank. Eyes met eyes and held.

Minutes, hours, ages passed. They enjoyed each other's company. There was no one else present. Only a few stragglers briefly disrupted their peace.

Janet rubbed the violet amulet. It vibrated in her hand, making her fingertips tingle. Bea looked encouragingly at her, rubbing her cheek gently.

– I have always loved the night, its dark passions, the young sorcerer finally said, – but Frances's words reminded me of everything it has cost me.

She turned towards her betrothed, not looking away anymore.

– It also reminded me of everything that is out there, threatening me, threatening us all. It is not very pleasant to ponder.

– I would say neither you nor we have much reason to be worried, Bea said with confidence in her voice. – You are already an experienced and powerful sorcerer, and what you are now is northing compared to what you will become. In *addition* to that you already have a small army of warriors at your beck and call, one that will grow in both numbers and skill, as the years go by. We will become a force to be *reckoned* with. Anyone taking us on will have to be some mean and powerful motherfucker just to survive the first few seconds of our encounter.

Janet giggled.

– You are such an incurable… optimist, are you not?

– I prefer realist, Bea shrugged.

They emptied their glasses, lowering them to their hips as their snuggling turned more intense.

The world went away for a while. Janet let it, desired it, and the world obliged.

– We are wild things, Bea breathed in her ears. – Grandmother's tribe got nothing on us.

Janet caressed her cheek, rubbed her lips with her thumb. Bea practically purred in her arms.

– You do not need to call her grandmother, at least not all the time.

– But I want to. She is your grandmother and thereby mine. What is yours is mine.

– What is mine is yours, Janet echoed, and nodded eagerly.

Bea filled the glasses again. She raised hers. Janet raised hers.

– To dark passions.

Glasses met and parted once again, and once again the sweet tingle echoed in their ears, and the beyond sweet nectar burned pleasantly in their throats and stomachs and seeded their minds.

They sat down on the bench deeper on the balcony, in an area reminding them of a garden.

– There is a prevailing restlessness in me I can never get rid of, Janet admitted.

– And rest assured that I do not want you to. I want you to do whatever you wish. We are going to live according to our desires, no one else's. Rest assured that our clans, mine or yours will never rule us, never decide how we will live.

A comforting hand squeezed hers.

– That sounds so right, she heard herself say excited. – So very right.

They kissed, lips to lips, body to body. The sound of the glasses hitting the floor and breaking hardly registered in their conscious mind and time just went away again.

When they returned to the others both looked beyond relaxed and pleased, with content, lazy grins dominating their features. Everyone could see with one eye their state of mind, what they had been doing.

Eleanor looked more than a little flustered. She had obviously felt it.

– Master feels better now? She inquired humbly.

Janet noticed that almost everyone studied her with concern. She realized that her attempts at hiding her apprehension had been an abject failure. Almost all of her guard had known how she struggled, with herself, with everything.

– I do, she replied. – Thank you, apprentice.

– The Blue Flame is just at the start of her remarkable path, Livy said. – The near, upcoming trials are merely one in a long row she must endure in order to gain her destined power and authority.

– Thank you, advisor, Janet snorted, striving to make her voice and behavior as snotty as possible, striving in vain to conceal the inevitable pride coursing through her.

Livy bowed and curtseyed with great skill, well into what she had deemed her important future role already.

– Leave it to Livy to call days of intense fucking a trial, Toby chuckled.

The laughter erupted easily from everyone's throats.

– Your squire does not yet understand his future role as a knight, My Lady, Livy said lightly, cleverly both joking and not, – but I am confident that he will.

Janet spotted easily the flash of affection in the boy's eyes when he looked at her and knew her valued advisor to be more than correct.

– All the Blue Flame's followers love and cherish their future queen, Livy added.

Janet saw admiration and awe in everyone's eyes, and once again knew the clever sorcerer to be correct.

They approached the southern triple cities. She knew that by noticing many big and small things, none of them overt. The subtle effects worked best for her. She did not need to watch the other passengers. There was no need to look out the window. She saw the circle making out the cities of Alobi, Josbar and Kalaho long before she spotted it with her eyes. When it eventually came into view, it was exactly as she had envisioned it in a thousand fevered dreams.

It was not really a circle, but a wheel, a turning wheel very distinct in the terrain. Janet saw it spin slowly and the smoke and fire and shadow surrounding it.

She blinked and it had become just a circle again. The sight of the turning wheel lingered in her consciousness, never truly going away.

The heavy, still distant drums began beating the moment they stepped off the landing bridge and sat foot on the ground, quickly growing louder and increasingly pervasive.

Two rows of people formed the welcome committee, a long alley continuing far into the city of Josbar. They stood there with tall torches in their hands and made most of those departing the airship very nervous. A low chant added itself to the sound of the drums.

– A fitting welcome when a daughter of the Bone People returns home, Livy stated with pride practically engraved in her being.

The wayward daughter felt that, the confirmation of the other's words, along with the lingering apprehension never truly leaving her.

– There are three clans, Illandra taught her, – one for each triple city.

– I know, grandmother, Janet said with infinite patience. – We belong to the Josbari, «The Fire of the Turning Wheel». We are the priests, the leaders of the clans. The Alobi is the smoke and the Kalaho is the ashes. They serve us as the swords and the arms of our society.

– You have researched the matter, Illandra said pleased. – Very good!

The priestess in training was allowed to briefly bask in the praise.

– But do not imagine for a moment you have gone deep, bashful daughter of my son. You will do that in the upcoming days and weeks and in the years to come, in order to truly become a part of the tribe and eventually claim your birthright.

Janet would have scoffed at those words, if she had not sensed their sinister truth.

Three people, one man, one woman and one young boy stepped forward, parting from those forming the human alley. They focused on Illandra and only on her.

– Greetings, High Priestess, the young boy said. – Welcome home.

– Thank you, Kalir, Illandra responded. – It feels good to be home.

The three stepped aside, and Illandra and those accompanying her walked on.

– No high ranking officials bother to show up to greet you? Janet inquired.

– A wayward, unruly High Priestess, her equally so granddaughter and her ragtag band of would be warriors? Do not be silly.

Janet looked with her twinkling violet eyes at the rows of people making a path for them.

– But citizens still show up in droves.

– I would say, Bea grinned. – If I should guess, I would say that almost half of the population of the southern triple cities has come out to witness our arrival.

– We are a very curious people, Illandra said. – No matter how much certain members of the council of elders would want to keep that from manifesting, they would not even dream of attempting such a feat.

Janet looked closer at those studying, assessing her. She recognized all kinds of emotions there, from fear to apprehension to awe and anticipation and even *elation*.

– The prodigal daughter has returned home, Bea said brightly, – and everyone is happy.

Illandra led them through the human alley to a strange building at the edge of the circle. It resembled a T, one with soft edges. The travelers walked inside. The low rumble of voices faded to something approaching silence.

The reception hall was pretty much a living room, or like a living room. A giant mirror decorated the western wall. There was a long, long table and sleeping mats for everyone. They realized that they looked at an all-purpose room.

– This is a guest house, Illandra told them. – You will spend the time before your preparation begins here. Food and drinks will be served and your needs will be taken care of for as long as you stay.

She turned towards Janet.

– We do not have much time. I can not be with you during the initial proceedings. You will need to navigate the stormy waters alone.

– I understand, grandmother, Janet nodded. – I am a big girl.

Illandra stepped close to her with fast, abrupt movements. She grabbed the girl and put her in front of the mirror. Janet allowed that, sensing the importance of her actions.

– Behold your birth tattoos.

Janet did, perhaps even more thorough than the thousand times she had already done so. They covered most of the left side of her face, with some reaching the other side, all connecting in what looked like a tree and its branches, ending up on her forehead.

– You are a left side dominant, Illandra said. – Only a few in our line have been such. It has always been yet one more sign of great power and potential of leadership.

She touched a point in Janet's face.

– This is mine, a slightly altered representation of what was uniquely mine until your father was born.

She traced the pattern further with her index finger.

– This is your father's, a slightly altered representation of what was uniquely his until you were born.

She reached the end of the line. Janet felt a little like a doll, a puppet in the more experienced woman's confident hands, but she felt excitement as well. This was the first time she was given any kind of detailed explanation concerning the tattoos.

– And this is what is currently the last, what is still uniquely yours, until the next pup has popped from your loins.

– When did the tattoos first appear, grandmother? Janet asked.

– No one knows exactly, Illandra replied, – but it was countless generations ago, so long ago that no one remembers their beginning. It has been speculated that it goes all the way back to the beginning of the Bone People.

– So, the tattoos made us the Bone People?

– Perhaps. We do know that all Bone People have them, and that everyone's tattoos are unique to each individual tribe member. You will get to learn more as your induction proceeds.

She kissed her granddaughter softly and pulled back. Janet looked startled at her.

– Btw, I would not brag about the former initiation you passed, if I was you. The Ceremony of Bones is an older, different rite of passage, for a different purpose.

Janet frowned.

– Translation: keep quiet about it? The girl queried.

– You possess many and valuable and crucial secrets. My advice to you is to guard them zealously.

The tall older woman turned and walked out the door without looking back.

– What was that about? Fran wondered.

She received no reply.

Several of those present knew, or at least had more than an inkling about what it was about. Janet sent them a strict look they did not really need. They kept quiet.

More than a little distracted, stimulated further, and more than lost in her own head by the bombshell dropped on her, Janet kept analyzing events and her own mind, her already elevated and stormy thoughts rising to yet another level.

She felt it, a tangible effect beside the anger brought on by added knowledge.

Bea walked to Janet and grabbed her hands.

– This is exciting, is it not, beloved, in spite of all the ceremonial crap we must suffer through?

Bea was very much Bea right then.

– Yes, Janet admitted. – Yes, it is! I want this, want to learn more about myself, about my ancestors, even if it is just my father's people and not my mother's.

– You will explore the history of the Blue Flame later, Bea said casually. – We will do so together.

And as if on cue everyone gathered around them, and made Janet feel the love and dedication and respect.

She felt like she melted in their embrace.

They disengaged, but everyone kept their attention on Janet. Livy stepped forward.

– What is your will, Honored One?

Janet shrugged.

– What happens next will not be up to me, she replied. – We have, by coming here, submitted to the will of strangers in the expectation that when it is done we will all be one of them. I will become what I was born to become and you will join my tribe and clan by association and betrothal.

Bea was blushing, she was actually blushing. Janet giggled. That was so cute.

There was a knock on the door, on the one Illandra had walked through leading inside the circle the triple towns made. Janet nodded in confirmation. Eleanor walked to the door and opened it.

A young woman stood on the stairs outside. A host of boys and girls accompanying her brought cutlery and steaming kettles and various accompanying items visible in the elaborate display cases.

Janet nodded again, and Eleanor relaxed and stepped aside. Janet had now a direct line of sight to those outside.

– Greetings, Janet, granddaughter of Illandra, Scion of the Bone People, the girl said. – My name is Zoe, I am of the Josbari. I and my entourage bring the night's supper.

– Bring it then, Janet granted.

They did. Zoe's entourage of ten followed her inside, practically in her slipstream. Everything, every little act they performed seemed to flow effortlessly, as if there was no expenditure of power in their movement. They put the hot kettles and warm plates and heated forks and knifes and spoons on the table in what seemed like no time at all and still made it look like they took their time. They lit candles and incense, and put everything in order both elegantly and effectively.

– What is your name, sweetie? John asked a girl with cute features, clearly patronizing.

– I am Loewe, sire, the girl replied, blushing. – I am of the Josbari, the clan of your…

She held back, clearly embarrassed. He grinned.

– Will you stay? He asked her boldly, making his intentions clear.

– I can not, sire, she said humbly. – You are the… intended of my clan sister, and can not have any… contact with others until after the ceremony is completed.

She reddened again.

– Loewe is shy, a boy said.

The others laughed.

They still surrounded her, subtly protecting her from John's advances. He shrugged and pulled back.

The serving of the night supper had been completed. The eleven boys and girls pulled back to the still open door.

Zoe turned to Janet with a clearly beyond patronizing attitude.

– The festivities will commence at the coming dusk, she informed the other. – I suggest that you relax and prepare as best you are able until then. We will live even deeper through the night during the scion's induction and celebration.

Janet struck her. It happened so fast, without any conscious thought at all. She fell and hit the floor.

– You will treat me and mine with respect, Janet informed her.

Zoe quickly bowed her head and bared her neck.

– My apologies, granddaughter of Illandra, she whispered thunderstruck, clearly fearful.

– You may leave, now, Janet shrugged.

They did. The door closed.

– That showed her, Bea said, very smug.

They sat down around the long table. The sight of them and everything in the room echoed in the giant wall mirror.
– Look at it, it seems so real, Frances whispered.
Everyone did so. The flames danced on her skin and the smoke whirled in the air between them, burned in their throat, and stirred their senses.
– That is because it is. Another world lives in all mirrors, everyone knows that.
Bea began serving herself without further ado and the others joined her.
Janet started feeding with the others, but the other in the mirror did not. The mirror image stopped and paused, studying herself with curious eyes. Janet joined her, and as she did so, all their movements were delayed compared to the other. It went on for seconds, until the mirror image settled on both sides.
Everyone looked at the Blue Flame, studying her even more closely, with greater awe.
Activity was picking up in the hours before dawn, not the other way around. Noise and sound and speech increased in volume and intricacy. Janet listened with half an ear, while feeding and enjoying the company of those sharing her journey.
– This, Dane mused, – the entire southern triple cities, is some setup.
– All the triple cities have their own, unique way of doing things, Jess said. – I guess we have not seen anything yet.
Janet realized startled that he had been almost all but invisible to her lately. Now, he briefly reasserted himself in her sphere, before fading, fading, fading…
Bea raised her glass. Everyone else did the same.
– To our union. It will echo through eternity. Long after we are dust, our fire will live on.
– OUR UNION, everybody choired.
They drank and kept drinking, but it never quite took off, and that, too felt right. Everyone present had their eyes on tomorrow, on the upcoming night and nights.
Pervasive sensations coalescing into images and sounds haunted Janet with increasing frequency.
The travelers rose from the table fed and content. They undressed and retreated to the mats. Through unspoken agreement no one was fucking anyone. Thoughts on tomorrow and the immediate future increasingly filled their being, adding to themselves, until they dominated all perception.
Sleep brought rest of a kind, but no true rest from what was haunting them. They slept during most of the day. The drums began beating at

noon, and though they did not wake anyone up, they all heard them. They imagined they saw the drummer, heard him as he started chanting, and making magick, smoke and mist. In the spots of mist and smoke and shadow they glimpsed their own faces. Reality mixed with dreams and continued doing so as they woke up and enjoyed their morning meal.

Torches danced in the night. Janet saw them, felt their smoke in her nostrils. Feet moved around the cabin, towards the center of the circle with one torch in each hand. She experienced it as real, as if everything happened right now. She glimpsed Illandra and the elders she remembered from her first encounter with them on the field outside Maximus' Folly.

Eleanor looked confused at Janet when they opened their eyes simultaneously. The spices adding to all the great tastes of food in their mouths burned on their tongues and in their stomachs and their increasingly excited minds.

Zoe and her cohorts returned with «the morning meal» (it was not morning) and left quickly, showing without resistance the respect the Blue Flame had required of them last night. The travelers treated them with the disdain they deserved, consuming the food in a relaxed frenzy even before they were out the door.

Twilight approached. Janet could practically see it, sense the minute changes in the air as the air subtly darkened.

The twilight lingered and as the minutes ticked away, it was clear it would last beyond, way beyond its normal duration. Janet observed how the darkening actually stopped, how the process itself froze.

The sound of drums picked up, in both intensity and proximity.

– It is time, Janet said.

The knocking on the door was harder, more insistent.

Eleanor rushed to the door and opened it, quickly stepping aside to make room for Kalir and the woman and the man accompanying him. Janet met them at the center of the floor.

– Greetings, Janet Kathryn Caldwell, Scion of the Bone People, the boy said. – I am Kalir of the Josbari.

– I am Csjesse of the Alobi, the woman stated.

– I am Seri of the Kalaho, the man presented himself.

– We have come to fetch you and yours for the trials, Csjesse said.

Each of the three held a collar with a chain in their hands.

– Others will guide your followers during the ceremony, Seri explained.

– The collars will keep you from becoming a danger to yourself and others during the trials, Kalir explained. – They will also aid you, educate you in the ways of the Bone People.

There was a sinister subtext to the trio's words. It made Janet shiver and burn. She fought with herself to stand still when Kalir stepped forward. He did not seem like a boy to her anymore. The spell rose from his throat. She writhed under its influence.

– Do not fight it, daughter of the Josbari, he spat, – or your life will be forfeit.

His words grew out of the spell and the spell grew out of his words in an even, uninterrupted flow

She sensed that he did not mean her mortal life. It was more than that - worse. She submitted to it, to him. He slipped the collar around her neck. She felt its influence immediately, how it dampened her powers and hummed in her mind.

Bea stepped eagerly forward, meeting Seri halfway. She seemed perfectly calm, but Janet, closely attached to her knew she shivered when he put the collar around her neck.

– You will not shame us, will you, brother? She challenged John.

Initially reluctant he did willingly submit to Csjesse.

A voice grew out of the incomprehensible buzz and solidified in Janet's head.

Greetings, great daughter of the Josbari, a woman spoke brightly, compassionately. I am Evian, your guide in your trials. Great power awaits you at the end of their path.

A pull, and Janet followed Kalir out of the house and into the lingering twilight of the southern triple cities.

Do not be concerned, Evian said soothingly. You are being prepared for the spell, becoming its vessel, until you are nothing but that spell, that glory.

And in that moment, the walk, the migration to the center of the circle began in earnest. Janet saw it, sensed it, not only because the spirit of the collar showed her, but through the still vibrant remains of her power. The city people left their homes in three waves. The wheel turned. Forming a triskele flesh burning like torches sought the giant bonfire, the daystar at the center of the circle. They gasped at its vast power.

The sound of the drums picked up, transforming into thunder.

Three collared youths were brought to the temple in the fire's shadow. Their three handlers removed the chain, but the collar stayed on. Boys and girls in their middle teens with wide, curious eyes and a very visible attitude met them in the entrance.

– We all serve the elders, the High Priests here, Csjesse stated, – and so, when you are here, by definition do you. After your initiation is complete you will serve them no matter where you go.

Everybody wore the same unassuming clothing as the three. Janet noticed quickly the dichotomy of their tattoos, though, revealing that they were hailing from vastly different bloodlines.

The youths surrounded them and began removing their clothes, playfully and with a wicked disposition, well aware of how their touching and rubbing worked on their subjects. Janet felt like a puppet in their hands, her dulled mind and will unable to offer any significant resistance.

They were led into a bigger hall. Janet looked startled at all the slightly older nude youths writhing on the mats covering the floor, at the shiny collars decorating their necks.

Janet, Bea and John were put down on the three remaining available mats. A frown crossed Janet's features. This was not only about her and Bea and John and their intent. This was…

– This is your initiation, Seri called out to them all. – This is you taking the step from initiates, to full-fledged member of the tribe. You will either succeed or fail. There is no middle ground. This is your final chance to back out. Once the first drop of the ointment falls on your skin, it will be too late. You will forever be bound to your fate.

Rhyme, Janet thought.

No one spoke up. How could they, with the pleasant hum their mind and entire frame had become? She suspected that the choice of everyone here had been made long ago.

His voice carried far on the waves, into the ears of everyone present. He struck out with his open hands, signaling for the youths dressed to begin working on the initiates.

Oil? Janet wondered.

The Oil of Awakening, the spirit of Evian spoke seductively and awestruck in her head.

The drops fell from flasks into palms. Palms rubbed against each other, heating the fluid.

Hot! She gasped the moment it touched her skin.

Every single piece of air and skin and fabric surrounding her turned so hot, so pleasant. She writhed subjected to cruel and invasive hands. A hand, very deliberately touched her cunt. She caught a glimpse of another wicked grin. Another glimpse revealed another hand rubbing John's cock. Bea's moan filled her ears. She imagined Eleanor somewhere close to her in that faraway guesthouse equally worked up.

They turned her around with skilled hands and kept working on her. Time went away. It just faded in her consciousness, supplanted it with something new and indistinct.

Kalir stood above her, spitting his spells. She realized dimly that she recognized the patterns of his tattoos that they were vaguely familiar… to her own.

A blink and she imagined she glimpsed Illandra. Another blink and she was gone.

Janet was standing. Awareness returned somewhat. They had been dressed again, all of them wearing simple tunics. The door opened wide before them. They were led through a confusing landscape of fire and green and brown and leering faces. They were supported, unable to walk properly.

Everything had turned into a haze, indistinct glimpses of surroundings and people. Janet had no proper sense of herself anymore. She had become one with the formless mass of flesh moving in and out of her vision, joined with it. The soft song in her head disrupted any coherent thought, keeping it from forming.

A procession moved through an uneven, shifting terrain, never truly settling in the eyes of those being led through it. Chanting filled the thick and sizzling air. Lines of sweaty bodies formed an alley along their path. The hums of many throats rose at the distant sky.

A hole in the air emerged slowly in Janet's vision. The next moment it faded away, as if had never been there at all. Faces covered by birth tattoos swam before her. Crows squeaked in her ears. She gasped, attempting in vain to get her bearing.

A girl held her chain. She took great pleasure in occasionally pulling it too hard, making Janet stumble and be in the need of support by those other youths supporting her.

– You are nothing but helpless children, the girl spat.

The words were hardly audible or comprehensible in Janet's cotton ears.

Yes, this is an initiation, cruel and tough, Evian informed her brightly. You are all blessed.

Blessed, Janet repeated in her head with a frown on her brow.

You will become an adult in name and fact, and you, of a prominent line of priests are particularly fortunate. Eventually all the secrets of the Bone People will be yours.

They reached a building, a structure, not really that tall, but they still felt as if it towered above them. A tunnel appeared in front of them. Their handlers dragged them through it. It felt like the darkness went on forever. A thousand feet fashioned the long march.

They emerged into a yard, a round space, where a tall fire burned at the center. People sat on stands broad like in a Greek or Roman theater. Square pillars connected at the top, forming a circle had been placed at even intervals around the seething daystar of dancing flames and shadows. Everyone on ground level cast long shadows here.

Relatives of those to be initiated and other interested parties gather here to watch and enjoy the proceedings, Evian droned on, more than happy to explain everything.

Today, many have flocked here to witness the spectacle of the Blue Flame, she added with unmistakable pride.

Janet could almost glimpse her face and even her detailed features through the static and haze surrounding her senses.

A small… hut seemed to fade in from nowhere. It stood out to the south, covered in mist. A woman, a priestess stood on its porch. All the collared youths stared blindly at her. They could do nothing else.

– Welcome initiates and novices, she declared. – It is time for your next step, for you to become full-fledged members of your tribe.

Look at her, she is magnificent.

No, she is not, Janet protested. She is just yet another stuck up, patronizing priestess full of herself.

Hush, Janet of the Josbari, it is time for you to be humble, to listen and not speak unless you are given permission by your betters.

The spirit's presence shifted subtly, stepping up its task as tutor.

There was a pain, was punishment, soft and mellow but stern, and unable to resist Janet just floated away and all her objections amounted to nothing.

– I am Myriam of the Josbari, the priestess called. – Come with me inside.

They followed her call, followed her inside.

A great hall revealed itself to them. Heavy eyelids rose ever so little. Their sense of wonder persisted. They stood at the center of the floor, facing the deep end of the hall. In that deep end a half circle of high seats faded into their consciousness. Women and men in robes and hoods sat there. The woman who had led them inside curtseyed before the High Priests. She pulled back, standing with her back to the wall.

– Greetings, the woman in the center seat spoke up. – I am Ione, High Priest of the Bone People. We have called you here in order to gauge your motivation and your heart and mind and spirit. If we deem you unworthy to proceed, you will go no further and your life is forfeit.

Awe mixed with anxiety in the dim minds of the youths standing before the High Council.

Illandra stood up, calling attention to herself.

– Janet of the Josbari, she cried casually, but with a loud and powerful voice, – step forward.

Janet did, obeying the word and will of her paternal grandmother. She kept staring straight forward, at the mist and nothing her vision had become.

Ione rose from her chair, an act creating no small commotion among her peers.

– The Blue Flame, the High Priestess mused.

Janet looked up, locking her attention on her, or attempting to.

– Look at her, the woman said to the others and shook her head. – Behold her in her mere pubescent glory.

They did. It was impossible not to notice their attention, their invasive probes.

– Burn for us, child, the priestess commanded.

And then the girl did manage to lock on to the regal woman.

Janet felt how the collar powered down, how that returned her powers.

The flames began licking her form, spreading to the very air surrounding her.

Eyes in the half circle facing her lit up in wonder, triumphant and possessive.

– It is such a fortunate coincidence, is it not? One of the others said with thick triumph in her voice. – One of the Bone People has become the heir to the Blue Flame.

– She belongs to us, now, Illandra said pleased.

Comments echoed among the High Priests. Janet felt it, even as her collar was turned back on and power and awareness faded into the hum of her mind.

– She is like this, now, in her infancy. What will she become?

– Everything we may desire.

– We will breed her extensively, of course.

The frown did not quite leave Janet's brow, but she never managed to make more out of it.

Ione sat back down. The restlessness among those on the high seat settled somewhat.

Illandra once again called sole attention to herself.

– Janet of the Josbari, why do you want to become one of the Bone People?

This is a question asked everyone brought before the High Council, Evian said, very helpful. No one is considered a member of the tribe and given clan until they have completed the trials.

– I want to know myself, the girl replied sleepily, – who I am and where I come from. I want to know everything there is to know. I want to share everything with my betrothed. What is mine is hers.

– You do this for your betrothed?

– I do it for her and for myself… and I do it for the t-tribe.

It slipped out of her, and she could not keep it from happening.

More thick triumph emanated from the half circle towering above her.

– You are just a girl after all, Ione spat, – are you not, eager to learn from your betters?

– Yes, the girl bowed her head in shame.

– But for you to be accepted, you must serve your tribe unconditionally. Do you do that, Heir to the Blue Flame?

– I do!

– It is your wish to serve your tribe and clan in all things?

The voice hit her like a blade. It dug into her, cut her open.

– It is, she gasped. – I submit myself to the service of my people and dedicate my life to the purpose of my birth.

– You will dedicate yourself to the tribe *above all else?*

– I will!

The girl was swaying, sweating, humming and floating off on the airwaves surrounding her. Illandra smiled to her fellow High Priests.

– You have never spent any time with your brethren, but you still feel loyalty to them?

– I do! Janet cried out. – I did not think I would, but I do! I grew up without knowing who I am and I was lonely, so very lonely.

She sniffed, suddenly overwhelmed with emotion, unable to keep it contained. The women and men of the high seats exchanged pleased smiles.

There was a lot more questions and answers. It ended eventually, but kept echoing in her mind. Janet was practically exhausted when she stepped back and a virtual oblivion claimed her.

– Beatrice Maximus Rosen, Illandra called. – Step forward!

Bea did, holding her head high.

– Why do you, an outsider want to become one of the Bone People, Beatrice Maximus Rosen, you, who can never be one in fact?

Bea attempted to focus and fight against the brutal intrusion of her mind, her very self, in vain.

– I want to share everything with my betrothed, she cried out, gasping in vain to get her bearing. – What is mine is hers.

– So, you are willing to throw away everything you are in order to please her?

The voice, unexpected came from one of the males to the right.

Bea blinked confused, bending, bowing her already weary head.

– No, I want to join you, join the Bone People. It is not just because of my sweet witch. I need to do this, in order to remove myself from my upbringing.

And then she felt shame as well, and it had been brought forth so easy. She lowered her eyes a bit more.

Those in the high seats looked pleased and smug at each other. Janet saw it, even as her eyes in truth saw nothing, except the emptiness revealed to her.

– She is a great… bonus, is she not? Illandra offered casually.

– You are correct, Illandra of the Josbari, Ione agreed. – She is! Another ancient power will come under our scrutiny and control. Everything is as it should be.

She turned towards the crumbling creature crouching in her shadow and spoke with a strict, cruel voice:

– Beatrice Maximus Rosen, do you forfeit your birthright and your loyalty to it, and embrace your new life as a member of the Bone People?

– I do, willingly and eagerly!

There were more questions and answers, exhausting and all-consuming. Bea felt like Janet did, like a wet rag. It ended eventually and she, like Janet fought to stay on her feet.

– John Maximus Rosen, step forward, a male priest cried.

The boy did, stumbling, sluggish.

– Why do you want to join the people, John Maximus Rosen?

– I want her, he mumbled. – She belongs to me, to *me*.

The High Priests exchanged glances.

– He is just as much a part of the ancient power that she is, and he will spread his seed around like wildfire.

– And we will control crucial parts of the Rosen line. They will be ours to command.

Janet heard it all, even though it did not quite register in her dazed conscious mind.

Others stepped forward, were heard, were interrogated and spoke their piece. The three outsiders heard it all, becoming a part of it, forever, uniting with their new brethren. It seemed to go on and on, never truly ending. The daystar burned in the sky. They saw it, or glimpsed it through the transparent roof. The two moons hung low, so low that they imagined they could reach up and touch them, touch the firmament of forever.

Ione stepped forward, creating a humming expectation in them all.

– Congratulations, she cried to them, – you have done well. You have been heard by your elders and passed through the needle's eye, and are ready for what comes next.

She nodded, to herself, to them. The collars powered down again. They all felt the surge as their power and awareness returned in full.

– Now, Ione, the high priestess of rattling bones told them all, – now, your trials begin.

The beat of one strike on the heavy metal drum shaking in the non-existing wind echoed through air and walls, flesh and bone, and feverish minds.

Chapter 19

The gauntlet seethed and burned in Janet's eyes. She sensed its viciousness like a living thing. Evian actually recoiled in her mind.

The four, Janet and three strangers stood poised at entering it, hesitating briefly before taking that one, decisive step.

The invisible labyrinth faded into their vision, the haze covering their eyes.

Janet was neither the first, nor the last stepping into its maw. She just knew that she did, that she had done so ages, many lifetimes ago.

Sweat did not pour into her eyes. Her eyes had become sweat. Acid fluid surrounded her on all sides.

They were out there, in the yard, on the arena, but at the same time they were somewhere completely different. A haze imposed itself on reality, on them.

They fell in the dirt and the mud. Not a single piece of exposed skin and clothing was clean. Their tunics were in tatters.

– This is your gauntlet, Ione told them. – Walk through it and set yourself free.

Three walked with Janet. She did not know them. She did know them, their thoughts, notions and desires. Everything turned into a seething cauldron in here. She glimpsed the arena through the layers of haze and mist and waves of energy.

She recalled the moment she took one step forward, how the gauntlet swept them into its maw, and there was no way out, except forward. Do not leave the path, the voice hissed, or your life is forfeit.

A narrow passage presented itself to them. One ka for each of them was spinning in the air, blocking their path. The shining blades twinkled and cut what could just as well be flesh. The four youths approached cautiously. Their naked soles touched the ground. Emily, moving far to the right touched the invisible wall. She shouted short and sharp as it burned her at the point of contact.

To most of those watching it seemed like there was only air around them, but those running the gauntlet could sense, feel and even glimpse what appeared to be matter close by. The illusion of solid air turned real.

One group of four was ahead of them, another was behind. They did their best to ignore their plight and focus on their own. There was a sound resembling angry wasps as each ka sliced through the thick air.

Suddenly one blade charged Emily. Words erupted between tight-woven lips. The blade seemed to hit something hard, something solid enough to release sparks.

– Please believe me when I say that you are in danger, in more ways than one, Ione kept speaking words haunting their awareness.

They ignored them and her as best they could, making the hardest of efforts in order to not be distracted.

– Those not able to join the tribe will not remain among us, Ione spat, – not even in our memory.

A ka was «fired» at Janet, thrown at her, as if by an invisible hand. She deflected it with her waves. It proved itself slippery, hard to control. She failed at gaining full control of it. It kept pushing at her shield, until it finally fell inert or seemingly inert to the ground.

They noticed it right before it happened, as a pressure in the air. Then their nostrils started bleeding. The wind, constant, unrelenting picked up, battering them from all sides.

The two last blades charged forward, as if alive, with an independent mind. Jackson screamed as one cut into his shoulder. The fourth spinning blade was caught in a combined energy discharge projected by the three others and disintegrated before their eyes, its pieces turning into shrapnel slicing them, until their powers and collective efforts had turned the pieces to dust. The blade stuck in Jackson's flesh turned inert. Its «intent» was clearly to harm, not kill.

The four charged forward, into a calm, but never completely calm zone on the path.

It was seconds, minutes, hours later. Tood bandaged Jackson's shoulder. Blood flowed freely. There seemed to be no end to it. The red had soaked all the white in seconds. Tood looked at the ka in his hand with disgust. It remained inert. He threw it away.

It was seconds, minutes, hours later. Small and big wounds burned. They moved on. The four winds once again battered them relentlessly. They heard a scream from ahead somewhere. It sounded like a death rattle, felt like an ice pick burrowed deep into their flesh.

Suddenly, it felt like the drums hammered her, hammered her physically. She blinked. The edges, the walls of the gauntlet, the invisible labyrinth showed… images, glimpses of different places, similar to what she had experienced with Malone in the coach between realms.

She practically recoiled from the memory, just as much as from the actual impact. A hand touching her lips drowned in blood.

The taste invigorated her yet again. She put yet another foot in front of the other. No air reached her lungs, no air at all, but she fought on.

Screams kept cutting through flesh and bone and simultaneously dazed and aware minds.

It felt like she was being ripped apart at the seams. In one glimpse, where fear, deep fear touched her she spotted the man with the horns.

She saw her father. He had killed himself with a knife, slit his throat and bled out in a circle of shingle and dirt. He had done it so she could live.

Or so she had been led to believe.

His body withered and shrunk, until only bones and rags were left.

The four slumped on the ground. They suffered and moaned under the onslaught of their horrors.

Tood screamed in terror and she wondered what he experienced that was so horrible that he would scream like that.

He remained pale, pale as the dead. It lingered in him, like a vile stench.

She reached out to him when they stumbled on later. He hissed at her.

– Do not *touch* me!

Emily grabbed her. More time had passed. A distressed Emily held onto her hard, digging her nails into her arms.

– Did we stop a while ago? Did we dream and experience horrible things?

Janet attempted to reply, to give some sort of answer, but failed to do so.

The gauntlet shook them and probed and invaded them. It had taken hold of their fragile bodies and minds ages ago, and did not let go.

– Someone… did this to us, Janet frowned. – They put us here.

– There are others, Jackson said with frost in his voice. – I can hear them.

Hear them screaming.

We all can.

The draft turned into a pull. It happened both fast and slow. They turned their attention, their pained eyes to the left, and what seemed like a vast hole opening in the air. They saw the path go past it, saw shingle and mud and dirt rise into the air and be sucked into a seething vortex.

– We must walk past… that? Jackson groaned.

It sounded like a whine to the others.

He looked weak. The blood loss clearly affected him.

– We must crawl past it, Janet heard herself say, – or we will surely be sucked into its maw.

She went down on all fours and then further down on her belly. She pushed her hands into the shingle, burying them in it, beneath it, in the cold mud, and began pulling herself forward. The others joined her. She sensed them, even though she did not see them, not anymore, when she clawed herself forward pull by pull across the treacherous ground and through the hard to breathe air.

Children of the Bone People will be strong, strong, strong, Evian hummed in her head. She ignored it, refusing to let herself be distracted.

Blood flowed from fingers where nails had been broken and even ripped off. She did not notice. Pain had become a constant, not a concern. She saw nothing, except the path ahead. The world had become hardly more than sparks emanating from clenched eyelids.

They were back on their feet, not stumbling anymore, but more like running, rushing forward.

Ghostly shapes appeared in front of them. Vicious visages bore witness to their intent. She struck out at them. Her hand went straight through the woman's head. The woman struck at her, slapping her in the face. Janet howled in shock and fear. It dawned on her that they reminded her of the Wraiths. They could touch you, but you could not touch them.

She snarled at them and struck again, and this time she hit flesh, vulnerable flesh. The woman fell back, out of her sight. Janet almost stopped in amazement, but only briefly. This did not distract her, not this either.

– *Become* rage, she shouted at her three companions. – Then you can touch them.

The rush of rage grew stronger, not weaker. She struck another of the no longer ghostly shapes. Triumph and hunger filled her.

She realized that they pulled back, that they mostly stayed away from her, even as they kept testing her, kept hounding and challenging her. This was a more physical, flesh against flesh part of the gauntlet, more similar to a traditional one, cruel but not impossible.

A scream rose in her ears. She and the other two turned. They watched Tood as he was surrounded by assailants and struck to the ground. It was as if he… collapsed, as if he surrendered to the forces gaining on him.

He was behind them. His three companions hesitated. They tried to turn back, but it was as if something stopped them, as if the path itself denied them that. The shapes grinned at them, challenging them to try, to keep trying.

Tood was dragged off. His repeated, ever louder screams, *shrieks* echoed in Janet's mind long after she had turned and moved on.

She saw herself keep fighting to chase Tood, never really getting anywhere, lost in the mist and the endless horror of the gauntlet, becoming one of its ghosts, its wraiths forever. She sniffed and dried tears flying like blood, and kept putting one foot in front of the other.

Days and nights passed like rain. Rain and snow and shingle and dirt and blood and pieces of bone and flesh kept hammering their faces, every piece of their skin. They stumbled and fell, stumbled and fell and rose a thousand times. Everything had become numb. Sensation ended, life, even existence ended and nothing was left.

Nothing, nothing, nothing…

They walked forever and there was no end in sight.

None, none, none…

An unending scream rose from her sore throat. Feet kept moving endlessly forward, moving, moving, moving…

She shook, startled and fearful, finding herself in a quiet room, filled with mist, looking at those gently massaging her sore and bruised body and mind. There was a memory, faint and treacherous that they had reached something resembling a finish line, and collapsed there, and been carried off by gentle hands.

They, the three of them, only three rested and writhed on mats in a rather small room. She recalled being bathed and dried, and her wounds being cleaned and treated. What seemed hardly more than hands and smiling faces oiled them and rubbed weary bodies and minds. She looked at her hands. They had been bandaged and stank of herbs. The pain brought by the sore hands seemed real, even if the rest of this, this entire pleasant haze did not.

She fought distraught the gentle hands handling her.

– Be at ease, warrior, a man said. – You have come home.

– Even if that is exactly what a treacherous mirage would say as well, a woman teased her with a cruel grin.

Janet relented, falling further into the pleasant haze, hardly even caring anymore whether or not this was the final, hardest test of the gauntlet.

They were dressed and led on into a bigger room, a hall. Janet and Bea caught each other's eyes simultaneously. Bea ran to her and embraced her. They kissed lips to lips in an endless stretch of overwhelming, wonderful emotion.

– This is real, Bea the mirage whispered in her ears.

Janet whispered similar silly assurances in her betrothed's ears, in a flow of sweet words.

They were put in front of mirrors, able to study themselves, rediscover themselves from the faint memory they had become. Beautiful, woven clothes covered them from head to toe. Their hair was made in small braids and deliberate fashion, accentuating their features.

– I look so different, Bea marveled. – I do not even mind the bruises that much…

She was practically glowing with pride. Janet felt very emotional and endeared when looking at her.

They were led outside, into the seething cauldron of the arena, with its crowd and waving hands. The council of elders waited for them at its center, right by the daystar fireplace burning like on an agora in the ground.

The flames danced, expanded, imploded in a constant transformation. The youths emerging from the gauntlet danced with them.

– One breath is the Universe, Jackson said.

His voice echoed so pleasantly within Janet. She moved casually on a ground littered with roses. The waves moved around her in new and exciting ways. Her fingers bent and created the world around her.

Like before they were called before the half circle one and one, in no particular or discernible order. Emily was among the first, the first, the second, the fifth being called. She stood out, somewhat, to the two remaining that had shared the walk with her. One of the men granted her her release, removed the collar from her neck. Everyone present could easily see how freedom incarnated coursed through everything she was. She practically jumped up and down, as she returned from the half circle.

Others stepped before the council and returned to the world, in an uneven stream of thoughts and action, in the unending twilight the world had become.

– Janet Kathryn Caldwell, Illandra called.

The girl split from those remaining that had shared the gauntlet with her.

Ione rose and met her halfway, creating yet another stir among everyone present.

– How do you feel, daughter of the Josbari?

– I find myself in a state of extreme awareness, Honored One, Janet replied courteously.

She stopped a few steps away from the commanding presence.

– Approach then.

Janet obeyed. The very air seemed alive around her and she was literally bursting with excitement.

– You, Janet of the Josbari lived apart from your people since your ill-timed birth. Now, you have come home. Now, you are free to follow your path.

She grabbed the collar, removing it in one simple movement. It brought no notable change.

Goodbye, the faint voice of Evian echoed in the girl's mind.

Janet curtseyed and pulled back.

She was surrounded by those who had shared the gauntlet with her and felt their heat, their comfort and joy as they embraced her and took part in her triumph. They had all been initiated by the cruel ways of the Bone People and would always have that bond.

One by one the youths born with concealed tattoos on their faces were called forward, and given their sign of approval from the council of elders and their chief priestess. It went on for quite some time, a time-span impossible to measure properly in the seemingly eternal twilight.

Janet and Bea held hands and enjoyed each other's close proximity more than ever. They kissed and caressed each other without more than a faint conscious awareness of it happening.

– Everything feels so much more powerful… potent, Bea whispered enraptured in her ear, speaking to both her body and mind with equal candor. – I can feel you, feel your Shadow stronger than ever before.

Janet nodded, attempting to speak, failing, and nodded again.

Jackson caught her eyes, as he bowed to Ione and left the stage to take his place in the tribe. She easily spotted the signs of slight fever as he moved, as he met her eyes.

– You fancy him, do you not? Bea wondered, not really wondering.

Janet did not really have to reply, in order to confirm her emotions to the other woman.

– He is cute, Bea nodded in acknowledgement, – and tough. Walking through most of the gauntlet wounded like that would have brought down a lesser man.

The hoarse subtext in her voice revealed her own interest.

The last with the elaborate birthmarks on their faces stepped out of the half circle. Only those like Bea and John remained.

– Those of you coming to us from elsewhere, Ione called, – approach.

They glanced at each other, realizing that she called them all up. Bea let go of Janet's hand and hurried to comply. John followed her, casting one, prolonged look back at Janet. His stare burned her.

The smaller group of people standing out gathered in the half circle.

– Congratulations! Ione praised them. – You have won your place among us. From now and to the end of time, you will be counted among the Bone People.

The smile spread slowly on their faces, also on Bea's. Only John seemed totally unaffected.

– You have earned your place here, Ione said. – In time you and we together will discover what that place is. You will get your engraved tattoos, the physical proof of your belonging, confirming what is already confirmed.

The collars loosened and fell off. The collective power of them all was felt by the gathering.

All of them bowed their heads in gratitude, except John, and Janet found herself appreciating that, found herself endeared by it, and she used that, used that momentum in an effort to get past her dislike of him.

They left the half circle, returning to those they had bonded with during their stay. And then… the council left the stage as well, joining their brethren. Ione made no visible or obvious move, but a cheer rose from the crowd, from everyone present. The drumming changed, first subtle and then in sufficient ways for everyone to notice. The celebration began with a surge of power and emotion.

– Sit with me, heir to the Blue Flame, Ione offered. – Feel free to bring along your betrothed and the intended father of your child.

– That is most kind, Honored One, Janet said.

The three of them followed the older woman and so did her council. Janet glanced at Illandra, as they made their way to the place intended for them, but her father's mother did not look at her and seemed oblivious and indifferent to her presence and her triumph.

– You would consider joining the circle of acolytes serving and training under the council, I trust? Your power and lineage clearly makes such a position mandatory.

– I would, Honored One, Janet replied humbly. – It is a great honor and duty.

She glanced at Bea, to see if there was a negative reaction, but her betrothed seemed just as taken by the regal priestess as Janet was herself.

They sat down on the pleasant seats at the special spot made for the council at the south point of the arena.

– We still have lots of delights ahead of us, Ione cried. – Let the festivities continue.

The general happiness picked up another notch. Everyone noticed that easily, had all become so very astute and sensitive.

They were served food and drink, enjoying in full the fruits of their hardship, and they knew it was only the beginning of… of all the delights. They felt a glowing expectation within and without.

Twilight deepened within the wheel. Janet could sense it, practically feel it. She did not have to ponder the matter at all. The certainty of it all, of everything happening around her, flowed through her mind like that familiar and great slow lightning. Her awareness had soared and kept doing so.

Kalir, Csjesse and Seri stepped forward, into the weak but distinct, coming from nowhere light marking a certain spot on the arena. Everyone or almost everyone noticed them. At that moment they invariably drew attention to themselves, just as they had not mere moments earlier.

Kalir, most of all drew Janet's attention. There was something about him, a quality he did not share with the others, with anyone. He hardly looked like a boy at all in her eyes.

When she looked at him he seemed bigger than his two companions, bigger than everyone standing close to him. He did not quite approach the council and Ione, but he clearly addressed them, addressed her, paying his respects. Ione moved a hand, virtually imperceptible, giving him her consent.

The gathering fell silent and focused its attention on the tall and big youngster.

– I am the storyteller of this eve, he began, speaking with a loud, clear voice. – I will give you an untold tale. This is the story that will be told on the Eve of The Nine.

A silent gasp echoed through the crowd. Everyone stopped whatever they were doing, for a moment or two. Even as they continued their chores, they kept listening to the penetrating voice.

Janet could do nothing but listen, noting easily the subtext of the spoken word. She felt like he was speaking directly to her.

– The Nine… the man child said, pausing, dwelling on the words, and their startling significance. – Their story is old, so old that it could just as well be nothing but a myth, a tale to scare naughty children. It will unfold slowly, imperceptibly, in such a way that most people will not see them coming.

She noticed his careful, shrewd wording and wondered if he, himself did.

It is neither a fairy nor a fair tale.

She hardly heard his voice anymore, imagining he spoke in her mind, to something deep within her.

They gained ascendance in the nine realms, or so the story goes, when the realms were in alignment, six-thousand five-hundred and sixty-one years ago. The Wheel of Fire and Shadow burned in the sky, and Big Red Moon cast its crimson light everywhere.

An entire cult, a massive movement ravaging many realms grew in their wake, one lasting for centuries, perhaps millennia after their passing.

And now many say they are returning, are ascending anew. Explorers, travelers, wise men, alchemists and madmen all say the same, in many a closed room, in streets and gatherings across the Ocean of Mankind.

There are also those claiming that they never truly went away from human life, that they in truth have been here… all the time.

The signs and portents are undeniably real. Big Moon has turned red. Jupiter's Cauldron is stirring up the biggest storm ever. The Wheel of Fire and Shadow is reappearing in the sky. The question we should all ask ourselves is what it all means, what the true significance is.

It is the year sixteen-hundred and sixteen, as it is measured in the Triple Cities, in the realm of Montan, in the land of Arcadia, and mankind's destiny, perhaps even its fate is up for grabs.

One generation ahead.

From each of the nine realms one of nine comes, all burning with massive power and a terrifying purpose. In one dramatic night of the moon their powers and their purpose will become one.

Three times three tomes tell the story of the Nine, and when it is done both they and mankind will be changed forever, transformed into something startlingly new and unrecognizable. Those finding and identifying those tomes will know the past, present and future in equal measure, and they will become gods, mighty beings beyond measure and understanding…

One story can never tell all. Not even many stories put together are more than a flicker of wisdom in eternity. I paint the images and the words, and they are only an imperfect vision of reality. The Ocean of Mankind can never be properly described.

But when I am done you will know, know the secrets and what was hidden and unspoken. You will know what most people have only glimpsed in their deepest dreams and nightmares, and their hollow ground, and yes, you will be changed.

Janet remembered every word. She could recall them all with stunning accuracy in her feverish mind, her chaotic and hazy thoughts. She imagined she could actually see them, see The Nine and feel every step they made, feel them like thunder in her bones.

The arena and her surroundings slowly returned to her consciousness, slowly turned solid and real once more.

– It moved you, did it not? Bea asked/stated, well before the echo of the words had faded.

She nodded, still not quite there.

– Of course it did, Bea said, replying to her own redundant question with a shrug.

Janet petted Bea on the cheek in acknowledgement before once more directing her attention at the storyteller.

– This tale has been told before on these occasions, I take it? She said aloud.

– It has been a longtime tradition, Kalir replied, – told to those recently initiated each year.

– For how long?

He nodded to her, to himself.

– It is said the story is ancient, that it was told long before the Bone People began.

She nodded to him, to herself, the low key excitement brought on by the story lingering.

– Nine is an important, even sacred number, is it not? Emily spoke up with an uncertain voice.

– It is, Illandra replied casually, – not only in the southern triple cities, but in Arcadia as a whole, and all over the Ocean of Mankind. We, the Bone People strive, in more ways than one to keep the memory of The Nine alive. They are an important part of our identity. It is said they aided Isis, the mother of our tribe before her ascension and that they even crossed paths with Al'rahan Amaro himself.

That made gasps rise from the assembly and made Janet feel hotter than glowing rocks. She managed with an effort to keep her mask, her carefully arranged expression.

She felt a hand on her shoulder and turned, and discovered that Ione had stood up again and touched both Janet and Bea.

– It was important that you heard our story, or at least that piece of it, she said softly. – More will come later.

– Thank you, Honored One, Bea said humbly.

– How long is it since you bled? Ione asked.

– It is almost a cycle ago for both of us, Honored One, Janet replied startled, realizing what this was about.

She felt the energy, as the priestess probed them both. It was done quickly, casually, not expending any effort beyond the necessary.

– These, our new sisters wanted to join the tribe, Ione cried aloud, easily making herself heard, – but that is not the only reason they have come here.

She deferred visibly to Illandra.

– These two are to be wed, with the sealing of a pact, Illandra cried equally forceful, – one that will benefit both houses, both clans and group of clans. It will bind them far stronger together and to the tribe than any casual ceremony. This is how it was done in ancient times, when our people were young. It is an event that will spread like circles in the water, one that may well echo in eternity.

And more blood stirred in Janet's veins.

– It is regrettable that you will miss the dance…

– We understand, Honored One.

– … but believe me when I say that you will get your worth of everything eventually.

Illandra said with a wicked grin.

Both girls blushed. They had no doubt what she was… hinting at.

– Have you chosen? Ione asked them.

– I have, Honored One, Bea said.

She turned and directed their attention to John by her side.

– This is my brother in blood. He is my chosen, the gift to my beloved.

Both the two high priestesses studied him, making him blush.

– He will do, Ione shrugged.

– I have not chosen yet, Janet said. – I wanted to find my gift to my beloved among my people, among those with tattoos similar to mine.

– You will be given ample opportunity to do that, Illandra said. – Eager males will present themselves to you and you will pick the best of them.

– I will! Janet nodded.

And Illandra smiled.

Something more stirred in Janet's mind. She looked to the side and Zoe of the Josbari stood there, with her ten selected.

– Greetings, Janet of the Josbari, acolyte of the Council, she said humbly and curtseyed. – I and my ten will serve you tonight and for the rest of the ceremony. Will you, your betrothed and the chosen of your betrothed please follow me?

– Sure, we will, Janet said casually, – will we not, guys?

– Why not? Bea shrugged.

John did not speak.

They rose and were instantly surrounded by the ten and one. Janet felt Ione's penetrating stare and turned to face her.

– The ten and one are your servants, but also your keepers, Ione said curtly. – There are rules to observe, ancient procedures not to be deviated from. This is another phase of what you have agreed to. Know that the rewards will be great.

– We understand and approve, Honored One, Janet acknowledged.

She and the sister and brother surrendered themselves to Zoe's mercy, and it did not feel like a sacrifice at all. Zoe's attitude had also changed completely. She was the servant of the Council and its acolytes. She was Janet's servant.

They walked, walked off the arena, leaving its buzz and burning eyes. Janet felt Ione's presence. She did not sense Illandra at all. They headed inside, to the catacombs. Janet sensed an entire world down here. It was a Roman arena, but its purpose was completely different.

– Big Moon will turn red? She asked Zoe casually.

– As you probably know, it did eighty-five years ago, Zoe replied, clearly eager and proud to contribute to the acolyte's education. – It is said it will do so again in fifteen years, on the day hundred years after the last time.

– Big Moon turned red in my dream recently, Janet mused. – That…

Zoe and her band fell on their knees and cast their eyes to the ground.

Janet and Bea exchanged amused glances.

– You may rise, Janet said curtly. – Please, resume your duties *immediately*.

They obeyed. Janet spotted awe and fear in their eyes.

– This girl is sorry, Janet of the Josbari, Zoe whimpered. – She will strive to better herself.

The ten and one moved on and the three moved with them. They penetrated deeper down into the catacombs. Janet attempted to note the turns made in the intricate hallways, but gave up quickly.

An endless labyrinth surrounded them on all sides, and they would be lost without anyone that could navigate by heart down here.

A light, a greenish light reached them from afar and embraced them, as they crossed yet another corner, made one more infinite turn. They reached a hall with steaming baths.

– Allow us to take care of you, Honored One.

Janet barely nodded, like she recalled Ione had done. It was sufficient. It felt good. She knew her triumphant, vindictive smile was a mirror image of Illandra's.

Shadows and mist danced above the floor, everywhere between the floor and the ceiling. The water, the pond twinkled in twilight. The three were led to the baths. Their garbs were removed, and they were grabbed and lowered into the steaming water.

They were bathed and cleaned again. It felt so pleasant, so beyond pleasant. They drifted away, and their thoughts did as well. The water sighed somewhere. Light and shadow and fire rose on random waves floating up and down, back and forth in the hall.

The dance began above. The Blue Flame sensed it. She did not need to reach out with her powers, her waves. She did feel hundreds of feet hammering the ground, but it was more than that. She heard their gasps, the labored breathing… and felt the females turn wet and warm below, saw and sensed dangling cocks harden and grow. Anticipation ruled them, as it ruled her.

The three rested on mats placed on top of rock beds. Zoe and Loewe massaged Janet. She writhed under their command. Zoe held a bottle in her left hand and filled her right palm with a greenish fluid.

– More oil? Janet inquired.

– It is called Sorcerer's Blossom, Honored One, Zoe said, with some of her old wickedness. – For obvious reasons.

– I have read about it in my book of shadows, Janet frowned. – Is that not used solely on…

– Yes, Honored One, Zoe acknowledged, – but there are occasions where exceptions are made and this is one of them.

It felt cold at first, but then it turned hot, hot as fire. Janet gasped and writhed on the mat. She caught glimpses of Bea and John. He was oiled by two boys. He looked beyond embarrassed when his cock began twitching and rising. The Blossom… befuddled the mind, making it more susceptible to the rising passion ravaging it. All three became harder to handle, breaking free from the hands holding them.

– Serve me, Janet groaned. – I demand…

Ione stood there, suddenly. She mumbled a spell. Janet and the other two froze. She heard the meaningless phrases repeated time and time again. They made her drowsy and easily handled.

Ione faded away. The need shook the Blue Flame hard, but she could do nothing to act on it. Neither her limbs nor her mind worked properly.

– You are already a sorcerer, Honored One, Zoe said, – but will still experience the Blessings of the initiation, and much, much stronger than you otherwise would. You are indeed blessed, and in time, if you are truly the one we have been waiting for, you will bless us all.

The mass clenching of bodies began above. Drums, gasps, growls and moans turned insanely loud.

Janet's senses acted erratic, were both sharp and dull simultaneously. Sometimes her vision was a haze and then, the next moment it revealed her surroundings with abject clarity. She writhed and moaned on the slab, totally at the mercy of the violent forces ravaging her.

This reminded her not of a building or construct at all… but of a cave, and she shook.

Sleep claimed her, and brought troubled and feverish dreams.

Big Red Moon turned her night to blood, and it had a face.

She heard herself mumble incomprehensible words or spells. They made no sense to her. Confusion and terror and lust ravaged her. She watched from above a rather large group of travelers cross a wild, untamed land. Big Red Moon was with them, with her, always.

It hovered right under the ceiling when she opened her eyes, only slowly, slowly fading.

She woke up, even as she was still dreaming. Half closed eyes focused gradually on the figures surrounding the slabs.

– Fair morning, Honored One, Zoe greeted her. – We stand ready to assist you further on these your great and exciting nights.

Her voice and behavior was clearly even more respectful. Janet turned her head and studied her, studied all of them. They looked… when she probed beneath their surface… they looked more than frightened. There was a *respect* there in their lowered eyes that did not resemble anything Janet had seen before. Something had definitely changed during their sleep.

– You may proceed.

Zoe nodded curtly to her charges and they went to work, removing the covers from the nude bodies and packing them in warm, pleasant blankets. Janet felt the heat, felt it penetrate deep within her, felt it heat her thoughts, her very self. They were gently grabbed and returned to the pool, lowered into its steaming heat. The first hour of morning brought more warm baths and more oil and warm hands and teasing fingers on sensitive and sensitized skin writhing on the pleasant mats.

They were fed spicy meat and pearly wine, sating their hunger for a while, a little while.

They were dressed again, in elaborately woven garbs. The soft fabric felt so good against the skin. They returned to the surface, surrounded by their eager and fierce eleven protectors.

– What did I do? Janet asked.

– H-honored One?

Loewe, who was closest, looked stricken at her.

They all did.

– What did I do last night, in order to make such an impression?

Everyone stopped. Zoe rushed forward and curtseyed before her, clearly waiting to be acknowledged.

– Speak!

– You told us, in not so many words that you were Queen Cathy of Arcadia, and expected to be treated accordingly.

– And you believed me? Janet said incredulous.

– The Queen was quite persuasive, Zoe whispered.

Janet and Bea exchanged humorous glances again.

– Surely you have realized by now, the truth of those words, betrothed, Bea said happily.

The eleven fell on their knees again, more stricken than ever.

– Ask for anything, Honored One, Zoe stated humbly, – and it is yours.

– On your feet! Janet commanded and noticed pleased the steel in her voice.

They stood straight before her before she had finished speaking.

– You will obey me and not the High Priestess.

– Of course, My Lady, Zoe replied promptly.

Janet sensed not the slightest doubt in her.

– You will treat me no different from any other acolyte during the rest of our time here.

– Yes, Honored One.

This time Janet's sigh was tinted with pride. She could not help herself, and sighed again.

She frowned, as they emerged from the catacombs, attempting to recall her dreams, her feverish visions. It was all just a jumble, a mirage impossible to catch… except it was real, *real.*

– Queen Cathy of Arcadia, Bea whispered in her ear. – Your humble and eternal servant loves the sound of that, and so does Cathy, does she not?

Janet found herself nodding in acknowledgment.

– It does have a nice ring to it, she admitted.

– That is my betrothed, the great jester, Bea chuckled.

The choir of voices greeted them as they stepped onto the arena.

Janet spotted the guys on the lower seat of the theater. Rosa cried out and waved. They all did. Janet and Bea waved back. It felt strange seeing them again, as if they belonged to another lifetime.

The Council sat around the round table. There were three available seats.

– There you are, Ione called. – Please, join us.

They did. Janet sat down closest to the High Priestess, and the others to her left. Breakfast was served. It was yet another feast of food and wine. The two girls and the boy started feasting.

– That is some appetite, Ione mused pleased. – You young people are so hungry, so needy.

Janet felt the truth of her words. She could hardly contain herself.

The low-level arousal she had had to contend with all morning stayed that way, even though she feared it could grow irresistible at any moment. Anticipation ruled her, just as she suspected it was supposed to do. Sweat kept wetting her brow.

She and Bea kept exchanging devoted stares.

– So, Janet of the Josbari, do the ways of your tribe sit well with you? Ione asked. – How do you feel?

Open and half open and closed eyelids replied with a dreamy voice.

– They do, Honored One. I feel good.

Good good good…

– And you Beatrice Maximus Rosen?

– My betrothed speaks truth, Honored One. My first encounter with my tribe to be exceeds all my expectations.

– In not so many days and nights you will be Beatrice of the Josbari. How does that make you feel?

– I can hardly wait, Honored One.

Bea blushed and grabbed Janet's hand and looked at her very much like a lovesick puppy. Janet was practically overwhelmed with emotion.

– You, all three of you are certainly a great addition to our tribe, Ione praised them, and they felt the heat of her praise. – You survived the initiation and thrived without the preparation all the children growing up in the tribe go through, I salute you!

Her hot stare drowned John. He shifted uncomfortable in his seat. Janet felt both glee and sympathy.

– Janet Kathryn Caldwell, Ione mused. – The Blue Flame of your generation, heir to a power that has not revealed itself for generations. That, in itself makes you interesting beyond words, but there is even more to you than that, is it not?

– Surely, the High Priestess jests, Janet mumbled embarrassed. – She knows well I am of the Josbari as well?

– Your Master, Ione said, dwelling on the word.

And then Janet understood, at least to a degree.

– The man that was your Master is not truly a Seer, but a time traveler, and through your bonding the two of you shared everything, including that, and with him lost to the Heights, you are the only one with access to that treasure.

And just like that the very thought set off a chain of thoughts in Janet's mind.

Young Peter had a conversation with his older self. Malone the Sorcerer told the boy everything he wanted to know. The memory was dim in Janet's mind, but still a memory, or very much like one.

– With that your usefulness to your tribe increases immensely.

The girl frowned, not quite able to wrap her head around it, but the voice of pride within her grew even stronger.

– I would imagine young Peter is out there, somewhere, Honored One.

– I would agree with that, Ione nodded, – but I am also fairly certain that his older self made provisions for that, making sure he is not to be found anywhere. My assessment stands.

The High Priestess rose, making everyone on the arena keep their eyes on her. Janet saw that she commanded attention with ease and that made the light of admiration in the girl's eyes brighten even more.

– Stand up, children, and grab your new life by the tail.

They obeyed. She clapped her hands.

The humming, already loud, grew louder in wonder and anticipation, echoing further within the two.

Three people carrying instruments emerged from the main gate and took the center stage. Janet recognized Kalir, Csjesse and Seri. They began playing their drums and flutes and guitars. Kalir began singing and chanting. His voice sounded almost impossibly loud amplified by the acoustics of the Greek amphitheater. She realized quickly that his voice was powerful in its own right. It filled the arena, filled people's hearts and minds.

– Dance for us, Illandra told the two girls.

They looked at her.

– Dance for us. Reveal to your tribe your life and passion. Tempt us with your wiles.

Both began smiling simultaneously. They stepped forward, displaying themselves to the gathering, allowing everyone to have a good look at them. Then, after a while they disrobed, removing all their garbs, displaying themselves some more, before joining the musicians at the center stage spot of the arena.

They began swaying as they walked, their feet quickly moving fast on the shingle. The rhythm and vibrations entered, invaded their flesh and bones and whirling thoughts. It felt awkward, just a little awkward at first. Public display of nudity was common and pretty much accepted in the society of their childhood and adolescence, but this had a slightly different and more poignant quality added to it. They pretty much danced for each other and hardly heeded the spectators. They embraced the spectators and their presence, the people on the large stairs of the gods becoming participants in their increasingly feverish minds.

The flutes rose to a higher level and tangent. The multitude of discord and raw beauty and passion existed side by side. Already excessive moves rose to a higher pitch. Flesh and hair and limbs flowed like mercury. Drums hammered even harder, doing so at every single hard and soft surface.

Bodies danced face to face, with swinging hips and constantly moving hair. Sweat poured and covered bodies already covered with oil. The wet and warm place below turned even wetter and warmer. They moved closer, dancing tight. Every breath felt so warm that it burned. They forgot awkward, forgot everything but the enticing sight and sensation of each other.

Janet pulled herself into the air and a moment later she had pulled Bea up there with her. It hardly took any effort, not to achieve and not to sustain. They kept dancing a body length above the ground. The drums beat faster. The two females danced faster. They were swept into the cocoon of Kalir's voice. The vibrations of the flute mixed with Janet's waves. Sweaty bodies clenched and began caressing each other. Fingers and hands seemed to be everywhere. They kept dancing, swaying while touching, kept performing without caring about those watching.

Time diluted again, stretching out like an endless rubber band, stretching, contracting in a never ending cycle. Lungs and limbs burned. Breathing became nothing but short gasps between eternal moments. They became the chanting, the music, the collective gasping of the arena, of its flesh and stone and deep recesses of shadow, mist and mind.

There was a pause, a prolonged beautiful discord. They noticed and frowned, even in their most savage part. It was there, in their deepest awareness everything turned immaculately clear.

It… happened. Skeleton trees swayed in the wind, the exquisite hot and wild wind. Janet saw it clearly, through the haze of her vision and consciousness both. Beatrice did as well. Janet sensed how she did, how the mirror revealed them both throughout infinity. A low moan escaped her wide open mouth. They stopped moving, froze a few moments before…

Something broke below. They frowned, not quite getting it at first.

The dam burst. Blood flooded their thighs. It flowed from their openings. Fear touched them briefly. The flow seemed to resemble a waterfall. The ground beneath grew wet and warm, turning into a warm, warm current sweeping them away.

Nausea overwhelmed Janet. Glimpses of faces on the arena flooded her consciousness, like everything did. The soreness below seemed to spread to her entire body, penetrate deep within her mind. She lost her focus, lost her strength. Both fell to the ground and rolled in the blood and the dirt.

They crouched there, still immersed in the dance and fiery emotions, their minds and bodies slowly returning to a lower than high point.

Chapter 20

Loud cries reached them from all over the arena. A few sounded alarmed, but most easily grasped what had happened. Janet glimpsed Ione and Illandra's smile through the film of red filling her eyes.

Zoe and Loewe and the others smiled as well, as they slightly cautious approached the two. The possessive desire in John's eyes was stronger than ever.

– Come with us, please, Zoe said softly. – Let us take care of you.

The two held hands as they rose. Both nodded. Skilled hands led them away and comforted them. Janet's waves went haywire and bathed everyone nearby in the still hot blood. The mumble and interest from the spectators picked up yet another notch.

Zoe rubbed her hands in the blood and licked it off her skin, and so did some of the others. The mumble turned to shouts.

– Cup your hands and collect the blood, Bea instructed them. – That way you can easily drink the blood of the Goddess.

They did so, still cautious, respectful. Janet glanced curious and a little anxious at her betrothed.

– There is so much of it. How can we be fine when there is so much of it?

– I have read about it, researched the matter, Bea shrugged. – The spells, the herbs, the very Ceremony of the Moon make the blood more potent and make it expand many times its ordinary volume the moment it is exposed to air.

– It is actually called the Ceremony of the Moon?

– It is, Honored One, Loewe said shyly, – and never in a thousand years has the name fit better.

The Blood Red Moon.

A soundless voice spoke in Janet's head.

– I am so proud that I knew something you did not, Bea grinned.

She kissed her betrothed on the brow.

– Soon, she whispered, – soon we will be together for all time.

– Soon! Janet agreed with passion.

They were brought back to the table where the council and John sat. The large fire burned their skin, heated their eyebrows. Blood kept flowing down their thighs, sweat pouring into their eyes. They swayed on weak legs before Ione and the council.

– She is so very desirable, is she not? Ione said to John. – You would love to make a baby with her?

– I would! He said hoarsely.

His cock pushed so hard at his pants that it hurt. Janet felt it. The shock of that sensation stopped her breathing, and she could not tell whether or not she was able to start doing it again.

Ione touched her cunt, eliciting a bit of blood from her and put the finger in her mouth, had a taste, a delicious taste based on her pleased grin.

The High Priestess rose. She was not quite as tall as Janet and Bea, but they did not see her as smaller at all. In their mind she practically towered above them.

– The time is almost upon us, she declared. – Now, everyone can bear witness to who the fathers are. You are not quite ready yet, but you will be, not that long after the final preparations are complete.

The final preparations… Janet and Bea nodded eagerly.

Ione faced the crowd. Anticipation seethed among them. Janet did not know exactly how, but Ione made the two girls feel it, its potent force. It still hurt below, but Janet did feel the beginning of renewed fever in her mind.

– Beatrice has given her betrothed a gift of passion and new life, Ione cried. – Janet wishes to return the kindness, to equal her future Companion. She requires a champion.

Quite a few males, mostly the young which Janet had shared the initiation, but also some older stepped down on the ground and gathered in front of the two girls and the high priestess. There was quite a bit of good humored and not so good humored pushing and brawling.

– The Blue Flame may choose whoever she wishes, Ione said. – Within the confines of the arena, no one may deny her anything. She may sit down and take her time doing the choosing.

– Thank you, Honored One, Janet said. – The Blue Flame thinks she may do that.

She and Bea sat down in the chairs offered them. These were ceremonial chairs, with elaborate decorations and pleasant seats. Hands reached out and grabbed each other.

Zoe and the girls and boys were there, offering them fruit and spicy pieces of meat. They accepted and devoured the food with a hunger standing out even for them.

Csjesse began beating her drum, beating it hard, each strike resembling thunder. The dance began without further ado. The males undressed, tore off their clothing and jumped into the hard, relentless dance.

The rocking shapes moved in pulls and pushes in Janet's crystal-clear vision. Arms and legs went up and down. Feet hammered against the ground. The haze and the mist made everything else indistinct, but not them. Cocks initially dangling between thighs hardened slowly.

Jackson appeared in her line of vision. His eyes sought hers across the vast distance of the arena. Each time he approached the council's spot he looked away, but increased his efforts.

– He is performing for you, wanting to catch your interest, Bea said casually, – which is perfectly understandable, since it is you he needs to convince.

She sounded bored, almost indifferent.

– You are quite correct, of course, Janet shrugged, – like you are about most things.

She kissed the other affectionately.

The dancers drew attention to themselves, by the force of their dance. Janet and Bea revealed obvious discomfort when shifting in their chairs. They were still sore below, but it did not seem to matter much.

Flesh mixed with fire. The huge burning at the center of the arena seemed to blend with the flesh and bone and sweat moving on the shingle and the dirt, practically bathing in it, getting covered by it. She glimpsed their skin, their faces, their eyes and whirling hair and their cocks through all that.

The dance eventually ended, having lasted forever. The dancers stood still, displaying themselves before the two girls, no, doing so before the girl with the violet eyes.

– Turn, Janet of the Josbari bade them, giggling patronizingly.

Some of them did, others did not. Jackson did.

Janet stood up. All sound faded away on the arena. Breathless anticipation lingered in the heated air.

– I choose Kalir of the Josbari, she said aloud. – He is my gift of joy and life to my betrothed.

Everyone's eyes went to Kalir. He stood fully dressed in a corner, practically concealed from people's immediate scrutiny.

Ione stood up.

– Janet of the Josbari has chosen her gift among the males present on the arena, as is her right, Ione stated. – Will Kalir of the Josbari appear before the council, please?

It was no query, no pleading, but a command.

Kalir walked to them, neither fast, nor slow.

– Greetings, Kalir of the Josbari, Janet said sweetly to him before he had quite reached them, overdoing it more than a bit.

– Greetings, Janet of the Josbari, he mumbled, striving to remain civil, knowing it would be on him if he was not.

– Let me present to you my betrothed, Beatrice Maximus Rosen, soon to be

Josbari, Janet said, very civil.

She walked behind the other big girl and pushed her one step forward.

– Greetings, Kalir of the Josbari, Bea said huskily.

– Greetings, Beatrice Maximus Rosen, soon to be Josbari, he mumbled, stubbornly glaring at them both, not quite able to keep up the pretense.

Bea reached out a hand, stopping it just low of his lips. He grabbed her hand and kissed it, allowing his hand to linger there, before letting go.

She turned towards Janet.

– Thank you, beloved, Bea said, – this gift does not seem too bad. It knows courtesy and other things besides. Methinks you have upgraded your taste lately…

– I have no illusions, Janet shrugged.

Ione took one step forward, once again commanding the attention of the gathering.

– In ten days or less the consummation begins, she declared. – It will continue for as long as it is needed.

A roar of anticipation rolled across the four youths close to the High Priestess.

Ten days… It seemed like forever to Janet. The twilight nights stretched out before her.

– This is a ritual revered by our ancestors. Ione admonished the four and the gathering. – No deviation or failure will be tolerated. A despoiling of any of the four participants will be punishable by torture and slow, slow death. The despoilers' death cry will last for a cycle. There will be no quarter given.

She looked mighty then, even more so than she usually did. Her words and sincerity pounded them all. A shiver passed through everyone present.

Four fairly large cages were carried to the center of the arena. They were placed in pairs. There were a slab and a bed in each cage. Chains with bracelets were attached to the floor on both sides of the beds.

– Ten more days and nights of captivity and trials, Ione said softly, – and then you are free to roam existence itself.

Janet glanced anxiously at Illandra. Her grandmother pretended not to notice.

Ione put a collar around her neck. The waves once more died in her mind.

There was no voice this time, only silence, the very death of voices.

She bowed to the High Priestess, submitting to her will. The other three did as well.

They were grabbed and led to the cages.

– My beloved is a cruel, cruel bitch, Bea whispered in her ear. – May she never forget that.

The encouraging words echoed pleasantly in Janet's head.

Something sounding almost like voices shrieked when the cage doors opened.

– The hinges do not look rusty at all, John remarked, – but they still sound like they are.

Janet touched the iron bars, as she walked inside. They looked as shiny as the day they had been made.

Everything felt old, felt ancient in here. Distinct smells brought associations of distant ages.

Voices, loud whispers rose in her ears.

She realized startled that her empathy, her ability to sense and feel had not been muted at all, but rather…

Illandra slapped a bracelet on her left wrist.

– On the bed, the priestess instructed curtly.

Janet could not resist her, not now. Practically sleepwalking she knelt on the bed. Illandra slapped the second bracelet on her right wrist. Two more clicks and the skin on her ankles also turned cold. She looked incredulous at her grandmother.

– I told you, grandmother said. – You are a sacrifice. At the moment of consummation you will be at your most feral, hardly more than an animal faced with an irresistible urge to mate, mate, mate…

Illandra tilted her head.

– There are legendary stories told of such beings. Our task is to see to it that you, the four of you do not become a danger to yourself and all the rest of us.

– I have changed my mind, Janet said.

– I have not! Bea grinned in anticipation from the distant cage. – And neither have you. Do not fool yourself, beloved.

She shook her head, looking at Bea, and her desire, her need started growing on yet another tangent.

– I want this, she mumbled, she acknowledged yet again. – I *want* this!

Illandra looked pleased at her.

– He is a curious choice, but then again I should not be surprised, Illandra mused. – You are indeed crafty and have an uncanny ability to see things clearly. It will serve you well, even in your most muddled moments.

She turned, walked out of there and closed and locked the door.

Janet shook the chains, with a less than satisfying effort. Even her anger was dull, unable as she was to properly connect to or at least to utilize her surface thoughts.

For some reason she kept hearing the sound of the rustling of her chains many hours later, even when she knew she did not move, also in her sleep. The sound of the three other sets echoed those of her own. Her dreams had already turned feverish beyond control, and this was just the first night.

She woke up the next morning filled with thirst and ravenous Hunger.

Zoe held her hand up and fed her food and spiced water from a cup.

– Spices, Janet mumbled weakly. – More spices.

– Precisely, My Goddess, the girl said eagerly. – It will aid you further on your Journey, help you ascend.

Ascend!

The powerful flames seemed to burn on all four sides of the cage, also between her and John. The sight, the very sight of him made her burn hotter. They fed her more spiced meat and water. It was as if she could not get enough of it.

The daystar burned from above, even in the midst of the long twilight nights. More than ever it seemed like it, and the two moons were right there, between her thighs.

She stood on her knees and shook the chains, and it felt like she made the ground shake. John shook his chains as well, and so did Bea and Kalir. It did not hurt, just adding to her frustration when the metal held.

They made her pee and shit in a bucket and cleaned her with soft touches. She looked at them with a blind stare, uncomprehending eyes.

She woke up from slumber to less slumber one night, twilight to people surrounding her cage. Their faces revealed themselves in every opening between bars. She spotted Illandra and several others… and imagined Myra there as well. It was not the Council. Ione was not there, and only a few of the others. Janet recognized startled some of those that had accompanied Illandra during the Ceremony of Bones on the plains outside Maximus' Folly.

– Look at her. Is she not magnificent?

That was Myra's voice, was it not?

And it was not the Myra her daughter knew, not the quiet and unassuming Myra, but a woman of mystery and power making Janet shake ever so pleasantly with fear and anticipation.

The next time she woke up, only the spectators on the arena were present. She did not see any of the priests anywhere. Myra was certainly not there. The girl frowned in more frustration. Thinking, awareness, reason faded with each passing moment.

The arena was filled with spectators all the time. They came and left, interested, but not interested enough to spend all their time there.

But the excitement was palatable among everyone, in every single soul she sensed. She felt it in her bones and flesh and her fever-hot brain.

The Council gathered in a circle, with Ione at its center. They prayed and chanted their spells, and the air changed to a thick and shimmering quality.

Janet shook the chains, rattling the cage, and growled at the world, and in her few, more lucid moments she wondered whether or not those in the circle wanted to suppress or enhance her power.

Night and day, night and twilight and day and dusk and dawn dissolved, mixing into one.

She watched the beast in the other cage, its straining muscles, its constantly erect malehood, and she saw the feral female reflected in its eyes.

He desired her, wanted her more than anything, perhaps even more than she wanted him. Pride coursed through her and overwhelmed the frustration.

She fell into deep sleep again, but there was no respite from the need. It just kept building and had long since passed the point of being bearable.

The herald, the girl which name the chained female in the cell no longer recalled struck the gong ten times. The female knew it was ten times, somehow, even though she could no longer count and articulate it. A loud, longing moan rose from her throat. She imagined herself jumping at the bars, pushing herself as close to the male in the other cage as possible.

The succession of clicks sounded so very loud in her ears. She frowned in confusion as she realized that the chains no longer bound her and that she was free. The sound of rusty hinges shrieked in her ears. She cast instantly her eyes at the door and discovered that it was open.

His door had slid open as well. She rushed forward without thought, rushed through both doors. He was just about free from his chains and was on his way up, when she reached him and pushed him back on the bed. She mounted him, pushed him into her wet and warm hole and began rocking up and down, hardly noticing the sound of the door to this cage closing and locking again.

They both growled and moaned constantly as they pushed at each other hips to hips. It did not take long, did not take many thrusts before agile bodies turned rigid, before she felt him push his heat into her and she splashed him with her water. They kept going without break. She was more aware this time, conscious of him moving in and out of her. The amulet dangled between her breasts, jumping on and off the sweaty skin as she moved. It was itching, seemingly moving of its own accord, creating an even stronger itch on her long since inflamed skin, caressing her swollen breasts and rock-hard nipples. She cried out in joy as the heat rode them yet again. She collapsed on him and overwhelmed him with kisses, and she felt him return his own.

He turned her around, making her back face him. Holding on to her hips he pushed himself deep into her. She yelped in profound happiness. She stood on all fours, while he was pumping into her from behind. She moved impatiently. He slapped her butt. She released another deep moan.

They rested on the bed, falling asleep, completely unaware of how many times they had exploded in pleasure. Eyes closed. Totally exhausted bodies rested.

Meat and fruit had been thrown on the ground. They sat on their hinges and fed impatiently, that hunger just as irresistible as the other. They were hungry. They fed. Desire rode them. They mated, and mated and mated. They were fed more spicy water.

He grabbed her again. She was not quite finished feeding and growled angrily at him. He put her down on all fours, pushing a hand between her legs. She relented instantly and rewarded him with a huge smile. The apple slipped from her weak hand. He pushed into her. She formed her body, her movement to his. They mated there on the remains of the food.

One morning she noticed the distinct outflow from below. He was still sleeping. She woke him up with excited sounds and movement, moving sensually in front of him, even more eager. He growled, clearly irritated. She grabbed his cock and began caressing it, rubbing herself against him, enticing him with everything she was.

He sniffed the air, clearly catching her heavier scent. His cock rose hard and painful. She grinned and moaned, extremely pleased with herself, with him. The distant sounds from the other cage heightened their fervor further. She writhed on her back, making herself irresistible. He mounted her in one single change of pace. They moved against each other, pushing and pulling, pushing and pulling endlessly. Pleasure without end began anew.

She had her first feeding after the night's sleep. He had as well. She fed him happily and opened her mouth in an obvious enticement. He finally got it and began feeding her.

They sat there, caressing each other, their fervor slowly building, building, building.

He pushed her at the bars. Her head was caught between them. She drew her breath in short gasps. Screams and shouts and growls from both couples once more filled the arena. She balanced on all fours again, while he pushed and pulled in and out of her from behind. Both bodies tensed and exploded in pleasure. He let go of her hair, and she fell slowly. Her head and front hit the soft soil. She stretched out on the ground, a happy smile accompanying the happy moan, slowly falling into the pleasant darkness, into yet another beyond content sleep.

She woke up with a frown on her face one morning, realizing that something was different. He opened his eyes and she saw the same signs of dawning intelligence and reason there. She kissed him on the lips and rubbed his cheek, feeling a catching in the throat when he returned the affection. They crouched in each other's arms a bit, before rising, welcoming the delegation, the Council and their entourage.

The door unlocked and opened. Ione and Illandra stepped inside.

– By now you have either conceived or you will not this cycle, Ione said. – This was occasionally done with more than one male, in order to increase the probability of success, but we should be okay.

– The protocols must be observed, however, Illandra said. – You will not be freed until your conception is confirmed.

Janet glanced at the other cage, where Bea and Kalir were given the same message, the one all four already knew well.

– Janet of the Josbari and John Maximus Rosen, Ione said formally, – will you please accompany us?

The four stumbled outside, accompanied by their honor guard. The low roar of the spectators met them, washed over them like the waves it was.

Bea and Janet made their ways to each other, embracing and fondling each other softly, not speaking, only feeling.

Kalir and Janet and John and Bea kissed. There was still a kind of lethargy in them all, as if they were not quite present, either in their bodies or their surroundings.

They turned and paid attention to the Council, and to the two women fronting it.

– You will all live the coming weeks like temple servants, Illandra told them, – but with special restrictions in place.

– You, Janet of the Josbari, Ione said, – will begin your tenure as an acolyte. You will have both special privileges and duties.

– I understand, Honored One, Janet said.

She felt lazy, content, still not completely awakened from her primal state.

– We all do, John said eagerly.

Janet glanced hotly at him, unable to hold back the show of affection and desire. It lingered and burned within her. She was unable to stop grinning.

The remaining spectators stayed while the procession crossed the arena and set course for the catacombs. They started leaving the moment the Council and those following it approached the tunnel.

The guys stood there waving. Janet, Bea and John returned the wave, just before they disappeared from view.

– You will meet them again soon enough, Ione told them.

Janet stayed her frown with an effort. Ione's patronizing was not evident, but there.

The entrance, this entrance felt like a… a portal. Janet sensed the shimmer in the air more than she saw it, and could not be confident that it was actually there.

She turned her attention away from Ione and studied Illandra instead, practically scrutinizing her, not making any secret of it.

– Is there anything you wish to say to me, granddaughter?

– Yes, there is, grandmother, Janet snapped.

Images, memories, distorted, unrealized came to her.

She turned back to Ione.

– Forgive me, Honored One. This one meant no disrespect.

She made all the right moves, and spoke with the correct intonations.

– It is perfectly alright, Ione shrugged. – We have all been young once. You will learn.

She did not include Janet's name or either of her titles, which was her right as High Priest. Janet's eyes narrowed ever so little.

They arrived at a fork in the hallway. Ione turned to Bea, John and Kalir with a stern look.

– The three of you will serve and await the final outcome in your way…

She turned to Janet.

– The Blue Flame will have other duties and objectives.

Zoe and Loewe and the others curtseyed or bowed before the big girl. She acknowledged them. They led her down the left hand path. Others followed the other three. Ione and Illandra remained.

The girls and boys led Janet and coaxed her, even as she hesitated and glanced behind her. This was a different hallway compared to the one she had walked before.

– Allow us to aid you, Honored One, Zoe comforted her softly. – These intricate hallways and their space may confound and even distress the most powerful acolyte, but soon you will know them by heart, mind and Shadow and be confounded by nothing anymore.

Zoe crouched a little, just a little, clearly waiting for or even expecting a harsh reaction, but Janet merely nodded, her curiosity and wonder overriding any anger that might be.

The memories of the never-ending pleasures, both those remembered by her mind and body kept riding her. The smile lingered on her face.

– The Goddess is happy, Loewe said. – Is the Goddess happy?

– That is what happens when you have uninterrupted sex for days, Janet shrugged deliberately.

Giggles filled the space of the ancient catacombs.

They reached a room with a large bed. Here, deep below the ground, there was a mundane-looking window. Janet looked out at a sunny and shadowy courtyard. The seemingly impossible sight did not truly confound her, at least not as much as she would have suspected.

Both the sun and the shadow burned and warmed her.

– This is the acolyte's private quarters, Loewe said. – No one except her and the High Priests and those ordered here by them may access these halls without her explicit permission.

– That is acceptable, the acolyte noted, grinning a little, – quite acceptable.

Her good mood, her low-keyed euphoria prevailed, in spite of the relative sluggishness claiming her.

The next few moments were a blur to her. It was one step, two steps forward and more gentle, supportive hands grabbing her. Then she rested on the mat on another, smaller rock bed in the bathroom next door. Steam and light and shadow danced in the air and close to her skin. They cleaned her with warm cloths and applied herbs on her sore parts and ointment on her aching body. She writhed in discomfort, even as the gentle rubbing began making its wonders on her.

Then, after a while more oils of various substance and usefulness were applied, and Janet began feeling wonderfully relaxed again. She once more drifted away. Eyes began flickering, but she did not fall asleep. Her consciousness drifted off, and kept doing so… until it was no longer a part of her body, but roaming free. A tall structure revealed itself. She recognized it. Maximus' Folly revealed itself to her, but one looking very different compared to how she remembered it.

The twin doors opened. They no longer displayed the Maximus insignia, but one completely different, a curious standard she did not recognize. She studied the doors at a glance and found them twice as thick. They had been laced with heavy metals. It took ten giant sentries, five on each side to open them.

An entourage brought itself into the vast domain of the castle. Once again she glimpsed the standard, on the door and on those walking these halls. She experienced it in a sweep. The standard was a stylized A, handwritten or seemingly so, cast in iron.

She heard the sound of frightened gasps. It distracted her, cutting off the drifting, the roaming. She opened her eyes and saw clearly, without distortion Zoe and the others kneel deep around the bed. They surrounded it, shaking in fright.

– I can feel the High Priest, Janet said drowsy, lightly. – She is right here, by our side. Perhaps you should not be so eager in your worship. The High Priestess may take offense. This is getting tedious, anyway.

She spoke louder, in a deliberately challenging tone.

– Be at ease, Honored One, Zoe said humbly, with frozen lips. – The High Priestess is very much aware of how we worship you. It is not unheard of or even frowned at, either by her or others. You are the yet unborn and she acknowledges that, like many priests before her placing a high value on acolytes. Even though her ways are often unfathomable that must surely be one reason why she chose to personally train you, take you under her mighty wings?

Janet kept herself from grinning with an effort. They did not realize that she had been jesting.

She had been sleeping, doing so on the large, pleasant bed. It felt like a long time had passed. She felt rested and content, cobwebs in her eyes.

– What did I do this time? What did I say?

– You addressed me, Honored One, Zoe said. – «Zoe, this one annoys me», you said, «chop her head off». You did so with your Voice, your grace. Your entire demeanor, almost your appearance changed.

They crouched in her presence. A different face, a clearly older and markedly different Zoe flashed briefly in Janet's vision before fading.

Janet sensed Ione again, her invading presence.

– Well, the acolyte said, – I clearly do not want you to kill anyone, no matter what my dream self tells you, at least not right now, so you may relax and resume your duties.

She rose from the bed and put her feet on the floor. A bit of the linen stuck to her oiled skin. She removed it with a casual pull. The others scrambled on their feet and surrounded her in humble affection and with lowered eyes.

They brought her to the slab again, to its soft and pleasant mat. Those not doing that began preparing her breakfast. The various scents played in her nostrils and eventually changed to tastes playing on her tongue.

She sat by the table not that long afterwards, still pretty much feeding like a wolf, stinking of fresh oils and herbs, writhing on the chair, the discomfort below far from healed. The oils and herbs had been mixed with such a skill that she was unable to notice any discrepancy in the mix, any wrongly applied blend.

They made certain her most casual and random desire was met, not too intrusive in their zeal. She kind of enjoyed it and found herself appreciating their presence.

– Sit down and eat with me, if you wish, she offered.

They exchanged glances and visibly hesitated.

– Feel free to sit down and/or eat with me, she repeated, fighting to keep the steel from manifesting in her voice. – No matter what your masters have instructed you to do. I, your true «master» set you free from obligations.

They did, even though some of them were always moving back and forth between the kitchen and the table, and moving by the table, eager to offer her more treats. Their smiles turned a little less respectful and she found herself appreciating that as well.

She raised her glass.

– Cheers to the festivities, to the initiation and to all we have endured and benefited from, she cried without raising her voice.

– Cheers, Honored One, Zoe said, clearly uncomfortable. – You are most kind.

Others repeated it. Those with glasses drank.

– See, it was not that difficult…

Uncertain laughter echoed around the table.

– We are not used to… acolyte kindness, Janet, a boy, Gareth said.

Janet could virtually see how everyone held their breath. When she smiled everyone relaxed.

– I guess I am not your typical acolyte, then.

– Not the typical anything, Loewe brazenly declared.

And Janet enjoyed herself even more in their company, even as other, less pleasant thoughts emerged.

There was more cheering and fun, as the meal progressed.

She frowned.

– I have a question, she stated, – and I expect it to be answered truthfully.

– Of course, Blue Flame, Zoe assured her, stricken again, used as she was with the acolyte's changing and random moods.

Janet leaned back a little, forcing herself to smile, to give them assurances of her good mood, pondering and analyzing before she spoke.

– I wonder about the tradition where all tribal members are required to kill his or her firstborn and its father or mother. Would you please enlighten me?

An expression of incredulity appeared on everyone's faces.

– I am happy to tell the queen to be that this is a brief tradition long since abandoned by our people, Zoe said, – abandoned centuries ago, no matter how much outside, ignorant scripture paints us in a bad light.

– You do not say? Janet mused, her eyes narrowing ever so little.

She stretched out and exercised on the floor afterwards, the way she had been taught and learned, in order to lessen the worse results of her recent excesses. The boys and girls watched her, the fast and deadly moves with unmistaken awe in their features.

She ended the exercise and returned herself to their care. They dressed her. The soft fabric tightened perfectly around her body. They did her hair and applied clan colors on the part of her face where there were no tattoos. In their hands she changed into something new and exciting and unexplored.

There was a… disturbance in her waves. She sensed a lone figure approach and stop just outside her quarters.

– Your pardons, My Lady, Zoe said.

She hurried outside. There was a brief exchange of words before she returned.

– Zarra, an envoy of the High Priestess seeks your audience, Honored One.

– Let her in, then, Janet granted her servant.

Janet turned and faced the entrance. She was ready.

Zarra stepped inside, stopping and curtseying before the acolyte after two steps.

She waited, until the Blue Flame gave her the nod.

– Greetings, Janet of the Josbari, she said, – I bring word from the High Priestess. She requests your presence in her quarters.

– That is acceptable, Janet responded as patronizingly as she possibly could. – You may take me to her.

The surroundings of her quarters and the sight of Zoe, of the gentle boys and girls faded in her vision and her mind. She followed Zarra down yet more incomprehensible hallways.

Shimmering, disturbances in the air and walls, ceiling and floor told her that she was close to the destination. The moment Zarra turned and they approached an entrance with an elaborate arch, Janet knew they had reached the end of their walk.

– Zarra will take her leave, now, if that is acceptable, the girl said subdued.

– It is, Janet shrugged.

Zarra curtseyed and faded away from Janet's attention.

The patterns on the arch reminded Janet of the tattoos and made her skin tingle well before she stepped across the threshold and then she felt like they burned her.

Ione stood at the other side of the room.

– Welcome, Janet.

– Thank you, High Priestess, Janet replied. – It is a pleasure being here.

– No need for such formality, child, Ione said pleasantly. – We enjoy less of it within the «confines» of the temple. Call me Ione.

– This is… the temple? Janet looked around with curious eyes.

– It is. Most parts of what you call the catacombs are. It has served as the spiritual center for our people for many generations.

– I like less formality, Ione, Janet said.
– I rather thought you would. Come, walk with me.
Ione turned and started walking. Janet rushed forward in order to catch up with her.
There was another arch, leading to an inner chamber and to another hallway filled with mist and shadows. The energy was palatable, both from Ione and the surroundings. She did not hold herself back here.
– Are you alright? The hallways can be jarring to those not used to them.
Pride coursed through the girl. She cocked her head.
– I am, and they will make sense to me one day and night. I know that!
– I know that, too, Ione confirmed.
Janet looked startled and sullenly at her.
– You are not just saying that to…
– This is not a test, Ione said good-humored. – You are an acolyte and eventually, unless you behave in a beyond loathsome manner, you will become a High Priest and lead your tribe to glory.
To glory!
The girl could not take her eyes off the radiant, confident woman, as she walked by her side. Ione was of the same age as Illandra, and like Illandra she looked far younger than her age. She radiated authority to anyone in her presence.
– I would like that, Ione, she said, striving to not sound too much like a young, eager girl.
Ione touched her jaw with feather-light fingers.
– I am sure you do. You show so much promise, potential already. It would be a shame if you made it go to waste.
– It would! Janet eagerly agreed.
They reached a special place. Janet did not notice at first, but Ione slowed down and let her lead. She stopped in front of a door without looking at the older woman.
– You sensed it? Very good!
– I can hear the music of the ether, Janet said. – I saw how pleased that fact made my master.
And less of the usual unpleasant thoughts and shame accompanied the boasting. She re-experienced not the humiliation at Malone's hand, but herself standing before his unmoving statue of flesh with a triumphant smile on her lips.
The door slid open. The girl glanced at the older, experienced sorcerer, noted her slight nod, before stepping inside.
The heavy door closed behind them, the loud crack sending shockwaves

through the ether of the temple.

– No one that does not belong may enter this place, Ione emphasized.

And the immutable pride once more coursed through the young sorcerer.

– You remain impressionable, in spite of your experience. Hunger keeps burning in your eyes. You are clay to be molded. Do you understand, Janet of the Josbari?

– I do, High Priestess, Janet replied humbly.

Ione nodded, very pleased. She walked to the altar at the far end of the room. Janet followed her there, drawn to the shimmering lights and twinkling shadows hovering in the dense air.

Ione reached into something Janet suspected was a concealed chamber. When she pulled her hand back out, it held a glowing, pulsing jewel. Janet could not take her eyes off it.

– Sit with me.

There were two chairs nearby, opposing each other. They sat down, sitting face to face.

The High Priest handed her a cup with a smoking brew.

– Drink! It is a drink carving you open, making you impressionable and ready for your task.

Janet drank. The bitter fluid burned its way down her throat. Her tongue turned numb, keeping her from speaking. She sensed how it did open her, prepared her for what was to come.

– This is the Crystal Ball of Amberlin, the High Priestess explained. – It has certain useful… properties of divination and revelation. It will help us discover your true nature.

– My… true nature?

She mumbled more than spoke.

– Precisely. Now, stare into its misty realm and gauge truths and lies, deception and clarity.

The acolyte obeyed. There was music, quickly turning louder, turning into a pervasive chant of imposing silence. One tiny glimpse brought a thousand roaming thoughts.

– Now, young sorcerer, tell me what you see.

Janet's eyes remained open, but her immediate surroundings, even Ione's imposing presence faded away. She was pulled into the shiny dark bauble and hardly felt herself as a body at all anymore.

It happened so fast, from one moment to another. Claws of fear gripped her and held her formless form in its mighty grasp.

Shapes raced towards her, away from her, and it was all the same. She blinked or believed that she blinked, but nothing happened, nothing changed. Her lips moved. Her tongue synched with them, with the throat deep below. Suddenly, she could speak. Suddenly, nothing impeded on her ability to do so. Sound formed from nothing, from the shapes slowly turning solid, turning real.

– I stand by a river… by Styx, the Dark River of knowledge and life. I feel its frothing waves. I know what this is. It moves me and I move it. I am one with its mighty currents. They hold no terror for me.

The Dark River!

A wave rose. She waved her hands and a wave rose in her wake. She shouted in joy.

– What do you see? The High Priestess asked with a hoarse and excited voice.

The girl frowned, attempting to put the many glimpses into words, into context.

– I see a row of trees with naked branches… They are withered and dead… I see them come to life and *bloom*.

Leaves appeared and then the branches themselves began to grow. Yellow, withered grass turned green and tall. Janet, the disembodied spirit laughed in near euphoria. Her wild amusement echoed through the void.

She woke up on the sofa, feeling very light-headed and weak, still laughing and chuckling, and the smile lingered on her lips.

Ione stood above her with another type of smoking brew in her hand.

– I am thirsty.

Ione handed her the cup.

– Drink the broth. It will reinvigorate and strengthen you.

She did, practically devouring it, and her parched throat turned less so.

– Nine, she whispered. – There were nine trees.

She had prepared herself in the few seconds she had been awake, and studied Ione when she spoke.

Ione turned a stronger shade of pale? Ione's skin flushed and turned a deeper shade of pink? Janet could not tell, and she fought not to reveal her frustration.

She returned the cup to Ione's open hand.

– You have emptied the cup, but you are still thirsty. You feed, but remain hungry.

– I am a big girl, Janet grinned.

– You are shrewd and cunning, Ione acknowledged. – Very good!

Janet bowed her head in deference, submitting to the powerful, more experienced woman in her presence.

– But my… my vision, what does it mean?

– Aside from the obvious? It is clearly too early to tell after just one session. We will examine the treasures hidden in your mind and flesh and spirit together, and identify all the big and small gems within and without we may find.

Aside from the obvious… Janet's eyes once again narrowed ever so little.

– Teach me, she implored the High Priestess, – please teach me everything I need to know.

A soft, comforting hand touched her cheek.

– Dear child, I will teach you far more than that. I will teach you everything there is, like all the high priestesses before me has taught previous acolytes, until you may touch the foundation of existence itself

– So, what is happening to me? Why do I keep feeling so… funny all the time? Other sorcerers settle in a kind of equilibrium, but not I.

This time Ione visibly and very uncharacteristically hesitated.

– We are not sure. We have debated and researched the matter, though, and believe we have found the answer, or at least a significant part of it.

The young sorcerer felt the excitement build within. She waited anxiously for her experienced peer to continue, but Ione still hesitated.

– You are waking up, becoming your true self, she finally said.

– My… true self?

– Yes, it is rare, but it happens. The lore, the ancient Books of Shadows speak of beings such as you, a chrysalis in human form. You are born and spend your childhood and adolescence as one person and become something distinctly different at some undefined point in your development. You have felt it, have you not, the stirring just below the surface? You will be even more than you are when the process is complete.

– Malone did that, did that to me, too?

– No, he merely exploited, hijacked your untapped power, making it appear prematurely. It will manifest. Nothing can stop that, except death.

Words, meaningless and unfathomable, slowly gaining meaning, slowly fathomed echoed within the acolyte.

– You need to prepare for that moment, Ione told her softly. – I will help you do that.

– Thank you, Janet said. – Thank you, High Priestess.

And Ione of the Josbari smiled.

Chapter 21

Janet woke up in her bed in her quarters, instantly alert. She sensed the change in the air, in her very surroundings.

Then she relaxed and a huge smile broke on her face.

She recognized the creature long before it reached the bed, before unruly hair and eager-moving limbs joined her on the pleasant sheets.

– I finally managed to get someone to take me here, Bea said exasperated, excitedly, in her very characteristic manner. – It was an ordeal, I tell you.

Janet sensed the boy as well. Her waves brought his scent and more to her. He stood outside in a rigid pose, shifting his body uneasily against the wall.

They kissed and fondled each other, overdoing the kisses beyond eagerness.

Both grimaced in discomfort as suddenly not so eager hands zoned in on the herbs-covered area between the thighs.

– I am still sore, Bea said subdued. – You?

– Very much so, Janet said and shook her head in regret.

– It is not very surprising, of course, Bea said, – not the way we cut loose.

She giggled.

– The boys are even worse off, I guess. Kalir's cock looked like a boiled lobster.

– It pleases me to confirm that John's looked similar, Janet said, joining her betrothed in a wicked smile.

– It is okay, Bea shrugged, – let us be content with fooling around a little for now. Being close to you will always be sufficient to me.

Janet blushed, and the warm, warm feeling within multiplied.

They snuggled there on the bed, caressing each other softly, lazily, content with enjoying the closeness and the pleasant sensation of skin against skin.

But even during the most intimate moments the flashes and sensations kept haunting her. She renewed the physical efforts, practically assaulting Bea with caresses. The distant look in her eyes reappeared the moment her eyes caught a glance of something not Bea.

The other noticed, of course, as astute as ever, grabbing her and pushing her gently away, holding her at arm's length.

– You are a little preoccupied, are you not?

– I am, Janet confirmed. – I am sorry.

– Do not be, Bea shrugged, looking at her with steady and affectionate eyes. – You are an acolyte. You are entitled. Soon, you will be able to teach your devoted followers and even more devoted Companion even more beyond valuable secrets.

Janet's face cracked in a huge smile.

– I love it when you talk like that, she said. – I love you so much.

She grabbed both hands of the other girl and drowned them in kisses, her eyes lit by gratitude and devotion.

– You are the one, she stated affectionately. – I am yours!

– You are the one, Bea echoed, swallowing hard. – I am yours! We will always be together.

And then, just then there were no distractions. Eyes occasionally distant filled with such devotion that the catching in both throats grew large and painful.

– I want us to be like this, want us to be together all the time, Janet said with dreaming eyes, a timeless time later, when they still snuggled, still was as close as a door and a key.

– I want that, too, Bea said. – Nothing will ever keep us apart.

Janet felt peace then, almost unequivocally, as if the world, and even the rest of the room, did not exist.

Somewhere… a baby was crying.

Janet froze. Goosebumps covered her skin in an instant. Bea looked puzzled and good-humored at her.

– You can not hear it? She wondered, fighting to keep the agitation and despair out of her voice.

– I can not! Bea confirmed softly.

The visions, the experience of everything beyond Janet's physical grasp rushed back in an instant.

– It is there, with me all the time, Janet said subdued, sullenly.

Bea touched and rubbed clammy skin.

– There will always be something, some part of her beloved Beatrice can not touch, she said. – But know that she will always be there, right there with her.

Janet crouched in her soft embrace, the prevailing touches and fondling and words comforting her.

– Sometimes I feel like I am drowning in it, she whimpered, – drowning in the Dark River. It will never let me go, I know that.

It was visible, almost tangible to her, a living thing moving within her, scratching her like the sharpest of blades.

– Hush! Bea soothed her. –Hush…

Her betrothed comforted Janet, but did not bring her peace.

– Something is wrong, she mumbled. – I can not put my finger on what, but something…

– … something is wrong.

A shadow appeared to her left, there one moment, fading the next. She could not grasp it, or its significance.

Bea smiled a little.

– You worry too much, you know that, right?

– I suppose…

Janet attempted to embrace herself with stiff arms.

– It is just that…

It was like something stung her. She looked astounded at Bea, at her hand burning her skin.

– Sorry, my love. You are so high strung. I just attempted to alleviate that.

There was a slight mark on her shoulder. A calm settled throughout her body, spreading to her mind.

Janet frowned.

– It is no more than an innocent spell of relaxation I found in an old tome. It is my hope that it might be of some help to your troubled mind.

Her doe eyes and soft touches quickly made Janet relent and smile.

– Thank you, you are so patient with me, so kind.

– Speak nothing of it, Bea shrugged again. – My beloved is so strong and so capable that I am proud of what little assistance I can offer her.

They moved closer, close again.

– We will soon be healed, Bea said frivolously. – Once again fully able to pleasure each other…

She kissed the other lips so close to her own slowly, deeply, with obvious joy. Janet froze again, realizing they were sharing breath. A tear rolled from the corner of her eye.

– We will relax, Bea soothed her, – and enjoy life in full.

– There is something out there, Janet said with her hollow voice, – something I can not pinpoint.

– Relax, Bea whispered. – Relax…

And slowly Janet turned calm and happy in the other woman's arms.

– Relax, Bea whispered. – Relax…

It echoed in her mind, even as she found herself alone, at dawn, when her beloved had left her and returned to her duties.

She returned to Ione after breakfast, walking alone, having learned to navigate the ancient hallways without aid, practically able to feel how her mind worked its magick, as the walls and air seemed to shift and move around her. Wonder and hunger lit constantly moving eyes. Ione handed her the cup. Immersed in the High Priestess presence, she drank it empty in one decisive swallow.

– Do not despair or grow impatient, Ione cautioned her. – You have been my student for a week, only a week, and have still wrested untold secrets from the corners and shadows of the realms. You are learning faster than any acolyte I have taught. Be content with that. Feel pride!

Janet did and kept doing so for each new thing learned and progress made.

– Only one week? She mumbled, her tongue once again partly paralyzed by the brew. – It feels like forever.

– The overwhelming sense of timelessness is common among powerful adepts during certain circumstances, Ione revealed to her.

Blood and spices and a thousand tastes and sensations surged through Janet of the Josbari.

The Crystal Ball of Amberlin, that was not a crystal ball at all, hovered above the altar. It twinkled in red and blue, shifting into violet.

She frowned, standing in the landscape of shifting red and blue and violet. It was clear to her that she at some point had grabbed the ball, but after that her memory turned into more mist and shadow and more time without time. The crystal ball touched her. She did not touch it.

The mist and shadow cleared and Ione stood before her.

– It is the Ascension, the young sorcerer gasped.

– It is one Ascension, Ione confirmed, – or rather one access to it, and to its bounty.

– But we are not truly inside of it, are we?

– No, that is its secret, to use it, but not attempting to subvert it or pass through it to whatever higher realms there are. Your master and countless others paid for that mistake, that childish, presumptuous act. The Bone People have drawn knowledge and gained wisdom from it for centuries. We, those of us passing the test possess the necessary maturity to not overreach our ambitions, the wisdom to deny ourselves its most obvious temptation and dangerous lure.

Yet another chill passed through Janet. Yet more cruel understanding grabbed her.

– In my youth I entered the temple like you did, a promising acolyte, filled to the brim with curiosity and desire to know everything. Do you know who my teacher was?

– My great grandfather, Janet heard herself say, – the same guiding grandmother Illandra.

– You are indeed very perceptive, Ione praised. – He was the father of her Companion, your paternal grandfather.

– Her mother ran away with another of my great grandfathers, did she not, – leaving her family behind?

– She did, and through him she joined the Bone People.

The impressions from the Crystal Ball of Amberlin, this particular Ascension access point ended. The two of them «returned» to the temple.

– Countless adepts have come to this temple, in order to be educated and in order to grow beyond their limitations. Many lines and traditions have come together here, in order to form new and unforeseen paths. The tattoos keep spreading like the branches of a tree or *the* tree.

Her words and particularly her emphasis echoed and kept echoing in the young sorcerer's feverish mind.

The fever did not leave her, but kept ravaging body and mind, present in sleep, slumber and when she was awake. The alertness never quite went away.

She sat there with her thumbs and index fingers touching and her legs crossed. Sweat poured from long since soaked skin.

– Focus, Ione told her. – Focus!

The High Priestess circled her and enticed her, pushed her into improving herself. The waves whirled in the restless air all over the room.

– You are emitting waves, Ione urged her. – They are an extension of your body and mind, and with proper control they can be a powerful and even deadly tool. They are a defense against the worst possible physical assault, a weapon to be feared wherever you walk. It can be blunt or sharp according to your will. Your will is your most important asset. You need to be at your best in order to properly utilize your talents.

A pin shivered on the table, in her mind.

– You feel it, do you not?

Yes!

– Then pick it up.

Janet focused, striving to blink the sweat from the sore eyes. The waves did not make a sound, but they were still like a roar in her mind.

The pin rose from the table, as if touched by a mighty wind. It fell on the floor several steps away. Janet collapsed on her spot, crouching there forever in repeated attempts at catching her breath.

– At some glorious future moment you will be able to pick it up and hold it easily, as if you were using your hands.

Janet rose on unsteady legs.

– You will now clean and oil yourself, Ione commanded. – Then, you may make your High Priestess her dinner.

– Yes, High Priestess, the girl said and curtseyed, before being on her way.

The chores did not really register in her conscious mind. They were just there, like a fly buzzing around her head.

She had an image of herself in front of the mirror, doing her hair and face and body, enticing glimpses of oiled skin, but it was indistinct, unreal.

Silhouettes of her surroundings touched her eyes, but hardly reached beyond that.

She put the plate with food and drink on the table in front of Ione, curtseying and pulling back respectfully. Ione began feeding without really acknowledging her acolyte.

Janet stood there, attentive somewhat, but still preoccupied. A waterfall roared in the distance. The sound of a thousand swords being drawn from their sheets and the subsequent battle-cry choir reached her ears.

– Sit with me, Janet of the Josbari, Ione, the High Priestess offered.

Janet did. She sat down in a chair close to the commanding woman in her presence.

Ione mumbled a spell, incomprehensible to the acolyte. The meat and the fruit and the herbs seemed to change, to be immersed in an eerie glow.

– Feed!

Janet hesitated only for a moment, before grabbing the food on the plate and devouring it piece by piece in a feeding frenzy she hardly even noticed before it was gone, and the food on the plate was only another memory.

It, and whatever it had become spread through her system, even to her waves. The images, sensations returned. They assaulted her, cut her open, made her bleed all over again. The memory, the full memory of the Ascension filled her to the brim, for one heartbeat, two… and then it once more faded to nothing.

– No! She cried in anguish and rage. – NO!

Her fist struck the table.

– More, she shouted, – I want MORE!

– And you shall have it, Ione said.

Janet stared stunned at her. She had changed, momentarily become something assertive and demanding, exposing a part of herself she did not want to share with anyone.

– Your true nature hides itself, Ione nodded, – and with good reason.

The High Priestess rose.

– Come, walk with me.

She had almost left the room before Janet managed to catch herself and rush after her, catch up just before the grown woman vanished behind the corner.

Janet virtually saw Ione's power. It emanated from her in calm, steady bursts, interfering with Janet's waves without her being able to prevent it. It was practically reflected in the very walls. Ione had made the temple hers, her place of power. Everyone and everything within these walls belonged to her. Janet shook in reverence.

They walked up a spiral staircase. It was the same here. Janet imagined that they were floating upwards, as they rode a warm wind up through the narrow tunnel, and that the stairs were not really there or quite unnecessary to their task of moving from the catacombs and to the high, high tower where they were able to survey the entire circle, all the southern triple cities.

The sight through the window opened up to her, as if she was sucked out through it, as if she hovered in the air outside and did not have her feet solidly planted on the cold floor inside.

The wheel turned below them, and they turned with it.

– This is a tower…

Ione spoke.

Janet frowned.

– But there is no tower in the southern triple cities, she objected, feeling ridiculous and small.

– Precisely!

The wheel below turned and burned and kept burning, its dark fire just as visible in the bright light of the daystar above as in the darkest night.

– This is a nice spot to live, Ione said. – Our people are somewhat content, but still unsatisfied. We yearn for more.

– More, Janet echoed.

– We have hardly left here, most of us, not in generations, not beyond a few necessary trips in affairs of state and journeys of study and recreation. Many of us have convinced themselves that our lives here are sufficient and even satisfactory.

The tower was windows, windows in all the directions of the sky. It was at the center of the wheel, just like the arena. Even the floor was a window, if she wanted it to be. Janet looked straight down on the seething fire.

The snow on the western peaks and higher-elevation valleys burned in white. They chilled her bones.

– But your great grandfather roamed. Your great grandmother came here from the outside. Your grandmother and father have shaken up the old ways more than anyone. So will you. You will take your tribe far and wide, farther than any of us has ever gone.

The Blue Flame envisioned it in her mind. Hammered and shaken by the visions, she knew her consciousness could never contain it all. The Blue Flame burned. She did not need to see herself with her waves in order to know that.

– You think of your friends, the High Priestess told her. – You may go to them, look them up.

The girl did. It took no more than a slight change of focus.

– They are educated in their duties as the Sorcerer's Guard, as the future high servants of the future High Priestess of the Bone People.

The words… the words and their implications were not lost on the acolyte.

They sat in a half moon circle facing their teacher.

– Your task in life will be to serve and protect the High Priest you have sworn allegiance to, the teacher said with stern voice and appearance.

– The Master of the Blue Flame, Livy stated. – I would die for her!

– And that is your purpose.

Livy bowed her head in acknowledgment and humility and joy.

The image faded away. Janet realized she had seen and heard everything she was supposed to see and hear.

The young girl sat in Lotus position on the floor. She was sweating hard. The attic of the high tower had faded from her surroundings long ago.

She collapsed on the floor, mumbling deliriously, casting spells in her sleep, her dreamless sleep. A sleepwalker stalked the night, the dream, the night terror, changing and shifting it all in order to suit her. Her throat, tongue and lips were just as much weapons as the rest of her body and her very consciousness roaming the ether. She woke up in her bed, somewhat rested a timeless time span later. Zoe and the others awaited her orders, provided the fulfillment of mundane needs. She rose from bed without lingering unnecessarily. They served her food and drink, and she devoured everything they put in front of her on the table.

She acknowledged that she experienced a certain impatience, in her zeal, her hunger for knowledge, but not excessively so. Her most immediate, physical needs were met. Her ever hungry mind desired far more. The days and nights just passed by like water.

She felt it, practically experienced the Dark River flowing and whimpered in her sleep.

John approached her. She had woken up a few seconds earlier. She smiled, pleased with herself and her extreme awareness.

He undressed and crawled into the bed.

– Hi, he said hoarsely, staring unashamed at her nude form without any of his former awkwardness and insecurity.

That kind of pleased her.

– Hi, she replied huskily.

Low-level arousal quickly rose to burning need. She writhed lazily on her back, eagerly awaiting his company. Fire exploded behind her eyelids. She writhed in his arms, seconds, minutes later, feeling his hard, hard cock move inside of her, feeling him in her mind, like she knew he felt her.

Felt her embrace him, on all levels. She could crush him, like she would a bug. That moment, with that thought brought release, brought another explosion of ecstasy shaking her to the core.

The night, the nights brought more pleasure, an unending ride of it. Sometimes she saw John's face and big male body. Other times it was Bea and her strong and curvy body she crushed in her embrace. Two sweaty faces haunted Janet's dreams. They became similar, interchangeable, even more so than their sibling resemblance would mandate.

The private ceremony took place the day they left. Ione handed Janet a sack of bones, literally. The girl looked awestruck at them, touched each and every one of the pieces and felt their power.

– These are remains of your ancestors. They contain pieces of their spirits and will aid you and comfort you in both good and bad times.

– Thank you, High Priest, Janet whispered. – Thank you so much!

That scene, like many others faded only slowly in her mind, her blazing memory.

The airship floated slowly through the air, heading north. Janet's hand reached to her neck, searching for the collar that was no longer there.

Bea, John, Illandra, Zoe and the guys, they were all there, sitting around her, smothering her in their devotion.

She recalled meeting the guys again, noticing instantly Eleanor's blushing face and realizing that the apprentice had felt at least an echo of what Janet and Bea had experienced. She saw, (saw again) in glimpses that the girl had sought out and mated with every single male in her path showing interest.

Toby, Rosa and Fran had also changed, also in their perception of Janet. After an entire moon of having been educated by the Josbari, they looked at her with new eyes.

Janet and Bea sat side by side, holding hands. It felt peaceful and right.

They rose, smiling to the others and left for the bathroom together. The sour vomit burned in their throats and threatened to erupt from their mouths the entire long stretch to the toilet. They knelt down on the stalls and the yellowish bile flooded the bowls.

Janet and Bea recalled Ione's smile when she removed the collars and everything repressed filled them up once more.

– You will venture into the realm, she told them. – You will return to us with abundance to share, and then we will all venture into the realms together, like a conquering army.

The two young women left the toilet together, like they had entered it, holding hands, sending each other affectionate smiles.

– Ione wants to use us, for her own purposes, Janet said, attempting to not sound too agitated. – We are tools for her to use in order to fulfill whatever agenda she is pursuing.

– You are a singular being, you know, unique in all the realms, Bea said with worship in her eyes. – It stands to reason that other, lesser beings would wish to bask in your presence.

– You always say the right thing, Janet marveled. – Where did you learn that?

– At home, growing up, the other young woman said with a sore subtext in her voice. – I was taught the finer points of etiquette from an early age.

– Do not worry, baby, Janet said softly. – Your betrothed understands.

– I believe my betrothed will always understand, Bea said, equally tender. – And you should not worry either. They will never manage to keep this woman down, especially not when she has her beloved by her side, and soon will have her for all eternity.

Her words, as always, soothed and excited Janet.

Illandra was still there, with them, when they returned to the others, just as enigmatic and ethereal as ever. Janet knew she was actually there, not being a mirage or a projection.

Ione had waved goodbye to them from her invisible sanctum in the sky.

Janet had not seen Kalir anywhere and still did not, as they removed themselves from the circle triple cities.

– I think I must still be asleep.

She frowned with the lingering smile on her face.

– I am certainly dreaming all the time.

Hands sought hands and squeezed affectionately. More kisses were exchanged.

Half closed eyes saw the ship float through the air, moving north, to destiny unbound. She saw it, being the ship, being the air it moved through.

Her waves moved, becoming the vast waterfall below, the seething river from which it sprang, and the below-surface Dark River spreading, spreading across the sea. Bea, Illandra and Eleanor, and the rest stared blindly at her, and she could not decide which dedication and worship ran deepest.

Illandra hid it well, but to Janet it suddenly had become very evident. What had previously seemed like dispassionate interest of a distant relative, showed itself to be something far more. Janet, startled fought to conceal her surprise.

John tried, tried hard to conceal his affection, but could not do so. She wanted to spit in his face, return his doggie worship like a curse, but could not do anything but to touch his face with fondness. She searched for jealousy or possessiveness in Bea's eyes, but could not find any.

– You will share yourself with all your subjects, Cathy of Arcadia, Bea said with her dry humor, – but you will reserve the best of it for me.

– I will! Janet declared, and it felt so right, so very right.

There was no sense of her statement being compulsory, an obligation, a pretense. It had been instantaneous, spontaneous, true.

Their mutual affection had just grown.

The warm laughter rocked them all softly.

The airship floated through the air, floated on warm currents. Janet's wings spread out, flapping, flapping. She laughed euphorically.

Soon, the happy voice whispered in her head. Soon!

The triangle triple cities appeared like a mirage below. A frown followed by a concerned look appeared on Janet's serene face.

– What is wrong, beloved? Bea asked softly.

– Nothing, Janet replied, strangely anxious, – nothing at all!

They did not dawdle after landing, but headed straight for the house on Altram Hill. The long walk hardly felt like that at all. The people waving to them and casting rushed glances at them did not seem real. Janet had seen spirits that seemed more tangible. The ferry brought them to the Island and more of the short, long walk. She felt every inch of their path, so much more astute and aware. They chose the other fork in the road. She chose it, for herself, and for all of the rest accompanying her. Excitement dominated whatever anxiety there might be.

The house towered above them. Janet walked straight through the non-existing door and kept it open for the others to enter. They rushed through it, filled with apprehension and boundless excitement.

Everyone stopped right inside and looked around in something way beyond awe.

– I feel it, Livy said brightly. – I *feel* it!

The surge charging through the others did not quite reach her levels, but was not that far behind.

– I feel the house. She turned towards Janet. – I feel you and your waves. I am yours in all things.

She bowed her head and lowered her eyes.

Everyone followed her cue, even Illandra, Toby and Rosa. Janet saw something else in her grandmother's eyes, too, something she did not quite get.

– We are imperfect beings basking in your glory, beloved, Bea said softly, – but command us, and your will be done.

The Blue Flame smiled and they smiled with her.

– Okay then, good people, she said to them, – this house is slumbering. We will wake it up, make it come to life. Get to it!

She clapped her hands, pushing them to step on it and they did.

The house buzzed with activity in the coming days. It had slept, but slept no more. At night, its buzz was quieter, but just as poignant. They imagined they heard breathing, and a beating heart. The sense of something, a living being waking up was altogether too real.

They glanced at the baby skull and bones on the shelf. The shiver of some of them added to itself, and made itself visible beyond doubt. Others, like Livy only looked more awestruck.

The neighbors quickly noticed the activity, of course, and stared at the perceived sinister structure in their midst with fearful and angry eyes.

There was more than enough space for everyone, even though they had to share rooms. Janet and Bea and Eleanor and Joan moved into the biggest room closest to the stairs. Eleanor and Joan slept on the floor, as usual, and were on hand serving every need of their masters.

Joan frowned and had done so since they had walked into the house, glancing around her and at Janet with anxious eyes. Janet ignored that, as she more or less ignored Joan altogether. She had all her attention on Bea, like her betrothed had all her attention on her. They hardly had eyes for anyone but each other.

Everyone gathered in the living room, like they did early every day and late every night. It was hard, even completely impossible to distinguish day from night within the confines of the house. The shimmering twilight from the southern triple cities seemed to have traveled north with them. It darkened the light and brightened the dark.

All items, each spot of the walls, floor and ceiling spoke to her.

Everyone with powers glowed. Even the mundane present shimmered in a pale light.

– My cruel master used me for his own petty purposes, she told them, – and then he dangled my reward, the prize for services rendered in front of me, and I accepted it, grabbed it with both hands. It was not his to offer, but it was mine to accept. I took it for myself, in an act of terror equal to his. It is mine, as long as I endure. It has waited for years without number for someone like me.

A deep chill of equal excitement and apprehension trickled down the spine of everyone present.

She no longer looked like a near-eighteen year old girl. During brief, slow flashes in time she appeared considerably different and far older.

– We will use this ancient abode, release its untapped power, utilizing it in order to fulfill Ione's dream, making it our own.

The fist she held up glowed and pulsed in the twilight, in the illumination of the candles and torches.

– I can feel the Queen's waves wash over me, Livy said with dreamy, excited eyes. – I experience beyond doubt and misgivings her mighty hand.

– This is a good thing, Livy, Bea said. – You express the truth we all know, one that will set us all free and give us a life undreamt of, one that not even the ancients dared imagine.

Everyone swayed back and forth on the floor, facing the Blue Flame and her betrothed. A low hum rose from somewhere and filled ears and minds and the space surrounding them.

Janet signed to her apprentice and Eleanor rushed forward and knelt in front of the two. She handed Janet two cups.

– This is the Brew of Unification, Janet stated. – Fully implemented it will become an elixir that will bind us all even stronger to this place of learning and belonging, tie us to it for all time.

She had her Book of Fate, her family Grimoire on her left, Bea on her right.

The low hum picked up. Livy, Zoe, Loewe and others eagerly attempted to emulate it. They did not quite succeed. It was notably different from a common and even uncommon human hum. It sounded more than strange, otherworldly.

Bea sent her yet another lovesick look of approval. They used it as yet another opportunity to embrace and caress each other. More laughter embraced her and made her feel warm and wanted.

Janet crossed her arms in front of her, holding one cup in each hand. She joined the low hum, and after some trial and error… she got it exactly right. The awe in those gathered at this place with her intensified further. The hum rising from her throat changed. She changed it, making the hum of the house follow her lead, transforming it through her desires. Goosebumps formed on all exposed skin. She began casting her spell. Her hum changed into words, or something resembling words, becoming guttural, accentuated. Blue flames surrounded the hands holding the cups.

The brews began steaming, becoming energized, boiling on the low burn of the blue flames. She emptied the content of one into the other. Steam turned to smoke, a slow, steady release showing no sign of ending.

The Blue Flame rose, a little awkward, focusing on not spilling the content of the almost full cup.

The other cup dropped from her hand. It hit the floor with a loud, metallic sound reverberating through the room, through the house and the ground it stood on, a sound joining the hum, the spell rocking them all.

Janet walked to each and every one present.

She turned to Bea first.

– Do you swear allegiance to Janet of the Josbari and the Blue Flame?

– I so swear, Bea replied, – on my life, in all things.

Janet put the cup at her lips and Bea drank. She swallowed and an ecstatic smile lit her face.

The sorcerer walked to Illandra next, studying her, staring her down. Illandra, startlingly lowered her gaze.

– Do you swear allegiance to Janet of the Josbari and the Blue Flame?

– I so swear, the seasoned sorcerer replied, – and in time, so will Ione and the rest of the Council and countless others swimming the Ocean of Mankind.

She drank from the cup put to her lips.

The others drank, one by one, not all of them as eager as Livy and Eleanor, but still submitting to the Blue Flame and her authority, the ancient power literally burning in her veins.

No one could avoid feeling it, not Rosa and Toby and the rest without powers either. They submitted like everyone else.

Janet touched their cheeks in affection. They returned it willingly and eagerly, as they drank of the brew, as further love and dedication lit their already shiny eyes.

– You were taught the tenet of the sorcerers and their Guard among the Josbari?

– We were… Honored One, Rosa replied, blushing. – We understand so much more, now.

Janet knew the teaching had not always been kind. She pondered it for a moment, before shrugging.

She walked to the center of the broken circle, raising the cup to her lips.

– I accept, she stated with a firm voice, one that did not shake, – accept your allegiance and the stewardship of the house, doing so for as long as I endure.

She drank, drank everything left in the cup. It burned on her lips, on her tongue, in her throat and throughout her body and self.

It spread, at the very least as far as the reach of her waves.

The land, urban and wild below the balcony stretched out forever in front of her. She stood there and enjoyed the afternoon heat, the slow humming of time. Even here, on the balcony the house brought twilight. The light from the daystar seemed to break and halt around it.

People passed the house below her, glancing at her and the house more than ever. Most of them were more than sensitive enough to pick up, to truly pick up on its seething energies. She dismissed them in her mind without any deep-felt consideration.

Joan approached her from the hallway. Janet did not reveal, in any way that she was aware of the woman being there. Joan stopped a few steps behind her. Janet sensed her mood, her insecurities and everything. She marveled at her own sensitivity, her ability to see several steps ahead.

– They call you Queen Cathy, the grown woman whimpered.

Janet turned and looked calmly at her.

– Yes, they do, do they not, she grinned.

Joan looked shocked, horrified at her.

Something ugly rose from Janet's core and she was unable to keep it from happening, from expressing itself.

– Yes, I am that Cathy you have sought, the Cathy that was Malone's complicit.

Joan, paralyzed by the onslaught of fear surging through her promptly fell on her knees and cast her eyes to the floor.

Janet looked down on her in contempt and triumph.

– It is a good thing that you know. It will make you better suited to serve me.

– Yes, M-my Q-queen, Joan whimpered.

– That is a good girl. You will now resume your tasks, and never stray from them *again*.

– Yes, My Queen! Joan cried out, surrendering even more to the tidal force governing her life.

– You are certainly not fit for anything else, the burning Blue Flame snarled in contempt.

A light prompting and Joan rose to her feet, her eyes cast down. Janet left the room and the eager servant trailed her.

Bea waited in the hallway. Janet stopped and Joan stopped behind her.

– It is a good thing that you are strict with her, Bea said. – She is a simple soul, in dire need of direction.

– She is all better for it, Janet nodded.

She frowned, unable to hide it and fully aware that Bea would notice.

– What is it, beloved?

– I do not really care much for that servant shit, you know that, but she makes it so easy.

– I do not mind, Bea shrugged. – I have been told my entire life that I am superior to others.

She shrugged again, deliberately.

– Most other people confirm that every day, every moment I watch them. You are a notable exception. I worship you and the ground you walk.

Janet blushed. The catching in her throat did not let her go. More hungry kisses were exchanged and a few heartbeats later she did not care whether or not it did.

– You have begun accepting yourself, Bea spoke softly. – They call you Cathy or Queen Cathy with increased frequency and you no longer mind.

Janet nodded, hesitant, but not denying the truth of her betrothed's words.

The twilight from the balcony hardly reached the hallway as more than a faint glow. The shadows easily overpowered the light. There was so much there, so much to sense and catch.

The house spoke to her, played its music to her, and even though she only listened with half an ear and eye, she had no trouble understanding its language.

– Master!

Eleanor said.

Janet, as usual sensed before she noticed Eleanor's approach, well before the apprentice spoke up. Janet and half a heartbeat later; Bea focused their attention on the girl

– James has arrived with the car, Master, she informed Janet.

– Excellent, Janet said. – We are good to go, then.

She and Bea walked down the stairs hand in hand. Eleanor and Joan walked in their slipstream as unobtrusively as possible.

They walked outside. Janet shut the door with a thought. The full force of the daystar hit her. She enjoyed its heat. The four of them entered the car and sat down. James, in his usual, impassive mode and with his soft touch made the wheels turn and they drove off.

The world outside moved slowly past them again. The car did not appear to move that fast, but still it did. People stared at it, and kept staring at them.

– They know the house is not for them, Joan said in a low voice, – that they can not enter it without the landlord's permission, and it baffles them.

– They know what it is about, Eleanor stated eagerly. – The old stories have only hibernated, never truly vanished from the collective consciousness.

Janet rubbed her lower arm. It was itching, but she saw no signs of inflamed skin.

– The world has become so peaceful, she said lazily. – I would like to keep it that way. We have so much ahead of us, I know that, but this slow, languid pace… suits me.

A crowd stood at the fork in the road, eerily silent. They stared at the car as it passed them.

– We have all the time in the world, Bea said. – The realms will just have to adapt to our pace. If not we will make them.

Hand squeezed hand.

Janet turned her head. The crowd had not moved.

They crossed the Island, or at least a fairly large part of it.
The eyes of onlookers kept displaying themselves in Janet's vision.
The familiar house of Learning appeared after the next turn. James drove into its yard not long after that. They spotted a few people in the building and surrounding area, but nowhere near as many as it would have been if it had been during morning and midday. Janet kept seeing herself and the guys and others in her mind's eye.
– Brings back memories, huh? Bea grinned.
– It does, Janet acknowledged, – but it also feels like it happened to someone else, like it does not relate to me at all.
– The butterfly hardly recall its time as a chrysalis, Bea nodded.
A soft kiss wet Janet's cheek.
Her betrothed's presence kept making Janet warm and fuzzy all over. And she knew it was mutual. The catching in her throat persisted and she did not mind, did not mind at all.
The car stopped. The four left the car. They stopped like one and drew breath, enjoying more of the afternoon's pleasant heat.
– They say our distant ancestors worshipped and honored the daystars as gods, Janet said. – It makes sense to do that. From a vast distance we recognize their power.
The four walked inside a place that in Janet's eyes was filled with vast shadows, once more quite different from how she remembered it. Echoes bounced off the walls of the empty or currently less traveled halls and hallways. This was a big place, with many rooms.
They descended the stairs and entered the basement. It was just as extensive, just as vast.
– The people constructing this building put a lot of time and effort into it, did they not? Bea said in wonder.
– They did! Janet agreed.
– It is quite the suitable place for the exchange of our vows, Bea stated both somberly and eager. – The fact that mother does not really approve also works in its favor…
– You are a laugh riot, beloved!
Janet chuckled, shaking her head.
Hands squeezed hands affectionately.
– This is so funny, Janet mused. – It feels like I am floating, floating like a spirit just below the ceiling.
A distant hum she could not quite identify accompanied the downright strange feeling.
– You are, Eleanor giggled. – You have been floating for *moons,* now.

The other three looked at her with fondness in their eyes.

– Like a spi - rit, Bea joked affectionately, like a twisted, very twisted parrot. – Floa - ting.

Janet laughed good-humored with the others, but the sense of floating did not leave her.

The happy laughter sounded like an echo, as if the actual laughter was not there.

Their walk ended in a small hall at the end of the corridor. They walked inside, a little short of breath, but filled with pent up anticipation.

Bea switched on lights soft and appealing.

The moment of added happiness made Janet breathe noticeably faster.

The hall looked completely ordinary, but Janet imagined how it would be just a few days from now. In her mind all the empty spaces filled themselves, seemingly responding to her expectations and yearnings.

– I like it here, she said. – It is a good choice.

– I knew you would, Bea smothered her.

Bea had picked the hall with the low stage, where the acting classes performed and trained. Janet found that strangely appropriate. Bea walked up on the stage and the other three followed her.

– All the guys should be up here with us, of course. The others, all the *snotty* guests may watch from a proper distance.

Janet giggled, squeezing the other's hand yet again.

– Our hands could just as well be glued together, she said sheepishly.

– Is not that the truth, Bea agreed brightly.

Janet looked around, studying the hall with critical eyes, very conscious of mimicking Bea's patronizing glare. She giggled some more.

– Do not worry, Bea assured her. – Everything will be ready in time. The moment we give our approval, handy workers will move in and transform this place in just a few hours into something both awesome and modest. It will not sicken us, but be like a dream come true, like the great event itself.

She moved behind her beloved, speaking softly into her ear.

– I want you to imagine it all, truly imagine it, visualizing it in your beautiful mind.

Janet did, in even more exquisite detail, as if it was actually happening right now. She closed her eyes, and the big, big smile growing around her mouth and spreading all over her face made anticipation and joy, powerful emotions beyond anything fill her to the brim.

Chapter 22

Activity picked up even a notch or ten more, in the house on Altram Hill. People moved back and forth in a rush, in a totally unrecognizable pattern defying understanding to a dazed and stressed, but happy Janet.

– I am floating, she hummed, – floating through an endless, warm, warm sea.

The bony hands in the shadows and dark corners were hardly visible anymore.

Janet and Bea tried out wedding gear, tunics, robes, hoods and dresses, the works, in quick, sometimes impatient succession. They posed before the big mirror, before each other and everyone around them.

Zoe, Loewe, Livy, Rosa, Fran, Joan and Eleanor helped them with the trial and error of pretty garments. There was much laughter and exaltation. Their happy faces faded constantly in and out of Janet's vision and attention.

The whirl of motion did distract her, but not considerably so from the sweet, blushing face by her side.

The parade of new attires to choose from never seemed to end. Janet felt a headache coming on. She rubbed her forehead.

– We could have had the clothes made locally, you know, Janet sighed. – There is an excellent tailor store just down the road.

She knew she had made a mistake before she had finished speaking. Irritation flared in Bea's already stressed-out mind.

– Mother will throw a fit if we wed wearing cheap-tailored garments, Bea said with her patronizing flair fully intact and realized. – Not that we will not make her pay for our compliance, but…

– I am not to be wed to your clans, Janet said embittered, her temper flaring, her delicate balance finally snapping, – but to you. I know that everyone else sees this as an *arrangement* between clans, but we do not… do we?

Suddenly they stood there, practically snarling at each other. Everyone looked shocked at them.

Joan rushed forward between them, very emotional.

– Y-you will be w-wed, Joan insisted. – You will be h-happy. I can not bear even the thought of that not happening.

– Of course, Bea said and touched her cheek in a comforting gesture. – You should not worry so much.

Half a heartbeat later Janet did, too.

– You must focus more on yourself, Janet said softly, – not so much on us.

It is not good for you.

It was like Joan did not hear her, as if she had not spoken at all.

Bea turned to Janet, shaking even harder.

– I am sorry, beloved, so sorry, she said subdued and down. – It is just that I want everything to be *perfect*.

Janet had already calmed down, and got equally emotional.

– I am sorry, too, she said softly. – Do not worry. Everything will be.

– Everything will be, Bea echoed.

The big smile broke on Bea's face. Big tears fell from her eyes. Janet dried them off her cheeks.

– If you ask me, it is no wonder that something finally snapped, Rosa said. – You need to relax and let us handle things, at least handle far more.

Both sniffed and nodded.

The search for the perfect wedding attire began again, hesitatingly at first, but then with increasing eagerness and urgency, though it was clear that Rosa had taken over as director, and she quickly showed herself to be so much better at it.

– I can enjoy this more, now, Bea said. – You?

– Indeed, Janet said. – I love trying on new threads. It was just that… that…

– I know, Bea said. – It just got to you. Rosa was correct. It is a miracle it did not happen sooner and that the subsequent explosion was not considerably more far-reaching…

Both grinned.

– I do think you need to be educated in the ways of the clans you are about to join, Bea said, – just like I have been educated in yours.

– I think you are right, Janet nodded. – I want to, want to know as much about you as possible.

Emotionally drained they ended the search and display fairly soon.

– There is nothing more to be gained by keeping this up any longer today, Rosa declared, speaking both to the two of them and the tailor sent by the Rosens. – We will resume tomorrow.

Janet had to laugh when she saw the shocked expression in the woman's face and even more when she glanced at Bea and saw that she hid her mouth behind a hand.

They dressed in informal clothing and walked outside. It was early evening. They had kept it going all day.

– Goddess! Bea shook her head. – I, in my ignorance believed physical exercise was tiring…

– You are absolutely correct, Janet said agreed vehemently. – In hindsight I do not find it strange that we eventually could not keep our rage contained, do not find it strange at all.

They giggled and gave each other fond gazes. Hands sought hands yet again. They enjoyed beyond enjoying the close proximity of the other.

Lips sought lips again when Janet froze and pulled away. Bea looked aghast, but curious at her, knowing instantly that someone or something had distracted her.

– The wall… Janet said. – Look at the wall.

They both did, at the even, unblemished surface.

– The magistrates broke into the house to look for Malone, Janet said, – leaving a huge, ghastly wound in the wall. It is not there anymore. Not even the lousy repair work they did is. The house has…

– … repaired itself, Bea mused impressed.

– And it has happened recently, after we…

– … moved in.

– And the mirror in the hall…

– … has also repaired itself.

A pleasant shake took hold of them both. Twin smiles lit up the close to twin faces.

Janet held on to that image in her head when she, with Eleanor dogging her tail walked down the road later. It was yet another warm, pleasant early evening, but one not even approaching the heat of her burning heart. She started humming without being aware of it, and the apprentice hummed with her, their beyond evident happiness not exactly bringing less stares from the locals.

The big black car brought dust and more stares. Janet and Eleanor stopped before it did. Eleanor opened the door only a heartbeat or two after it had. She bowed her head with the smile on her lips. Janet had a hard time distinguishing between her joy and her own.

She sat down in the pleasant seat and the apprentice joined her. The car drove on.

Janet did not really pay any attention to the scenery this time, even though it differed slightly from what she was used to. The Rosen estate appeared in her vision long before it did in fact. It was like a dreamscape growing out of the very land itself. She shivered in disgust and attraction both.

The gate was open, as it always was, and as always: none of those passing by outside walked inside. The car passed through it and rolled all the way up to the main building, and stopped before the main entrance.

This time it was James that opened the door for her, as if everything was coordinated and decided upon in advance. The thought made her grin. She stepped outside. Eleanor slipped out behind her. James walked ahead of them and opened the door, the big and heavy door. They walked inside.

James disappeared sometimes after that. Janet was busy with taking in the sights. She felt the dwelling far more pronounced this time, compared to her previous visits. The bright light in the dining room brought a dramatic contrast to that in her house.

The family, Justin, Madge, John and Turner sat in the sofa, just like the first time. They rose when Janet walked into the dining room.

– There you are, my dear, Madge said. – Welcome!

The girl frowned, but did feel welcomed, somewhat.

– It is very good to see you again, Janet, Justin said and extended his hand.

Janet took his hand.

– Yes, so very good seeing you again, John said flustered.

– Thank you, the girl said softly. – Thank you so much.

Turner did not say anything.

It was John that pulled out the chair for her this time, hurrying in order to beat his father… to the punch.

She could not help but blushing.

He had changed, had become more mature, reflected, everything. They were like two adults facing each other, with the relative calm that brought.

No one spoke to Eleanor, clearly aware of what an insult that would have been to the sorcerer. The apprentice placed herself behind Janet, and stood there, still and rigid.

The starter was Unicorn Soup, a spiced fluid matching the pale wine and Janet's buds well.

– Once again, we are so happy to have you here, my dear, Madge said and grabbed her hand, frowning a bit when she noticed the distinct vibrations.

– Thank you again, mother, Janet said courteously.

She finished the first helping of the soup, and started on another. The moments flowed fluidly between each other. She found she could actually enjoy herself (sort of) in their company. She consumed the soup in fast, furry flashes, hardly even taking a break between each time she put the spoon in her mouth and exchanged words with her new, upcoming, extended family.

– My appetite has increased significantly, she grinned. – It is like I can not get enough food, no matter how much I *devour*.

– I can imagine. Madge beamed at her.

They all glanced at her still more or less flat belly.

– Fortunately I have no trouble keeping fit, she added. – I and Bea and the guys train harder than ever, and we keep walking all over the triple cities, except when you guys insist we use James.

– And the baby is… healthy, Justin wondered, revealing a slight anxiety.
– Both the mother and the baby are healthy, father, she said lightly. – We are not made of glass, you know.
That word… made her frown. She pretended not to notice his brief, closer scrutiny.
The main evening meal with wine and veal was served and digested. Metal and glasses met and parted. Janet drank mostly lemonade, but kept devouring the food, as if she had not eaten in days.
– So, you have decided on that old learning house? Madge frowned, pushing the conversation towards a desired subject with great, proven skill.
– Yes, mother, Janet responded brightly, as if she did not have a single worry in her life. – We are so happy about it. They, in their generosity actually approved of us using it. It is exactly what we were looking for. We are *so* fortunate! Cheers!
Madge's frown deepened. Janet had to stifle a giggle.
– Mother just wants a well-attended ceremony, John remarked, – and that abysmal basement is rather small for the occasion.
Janet looked at him with fondness in her eyes, making him blush, which pleased her to no end.
The table, the entire room constantly revealed and re-revealed itself to her. Its people did as well. John stared at her. His mouth was not exactly open in an incredulous gap, but his father still noticed his condition.
– What really happened in those small villages down south? Maximus wondered with the usual spite in his voice.
Janet did not reply. She looked at John, prompting him to speak.
– We learned many things, cousin, he drawled with triumph in his voice, – great, unspeakable things you can hardly imagine, and we are all better for it. We met many of our cousins and distant cousins, and too many to be counted shadows in the night, a great marching band of ghosts and ghouls, and…
– That's enough, John, Madge cried out with a calm only marginally held.
He relented and fell silent.
Both his father and mother looked at him as if they saw a stranger, even though Justin did reveal a strange, almost invisible smile to the sorcerer's improved senses when he looked at his son.
– It was a resounding success, Janet shrugged. – Our clans will merge into one, and be the mighty force far beyond the paltry squad you envisioned, Justin.
– That is… good to hear, Justin said.
She smiled seductively to him and raised her glass.

After a short hesitation he did raise his glass as well. Glasses met and parted. The sound reverberated through flesh and air, and calm and feverish minds.

– The wedding ceremony will be great, mother, she said eagerly. – You will see! They will speak about it all over Arcadia, the Territories and beyond for generations to come.

She even sounded like Bea, she knew she did, before she had it confirmed by studying the others around the table.

– This veal has such a great taste, she said. – It is like it is begging me to be eaten, to be *consumed*.

That word, for some reason made a tear form in the corner of her eye.

The dining continued with its strange ways, both to her and her hosts. She hardly felt like a stranger at all and dominated the conversation, feeling very smug about it.

– I can recommend the Journey south, she said excited, filled with irresistible enthusiasm. – The terrain is so beautiful, so remote compared to our more civilized parts of the realm. I can imagine, just imagine why my great grandmother wanted to go there, to loose herself in the wilderness and ragged landscape.

She kept speaking, like the daughter of the house having returned home from an extended leave. They all looked at her for various reasons with darkened eyes.

It had turned fairly late when a servant led the two girls upstairs. Bea's room was at the end of the hall. It was big, spacey, so different from Janet's tiny closet at Myra's house.

The servant left them. The door closed behind her.

Janet made a prolonged yawn. It rose from deep in her spine and ended while her mouth slowly closed.

– You may undress me, now, apprentice.

Eleanor opened her mouth to speak, but only a squeak was heard. Pain edged lines in her face.

– Karmak is very disappointed with you, now, Janet said, – and so is your master.

Janet struck her, and she fell and hit the floor hard.

– In the following days I want you to observe the servants of this house closely, apprentice. They are so well behaved and attentive, such a standard to uphold.

Eleanor crouched on the floor, shaking in fright and shame. The Blue Flame knew she was listening and listening good.

– You may resume your duties, now.

The apprentice choked in relief and rose in a smooth movement, keeping her eyes down. She proceeded to comply with her master's initial command.

She had become skilled. Janet enjoyed her eager servitude, her soft, but fast movements.

– Well done, apprentice. You may feed, now.

The distressed girl complied, feeding herself the scraps on the plate she held in her left hand with a hunger delayed until desperation.

Janet climbed into the large bed. It felt so pleasant, like she was drowning in it. Eleanor already crouched on the carpet, moaning softly, already in the first throes of sleep, her entire self complying with the sorcerer's wishes.

Janet slept and writhed on the bed.

Bea and Janet walked down in the basement, the cave of their house, to the altar and the Ascension. It glowed and pulsed above them. They felt and recognized its power, and shivered in its presence. Janet put the Book of Fate on the altar.

– We can do this, Bea said. – Remember what Ione told you; it is safe to use the Ascension if you do not overstay your hand and try to reach for the Heights or some other lofty prize.

– I am not comfortable with doing this, Bea. I do not exactly enjoy myself down here, you know.

– We need to do this, Bea insisted, – need to put up wards, defenses against potential enemies striking at us. Everyone knows where we will be at a given point in seven short days, and it is not here, at our Place of Power, where we are at our strongest. I will wager that the dangerous and the craftiest of them will use the opportunity for everything it is worth. And who is better to use the power of the Ascension to her advantage than the Master of the Blue Flame?

Flatterer, Janet thought unprompted, feeling the heat of the other's admiration again.

– The sign on the wall, remember? It was a sigil, was sigil magick and has some very sinister properties. You are tense, on guard and right to be so. Enemies will strike when their targets expect it the least.

The sigil burning on the wall had burned her.

– And the attack on the heath. If Illandra had not acted swiftly and decisively then we would probably not *be* here at all.

Janet raised a hand, stopping her betrothed's tirade.

– You make good points. By Hel, it is my points, really. It is just that I do not…

A draft, something akin to a cold breath swept the altar and surrounding area.

– … like it down here.

They stood there, embracing the other, breathing together, their hearts beating as one.

– There is no escape, Cathy, Bea told her. – There never will be. The Blue Flame and her army will become powerful, become feared, even more, far more than she and they currently are and other powerful beings and groups of beings will do anything in order to thwart her Ascension. Accept your destiny. Embrace it!

Janet sniffed and nodded, in determination and growing anger.

– Will you help me help you, sweet witch?

– I will, Janet replied. – We do need to do it. If anything happened to you I would…

Bea's face lit up in quiet ecstasy.

– Hush, she whispered. – Hush…

They stood there for a while, a time without time.

Janet liberated herself reluctantly from her beloved and opened the Book of Fate, opened it on exactly the right page, doing so on her first attempt.

– «I whisper these words of malice and spite, and dream them true».

She shivered in a sudden cold spell, a strike on the senses only increasing in strength when she read, when she did whisper the words below.

– «I spite thee, world, a spite you so well deserve. I crucify people and leave them on the wood to hang, and return at night to admire my great work».

Bea joined in. They sounded like a choir at first, but then only as one, powerful voice.

– «The first approaching Enemy Mine I will treat nicely. I will give her/him/it a welcome for the ages. There will no end to my kindness».

Images, sensations began forming around them, erupting like a slow-moving stream.

Eleanor rolled sideways on the carpet, frantic, frightened and furious, eager like a dog on a leash to do her Master's bidding.

– «The second intrusion I will meet with steel and sharpened points. I will strike terror in the heart of everyone moving against me or considering moving against me. They will be like prey hiding and crouching in a dank cave».

Swords were drawn a thousand times. She heard them, as if it happened only a step or two away.

– «Arcadia is a fortress with no walls, reaching out to cover and covet the Ocean of Mankind. I possess this place of Ascension and Age, and use it for my gain. The dry and wet bones of my foes will become my throne».

Everyone in the house heard them. Illandra smiled, even as she bared her neck to the presence in their midst. The two below reached out, beyond the house, zooming in on the building quite a distance away, suddenly feeling like no distance at all. Words rose beneath the words, archaic and guttural and mighty. Janet of the Blue Flame heard them and spoke them, and Beatrice Maximus Rosen echoed them in perfect sync.

– «I take possession of this house of joy. Its walls will become the shield no one but I may break. Our path will become the trap of those wishing us harm. Sweet traps will ensnare them and subdue them and make them drown in the beautiful Dark River of our kingdom. I am the Dark River. I am the irresistible force moving in the night and I will not hesitate to utilize my might».

The words faded, but lingered. The power grew and multiplied. Janet closed the book, even as it did not wish to be closed. She let it go, even as sticky fingers held onto it.

The quiet storm fell silent, even as it kept raging. Bea stared at her with absolute astonishment and boundless love in her eyes.

Janet writhed on the bed in violent unrest. She rose on mighty wings, moving without moving. Bea slept on the bed they shared, whimpering, night terrors relentlessly rocking her.

Big Moon rose above the horizon, full and red. Blood flowed from it like a waterfall. The burning wheel formed in the sky, its hissing flames touching everything, burning everything it touched. Far out, at sea something unspeakable stirring for a long time erupted in water and wind, boiling above and below.

Janet awoke the next morning, soaked in sweat. When she after a few moments turned her head and looked at Eleanor the girl was already kneeling, looking up with a few anxious glances burning in worship. Janet ignored her, as she stumbled out on the floor, fighting all the way to the bathroom in order to keep her balance on unsteady legs. She knelt by the toilet bowl, managing that feat just as vomit flowed from her sore throat.

She drank lots of water afterwards and kept doing that when she had the shower. It was just her cleaning herself, none of the pleasure she usually associated with it.

Madge waited for her when she emerged from the bathroom.

– Good morning, the sweet older woman greeted her.

– Good morning, mother, Janet replied, somewhat coherent.

– Ah, I see you are just as grouchy in the morning as your betrothed. It was to be expected, I guess.

Janet did not respond.

Everything seemed off, nothing right.

– I took the liberty of selecting a choice of new, fitting attire for you. Please try it on.

The garments she had worn yesterday were nowhere to be seen. She shrugged and succumbed to the dominant will of her mother to be.

– The two of you are pretty much the same size, the woman prattled on, – so I would not really have had any trouble gauging your measurements, even without the timely assistance of the clan tailor who has offered you her wedding fits all week. But know that these and all the others we will procure for you are *your* clothes to own and use. I will send for our tailor later again, of course, to make everything a perfect fit, also when you start filling out.

Janet did not really listen to her. She stood before the mirror and felt and beheld her new self. With garments much closer to those Bea wore, she looked even more like her. A warm feeling of gratitude and disgust swept through her, as she touched the fabric and turned in front of the big mirror.

The two of them had breakfast alone later.

– I can not wait to show you off to my friends, Madge giggled, actually giggled a bit, a feat that made Janet stare incredulous at her. – It will be worth it just to see whether or not they will be fooled. Some of them will be, but not the sharpest of them. You are prettier than she is. You do not have her… rough edges.

Is that what you think? Janet thought glumly.

She had to rush to the bathroom not long after breakfast in order to vomit again, and she emerged from it pale and sweaty. Madge inspected her with concern in her eyes.

– You look fine, dear. Do not fear this unpleasantness will last. I had some trouble with it as well, but it did stop fairly soon, before becoming too troublesome.

– It is the smells, mother, the girl mumbled. – They are overwhelming. I thought my sense of smell was overwhelming before, but I had no idea.

– Yes, yes, Madge said distracted, while she dried a piece of vomit from the girl's jaw. – But remember that we are here for you, that we are all here for you. Everything will be fine.

She did Janet's hair, made it into the two braids very similar to the way Bea had had it fashioned when the two of them had first met.

James drove the two of them around the neighborhood that day and the next. Other drivers drove them on the mainland. Madge displayed Janet like a trophy. Some of the people they encountered were fooled, in spite of the difference in hair color and looks between Janet and Madge's daughter and of the persisting happy news and rumors, but others, with their sharp eyes and mind were not.

– Janet is of a long lost branch of the clan that has returned to us, Madge prattled on. – We have now two daughters instead of one. It is such a fortunate turn of events.

Others studied the young woman with curious and cruel eyes. Janet did not have to wonder if they knew what she was.

Nothing or very little was stated openly, but a lot was implied.

Her senses cried danger and she had to make an effort in order to not power up and expose herself completely to everybody.

She knew what this was.

Maria was there. That made sense to Janet. The girl had, after all served the Rosen and Maximus clans before, during the Samhain festivities. Janet had wondered about that and about her.

She remained the servant. Janet observed her. Observing her, it was not hard to see that she served a woman, one that clearly was one of Madge's confidants.

– Janet, over here, Madge called to her.

Janet heeded the call and walked to the three women standing a bit to themselves, in what was clearly a choice.

– Janet, Madge said, – this is Josela Martins.

Janet knew of her. She was one of the dominant players in the triple cities, owning several pleasure domes and other ventures.

– Greetings, My Lady, Janet curtseyed.

– Josela, may I present my future daughter, Janet Kathryn Caldwell.

– Greetings, Janet, Josela said, clearly amused. – Know that you do not have to pretend with me. I am far better informed than most other citizens, including those gathered here today. The best way you may show respect is to acknowledge that, and I will aid you by not blurting out your full row of names.

– Very well, Josela of the Martins, Janet straightened.

– You are such an interesting person, Janet, Josela kept going her one way speech. – Maria here has so much good and so many interesting things to say about you.

Maria stood there with lowered eyes, not really present, behaving very much like an underling, a servant.

– You want to ask me something? Josela told Janet. – You are curious, are you not?

– Maria has powers, Janet said slowly. – But she is not a mage or a sorcerer…

– Maria's clan has been serving mine for centuries, Josela said, very smug. – Her ancestors were bound to mine, and thus it has been since.

Janet looked flustered at her, with sudden sweat covering her forehead.

Maria was not a servant. She was a slave, trained from birth to serve the Martins clan unconditionally.

Janet could not keep herself from shaking.

– You are well read, are you not, and know the lore?

Janet heard her voice as if through water. She finally managed an abrupt nod.

– But young and naive as you still are, in spite of everything you have experienced, you had not truly considered the significance of that particular knowledge.

Janet did not voice a reply or respond in any other visible way.

She wanted very much to reveal herself, to show Josela and everyone else present what she truly was. The first blue flames manifested around her fingers, those no one but her was able to see. She remained in her passive and irresponsive mode.

– You are a very beautiful girl, Josela said. – I look so much forward to your wedding.

She was invited, of course.

– Thank you, Janet heard herself say.

She knew people could not tell her state of mind by watching her. Her surface remained calm. She walked among them with impunity. They did not truly see her. Chaos kept ravaging her insides and she could not quite keep it together. She stood on the balcony watching the vast estate surrounded by fences without really knowing exactly how she had arrived there. Vacant eyes stared at the well kept garden. The invisible flames on her hands kept flaring. Blood kept boiling in her veins.

A man approached her from behind. She turned just as he stepped out on the balcony.

He approached her in a non-threatening way, and that told her something about him.

– So, Janet, are you enjoying yourself?

He asked casually.

They had not met or spoken before. She did not know him. He did not present himself, and used only her given name. It was not an insult in all situations among strangers and in the sorcerer community, but it could be. It was the way a child or a close friend was usually addressed.

– I know what you mean, sire, Janet said, playing the insecure young girl to a point. – My guess is that these get-togethers can be quite boring for most, but I have no trouble seeing that the Rosen and Maximus clans have such an interesting gathering of acquaintances in their circles.

She read a shadow… a different face on his face, similar in a way, she surmised to her tattoos. His second face looked at her with its wicked, wicked eyes. He was indeed a sorcerer.

– You have made quite an impression, young lady, he said offhand, in quite the friendly manner, – but nothing compared, I suspect to what you will eventually do. Your reputation is certainly not unwarranted. I, for one look very much forward to that day and that night.

He faded away like mist. It was not that she could not see him leave. She could, but she still could not get a grasp on him. The deliberate shrug did indeed look strained, she knew it did.

– You are upset.

– Huh?

She looked around her, and realized that she sat in the car with Madge, on their way back to the Rosen land.

– I can tell, Madge said, – just like I can tell when Beatrice is. You both wear your emotions completely in the open, easy to read.

– You are correct, mother, Janet said and bowed her head. – I can not help myself. They are a cold, callous crowd.

– You are young yet, Madge said softly, – and new to our ways. You will learn.

The young girl, the Rosen past and future sat cross-legged in her room, attempting meditation, in an attempt at calming herself, her shaking insides.

It did not work. She could not even reach a modicum of calm.

She struck out with her hand, releasing waves in all directions, without control. The big glass of water on the table shook. She struck out with her other hand, replaying the previous event. It did not work. She sat still for ages. It did not work. Her eyes would not close, not for more than a moment at the time. She could not free herself from her surroundings.

Justin took her on a guided tour in the hallway of portraits and lineage. It was a considerable stretch of wall.

– The story of our clan goes way back, before the first English and even the first Spanish and Portuguese arrived here.

She looked at the portraits, and the meticulous lines of Lineage. Bea was one end. She was another. John was a third. There were others. Jenny, her Rosen great grandmother and eventually a tribal member of the Bone People was the sister of Bea's great grandfather. One of his daughters, like Bea's avatar on the board, had a red cross attached to it. There were others. They were demon hunters and more.

– You guys are really serious about this? Janet said.

– It is the driving force of our lives, Justin nodded. – It should be in yours as well. Your mother and Illandra most certainly have a lot of facts to contribute to your lineage.

– It is all in the book, Janet shrugged, – in the Book of Fate, not always instantly discernible, but There.

His eyes lit up like stars. He and Bea had the same eyes.

– You have no doubt asked yourself how it would have been for you to grow up here, in this house and in the clans, like she did. Today and tonight and in the coming days and nights, you will get even more of an idea of how it was.

– I already know how it is. You all look at me with your dark clouds, in a continued attempt at putting me down, controlling me. This house smothers me, strangling me like a heavy blanket, exactly like it does her.

He smiled.

– The two of you are remarkably similar, you know, and I do not mean in appearance only. We have felt compelled to rub our eyes in disbelief several times during your thus far brief visit.

– John has made considerable headway on his growth while he was away at those small villages down south, she said casually. – You have most certainly been on the right track all these centuries. The deal you made was worth it.

Now, there was a reaction in his big eyes.

– Bea has told me your secrets, all the clan secrets. She has hardly shut up about it.

He smiled.

– It is just as well that you know, he said. – It will make everything easier, make it even easier for you to become one with them all, to be their keeper.

She sensed frustration in him, but that did not rock his confidence.
That did not either. He kept speaking, both in her ears and her extended awareness, knowing well what kind of effect he had on her.

– I have considerable training in military and counter-intelligence operations. Hers, being what she is, is even more extensive. It is a remnant from the time of our ancestors when war and strife ravaged our existence. She will focus on that and will be your arm, like the others will be your fingers, allowing you to focus on what truly matters.

He was so… elegant, intense and articulate. She frowned and did not care if he noticed.

– I love her, father, she said subdued, – love her so much that it hurts being away from her.

– But you do, anyway, making the sacrifice because she asked you to do it.

She nodded meekly.

He reached out with a hand, touching her cheek in a comforting gesture. It was not surprising to her when he stepped closer, stepped close.

– I can not fuck you, father, she said with a hollow voice. – That will be the one thing she will never forgive me for doing.

They stood there, facing each other briefly.

She turned and left him there, in the long hallway.

She walked back, all the way to the house on the hill, taking her time, not really in a hurry. It felt good, and while she did so, her calm returned somewhat. The walk did for her what continued efforts at meditation had not done.

The warm wind played with her hair and skin, her good mood slowly resurfacing and expressing itself. Her legs, feeling weak all day regained their agility.

Eleanor walked close to her, sometimes by her side, sometimes behind.

– It is such a great day, is it not?

– It is, Master, the apprentice nodded empathically, unable to hide her joy, her enthusiasm.

Janet chuckled and hummed, all the way back to the house on the hill.

Bea waited for her on the porch.

– I jumped from the balcony, she informed her beloved with a happy glee. – I felt a burning need to greet you out here, and not a second later.

They embraced quietly. A somber quality appeared on Janet's face.

– You were right about them, Janet sniffed, gritting her teeth, focusing hard on keeping herself from stuttering. – I actually think they might be worse than you described, though.

– I was pretty confident that would be your conclusion, Bea said lightly.

Janet grabbed her hands, clutching them and kissing them fiercely.

– I think perhaps our enemies are far closer than we thought, Janet hissed, – at least some of them.

– I think so, too, Bea agreed.

– They will be there when we exchange our vows, Janet snarled.

– Let them, Bea shrugged. – Let them watch our happiness, our dedication to each other.

Janet pondered that for one heartbeat, two, before nodding.

They walked inside, with yet another unspoken agreement between them.

Janet noticed something, a disturbance the instant her feet touched the floor.

– The house has…acted up in your absence. Without its master present, it becomes wily and wicked against any other inhabitant. It serves you and does not care that much for the rest of us.

– Has anything happened? Janet said stricken.

– Something has. Hands grew out of the walls and grabbed Livy. We managed to get her free, though, by coaxing and beseeching the house. My guess is that it wanted to eat her.

– It did. Janet frowned. – It is a hungry *beast.*

– Thank the gods that its master will be here to protect the rest of us then, shield us from its unsavory appetites.

– You are so funny. Janet shook her head. – So very, very funny…

They waited for her in the living room, at the center of her Place of Power, with today's main meal and their affection. The catching in her throat grew hard and sore.

She sought out Illandra later, in a fairly calm moment

– I wonder if anything is wrong… with me, Janet said, going straight to the point. – Have you noticed anything, anything at all?

Illandra did frown and look concerned at her.

– Just the fact that you say that is cause for concern, grandmother said. – Stand still!

Janet did. Illandra surveyed her, probed her and gave her a thorough examination. Janet's skin tingled.

Illandra eventually shook her head.

– I can not find anything, she said, - nothing conclusive, but there is something, the same delocalized danger we have discussed before. Promise me you come to me if anything seems off, no matter how trivial it may be.

– I promise, grandmother, Janet said. – Thank you!

She kissed the older woman on the cheek and ran off, returning to Bea.

It did keep her awake a little bit longer that night. She lay still by Bea's side and listened hard to everything surrounding her. The house never stayed quiet, but there was nothing uncommon, nothing she could pinpoint.

The preparations for the exchange of vows kept her busy during the last few days and nights before the big day, no matter how much Rosa kept running things and took the load off the two main participants. The excitement kept surging, and everyone was caught in its inevitable maelstrom.

They returned to Circle of Nine the night before the day. The living room of the house on the hill changed into the busy and noisy tavern, and sometimes Janet was tempted to believe they had not physically moved at all. Everything just flowed from one moment of engaging exhilaration to the other, and she felt how she was carried away, allowing herself to enjoy fully the ongoing celebrations.

– We will drink a lot before, during and after the upcoming great festivities, Bea declared. – Let us have a toast or ten to all the great things in our lives.

Muted, but happy cheers accompanied and followed her words. Dark moody music swept them and the room and everyone in it in equal measure.

Janet looked at her, beyond devoted. They all drank.

It was later, feeling like much later.

– To the great things in our lives, Toby raised his glass.

They all drank.

The mood rose in her, just as certain as the drink descended into her depths. She saw Bea's face only in glimpses, in pieces. She reached for her, pulling her close, clutching her in stark desperation. Bea chuckled softly and comforted her in her distress.

– Tomorrow?

– Tomorrow is far away. Time is now.

Soft lips met hers, met hers a thousand times.

– To… Rosa made a failed attempt at speaking. – To the great things in our lives.

She sniveled.

They all drank.

– To the lovely couple, Jess cried.

Janet and Bea beamed at him.

The evening passed, passed away. People walked through the passages, walked back and forth in a seemingly endless stream, one both slow and fast.

Janet frowned, unable to catch the strange dichotomy suddenly haunting her. People passed the passages outside, on the street. Janet watched them, their wicked eyes.

Bea took another huge, excessive sip of her glass. Janet cast worried glances at her, unable to help herself.

– Do not fear for me, Bea whispered in her ear sometimes later. – I am exactly where I am supposed to be.

They did not truly get drunk, not on the fairly modest intake of alcohol, anyway. They kept riding the elevated state of consciousness. It lingered and grew within and without.

There was… something invading the room.

Dissociation continued to haunt Janet. She sat around the able. She found herself outside in the street, among the many wicked eyes. There was no fixed point she could focus on.

– I am not here, Eleanor said abruptly, with a detached expression in her eyes.

Most of those present looked incredulous at her, not getting it at first. Janet, however, did.

– This can not be happening, Eleanor said with Janet's voice. – I am not here, not there or anywhere. I do not know where I am.

All of them nodded to themselves, not looking at Eleanor, but at Janet.

Janet felt Bea's hand on her cheek, a comforting touch in the confusion marring her.

– It is your power, Bea said. – It makes your perception exist in a state of constant drift.

Janet sat there struggling with it, really struggling with it for a while, feeling totally dislocated, drifting aimlessly through the Void.

Until she suddenly returned, and the table and the flesh she touched, the smile on her face once more felt solid, felt real.

When she touched each hand, each face close to her, it was as if it was actually there and not far away. That conviction persisted later, when she made her way to the bathroom. Foreign people and sensations surrounded her on all sides, but she sensed the presence of the guys and the guard.

We will always be there for you, Eleanor formulated, somewhat coherent in her increasingly intoxicated mind.

A warm, warm glow burned pleasantly the sorcerer's flesh as she stumbled on the last few steps to the toilet bowl, and as she sat down on the cold seat and it chilled her skin.

The four walls moved around her. Everything moved.

The mirror outside the door moved and stretched, becoming the entire room, the entire three-dimensional space.

She appeared back in the hallway, and he stood there, waiting for her, just as she had known he would.

Jess of the Orchards looked red-faced and embarrassed at her.

– I have been… recalled, he said exasperated. – It is no big thing, except by its ill timing. They do this all the time, in order to keep me on their leash.

– You should go, she said softly, faking her reaction, hiding her contempt, – pretending their authority means anything to you, savoring the just reward you one day will serve them.

– Yes, he cried out, grabbing and kissing her hands, the tiny rescue she kindly dangled in front of him. – Yes!

He was gone, from her attention and her mind.

Something happened as she made her way back to the others, to those loyal to her above else. A sensation grabbed her.

Eleanor rushed forward to greet her, excitement brightening her eyes more than her childhood friend had ever seen.

The room buzzed with excited and alarmed voices. Janet understood, realized what was happening before she saw the ale and water and many types of fluids and vapor float in the air. Several males and females coughed and coughed hard, as fluids were drained from their bodies.

– I felt… light, Master, Eleanor said brightly, – and dizzy, and then…

It was her power. It had manifested in a quiet moment without stress and expense and attempted focus. Janet mirrored the apprentice's wide grin.

The manifestations faded. She gained a modicum of control, enough to stop what she was doing. The various precious fluids stopped floating and leaving people's body, stopped killing them.

– My spirit quest is seriously approaching, then? Eleanor wondered with sizzling hope in her voice and full body expression.

– It seriously is, her master confirmed.

– This calls for a celebration, does it not? Dane joked.

A few at the neighboring tables looked curiously at him, at them, probably wondering if it was possible to «celebrate» more than they were already doing.

But as the celebration continued, with Janet and Eleanor being happier than ever, the people on the neighboring tables and more were drawn in, enticed by the joy and passion burning at that particular perceived set of center tables. The number of toasts and cheers picked up significantly, the glasses raised high above heads too many to be counted. Blobs of light and shadow formed and spread in the room, underexposed and overexposed frozen and moving images slipping in and out of Janet's consciousness.

They were walking, stumbling down and up countless streets with unknown people, toasting with them, as if they were old friends. Flesh, brick and mortar merged in Janet's mindscape, becoming one and the same.

– TOMORROW, they sang and howled, – TOMORROW IS ANOTHER DAY… IF TOMORROW COMES.

They fell asleep on couches in a big, unknown house somewhere, stretching their bodies and minds with happy and content grins.

Janet woke up in such a place, as the first stirrings of dawn flooded the hall. She stretched and yawned happily. Bea slept by her side, and woke up just a few heartbeats after her.

Her knees below the skirt-line were bruised, dirty and bloody.

Bea's were not. They were unblemished, clean.

Janet shrugged and leaned over and gave her betrothed a morning kiss. Bea returned it, equally affectionate.

Bea slipped into sleep again, innocent like a baby, but Janet was unable to do that. She frowned and subconsciously and consciously reached out with her power.

There was a large window to her right. She looked through it without moving, at buildings and streets on the edge of Auburn, at its far southern and eastern point. The sound of waves, of waves striking the shore echoed in her ears.

And beyond that other waves echoed in her mind, doing so with increased frequency and power.

She shook Bea awake again.

– Come with me! She called eagerly.

Bea shook her head a little, before smiling, before joining her Companion-to-be on the floor.

They walked outside, in the sharp morning air.

– This is weird, Bea mused. – I do not think I have ever been to these parts of town before, not ever.

The waves striking the shore grew louder, turning to music in Janet's head.

– Can you hear it? She practically hissed in her excitement. – Can you hear the music?

Bea frowned. Then her face cracked in an excited smile.

– I can! *I can!*

They started rushing forward, and not before long they were running. Buildings and houses faded away around them.

They stood on the southern and eastern point of the Island, casting their eyes and attention out at the vast sea. There were no more islands or reeves or islets in this direction, only the vast, vast sea.

Somewhere out there, at a fixed point their eyes could not spot, Jupiter's Cauldron was acting up, whipping up a storm. Dry water wet their skin.

– I feel it! Janet shouted. – It is unequalled, more powerful than the Ascension or anything, anywhere.

Bea did not speak. She seemed to be struck mute.

– The Cauldron does not actually speak. It is just noise, perceivable chaos, but still seething with power that might be caught and utilized.

Hand found hand and held on, held on for dear life.

They stood there for a very long time, silent, struck with equal parts awe and terror.

Chapter 23

The companions-to-be and the maids gathered before the mirror again.

Janet Kathryn Caldwell and Beatrice Maximus Rosen, soon to exchange vows stood in front of the mirror in the old house at Altram Hill.

They tried out and fit the final selections of wedding garments. Eleanor, Livy, Rosa and Joan stood around them, gawking. The two Companions-to-be did not really change their minds with one final tryout, and ended up with the same outfit and appearance they had decided upon earlier, the totally identical robe and the hood, the same hairdo and everything.

Janet had bandaged knees camouflaged as clothing… and so had Bea.

Nothing, or almost nothing, made them look different from each other.

– It is funny, Bea said. – I still feel like time is crawling.

She began painting pale, almost invisible tattoos on her face matching the invisible Janet had been born with. Janet focused on making them visible to her while she did the work. Janet painted herself, painted visible tattoos on her face as well, copying the invisible.

They stood side by side in front of the mirror afterwards, their differences even less, their similarities even more pronounced.

– This suits you, Bea stated with conviction.

– It suits you! Janet grinned with love in her eyes.

– This is so fitting, Bea said. – We are one!

One, Janet breathed.

The rather large group of people began their migration, leaving the house on the hill and making their way down the road. The companions-to-be and their four maids sat in the slow-moving car with its open windows, and the rest walked on both sides of it, like an honor guard.

The warm, pleasant air filled the car, the draft just about strong enough to make the passengers sweat less than those bathing in the burning light of the daystar.

The wheels turned and those inside and outside the car breathed in sync with them.

There were two distinct shadows on the ground on this day, one weak and one strong. Big Moon paired with the daystar, resting in the opposite horizon, visibly glowing in the middle of the day.

– We are the Children of the Moon, Livy said excitedly. – Even when the daystar reigns supreme it is still there for us.

The dichotomy created a strange twilight in the shadows, one even visible in the most powerful daystar light.

In blinks and flashes, for just a few moments Janet saw Big Moon turn red. She saw it swallow the daystar and turn day into night.

People watched the procession, watched it closely, while still attempting to not reveal their attention openly. Janet spotted a stumbling old woman as she reached the main road. A shadow covered her frame. She looked bewildered and lost.

The car turned a corner and Janet could see her no more.

– You will be *so* pleased! Rosa said with a very smug grin. – I am so confident about that fact that I am willing to bet that you will declare me your omnipotent queen for at least a year.

– NO BET! Bea and Janet choired.

The car made a turn into the better public road. The man with the horns stood there, turning Janet frantic.

– Stop the car, she shouted. – STOP THE CAR!

The car stopped. Janet had looked away for a moment, just a tiny moment, but when she looked again the man was gone. She looked at the others in the car and those outside looking inside with concern with crazy eyes.

– He was t-there, she stuttered. – He stood there, s-staring at m-me.

Bea rubbed her back, steadily back and forth, slowly calming her down.

– Okay? She said gently after some time.

Janet nodded with a determined and furious look in the violet eyes. She nodded again.

– Drive, Bea ordered James casually.

He did, with the same gentle treatment of the engine. It hardly felt like the car was accelerating at all.

The hot wind warmed them, chasing off chilling thoughts. The turning of the wheels had a soothing effect on twitchy nerves.

Janet, remaining off-center, sat there twitching, picking on dust on her robe, even when there was clearly no dust left. She fought to conceal the flickering glance in her eyes. Rosa looked concerned at her and that in turn made everyone else look concerned at her as well.

– Sorry, she apologized. – It is not just that… man. I just can not… can not relax, you know.

– I wonder why, Rosa joked.

Janet laughed, and relieved, the rest did as well.

Bea held Janet's hand, rubbing her palm, and it eventually made her feel so wonderfully relaxed, made her close her eyes halfway and enjoy the rhythm of the movement.

She looked, with those half closed eyes at what seemed more and more like her mirror image. Only the eyes told a distinctly different story.

– This is a good day, she emphasized. – This is a very good day. No one shall be allowed to ruin it. *No one!*

Others including Bea, especially Bea mouthed her oath.

Today's route was quite familiar to her, but it still seemed different, different today. The turn ahead did not look quite like it had the previous time she had passed here. The house on the left had been white and was now green, pale green. The frown cut deep, no matter how hard she fought against that happening.

And then, as if prophesized she got dizzy. It was like the car tumbled over, or was about to.

– Damn, nausea… is…

She stopped, making fists of her hands in fierce resolve.

– What else is new? Bea joked glumly. – It would be too much of a good thing if we avoided it today, I guess.

– No, not that. This is… different. It is as if the car is tilting, driving on two wheels or something. My… balance is way off. I doubt that I could stand up.

– I will support you, Bea said with that endearing look Janet loved so much.

The dizziness faded slowly. The car moved forward in a normal manner and not like it drove through a forty-five degrees curve anymore.

Images, never that distinct faded in her mind, and she could not retrieve them, no matter how hard she tried.

She made a concerted attempt. The more she tried, the more the impressions seemed to slip away, beyond her reach.

More than one group of waving people had placed themselves along the route. It made Bea and Janet inadvertently smile to each other.

– The secret is out, Bea shrugged. – That was inevitable, too.

The crowds grew even bigger as they approached the familiar building. The car drove into the yard and eventually stopped in front of the main entrance. They stepped outside in the warm, warm day. A cheer rose from the crowds. They kept their distance, were not intrusive, or at least not excessively so. Bea and Janet, in their mounting joy waved.

One crowd was distinctly different from the rest. Several of them held up big posters. One in particular caught Janet's attention.

THE ROSENS AND MAXIMUSES ARE A PLAGUE
A DRAIN ON OUR SOCIETY

– Do not mind them, Bea shrugged.

– I do not! Janet assured her.

– Sometimes commoners can get it right, though.

– They can? Janet blinked. – You think so?
– Of course I think so, Bea said empathically. – Have you not been paying attention?
Janet nodded, not quite pleased with that, and nodded again.
– My guess, Bea said, – is that you have not spoken up, or not spoken up as much as you wished in a misguided desire to «shelter» me, but let me assure you that we are on the same page on this, on this as well. We will change things, shake them up until we have spit on all or almost all our ancestors…
Janet squealed in delight and embraced her, the impulsive huge smile painted on her face.
The big, heavy doors stood open, wide open, welcoming them. They walked inside.
– You just walk down and take a look, Rosa said, the adult, practical ceremonial master. – The rest of us still have a million things to do. You just relax and enjoy everything. *Please* do!
They grinned at her in gratitude, and waved to the guys and the guard as they, in accordance with Rosa's strict orders slowly and pleasantly, without stress descended the stairs.
– She is clever, Bea acknowledged, – leaving us in peace to do our thing.
They made their way down the darkened hallway. Janet started humming with the smile on her face growing even wider.
– You are humming our song, Bea marveled. – That is so cute!
She joined in. Janet felt it as she did. Their auras, always touching and humming together, spread to fill the shadowy space.
Janet frowned, a bit puzzled.
– Your power is clearly growing, she insisted. – You should not be able to do that. You would not have been just a little while ago.
– If it is, I have you to thank for that. Your encouragement and comradeship have meant the world to me.
Stars twinkled in Bea's eyes.
– I, myself do not feel so good, Janet said with frustration in her voice. – As I said, it is not just the morning sickness. I do not know what is wrong with me.
– We will find out, Bea said, visibly concerned. – You have indeed been a bit under the weather for quite some time. We will take you to advanced health-workers, experienced sorcerers far better than overrated Illandra and whoever can help us find out what is ailing you. If someone is doing this to you, they will pay dearly for it, pay a thousand times.
Now, it was Janet turn to look at Bea with puppy-look eyes.
The two companions-to-be reached the open door to the fairly small hall.

They stopped on the threshold, taking it all in.

Two mouths opened and stayed open in wonder.

The hall had not been that much changed. They still sort of recognized it.

– This is…

– This is…

– That is certainly one for your clan's carpenters, Janet whispered.

– And Rosa's design, Bea said exalted.

It resembled a place of worship and magick with its decorations and changed general appearance.

It… welcomed them.

– I did not think she had it in her.

– I did, Janet said, – but this is the best I have seen her do.

– To be able to create something like this…

Bea shook her head in wonder.

There was something, something in her eyes that made Janet look closer at her.

But then, a moment later it was gone.

– Not long to wait, now, Bea said with her sweet and blinding smile.

– We have been so patient, Janet agreed, – but now the wait is done.

They held hands, facing each other. They spoke as one. Spells flowed from their lips. The room changed further, into a fortress that only a few would notice.

– That was easy enough, Janet noted. – I sense no fatigue, no drop in my physical or mental performance.

She shook her head, dismissing her worry, focusing on the radiant girl in her arms.

– We can not do anything with those within the fortification, Janet said, – but this will keep everyone else out, the only exception is if any of the gods decide to return from their long exile.

– My firm conviction is that even they will hesitate before fucking with Queen Cathy and her Guard, Bea grinned, always in an upbeat mood.

More lovesick looks were exchanged. There seemed to be no end to them. Two pair of eyes twinkled and twinkled and twinkled. They both giggled softly, as they broke physical contact.

– Letting go feels like…

– … feels like death.

They choired.

Unable to tell who had started the sentence and who had completed it.

Janet smiled to herself.

They heard the steps from the hallway, heard them grow steadily louder and turned towards the sound. A woman appeared in the door. The lone figure stood before the wide opening. They recognized their former teacher, in her scandalous modern Roman toga.

– I thought I would find the two of you here early, she said.

– We like to take things slow, Gaia Ofolus, Bea said lightly, – to have much time on our hands doing both important and unimportant things.

– That is funny, Gaia said. – I always saw the two of you as fundamentally impatient.

The two teens exchanged secret smiles again.

– You have clearly learned to enjoy life, the older woman said. – That is twice the feat when it comes to both of you.

They nodded solemnly, knowing exactly what she was hinting at.

– I have always counted you among my brightest students. When do you plan on returning?

– We are not, Gaia Ofolus, Janet stated. – Our days of public learning are done.

– I thought as much. You have long since found other avenues to explore. I envy you!

She was good at this, at hinting, and still making herself understood.

– Rosa was always great at decorating. I would presume that her public learning is also in the past?

It was not a question. They did not voice a reply.

– It was great meeting you here, Gaia Ofolus, Bea said. – I am afraid we must prepare further. Time is nigh!

– Do not fret, dear. Rest assured that I appreciate the invitation, though, and that I will be here.

Madge had issued the invitations, of course, both to Gaia and her influential father. The two young women kept a straight face.

She left them, very courteous. They forgot about her, even as the sound of her steps faded away in their ears.

– I think she does envy us, Bea said patronizingly. – She has always yearned to take the more decisive steps out of her father's shadow, doing so beyond the few, paltry moves she has made.

They walked to the altar, lighting the big candles there. There was one color for each candle, combining to brighten the shadows in this part of the hall.

– We light these candles, they choired. – We light them to illuminate the path for ourselves and others, in this realm, and others close and far away.

They both stepped back.

– This is so right, Bea said.

– So very right, Janet echoed.

– A chill is trickling down my spine, Bea said.

– Thank the Goddess, Janet sighed relieved. – I thought I was the only one with second thoughts.

– It is a happy trickle, Bea grinned deviously.

They kept quiet for a while, grinning happily at each other.

The fires, all the fires in the hall began rising, stretching, brightening, darkening the very air they breathed.

– Can you hear it, beloved? They are playing our song.

She could, even before the first chords of the choir began echoing through the hall and hallway. The two of them turned and walked through the door, into the hallway, where the four maids waited with eager smiles.

Rosa and Eleanor took Janet's hands. Joan and Livy took Bea's, leading them away.

There were two smaller rooms at the other side of the dark trail. Janet was brought into one and Bea into the other.

Myra waited for Janet, like Justin and Madge waited for Bea.

The pleasant, pervasive heat smothered Janet.

Rosa and Eleanor quietly left them and closed the door.

– Look at you, Myra said softly.

And Myra did look at her. Janet felt the act warm her and prickle her skin and the edge of her thoughts in a way she knew Bea's parents could never do for Bea.

– You have grown up. Through hardship, passion and strife you have found the first major pieces of yourself. Welcome, o'witch of the Blue Flame.

Myra touched the violet jewel. Janet felt it, a charge burning her veins and skin and mind alike.

– Has the Blue Flame always skipped generations?

The question burned on her lips.

– No, her mother said, accommodating her curiosity. – It used to manifest in every single child born to us. We were many once, like the Bone People, very much like them.

– Now, there is one being both, Janet stated.

– Yes, Myra said, – there is. Finally, there is!

She tied little ribbons in Janet's hair, and a chain of rope bracelets around her right arm. Janet stood there and allowed herself to be fuzzed over.

– I remember so little of father. How was he like?

Myra paused a little in her chores, brushing hair from Janet's forehead.

– He was strong, powerful, going his own ways, no matter what tradition and clan demanded of him. He sacrificed himself so you could live.

A hard catch grew in Janet's throat.

– But *why?* You could have gone anywhere, into the territories and even other realms.

– Your place is here, Myra said quietly. – He knew that.

The sore feeling did not go away, but Janet nodded in something at least resembling understanding.

She wanted to say more, but held her tongue, hiding her anger and resentment and her further knowledge of the subject, exposing only her anguish. Myra fuzzed a little more. Janet let her. She studied Myra with suspicion on her mind, but saw nothing there reminding her of the very different Myra that had stood outside her cage before her savage mating with John Maximus Rosen.

There was a knock on the door. Myra walked there and opened it. Bea stood there with the four maids behind her. The four giggled in happiness and anticipation.

– You will now spend your final hours unbound in contemplation, Myra said, – until you reveal yourself to our clans, to the realm, to all realms as One.

There was something in her voice and expression, something in the wording beyond the words. Janet pondered it briefly, before losing herself in Bea's eyes and presence.

Mother and the maids left, closing the door behind them.

Bea was visibly upset. She did not attempt to hide it either, but hid what Janet suspected was the deeper wound, and that hurt a little, no matter how much Janet understood or strived to understand.

Bea allowed Janet to fuzz over her, just a little withdrawn. They stood close, once more breathing each other's air and fragrant. Janet felt how Bea slowly returned to her cheery self.

– Do not let them bother you, Bea said. – I do not, at least not for long, not beyond the moment.

– I understand. Janet nodded. – Just remember that you are not alone with your burden anymore.

– I will, Bea stated. – Remember that you are not either.

– I will!

Janet nodded empathically and somberly.

They sat down and held hands, while the activity slowly picked up outside their little space.

– I kind of like this particular tradition, Bea said. – The two companions-to-be spend an entire afternoon together with nothing but themselves as company.

– It is the final chance to pull out with dignity, Janet said. – The moment we leave here, we will have to do so in full scrutiny of our clans and curious strangers.

– That is true. When you wed into the Rosen and Maximus clans you join their entire, sinister network.

The bitterness was still there, no matter the levity, how much she attempted to hide it.

Time went away for them, as it often did, but they noticed bits and pieces of what went on outside their bubble. Without really making a conscious decision about it, Janet reached out with her waves, made them flow the hallway and the hall. People gathered. They sat down in chairs facing the altar. Illandra walked up there, making her own preparations with spells and incense. Janet noticed how some in the gathering reacted to it, frowning, not exactly hiding their aversion.

The two of them rose, making themselves ready. It would not be long, now. They fuzzed over each other more than a little, «correcting» some arrangements here and there. Janet got a remote look in her eyes, as she got momentarily distracted.

– What is it? Bea wondered, noticing easily the other's slight change of mood.

– I would have thought Jason would be here and he is not. I would have sensed him if he was.

– Jason? Bea frowned.

– The Wanderer, Janet said in a hushed voice.

Bea thought about it for a few seconds, before her expression of awe changed into a shrug.

– All guys are the same, you know that.

Janet chuckled, the laughter once more coming easy. The puzzled look in her eyes remained.

– We never told anyone, except the guys about him, you know, about his connection with me, with us both, and as unlikely as that is, neither Illandra nor Ione or anyone else found out, not during all the time we spent under their wings, their scrutiny and «care».

The last word was spat out, like a curse.

– It is our secret, Bea said.

Our secret, Janet breathed in agreement.

There was the expected knock on the door.

– Enter! Janet called.

The door opened. Four giggling maids stood outside.

– Janet Kathryn Caldwell and Beatrice Maximus Rosen, Rosa called out. – Please allow us to escort you the final stretch to your happiest of moments.

The two of them stepped outside. They were grabbed gently in both arms and led away across the Abyss to the other side of the frothing river.

The small procession entered the hall. The maids walked left and right of both the two companions-to-be. The elevated mood of the gathering struck them all.

She had been correct. Jason was not here. Janet did not see or sense him, and she knew she would.

John and Jess also brightened the event with their absence.

A thrill of excitement surged through Janet, through Bea, as they spotted Illandra at the elevated stage, in front of the altar.

Zoe began playing the flute, playing haunting music reminding everyone present of times long gone. Loewe played the drum. No one else played anything, but Janet still imagined the other music, the other drums, the choir rising from the Dark River itself. Goose bumps erupted on her exposed skin. Bea noticed and once again squeezed her hand in a comforting gesture.

– I do not know what is wrong with me, Janet whispered. – I do not get stage fright or anything. Not ever!

– We, you do, now! Bea grinned affectionately.

They walked to the altar, where the High Priestess awaited them, on a carpet, a path decorated with flowers and vines and wild growth. The wild growth stretched and moved around their feet and that and the guests' reactions made Janet feel good, very good.

The flute and the drum faded. The two and four stood before Illandra of the Territories, Illandra of the Josbari, of the Bone People. They bowed their heads in her presence, Janet and Bea doing so only briefly, hardly noticeable before holding their heads high.

– Janet Kathryn Caldwell and Beatrice Maximus Rosen, is it your intention to become Companions, to join with the other in Life, Death and Eternity?

– It is, Honored One, they choired.

– And your clans approve of this union?

– They do!

You would know, Janet thought a little naughty.

– You have requested the age-old ritual. Do you insist on this?

– We do!

– Then, by the power of my birth and before the witnesses and the gods I will wed you, tie you together in a union no one but the two of you may break.

She raised her arms, stretching them to her sides, thumbs and index fingers connecting. The humming, the words of spells flowed effortlessly from her lips. Her face changed, becoming cast in Shadow. Arcane energies flowed from her and cut into them. They felt it as it happened and continued happening.

They gasped in joy and pain, shaking like rag dolls, and just as helpless. Janet glimpsed indistinct faces watching it all from afar, their shock and interest.

– Your hands, give them to me, Illandra snapped.

One gave her the left hand, the other the right, those closest to the other. The sorcerer grabbed them and held them both in one grip. She bent down and picked up the knife, the glowing blade from the altar. She made the incisions in the wrists, making the blood flow. Then she pushed them together and squeezed.

– Sisters in spirit, join in blood, in mind and Shadow.

Blood flowed from both and into both, from the other. They felt it, a beyond poignant sensation, a burning that spread from their lower arms to the shoulder and to the entire body. Blood joined, mind joined, Shadow joined. Those watching saw two dark shapes materialize and mix, and the two saw it with them. The process continued relentlessly and made sweat flow from their brow.

– Recite your vows, give voice to your dedication.

She let go of the wrists, wrists falling down, but not separating, staying glued skin to skin.

Words, practically unprompted started flowing from wet lips in perfect sync.

– What is mine is yours. What is yours is mine. I give myself unconditionally to you. I take you as mine for all time. I do not end with myself, but with you. I do not know and do not want to know where I end and you begin. There is no need, no desire beyond that. We are One!

They kept gasping, heaving for breath, as throbs of happiness kept surging through them.

Wrists glued together broke contact. Hands fell down. Only a tattoo that seemed to have always been there marked what had been.

Toby, Dane and Fran joined those on the stage.

– Nine, Illandra said, – you are nine. Dance, companions that will soon be, depart and return to each other.

The drum began beating again, very slow, with its beats far apart. Its sound still lingered, like with a gong, reflected from the floor, the deep, dark floor. It rumbled deep below it and in their warm, warm bones.

The happy smiles stayed on the two's faces as they parted, as they began swaying and dancing on the small stage, before the altar of their dreams.

Janet felt like she was flying. Extremely light on her feet, in her euphoria she nearly was. She focused on the dancing, on the moving of her feet, on their contact with the floor, the dark, shiny floor.

They performed for each other, only for each other. Boundless euphoria, as impossible as that felt gained even another level or two. The other eight close to them faded away, vanished completely, even as they noticed that they, and also some others spontaneously leaving their comfortable seats began swaying as well. The two danced, sizzling like two daystars circling eternally, doing their never-ending slow shake of boundless attraction. Slowly, painfully slowly they closed in on the other again, excited in spite of the painful path, one seemingly wrought with hurdles.

Faces swam for their eyes. Bea's mother frowned, the frown very visible in the suddenly so distinct features, clearly disapproving of this public display of passion.

You have yourself to thank, you fake ass, Janet thought and stifled a giggle.

In one sweeping twin whirl they returned to the other. Hand reached for hand. Hands clasped. Something similar to an electric current made more gasps rise from open mouths. An impossible image of a thousand daystars filled their vision. Both stood there, swaying, their contact never truly broken, their shadows never really apart.

They rushed forward, stopping before the High Priestess with eager smiles.

She studied them. They let her, the thought of grievance hardly touching their mind at all. Deep, constant blushes rode them.

– You are *one,* now and for all time?

– We are, Honored One, they choired.

The regal, older woman looked like she pondered the issue at some length, extremely skilled at doing so, making the first sting of uncertainty touch them. She stood there for what felt like ages, totally inactive, making no sign that she would ever move.

She crossed her arms in front of her and grabbed both pairs of temples. They felt it yet again, the potent charge through their flesh, their very being.

The priestess stepped back.

– I grant you your blessings, Illandra declared, – grant you what is already yours. Be forever joined.

She stepped further back, pulling away, leaving the stage to them.

Janet and Bea looked at each other, casting the first glances at their surroundings. The guys rushed in from all sides, embracing them with impunity, drowning them in wet kisses and happy tears.

Rosa embraced Janet hardest of all.

– I am so happy, she cried. – This is such a great day. Congratulations, both of you.

She turned slightly, including Bea, embracing her equally hard.

– Thank you, they choired in perfect sync, shivering with the guys in the euphoria and emotional aftermath.

– And I am happy to confirm to you that what we have experienced so far is the mere start of the festivities, Rosa said mischievously.

– That makes me so happy, Fran sniffed. – I am convinced I will be more dead than drunk tomorrow.

The euphoria and raging emotions brought more shaky and happy laughter.

Janet noticed Bea's grin and found it… odd.

She shook her head, dismissing the thought, forgetting it the moment it surfaced.

– How does it feel?

Livy asked eagerly, beyond curious.

– It feels great, Janet replied, – so pleasant and…

– … and deep, Bea said. – Even more than before we are truly one. What we only imagined and yearned for have…

– … have become true, Janet said.

Eleanor stood there, breathing with them to an even bigger degree than the others, her happiness added to theirs.

The guests had stood up from their chairs. Some were about to leave. Others lingered, gathering around the Rosens and their nearest network. They looked pleased, looked smug. Janet assumed it had been a successful afternoon for them as well.

There was no way she could keep her emotions concealed, but she did make an attempt and was exposed a moment later.

– I can not be myself in public here, not like with…

Eleanor spoke, but everyone knew that it was, in truth Janet that was speaking.

– … the Bone People, Bea nodded and looked at her with nothing but love and understanding. – I know.

Madge and Justin found back to each other in the relative chaos below. They waved. Janet and Bea returned the wave, a little excessive. The older companions looked like they would start on their way towards their old and new daughter, before they stepped down from the stage.

– Uh, huh, here they come, Toby mumbled.

Janet hardly noticed his words. They did not seem important, somehow. So much was happening in her immediate surroundings, so much satisfying and great.

Her arm itched again. It was the arm with the hand holding on to Bea's.

– So close, so far away, Eleanor said with her hollow voice and remote-looking eyes.

Janet frowned when she studied her, practically scrutinized her.

– That was not me, she insisted bewildered.

Bea looked patronizing at her.

Janet cried out, as the skin on her wrist turned red and swollen. A moment or two later she felt pain on her shoulder as well. She exposed it, brushed aside the clothing with a quick burst of speed. Dull pain grabbed her.

The sigil, strange tattoos and other symbols drew themselves on her shoulder and arm. They burned themselves on her skin.

Alarmed beyond alarmed she attempted to fight off the sinister influence assaulting her. She attempted to use her mind or cast spells, in vain.

Sleep and fatigue, a tearing sound cutting into her overwhelmed her in one sinister sweep.

She knew what this was. Dull panic and horror grabbed her.

In the half heartbeat before she lost consciousness she felt a force of some kind leave her. She recognized dimly the force-field she and Bea had made. It spread outwards, outwards, outwards. She (and Eleanor) fell and hit the floor, but she did not feel the impact, only a general sense of it, as it happened. Consciousness faded, slow enough for her to see Illandra fall as well, and Livy, and…

Then time ended and darkness ruled for a long, long time. She floated in a dark current, a puppet unable to move, unable to do anything other than float, float, float…

Pain, non-localized, sore rolled over her. She had a sense of herself writhing on the floor or in the air, or stuck to something, something she could not in any way touch or sway.

Her eyes opened slowly, painfully, as if she had to strive, strain herself for every little chink opening up from her cavern.

Delirious, she thought dully, through the red haze of the incomprehensive illness.

Bea's face manifested immensely slow in her infested vision, through strong, unhealthy colors. It was as if Bea was high above her and not right in front of her.

– Do not try anything funny, my love. It will not be pleasant for you if you do. I would rather not gag you. It is important that you scream when the time comes.

It was as if there was a gag there, at least partly blocking her from crying out or form desired words (spells, spells were bad, bad, bad girl).

She managed to turn her head just a little, but that was all. She seemed to be frozen in her position, unable to deviate significantly from it.

Janet looked at Beatrice with eyes like wounds, with a persisting, horrible incredulity engraved on her face.

Beatrice grabbed her jaw and turned her head back and forth a few times.

– That is it, beloved, take a look at the delights. I give you permission.

Piece by piece the horror revealed itself to Janet. She hung suspended in the air. There was nothing perceivably solid making her stay in place. It was all air, smothering, sinister air. The others, Toby, Rosa, Eleanor, Fran and Dane hung opposite her, equally helpless. Joan knelt unmoving on the floor, her eyes cast down. Illandra hung higher in the air, close to the ceiling, enclosed in some kind of filament. It covered her completely. Janet could not actually see her, but still knew it was her. Livy's imprisonment also seemed slightly different. She was in a cage of some kind, one consisting of air no more visible than what bound Janet, but just as effective.

It was visible, kind of, when she squinted her eyes. It hurt more when she did it, but she kept doing it.

Everyone else present stood outside the force-field. Some of them kept trying to leave the hall, but another field kept them from doing so.

– You want an *audience?*

She blinked.

Bea smiled at her.

– I am quite confident that you will value everything eventually. I prepared both myself and you for a long time. Being single-minded and dedicated is so very helpful.

The memory of the glowing sign on the wall flashed slowly through Janet's mind. So did other things and events in hindsight gaining special significance. She saw Bea stand nude and cast her sinister spells, reading from her Book of Shadows.

A frown formed, seemingly by itself on Janet's swollen face, her confused and distressed features, one deep and sore. The soreness burned her very soul.

A horrible sadness grabbed her.

Tears, one, two three, no more than ten trickled from her left eye. Bea's smile softened. She reached out with a hand again, to Janet's jaw. Janet pulled her head away. It hurt, but she turned away.

– Fine, be that way.

Bea struck her. The fist hit her jawbone. Blood flowed from her mouth. Bea dried the blood off her skin with both hands.

– I regret the need for this, but pain and blood is essential for the spell.

The spell… Something dawned on Janet, something more and even worse.

– Yes, I did not do this just for show. There is more to it, a purpose, one holy and grand.

She looked mighty then, beyond insane and mighty. Janet shrunk in her presence. A misery beyond, far beyond her predicament swelled within, in her hollow insides. She felt bloated, like a balloon.

– I have been working my ass off to get this rolling, you know. You should be a little more grateful, at least show a little appreciation.

Janet expected more tears to flow then, but they did not.

– I worked in secret, my intentions and desires hidden, obscured behind veils of benevolence and the holy love I feel for you. No one, not you, not Illandra, not even Ione, the High Priestess, Ione, that obnoxious, arrogant bitch could see through me.

She activated Joan with a tiny, hardly visible move.

– Get on with it, slave, she snapped. – Earn your keep.

– Right away, Master, Joan whimpered.

Joan began working with the bowls on the floor. They circled her. She rotated clockwise as she worked with each of them. Working fast and effective she cut the meaty part of her hand with a small blade. Blood flowed from her cracked skin and into the first bowl. It turned warm and smoky as it hit the herbs chirping and moving down there. There were five bowls.

– I do not really need to voice my commands, of course, but I enjoy doing it, enjoy commanding the slut around, even though she is not much fun, eager to please as she is. It is more like giving orders to a loyal dog.

Bea talked and talked and talked, clearly loving the sound of her own voice. Janet wished she would stop, just stop. Her head hurt. Her jaw hurt. Dizziness and nausea kept charging her in waves, overwhelming, pacifying her. She choked in her ongoing, relentless distress and kept choking. She wished she could stop, just stop.

Bea reached out with her hand again. This time Janet did not pull her head away. Bea rubbed her cheek. Janet leaned against it, experiencing a brief moment of peace.

– That is a good girl, Bea whispered. – It feels good, does it not?

Janet sniffed, half nodding, half unable to hold her head high.

Joan was done with the five bowls. Smoke rose from them in an even stream. Joan rose with a cup in her hand. She walked to Bea and Janet with her head bowed in submission.

Bea struck Janet again, struck her again and again with deliberate, directed brutality. Something broke somewhere. That, too, like everything else in this horrible night terror seemed to go on indefinitely. Dull pain turned sharp and then dull again. It happened a thousand times.

Janet's head hung low. Blood and saliva and pieces of skin dropped from her slack mouth and jaw.

Bea looked at her with the so very familiar soft smile.
– Look at you. You had a secure future, had your life mapped out, as an acolyte of the High Priests, selected to become one of them. With one stroke I take it all away. Ione's plan for you will be nothing but dust.
Joan held the cup under Janet's jaw, doing so until blood and fluid had filled it halfway. Bea cut the fleshy part of her own hand. She filled the second half of the cup. Joan returned to the five bowls and filled them with the blood. She walked to one and one of the five hanging there like butchered meat, and gave them to drink. Rosa was first. She drank with only half-hearted resistance, clearly under the sway of Bea's spells and indomitable will. Joan walked back and forth, until they had all drunk, had drunk the bowls empty.
Bea kept fixing her wicked stare at Janet. Her big eyes swam in Janet's befuddled vision and consciousness.
– We will become one, my love, and with that single act I make all my father and mother's dreams ashes, and I will ascend, superseding all their expectations.
– Ascend? Janet spat, experiencing a slight rise of her dull anger, her voice drowning in blood.
Her voice sounded like dry leaves rubbing mortar.
– You will understand…
– Oh, I understand perfectly. Janet suddenly spoke with a well-modulated voice, in spite of the blood filling her mouth. – You approached me like a predator does a prey, homing in on me with a shrewdness and determination fooling me completely. You are a great demon hunter, «beloved».
– You are so wise, sweet witch, in spite of your childish outlook on life.
A rage worked itself up from Janet's depths. She could not hold it back even if she tried, and she did not want to. It did not quite get there, but lingered like stagnant water in a still pond.
– I hate you. I hate your guts, bitch!
Bea shook, as if being struck.
Then she brightened and shrugged.
– Soon, very soon, it will not matter.
She muttered a spell, and Janet felt her numb and dull self return.
– You are easily handled, see? I have prepared myself painstakingly.
Even the laughter hurt in Janet's ears.
Livy hammered at the wall of the cage, lost and filled with despair, gaining Bea's brief attention.
– Take me instead, the young sorcerer begged.
– You would do it? Bea asked her, clearly intrigued. – You would give your

life for her?

– I would!

Then, in a deliberate act she bowed her head in submission.

Bea laughed some more, very patronizing.

– Do not worry, I will take you, will take you, too, but not quite yet.

Bea turned her attention back to Janet.

– We are ready, she stated, nodding, nodding again. – Everything is set. We are finally ready.

She picked up something from the floor, something Janet could not quite fathom at first. The four short and thin rods slowly gained ascendance in her vision and mind.

– The Rods of Malarki, Bea boasted. – I found them in storage at the Center of Art and Antiquity. No one knew their properties and true function. They had no fucking idea!

Janet knew their purpose. She moaned in more paralyzing terror.

Bea pushed the first rod into her, pushed it straight through her stomach. Janet screamed. It hurt, hurt a lot, even more then it should have done. She hung there, breathing hard, hardly able to reason at all. Bea pushed the second rod into her, pushed it through her chest, narrowly missing her heart. Janet screamed again.

– Yes, scream, my love. Every time you do that is beneficial to me. You are mine, now, mine for all time.

The two remaining rods were pushed through the thighs. Janet wanted to scream, but could not anymore. She had no voice. Her body shook in violent cramps.

– That was actually great. Thank you so much…

Bea held up a hand, formed into a hex, both weaving and speaking her spells, each word and intonation cutting into Janet like the dullest blade.

Janet's attention was pulled to… pulled to Eleanor. She understood why in an instant and shook her head.

– You are her mentor, her Master, Bea whispered seductively. – Exercise your right.

My… right?

Janet, sick to the bone looked even more terror-stricken at the vulture hovering over her.

Janet resisted, but it did her no good. The deeper contact was practically instantaneous. The light report that was always there grew to a storm. The apprentice moaned in fear, in useless protest. Janet's mind, dominating hers brushed aside the few, feeble hurdles. She filled Eleanor's consciousness with her own, supplanting, eradicating what was there, and there was nothing she could do to keep that from happening.

– That is it, Bea whispered enthralled. – Remove every shred of her.

Janet sensed it as it happened. All Eleanor's lights faded to sparks, then to embers… and then to nothing. Janet had four eyes, four nostrils, four ears, double for everything. She shook both her heads in abject denial. A horrible feeling of dread washed through her like lukewarm water. Bea walked to her, to Eleanor's body, what was now only one more vessel for Janet's consciousness.

– Yes, I can see you in there beloved. This is so exciting, such a triumph.

Janet saw both her front and back. Her consciousness flowed back and forth without her having any control over it. It weakened her further, even as the strength of Eleanor's life force boosted her own.

But she could not use it, could not gain any control worth its name.

– That was easy, was it not?

Bea held her hair, held Eleanor's hair, pulling her head up. Janet stared dully at her.

– THAT WAS EASY, WAS IT NOT?

– YES, YES, YES! Janet cried out in misery and sick, numbing fear.

– I knew it was. The next four will be harder, but that is how it is supposed to be.

Janet stared uncomprehending at her, through veils of tears, through Eleanor's dry eyes.

– Now, do the same to them. Make them empty shells for us to fill.

Janet shook her head defiantly. It happened so fast, like an instinct, impossible to hold back.

The next moment she cried out in vicious pain. It devoured whatever remained of her will, reducing it to nothing. She became even more the function, the vessel Bea envisioned.

– Please, she wheedled. – Please, please, please… stop. I beg you, beg you, beg, beg, beg…

Her words just faded into incomprehensible gibberish. She collapsed in body and mind.

– Hush, my love. Bea rubbed her face, Janet's bloody and broken face, kissing her brow. – Just a little further, now, and all will be well.

– I love you, Janet's sniffed, – love, love love love

Bea's features softened, before hardening once more. She straightened, pulling back, returning to a pre-prepared spot on the floor. Janet knew what that was, knew it was where she would receive all the energy, all the power drawn from everyone else within the inner force field.

She began her swearing, her curses. Janet felt each and every one of them, felt yet one more brutal intrusion. She reached out, unable to resist to the other four, using both Eleanor's and her own assets.

It began. Rosa's memories mixed with hers, with her conception of her friend. She watched Dane grow up with the Deep Purple tribe and clans, with the accompanying emotions.

Outside, some of the gathered sorcerer's made half hearted attempts at breaking the force field. Others stared in sick fascination at the spectacle within. It changed nothing.

Toby smiled at her, with his sad, sad puppy-look. She started sobbing in her mind's eye, but nothing revealed itself on the surface. Fran faded away, fell into a well dark and deep.

Energy flowed from the four to Eleanor, and from Eleanor to Janet. It seethed in the air, practically visible. Power filled Janet, but she could not act on it. She had no connection, no access to herself.

They began disintegrating, literally falling apart. They filled Janet, their essence and characteristics and even parts of their physical forms and characteristics were sucked into hers, altering her appearance. Her features changed. Her hair changed from one color to many.

– Yes! Bea shouted in ecstasy. – YES!

Gasps of horror erupted from those watching. Their shocked faces looked like a display wall on a gallery.

A thousand thoughts surged through Janet's thoughts, Janet's set of minds in a moment. She watched dispassionately both those shocked and those not, those looking at the performance of the current demon hunter with approval and interest.

The four had become dust. Only their clothes and small pieces of flesh and bone remained. Eleanor, Eleanor's shell and Janet were still whole, still whole and…

One thought solidified.

And *kicking*. Rage filled her, swelled her. Dispassionate, calculating rage, what she had kept hidden, both from herself and others manifested in a blink of an eye. She spotted the frown on Beatrice Maximus Rosen's brow. Eleanor's lips moved, spat a curse, the vilest of curses.

I give myself. I surrender myself to death and decay. I do it all for *vengeance!*

Many sentences and phrases and spells and curses spoken as one, coalescing into that one, final sentence.

Eleanor's shell crumbled to dust as well, joining those of the other four.

The balance shifted, was violently disrupted and changed.

Power undreamt of filled Janet, her body unscathed. All her shackles crumbled. Blue flames surrounded her. The tattoo birthmarks burned in an

eerie, intense glow. She stood there, shaking with hatred and loss.
Bea shouted stunned, paralyzed.
– You did not? How could you? I can not fucking *believe* it.
She shook her head and began shouting in an impossibly loud voice:
– NO! NO! NO NO NO No no
The last of her repeated denials drowned in a roar.
Janet rolled her hands, her entire body and self into a fist. She visualized a dagger, imagined that she buried it deep within the other's flesh and that it made blood flow and ripped apart flesh. The black, black, all-encompassing rage flooded her. The raging waves shook Beatrice Maximus Rose violently. Her loud, unheard scream was cut off. In one single destructive burst her head was separated from the body. Blood jumped from the jugular vein and all over the room. The body crumbled. The head hit the floor with a dump sound. Her scream of shock, denial and incredulity and juvenile protest persisted, as if she was still breathing, as if she was not a heap of rotting flesh on the floor.
Janet of the Blue Flame stood there revealed, for all those with knowledge to study and behold. She was well aware of it and did not care for a moment, about anything.
And then there was care, was emotion, as she looked down on the lifeless husk by her feet.
– You believed you spoke with Cathy almost all the time, the sorcerer choked, – thought you faced her mindscape, her vulnerable core, but you hardly ever did, and had no idea what she is like.
She smiled, a cruel, horrible, twisted grin shaking those watching, making some of them pee on themselves. She smelled the stench without effort.
– But now you know…
The force field disintegrated, fading away as if it had never been there in the first place. The sigil and marks on Janet's arm faded to nothing. She started pulling out the rods. It hardly hurt, hardly hurt at all. The wounds did not really bleed that much.
Joan crouched on the floor, sobbing and shaking hard.
Livy's cage crumbled and dissolved. The filament holding Illandra vanished. Janet, as an afterthought caught the unconscious woman in her waves as she fell, and put her down on the floor, not that rough.
Livy stepped forward, intruding on Janet sphere like a buzzing fly, shaken, but filled with a stronger than ever awe.
– My Queen…
– Do not call me that, ever again, Janet snarled.
Livy fell on her knees, stricken with a fear and awe without peer, one

beyond worship and submission.

Zoe and Loewe stood frozen with the rest. They could not even be said to be breathing.

I am so proud of you, beloved, the dismembered voice spoke to the young, so very experienced sorcerer from afar.

Janet listened to it for a moment, before dismissing it, dismissing the very thought and reality of it.

She turned towards those standing frozen on the floor, crumbling in corners and shadows, those fleeing the fastest they were able. A door slammed somewhere.

– You did this, she told the Rosens and the Maximuses and their guests of honor. – You made her into what she was.

The Blue Flame burned, seething with cold, dull emotion. She noticed, in yet another afterthought, that the door to the backyard stood wide open. She walked to it, covering an endless stretch of gray, stepping through it without looking back.

Janet Kathryn Caldwell stumbled into the eternal night.

Falling

is the first of three books telling Janet's story as a young girl.

The other two are

Forsaken

and

Fallen

Author's word

It took more time than I initially believed to be the case to complete this one. The story turned out to be much longer than I initially thought one would be. It needed a far more detailed backdrop, and thus I provided it.

It always feels strange to write the final scene, the words and story you have waited for years to complete and carried in your mind even longer. I had, have notes, of course, but not the complete, fleshed out ending, even though there have been occasions where I have written the final chapter first or early, like with Your Own Fate.

I started on book two of the trilogy months ago. I wrote the fallout of the ending before I wrote the ending.

This is the fifteenth novel I've written, and just pondering that fact makes my thoughts flow. It's different from all the other books I've written, like they're all different from each other. That has been my tenet from the start, and I know now that I will always stick to it.

I have secrets with this novel, this book, like I have with all the others, first hand knowledge of the story and of the motivations of the author that I will take with me to the grave…

I quite enjoy that.

In order to finish the story faster than I otherwise would have done, I have much more than usual written solely on this one. I have not exactly ignored the other four novels I'm currently writing, but they have been on the backburner for a while. Now, they slowly re-emerge to the foreground of my attention, which is fun in itself.

Usually I don't use archaic and little used wording and phrases excessively, but this time I have sort of encouraged my own use of it, practically excelled in it. You will quickly realize why.

One very interesting item: Writing this novel has shown me, even more than before what life and writing is, how similar life and writing are. One decision or act, once made reverberates from that point and changes the rest of your life in smaller and bigger, often irreversible ways. I make a decision in chapter fourteen, something not given in advance, something not strictly necessary for the story, and practically everything changes. I had no idea, no conscious awareness of where it would lead. It felt like a logical progression at the time, a way of developing the plot, but the result, totally unforeseen resulted in a number of other changes later on that again would lead to other changes and so on.

The overall story would have managed fairly well without all that, but it would have been a much shorter, less interesting, meager result. It's very funny and fulfilling; I seek variety and depth and realism, and the end result is far superior to what I at that moment in the past could imagine. The novel grew, and I grew with it.

One word may change everything, and one act alone may transform you and your surroundings, your very world, for better or for worse.

I had confirmed to myself another tenet of mine, another general rule: Don't rush things!

It's such a pleasure being an author.

December 26, 2007 – June 25, 2015
Printed version ready and done November 8, 2015
Final proofreading complete January 26, 2016

FORSAKEN

The name Forsaken has no religious connotations. It has far darker meanings than that…

Janet of the Blue Flame is truly forsaken, by everything and everyone she once held dear.

Her heart and soul have been ripped out, her mind violated beyond repair. The cruel violet eyes are dry. There are no more tears left. She is hardly more than a shade drifting through the dark corners of the world.

In a tavern without doors she sets out to drink herself to death.

Weeks later, after already legendary binge drinking bouts to end all legendary binge drinking bouts a man comes to her with a proposal. He wants her on «his team» of sorcerers, one he wants to take him on a tour across the nine realms and beyond. She does not know why she agrees, whether or not it is because death has lost its appeal to her or because it has not, or because she just does not care.

There are maps, ancient lore describing the path they must take, and Janet has traveled parts of the Journey before, enough to know some of its perils, enough to scare her, if anything can scare her anymore.

Janet of the Blue Flame is set loose on this realm and all the next, like an attack dog that has broken its chains.

www.ingramcontent.com/pod-product-compliance
Lightning Source LLC
Chambersburg PA
CBHW060604310726
48982CB00008B/1232/J